The Boy and the Battleship

The Navy Cadets

C.R. Cummings

Also By
CHRISTOPHER CUMMINGS

The Boy and the Battleship

The Navy Cadets

C.R. Cummings

DoctorZed
Publishing
www.doctorzed.com

Published 2014 by DoctorZed Publishing

DoctorZed Publishing books may be ordered through booksellers or by contacting:

DoctorZed Publishing
10 Vista Ave
Skye, South Australia 5072
www.doctorzed.com
61-(0)8 8431-4965

ISBN: 978-0-9923909-7-6 (sc)
ISBN: 978-0-9872495-8-6 (e)

National Library of Australia Cataloguing-in-Publication entry

    Author: Cummings, C. R., author.
    Title: The boy and the battleship / Christopher Cummings.
    ISBN: 9780992390976 (paperback)
    Series: Cummings, C. R. The navy cadets ; 1.
    Subjects: Military cadets—Fiction.
          Terrorism—Fiction.
    Dewey Number: A823.3

Cover image © gio_banfi | istockphoto.com

Printed in Australia
DoctorZed Publishing rev. date: 05/02/2014

Dedication

To my mother,

the late Cynthia Adelaide Cummings (nee Wickham),

a sailor's wife,

for her love and support

and for her sound advice on relationships and life.

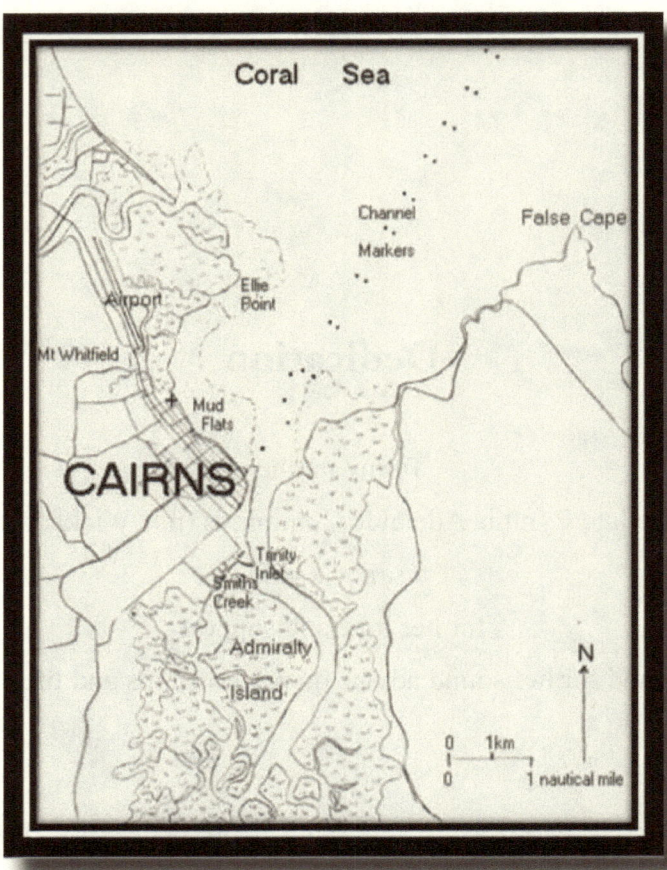

Map 1: Coral Sea

Chapter 1

THE DESTROYER

It was a perfect North Queensland winter day: clear blue skies, a crisp fresh breeze, and a sun just warm enough to be pleasant. Twelve-year-old Graham Kirk breathed deeply and looked out over the ruffled chop the wind had churned up on Trinity Inlet. He felt wonderfully alive and excited. Sniffing the sea smells with a mixture of pleasure and nostalgia he turned his gaze back to study the ship.

Graham was standing on the bow of HMAS *Hobart*, a guided missile air defence destroyer. The ship was visiting Cairns after exercises in South East Asian waters and, unusually in these times of heightened security after the 'War on Terror', was open to the public. Graham and his friends had leapt at the opportunity and they had just spent an hour climbing everywhere they were allowed to climb.

Graham's gaze moved intently back along the anchor chains on the focsle, over the steel breakwater to the forward 125mm gun turret, before travelling up the front of the superstructure to the bridge windows; and on up to the lattice work of the mast, with its array of radar scanners and aerials. *What an impressive sight,* he thought. *I wish I was old enough to join the navy now.*

He sighed wistfully. Ever since he could remember his one ambition had been to become a naval officer. Earlier that morning he had watched the destroyer sail in from the Coral Sea. As it came into port if had looked most impressive: long, sleek and deadly; the grey and black ship sliding silently over the grey-green waters of Trinity Inlet against a backdrop of dark green, jungle-covered mountains. The memory sparked one of his favourite day-dreams. In it he was the captain of the destroyer. The ship would make a majestic entrance after some heroic deed—with all the people down on the Cairns Esplanade watching. Before the admiring eyes of his schoolmates the suitably modest captain steps ashore to a hero's welcome—a welcome in which Cindy would play a suitably romantic part.

Perhaps I have just rescued her? Graham pondered. *Maybe from a cruise liner which had been taken over by terrorists or pirates?* He liked that idea and smiled.

And there was Cindy!

She had just hurried into sight. Seeing her sent a sharp stab of guilt and anxiety through Graham. The day before he had made a naughty suggestion to Cindy and now he was concerned that his bad behaviour might get him into trouble. Cindy was a Year 10, three years older than him, and was a very attractive brunette with a shapely body that her school uniform did little to conceal.

Scorching fantasies about her burned through Graham's mind and he squirmed with a mixture of arousal and anxiety. A few weeks before he had reached puberty and that ecstatic experience was seared into his brain. Since then Graham had found his whole being stirred into seemingly continual arousal. His interest in girls was now firmly alive. And Cindy had not responded negatively to his hints and innuendos. But now he worried that he had gone too far.

Suddenly she saw him. To his intense relief she smiled. "Hi Graham! What ya doin'?" she called.

"Just studying the ship," Graham answered, his heart beginning to hammer with the instant excitement he now experienced when he was in her presence. "What are you doing?"

Cindy glanced behind her. "Trying to avoid my little brother," she replied.

Her little brother Max was a class mate of Graham's. He shrugged. "I haven't seen him. He might be with Pete and Steve." Emboldened by her friendly greeting and by being alone with her he said, "Are we going to meet again?"

"Only in secret," Cindy replied. "I don't want to have any trouble."

"When?"

Cindy again looked behind her. Her eyes were alight with mischief. "I don't know. I will see when we can organize something. I will see you later." With that she hurried off around the other side of the superstructure.

Graham was left aroused and hopeful. *Maybe?* he wondered. He stood there in a state of euphoria, amazed that an older girl had even spoken to him. *She is really attractive,* he thought, knowing that he did not really like her and sensing that what he was experiencing was just pure lust.

That notion sent several waves of guilt through him; firstly for doing such things at all and secondly for being disloyal to Thelma, the latest object of his adoration.

And there was Thelma.

At that moment she and her black-haired friend Janet Ozgood appeared out of a doorway behind the gun turret. Thelma was in the same class at school and Graham had only recently noticed her. Now he thought the sun rose just because of her. Actually she was a fairly plain looking girl with a straight nose, hazel eyes and hair the same colour as his, mousy fair. But she was nicely shaped for her age with quite a big bosom and she always looked happy.

For a moment Graham admired her, and unconsciously compared her with her friend. *Janet is prettier,* he decided. *And she's got bigger boobs and better legs.* At that he felt a twinge of disloyalty and rationalized. *Anyway, what can you expect? Thelma is only in Year 8. She will develop as she gets older. And besides; Janet is a...*

Graham struggled to form an opinion but failed. He was a bit in awe of Janet. She always looked and acted so cool and grown up. Instinctively Graham sensed that she would never be the girl for him, however beautiful she was.

The two girls turned to talk to a young man Graham had never seen before; a man of about twenty with long blond hair tied in a pigtail. *He's a scruffy looking jerk!* Graham thought, resentment fuelling his uneasy jealousy. The man said something and both the girls laughed. Then they moved out of sight along the starboard side.

"Hello Graham. Having a good day?" asked a girl's voice.

Joany! Graham recognized the girl who had appeared beside him. Joan was another Year 10 girl. She was a pretty blonde with shoulder length hair and ruddy cheeks. "Hi Joany. Yes thanks," he replied.

Joany nodded. "Good. See ya," she said. She wandered on across the deck and for a moment Graham admired her nice curves and good legs. The fact that another Year 10 girl had bothered to speak to him got him all flustered and set his fantasies working.

From the port side appeared Graham's friends: Max, Peter and Stephen. Behind them was Kylie, Graham's little sister. Last in the line was Margaret, Kylie's best friend, and Graham's devoted admirer!

Peter waved and moved to join him. "We wondered where you were," he said. "We went looking for you down at the blunt end. Have you seen all you want to see yet?"

Graham smiled. "No, but they won't let me look in lots of the places I'd like to go. I wish they'd let us look down inside, in the engine room and places like that."

Stephen shook his head. "I can't see them allowing that," he put in. "They'd be too worried about things getting broken or pinched I reckon."

"Or sabotage," Max suggested.

"Sabotage!" Graham scoffed. "What rot! Who would do any thing like that? And what could a person do that would matter anyway? We were all searched before we were allowed on board."

Kylie joined them. "Some of those Peace Protesters perhaps?" she said.

"Peace Protesters! Fair go Sis. This is Cairns, not Sydney. Where would you find a demonstrator here?" Graham scoffed.

Kylie pointed over the side. "There are some on the wharf right now," she replied.

"Where?" Graham was astounded, and annoyed. He resented any criticism of the navy, or its role. To check he walked to the port rail and looked down at the wharf.

To his astonishment he saw that his sister was right. Half way along the wharf, near the gangway leading onto the quarterdeck, were a small group of people with placards. They were just standing talking to the navy people there. Graham felt a rush of indignation. He counted the demonstrators.

"Oh, there are only seven of them."

"It's been enough to attract the TV people," Peter said, indicating a TV news crew heading along the wharf.

On seeing the media crew Graham felt another surge of anger. *Mob of bloody vultures!* he thought. "They just exaggerate and make things worse," he said. What also annoyed him was that the media seemed to be grossly ignorant of even basic knowledge about the navy and often made the most elementary errors in fact. He watched them with sour distaste.

Stephen leaned on the rail next to him. "The TV station probably paid the demonstrators to turn up," he offered cynically.

Margaret was shocked. Her usually cheerful, freckled face wrinkled in a frown of distaste and disbelief. "Oh Stephen! That's a horrible thing to say," she cried.

Stephen shrugged. "It's been known to happen before," he replied.

"It has not! You are just making it up," Margaret said.

"Sorry Marg," Peter put in. "But it has happened."

Kylie stepped in. "Where? When?" she questioned angrily.

Peter shrugged and looked embarrassed. "I can't think of a specific example, but I have read about it."

Kylie sniffed in disbelief. Margaret looked worried. Graham felt annoyed that it was all spoiling their visit to the warship. "Never mind them. Let's go and visit the bridge again," he suggested.

"No. I want to go home," Kylie replied. She was a pretty eleven-year-old, in the same class at school as Margaret. She loved her brother but enough was enough.

Max chipped in. "I agree. I'm thirsty and my feet are killing me. Let's go home."

Reluctantly Graham agreed. The group made its way along the port side in single file. Graham went last. He looked around him continually, noting details and absorbing the atmosphere: the smell of paint, oil, saltwater and machinery; and the naval personnel in their various uniforms.

Even though he was only 12 Graham was already very familiar with ships, mainly because his father was not only a Master Mariner but also owned several. With his older brother Alex and, to a lesser extent Kylie, Graham had grown up with, and on, ships. Captain Kirk operated two tugs, a large barge (a converted Landing Craft Tank) and a 250 ton freighter. His business took him all over northern Australia and the South Pacific. Sometimes the children did not see their father for weeks on end. At other times they went with him as unpaid crew, particularly during school holidays.

To Graham merchant ships were all very well but they lacked the glamour and excitement of warships. His heart was set on the sea as a career—like his dad in the Merchant Marine if he had to; but for first preference as a naval officer. As he followed the others along the narrow strip of deck between the railings and the superstructure he studied all the details such as fire fighting equipment, pipes, bollards and cleats and various boxes and doors.

At the stern they found a helicopter had been rolled out of the hanger onto the small flight deck. This was sufficiently interesting to distract the others and they joined the queue to have a look inside the machine. Graham wasn't particularly interested in aircraft but he knew they were important in naval warfare so he studied the helicopter and then looked around to take in the details of the flight deck.

As he did he found himself looking at Cindy. She was standing over near the starboard side and was chatting to a young sailor. To Graham she looked very attractive. *She looks older than she is,* he thought. Then he frowned at the way Cindy giggled at something the sailor said. She rolled her eyes and put her hand on the sailor's forearm. *She is flirting,* he thought. The sight somehow disturbed him but he could not account for it, not wanting to admit that he might be jealous. *She is too young to be behaving like that,* he told himself. *Anyway, it isn't Cindy I like, it is Thelma.*

Graham looked around and noted that Thelma and Janet were also studying the helicopter. To Graham's annoyance he saw that Thelma was talking to another youth. *It is that Edmonson jerk from Year 10,* he thought resentfully. This time he did admit to jealousy. Edmonson was another of the type Graham considered to be 'long haired gits' and he could not imagine what Thelma saw in him. But he did realize that Thelma was not really aware that he existed. *I must get her to notice me and then I will ask her for a date,* Graham decided.

At that moment he was bumped and glanced to see that it was Margaret. She gave him a smile. "Your turn in the helicopter," she said.

Graham felt a spurt of anxiety. *I hope Thelma doesn't see Margaret with me. That might wreck my chances,* he thought. In fact Margaret was starting to annoy him. For several years she had been Kylie's best friend but had also made no secret of her admiration for him. At first it had been very nice and flattering but now he found it cloying and irritating. Twice in the recent past mates of his had teased him over being friends with Margaret, calling him a cradle snatcher who was interested in young girls. The fact that Margaret was only in Year 6 at primary school did not help.

It will be a real shame job if Max or his mates notice. I wish she'd go away, Graham thought. But thinking that made him feel ashamed and guilty as he was very aware that Margaret was a very nice person and he really did like her.

Graham gestured to the open doorway. "You go first," he said.

"You are sure?" Margaret asked, her plain, freckled face crinkling into a smile.

"Yes. Up you go. I will follow," Graham replied. Unable to help himself he smiled back and her soft brown eyes danced. She nodded and climbed up into the helicopter. As she did Graham noted her tubby bum and freckled legs. *She is nice but she can't compare with Thelma— or Cindy.*

As he stood waiting Graham again looked at Cindy. *She is really very curvy for her age,* he decided. Then Graham felt another spurt of jealous annoyance as Cindy shrilled with laughter at a joke the young sailor told her. Once again she very obviously flirted with him.

Cindy suddenly looked towards Graham and their eyes met. A flush of guilty shame made Graham look away and he pretended he hadn't been looking. To add to the appearance that he hadn't been he climbed up to look in at where Margaret was sitting in the pilot's seat. She was asking questions of a young man in a flying suit. Kylie sat in the other seat and was also flashing smiles at the young man and that also irritated Graham. *She shouldn't behave like that either,* he told himself.

Margaret and Kylie both moved back through a doorway into the fuselage of the helicopter and Graham was next to climb in and take a seat. Another youth followed him and the young pilot quickly explained what various controls and gauges were for. Graham nodded politely and then moved back to check out the interior. Then he climbed out a side door and joined the others on the flight deck near the tail of the helicopter.

For a few minutes Graham just watched what was going on around him, his interest divided between the girls and the naval activity. He surreptitiously observed a lieutenant giving instructions to two Petty Officers. Graham took in all the details: the white, open-necked shirt with the black epaulets and their double gold rings; the white shorts, socks and shoes; the peaked cap with its glossy black brim and gold badge. He tried to imagine himself as such an officer, only to have his day-dream disturbed by chanting and yelling from down on the wharf.

Graham hurried over to the rail and saw that some of the demonstrators on the wharf were trying to force their way up the gangway. The lieutenant came hurrying past asking people to move back. A group of ratings in grey and black camouflage overalls appeared through a watertight door. Several police came out of a building onto the wharf. There were more shouts from the demonstrators and the chant, "No more war. Make peace. Build schools, not battleships," could be heard.

This was orchestrated by a thin man with black hair and a pointed beard. The man stood to one side and shouted into a megaphone; "Make love, not war! Make love, not war! Turn the swords into ploughshares! Turn the battleships into scrap!"

"This isn't a battleship," muttered Graham in annoyance. "It's only a destroyer. He's just ignorant."

"You are the one who is being ignorant!" cried a girl's voice beside him. Graham looked and then felt a stab of anxiety. It was Thelma's friend, Janet. And Thelma was with her. Both girls pushed through on Graham's left to look over the rail.

"He should get his facts right before making a fuss," Graham grumbled, aware that he was scared of antagonizing Thelma.

Janet snorted. "I'm sure he knows what type of ship this is," she insisted. "He is speaking metaphorically—warship, battleship—who cares about the difference. They are all designed to kill people!"

Graham was astonished at Janet's vehemence and did not know what to say. Luckily for him they were distracted by a scuffle which broke out at the gangway as half a dozen police tried to move the demonstrators back. A girl's shrill scream cut over the hubbub. There were shouted obscenities and loud yells. The bearded man with the megaphone took up his chant again, "Make love, not war! Make love, not war!"

"I like that love idea," Stephen chuckled. He leaned over the rail just beyond Thelma and pointed. "It looks like Mister Rabble-rouser has already been practicing what he preaches if that girl beside him is his girlfriend."

Standing beside the bearded man was a tall, blonde girl clad in a sarong and white cotton cheesecloth top. She had very large breasts and obviously wore no bra.

Janet bristled. "He's not a rabble-rouser—and don't be crude around me Stephen Bell!"

Stephen turned to Graham and smirked, which annoyed Janet even more; and embarrassed Graham.

Thelma now weighed in: "That's right! It's a free country. People can demonstrate if they like!"

Graham didn't argue. He was now acutely conscious that Margaret was pressing against his right side, though whether from accident or design he could not tell. *I don't want Thelma to think I have a girlfriend!* he thought in near panic, hoping Thelma would not notice. Then he felt guilty and ashamed of such thoughts. *Poor little Margaret; she is nice kid,* he thought. *But she can be a pain!* Once again he wished she would go away. Besides, she was not only too young, she was very plain: brown hair and brown eyes, freckles; still in the puppy-fat stage with no figure—no waist and breasts that resembled mosquito bites.

Not like... well, like Thelma's, he thought. Hers were quite big and nicely rounded. *But not as big as that blonde's in the cheesecloth top,* he noted with fascinated interest. She was jumping up and down so that her large breasts quivered and bounced. *Or like the black-haired girl the police are dragging down the gangway.* She was also wearing a cheesecloth top, sarong and sandals. From her mouth poured a flood of obscenities and insults directed at the police.

Janet gasped and pointed at the black haired girl. "That's my sister! Hey, let her go you pigs! Let me through!" she screamed. She began pushing through the crowd towards the gangway. Thelma followed. Graham stared open-mouthed. Her sister! No wonder Janet was so touchy about the demonstrators! It made him feel like a real drip.

"I didn't know Janet had a sister," Peter said.

"Pretty good figure too," Stephen added.

Kylie snorted. "Pretty common! Listen to the gutter language!" she snapped.

"You'd scream too if the cops dragged you off like that," Stephen replied.

Peter shook his head. "She should practice what she preaches and protest peacefully," he commented.

Their attention was taken up by the protest. The demonstrators began to give the navy sentry at the bottom of the aft gangway a hard time, taunting and pushing at him. He called on a small radio which the demonstrators tried to snatch from his grasp. Then he was jostled, his cap snatched off his head and the information pamphlets he was holding were grabbed and flung into the air. He was abused and called insulting and hurtful names. Seeing that made Graham feel both angry and resentful.

Four more police, including a senior officer, arrived in two paddy wagons. Arrests began. There was a lot of shouting and running around and a couple of minor scuffles. The TV crew was joined by a second one from a rival network. A crowd gathered at the entrance to the wharf. Then the demonstration just seemed to fizzle. The demonstrators appeared to just disperse, as though on cue.

It was then that Graham noted the youths at the ensign staff at the stern of the destroyer. For a moment he could not make out what they were doing and then he saw it was Edmonson and the scruffy youth who had been talking to Thelma and Janet. Edmonson was untying the halliards.

Graham was puzzled and stood back from the rail. *What are they up to?* he wondered. Even as he thought this Edmonson looked around in such a furtive and guilty way that Graham was sure they were up to mischief. Then he saw the scruffy youth pull the halliards loose and tug at them, obviously trying to work out which was the downhaul.

"They are trying to pull down the flag," Graham cried. Even as he said it he knew he was wrong. It was actually the naval white ensign so to him all the more precious.

They are going to desecrate the flag. I must stop them! he thought.

Chapter 2

TROUBLEMAKER

As he started walking towards the two youths Graham saw that the scruffy looking one was pulling coloured cloth from under his shirt. *What on earth is that?* Graham wondered. And then he saw what it was as the youth shook the cloth free. It was a peace flag with the peace symbol on a white background and with a rainbow curving across the flag above the black peace symbol. *He is going to put up the demonstrator's flag,* Graham thought.

Seeing Edmonson start pulling down the white ensign caused Graham a spurt of anger and he broke into a run. *I must stop him,* he thought. Seeing that he would probably be too late to prevent the white ensign being lowered Graham let out a bellow. "Oy! Hey! Stop that! Stop! Help me!" he shouted.

The yell alerted the two demonstrators and both their heads jerked around to look. Graham shouted again and dashed over to grab the halliards. He was just in time to stop the white ensign touching the deck. "Stop! Stop that!" he shouted. "Don't you dare desecrate the flag."

Graham's actions had been so fast that the pair were caught by surprise. For a few seconds they stared and made no move. It gave Graham time to get a firm grip on the halliards. He began to try to sort them out to re-hoist the ensign.

The scruffy youth reacted first. He lunged at Graham and grabbed his arm and the halliards. "What the bloody hell?" he cried. Then he tried to pull the halliards from Graham's grasp. "Let go, toad face!" he yelled.

Edmonson now recovered and also tried to pull the halliards away. Graham clung on grimly, just managing to keep the ensign off the deck. He had the satisfaction of noting that the scruffy youth had let go of the peace flag which now hung down so that it was being tangled around his legs and trampled on. *Good!* Graham thought.

The scruffy youth tightened his grip and then began to punch at him. "Let go you little turd! Let go!" he snarled. The punches weren't well directed but still hurt. They struck Graham on the shoulder and side of his head and he felt sharp stabs of pain and what felt like hammer blows which caused him to partially black out. His response was to hang on even tighter, despite being aware that he was in danger of blacking out.

Half stunned Graham fell to his knees, landing painfully on the steel deck. More punches hit him and he felt Edmonson clawing at his fingers, trying to prise them loose from the ropes. *Hang on!* he told himself.

Suddenly Graham's head was whacked against a steel projection. *Bollard or fairlead,* his reeling mind told him, even as he saw stars and slid in and out of consciousness. His fingers weakened but then he stubbornly tightened his grip. Hands grabbed him and he felt himself being dragged.

"Toss the little mongrel over the side," snarled a voice.

That did get Graham struggling. He had no desire to end up in the water. He had often seen very large fish there and had heard numerous stories about sharks or crocodiles lurking in the murky water of the Cairns Inlet. In his semi-conscious state he was aware that hands were pushing and dragging at him and that he could feel the bottom wire of the guardrail.

Out of the corner of his eye he saw water. *My head is over the edge!* he thought. And the water looked a long way down, at the bottom of a grey steel cliff, deep and dark green. Fear galvanized him into a bout of furious struggling while he grimly maintained his grip on the halliards. Fingers tried to break his grip and there punches and kicks.

But there were other voices too, shouts and yells to stop. Boots pounded on the steel deck and Graham heard Margaret screaming. "Let him go! Let him go!"

He opened an eye and saw her then. She was pummelling the back of the scruffy youth. He angrily tried to fend her off while still hitting at Graham's hands and wrists. Then Peter and Kylie arrived and grabbed at the youth and Edmondson. More angry shouts and loud cries sounded and more people appeared. Graham saw Cindy and Stephen and then navy uniforms.

Strong hands held him. The youth was hauled away and stood up, held by Peter and a sailor. Then more navy people arrived and Edmondson and Margaret were separated and held firmly. Another sailor knelt and took hold of the halliards. "Let go!" the sailor snapped.

Graham noted leading seaman badges as he obeyed. To his satisfaction the leading seaman quickly re-hoisted the ensign and belayed it, then stepped back and saluted.

Good! Graham thought. *I saved the flag.*

The officer in whites appeared. "What the devil is going on here?" he demanded to know.

Graham found he was unable to speak. He was so upset and numb that all he could do was sigh and lie back. Then more strong hands seized him and he was hauled to his feet. It was just as well they were strong as his muscles felt very weak and his knees buckled.

A sun-browned, middle-aged face swam into Graham's focus. "Are you all right boy?" it asked.

A Chief Petty Officer, Graham thought as his eyes focused on the man's rank slides. He managed a nod but still felt too dizzy to stand unaided. Another sailor grabbed his other arm.

More people arrived. A crowd began to form and the officer ordered some of the sailors to hold them back. Then he turned to the group again. "So, what is going on?" he snapped.

The scruffy youth answered first. "This kid started pulling down the flag so we tried to stop him," he said.

Graham was stunned. For a moment he was speechless. Then indignation flared and he cried, "I did not! They were pulling down the ensign and were going to put up that peace flag. I tried to stop them," he said.

"Liar!" Edmonson shouted.

The lieutenant gestured and Edmonson was held back by two sailors. "That will do! What peace flag?" he asked.

Graham steadied himself and looked down. There was no sign of the flag. He shook his head and looked around. "There was one. They must have hidden it," he said.

The scruffy youth glared at him. "There never was one!" he snapped.

Margaret spoke next. "Oh you liar! There was! I saw it. You pushed it over the side when we arrived," she cried.

The scruffy youth gave her a hateful glare and denied this. The lieutenant was joined by a lieutenant commander in work camouflage. The lieutenant commander finished speaking into a mobile phone and then pointed forward. "We will sort this out without any more name-calling thank you. Please move with these men. Buffer, take them to the hangar and separate them," he instructed.

"Aye, aye sir," replied a burly Warrant Officer. He gestured to his men to move their prisoners.

As the seamen tried to move the scruffy youth he began to resist. "Let me go! You have no right to touch me! Let me go or I will take you to court for assault," he shouted.

The lieutenant commander just shook his head. "Move them Buffer," he commanded.

Once again the scruffy youth yelled loudly. "This is illegal! You have no right to arrest me! Let me go, I know my rights. This is Queensland, not some police state. I will have the police onto you."

The lieutenant commander faced him. "It isn't Queensland. You are on a vessel of the Royal Australian Navy so Commonwealth law prevails. Now, go quietly so we can sort this out or I will have you arrested and charged under the Anti-terrorist legislation."

Graham saw a look of shock cross the scruffy youth's face and he went pale. "I'm not a terrorist! I was only demonstrating," he muttered.

Edmonson looked scared and blurted out, "We were only trying to make a point. We just wanted to put up our peace flag to show that we don't approve of war or warships."

The lieutenant commander nodded. "Good. We will just get some facts and then you can go. Ah! Here are the people we wanted. You wanted the police young man? Well, here they are, Federal Police."

Graham looked around and saw two uniformed Federal Police walking quickly towards them. Under the urging of the senior policemen he and the others were led forward past the helicopter and into the hanger. Here they were separated and seated, each one guarded by a sailor. By then Graham was feeling very anxious. *Are we in trouble?* he worried.

But he was pleased to see that Margaret, Kylie and Peter were with him. There was no sign of Stephen or Thelma or Janet. Nor were Max and Cindy present. The fact that some of his friends had apparently chosen to slip away upset Graham a bit as he was concerned that he might need them as witnesses. *I can always tell the police to ask them if I have to,* he thought.

Once they were all seated under guard and their names and addresses written down the senior Federal Police officer asked their ages. As all but the scruffy youth were under eighteen, he said, "Because you are minors you are entitled to have a parent or other responsible adult present when we question you. Who would like that?"

Parents! Graham thought with a gulp of anxiety. He did not want that. *I've been in enough trouble at school and at home recently,* he thought. When asked he vigorously shook his head and then fixed Kylie with an intense stare. She met his eye and gave a wry smile. "We had better have our mum here," she replied.

"Kylie!" Graham cried. "I don't want mum and dad to know I've been in trouble."

Kylie shook her head. "We'll have to," she replied.

"Why?"

"Because mum has a right to know; and it will slip out anyway. Alex will hear about it. Then mum will feel hurt that we have kept it from her. Besides, she will be able to tell," Kylie replied.

"How?" Graham asked, even though he had a pretty good idea.

Kylie confirmed this. "Because you are developing a beaut black eye and there are a couple of bruises on your face," she said.

Drat! Graham thought. He shrugged. "OK, I suppose you are right." So both he and Kylie asked for their mother to be phoned.

Both Margaret and Peter declined. A solid, middle-aged civilian in a grey suit was shown in by a rating. The man nodded to the senior police officer and showed an ID card to the naval officer. From the officer's reaction and deferential respect he was shown Graham made the assumption that the man was important. *I'll bet he is a secret service agent, ASIO or something,* he thought. That thought got him even more anxious and he felt his stomach turn over. The man was taken forward through a door.

Then questioning began. For the next hour Graham sat in the hangar, anxiously preparing to be questioned. The scruffy youth was taken away first, leaving a worried looking Edmonson who kept darting Graham resentful glances. To Graham's surprise the scruffy youth did not return and nor did Edmonson after he was taken away.

Why are they taking so long? Why don't they ask me first? he wondered as Peter was led out through a door at the forward end of the hanger. Margaret and Kylie both gave sympathetic smiles before a guard shook his head and said, "No communication."

Kylie huffed. "We were only smiling," she said. "Not communicating."

The rating gave a shake of the head. "I don't care whether it is smoke signals, flashing lights, waving flags or Morse Code. No communicating."

Silence returned. Graham sat and brooded, worrying about what their parents would say when they got home. By this time his bumps and bruises were beginning to throb and he also worried that his mother would make a fuss over them.

Then, to Graham's mingled relief and regret, his mother appeared. She came in with another officer and when she saw him and Kylie she shook her head and looked anxious. She was not allowed to speak to them and was also led forward. Then it was Kylie's turn to be questioned. She stood up and gave Graham a very definite smile and then poked her tongue at the guard before scuttling through the doorway. The guard started to look annoyed but then grinned. That set Margaret smiling and Graham smiled back. The moment the guard looked away Margaret lowered her left eyelid in a definite wink. That made Graham feel even better and he smiled some more, only having to wipe it off his face as the sailor turned back.

He was last to be questioned and was led forward to a cabin where a lieutenant commander and two policeman sat on one side of a table and his mother on the other. Behind the two uniformed policemen sat another naval officer and the middle-aged civilian in the grey suit. Graham met the man's eye and felt his stomach churn with anxiety again. *I might be in real trouble,* he thought.

As Graham seated himself beside his mother she gave him a sympathetic but worried smile and squeezed his hand. Then the interrogation began and the questions instantly took the smile off his face. To his amazement the police seemed to think he had started the incident.

"Those youths said that you began pulling down the flag and they moved to stop them," one policeman said.

"That isn't true!" Graham cried.

He looked at the row of faces—two police, two navy officers and the stony-faced middle-aged civilian and felt his stomach tighten then churn with queasiness. He then described exactly what he had done. He was very glad his mother was there.

The lieutenant commander looked up from the notes he had been taking. "You have used a lot of nautical and naval jargon in your description. You seem to know a bit about ships. Why is that?"

Hearing that made Graham feel better. "Because I am very interested in the navy," he replied, adding, "And I want to join when I am older."

The lieutenant commander nodded and wrote this down. "All right, good. Thank you. That will be all. If you gentlemen are finished we can send him on his way?"

The senior policeman nodded. "Yes. We have his name and address if we need to follow up. OK lad, off you go. Take him out please. Thank you Mrs Kirk."

An Able Seaman who had been standing behind Graham touched his arm and pointed to a side door. "This way please."

For a moment Graham stood there with his mind racing. *Is that all?* he wondered. Then he nodded and went through the now open door. His mother followed after a few quiet words from the lieutenant commander. Graham and his mother were led along a passageway to another cabin where he found Margaret, Kylie and Peter waiting.

The Chief Petty Officer guarding them spoke briefly to Graham's guard and then said, "You kids can all go now. You will leave the ship and not return."

That hurt. Graham felt a spurt of irrational resentment. *I have tried to do the right thing and help the navy and now I am being banned from visiting the ship!* He knew that the ship was only open for visitors that day and would leaving the next day but it still rankled.

The friends were led out on deck and disembarked via the aft gangway. As they stepped off the gangway and began walking towards the exit another group of demonstrators appeared from the shops across the wharf. These had placards and were chanting slogans. Graham noted the long-haired youth with the pony tail and his blonde girlfriend and also Janet's sister.

The sailor guarding the gangway moved to stop them and Graham felt a strong urge to turn back and help him but was stopped by his mother. "Stay out of it Graham," she said. "You are already in enough trouble "

So Graham could only stand and watch and that made him both

upset and angry as the demonstrators shouted and jostled the sailor. His cap was snatched off and thrown into the sea and he was abused and spat on. More sailors appeared at the top of the gangway and began hurrying down to help the sentry. At that the demonstrators turned and quickly walked away, dispersing and melting into the crowd that had gathered.

What unpleasant cowards! Graham thought. He felt very sorry for the sailors, especially the one who'd been standing at the bottom of the stern gangway handing out information pamphlets. As the children watched another sailor took his place and began welcoming the people who were waiting on the wharf but were now plainly unsure whether to come on board or not.

Mrs Kirk shook her head. "Come on children. Let's go home. This is no place to be," she said.

As the friends made their way across the wharf Graham looked around to see if he could see the scruffy youth and Edmonson. There was no sign of them. *The demonstration appears to be over,* Graham thought, noting several uniformed police moving onto the space between the ship and the buildings.

Then Graham looked around for Thelma and Janet. He saw that they were on the wharf down past the stern of the ship—and they were talking to some of the demonstrators. These included Janet's sister, the bearded man and the big-breasted blonde. It was obvious that the girls knew the people. With a sharp pang of jealousy Graham noted that Thelma was talking earnestly to a youth. With dismay Graham realized he knew the youth.

That is Jerry Denham from Year 12! he thought. The sight cast him into even deeper gloom. *Oh, how can I compete with a Year 12?* he thought. Worse still he had defended the navy. *What will Thelma think of me now?* he worried.

Feeling distinctly dejected Graham followed his mother and friends across the wharf. After a few paces he stopped and looked back up at the destroyer, savouring the sight of the grey mass of steel with its clutter of aerials, boats, pipes, signal lamps, boxes and other fittings. To his mild annoyance Margaret stopped beside him.

They were joined by Stephen and Max. Max raised an eyebrow. "What happened?" he asked.

"What happened to you more like!" Graham retorted.

Max shrugged. "There were so many sailors rushing to the fight that I didn't think you needed me," he explained.

Graham glanced at Stephen who adjusted his glasses as though they were sufficient excuse for not joining in. Peter then described the interviews.

"Did they believe you?" Max asked.

Graham shrugged. "I don't know. They didn't say."

Peter nodded. "I think they believed our version of events. Anyway, it was four against two in the story telling," he commented.

Stephen again adjusted his glasses. "What did Edmonson and that other jerk say?"

Peter shook his head. "No idea. They questioned us one at a time in another room. Where are they anyway?"

Stephen pointed along the wharf. "Over there with Janet and Thelma and that mob," he said.

Once again Graham glanced towards Thelma and saw that she was looking at him. So were most of those with her. *I hope she doesn't notice Margaret,* he thought. A feeling of mild discomfort swept through him as the demonstrators returned the scrutiny.

Graham looked away and as he did he noticed Cindy talking to two sailors over near the entrance to the wharf. *She is a real flirt!* he thought. He felt relief when Max called her to join him. "Time to go home," he said.

Cindy nodded and pouted but then said goodbye to the sailors and walked over to join them. As she did her eyes briefly met Graham's but she gave no hint of any secret between them.

Mrs Kirk stopped at the exit and looked back. "Come on you children. We are going home."

"Good idea," Peter agreed. "I think we have seen enough today."

Graham didn't agree and as the others began walking away he turned to have one last look at the destroyer. Kylie looked back and called in an exasperated tone: "Come on Graham, you've seen enough of the battleship!"

"It's not a battleship!" Graham responded testily. "Battleships are much bigger; ten times as big—no more!"

Max stopped and called back, "How would you know? You've never seen one!"

"I've seen pictures of them," Graham replied defensively. He was a little hurt by Max's thrust. If there was one thing on earth Graham wished to see it was a battleship. He had read dozens of books about them and was fascinated by the steel monsters. "I'd really like to see one," he added.

"Fat chance of that," Peter observed. "There aren't any anymore."

"Yes there are!" Graham cried. "The Americans still have some."

Peter shook his head. "Not in service. They have all been decommissioned and are museums," he replied.

"Not all. I think some are still in mothballs," Graham answered.

"Mothballs!" Kylie tittered. "Do they have a problem with silverfish and cockroaches?"

Graham was not amused. He sniffed and said, "Probably. And rats. They seal the ships up to preserve them in case they need them again. The US Navy has still got one or two of its four Iowa-class battleships in their Reserve Fleet, I think."

Peter nodded. "The last I read was that they have only two still in reserve: the *Wisconsin* and *Iowa*. The *Missouri* and *New Jersey* have been sold and turned into museums or memorials," he said.

"Didn't the British have a lot?" Margaret asked. "We saw that in a video in History the other day."

Graham nodded. "Yes, they did but they've all been scrapped for half a century or more now," he replied. He almost sighed aloud with regret at the thought. Into his mind came a film he had seen, an old black and white Newsreel, which showed a line of British battleships in line astern. He had found the sheer majesty and power of that scene awe-inspiring.

As they began to move Max said, "The last British battleship was the *Vanguard*. It was scrapped way back in the 1960s," he said.

Graham looked at him in mild surprise. He hadn't expected Max to know something like that.

"Come on," Kylie said. "Let's go home. I'm hungry."

They resumed walking along the wharf towards the entrance. Graham came last, his eyes still feasting on the ship; with glances to see where Thelma was. To his disappointment he could no longer see her. The demonstrators all seemed to have vanished too. He shrugged and turned his attention back to the destroyer. Margaret walked beside him but said nothing. As they reached the entrance they had to wait while a group of people in navy uniforms came through the doors from the other direction.

Navy Cadets!

Graham stared at them in envy. That was his immediate ambition. As soon as he was thirteen he was going to join the Navy Cadets—and his birthday was only six weeks away!

"G'day gang!" called a voice. It was a boy from their class: Andrew Collins. Graham managed a reply but his voice was choked up by surprise and envy. Andrew was already a cadet. Graham ran his eyes down from the grey sailor's baseball cap, over the grey and black mottled camouflage uniform to the black leather boots. How he longed to wear that uniform! Or, better still, one of the Petty Officer's or officer's uniforms with the peaked cap.

Thelma would be impressed then, he thought. Graham imagined himself dressed that way. Into his mind came a photo on the side table at home of his father in a naval uniform. *I'll look good,* he told himself with pleasant conceit.

Stephen eyed the navy cadets and nodded with approval. "There are a couple of good lookers in that mob!" he commented, indicating several girls in uniform. "I might join."

Graham looked and saw that Stephen was right. Some of the girls were very pretty. He had recently reached the age where girls interested him very much so he studied them carefully.

Max nudged him. "I like the look of that one with the black hair," he commented.

"No Max," Stephen said. "You can have the fat one. Strewth! Isn't she huge! You watch the stern of the ship go down when she goes up the gangplank."

Kylie gasped. "Stephen! Don't be awful!" she chided.

Graham stood and watched the cadets file on board the destroyer. They were met by an officer and several ratings and were obviously going to get a special guided tour. *To see all the things we weren't allowed to,* Graham thought enviously. Regretfully he turned and followed the others.

Chapter 3

PLASTICINE PEOPLE

At the front car park Mrs Kirk told the children to go straight home. She could not give them a lift in her car as they had all ridden their bicycles. Graham badly wanted to stay, both to see the destroyer and to see Thelma but knew he could not disobey. *I'm in enough trouble already,* he thought. So he joined the others, unlocked his bike and began pedalling. After four blocks Peter and Stephen called farewells and turned right along Lake Street. About 20 minutes later, Graham, Kylie, Margaret, Max and Cindy reached the corner of the street fronting the Kirk's house. Max and Cindy turned left while the others turned right. "See ya later!" Max called.

Graham nodded a reply and then met Cindy's eyes. She gave a mischievous grin and also said goodbye. This time Graham was more enthusiastic. *She is a real flirt,* he thought. For a few moments he eyed her female shape as she pedalled away. *A very shapely bum,* he noted with approval. He would have liked to watch for longer but did not dare lest Kylie and Margaret notice his interest.

At the front gate of home Graham dismounted and said to Kylie, "I hope we aren't grounded after that fight."

Kylie shook her head. "I don't think we will be. I think mum believes us," she replied.

Feeling sore and anxious, Graham wheeled his bike around the side lawn and placed his bike under the back of the house next to his mother's car and went up the back stairs followed by Kylie and Margaret. Mrs Kirk was already home and in the kitchen. With her was Graham's big brother Alex. Mrs Kirk looked up from what she was doing to give Margaret a greeting. Graham saw that she was sifting flour for a cake or scones.

To test her mood Graham said, "Can we have some afternoon tea mum?"

Mrs Kirk looked at him and frowned. "No. It is much too close to tea time. You should have come home straight from school. Now let me look at your face."

Graham swallowed and moved to let her look. As he did Alex grinned. "What happened to you little brother?" he asked.

"There was a fight," he admitted.

"A fight! Who with? Why? What happened?" Alex asked. He and Graham had often fought and Alex was frequently in trouble at school for fighting so it was something he understood.

"A kid from school. It was nothing," Graham answered.

Kylie shook her head. "Oh it was so! It was with two anti-war protestors who tried to take down the flag on a destroyer," she said.

"Ensign," Graham muttered, annoyed that she had used the wrong term.

His mother waved him to silence. "Never mind that. Stand still while I check these bruises," she demanded.

Reluctantly Graham stood while his mother fussed and tut-tutted. Then he described to Alex what had happened, Kylie adding bits he omitted.

"Why did you do it?" Mrs Kirk snapped.

Graham squirmed and shrugged before saying, "Because I didn't want the navy flag—ensign—pulled down by two ratbags," he replied.

"And why were you at the wharf? Who said you could go there?" Mrs Kirk demanded.

Graham shrugged. "You weren't home so we thought it would be all right," he answered.

Mrs Kirk sighed and looked up at the ceiling then glared at him and pressed her lips into a firm line. After a few seconds she said, "Graham! I know you have been in a bit of trouble lately but it doesn't help if you don't tell me. I don't want any sneaking. There must be trust."

"Yes mum."

"Don't go places without asking permission please," she snapped. "And that goes for you too Kylie, and you Alex," Mrs Kirk said.

"Yes mum," they chorused.

Graham now voiced another anxiety that had been gnawing at him.

"What do you think dad will say?" he asked. He was quiet sure that his mother would tell him.

Surprisingly Mrs Kirk smiled. "I think he will say what I am also thinking: that any child of mine who fights to keep his country's flag flying deserves a medal. I think he will be proud of you all."

Graham glowed inside at that and for a moment he met Margaret's eye. She positively beamed hero worship back and he had to smile and then look away.

Mrs Kirk then said, "Margaret, I think you had better go home now. It is getting late. It will be dark soon. You are not in trouble and you are welcome anytime but I need to speak to these children in private."

Margaret nodded and looked embarrassed. "Yes Mrs Kirk. Goodbye Kylie, Goodbye Graham," she whispered. She cast a lingering look at Graham and then turned and walked towards the front.

Kylie called after her, "See you tomorrow!"

"Yes."

After Margaret had gone Mrs Kirk got them to retell the story and then she shook her head and looked thoughtful. "Well, I hope there are no repercussions," she said. "Now Kylie, you go and have your bath while I doctor Silly Boy."

So Kylie had her bath and then Graham was sent to have his. After that, wanting a bit of peace and quite to recover in, he went downstairs to the Ship Room, a large enclosed area under the house. The house was a typical 'Old Queenslander' set in its own allotment with gardens at the front and lawns all around. The back of the block was taken up by vegetable gardens, a fowl run and a big mango tree.

The timber house was on high wooden posts with the living areas upstairs. Downstairs under the front veranda were a fernery where Captain Kirk cultivated orchids and ferns when he was home, and an aviary. Behind them, under the main part of the house were the Ship Room, tool room and store room. Behind them were a carport and laundry.

The Ship Room took up almost half the area. It was a large room about 10 metres square, interrupted by six of the house posts set in the concrete floor. Graham had become the sole user of this room largely by default: no-one else wanted it at that time. For the last three years it had developed as his private domain where he kept his model ships and played games with his 'Plasticine People'.

These were tiny model people about 2cms high that he had made. Initially they had been created as crews for his model sailing ships, but this had soon evolved to include whole armies. Graham had liked model building as long as he could remember. His first attempt at scratch building a model had been at age 6. His father had built a model of a pearling lugger, carved from a piece of timber, painted with varnish and rigged with bamboo masts, cloth sails and cotton rigging.

Graham had so admired this he had tried to emulate it—with sufficient success to give him pride in his own creation. He had been working slowly at model-making for years. About four years earlier his literary horizons had taken in the *Horatio Hornblower* books by C S. Forester. These were a window on a wonderful new world and led him on to several more book series about sailing ships during the Napoleonic Wars: notably those by Patrick O'Brian about Captain Aubrey; and by Dudley Pope about Lord Ramage.

Inspired by these books, Graham had begun building models of 18th Century warships. The urge to play games with them followed. He had built a crude waterline model of a small Sloop of War which he called HMS *Investigator* (although it bore no real resemblance to the original sailed by Matthew Flinders). But something seemed to be lacking— people. An experiment with HO Scale plastic people was unsatisfactory. They cost money, had to be carefully painted, came in odd poses, and kept falling over and getting lost when he pushed the ship around the lawn.

Next, Graham experimented with plasticine, having watched Kylie make some little people for a school project. His first attempt had a wire skeleton over which he squeezed different coloured plasticine. But he did not like it. The little man kept falling over. Also his bones would show through after he was handled.

Another experiment with plasticine had led to a simple little man of four colours. His head was a tiny ball of orange about 3mm in diameter. The body was a blob of blue with two arms squeezed out sideways and two tiny yellow buttons, each smaller than a pinhead. All this was set on another blob of white plasticine, which represented the lower body and legs. After some trial and error Graham had given up attempts to make the little man stand up on legs and now simply made the lower part a flat bottomed blob. The magic of imagination endowed the little man with life; and allowed the deformity of the legs to be ignored.

Jack, as he was christened, was a success. He was placed at the steering wheel of the *Investigator*, where he still stood. Experiments quickly added more clothing details to other little people: black, 18th Century sailor hats, tricorn and bicorn hats for officers, finely rolled yellow plasticine for gold lace and gold epaulets.

Research into costumes and uniforms was the next phase. A marine in a red coat with gold lace and white cross-straps had been so impressive Graham had made a dozen more, arming them with pins to represent muskets with fixed bayonets. Some details were not successful and were abandoned: hair on men except for beards or moustaches; eyes, noses and hands.

Soon Graham had hundreds of little people: sailors, soldiers, marines, pirates, smugglers, civilians. Inevitably the French, Spanish and Dutch had to be made to provide enemies. An American Clipper model was included in the game, even though it wasn't the right scale. Indeed scale had not been a conscious consideration. Graham had not constructed the models from plans but from pictures, using instinct and looks to judge scale.

The next development had been a demand by his brother Alex to play. Alex had insisted on being both the pirates and the Americans. His models were relatively crude and Alex was a sore loser so the games often led to fights.

Inevitably Kylie had been roped in. She then took the bit between her teeth and set up her own country. She had only a few ships but was very good at making people. She made a whole army of soldiers with black shakos, dark green tunics, white trousers and white cross-straps. These were the Lucranians. She made a King, a Queen and a Princess then built a white painted cardboard castle for them to live in.

Alex had responded by making the Prussian army, all black uniforms with silver or white details. Using these he kept invading Lucrania. Graham had become interested in Napoleon and steadily built up a huge French army. But as the others were only intermittently interested in the game he usually fought against himself; using a dice to decide casualties.

Indeed arbitration by the dice was insisted on by their father; in an attempt to prevent arguments becoming fistfights.

This had led them into wargaming, evolving their own rules; or adapting those from books on the subject.

A TV series called *Cities of Gold* had led to more model construction, of Aztec temples and houses, jungles which were mostly made of two dimensional cardboard trees with trunks stuck in blobs of plasticine; plus hordes of wild Indians, cannibals, head hunters and other savages; as well as both Incas and Aztecs. Graham next made the Conquistadors. Their armour was cut from the thin aluminium foil found in the top of Milo and coffee tins.

Over the years the interest of Alex and Kylie had waxed and waned. Kylie became something of an expert at constructing model buildings to scale (1cm = 1m). Only Graham consistently continued to build model ships and to play with them. Now Graham had seventy-five of them, ranging from huge Ships of the Line nearly a metre long down to tiny schooners and native outriggers. Some were very poorly put together— rush jobs to meet some emergency; but a few were examples of genuine craftsmanship, of which Graham was secretly very proud.

So Graham now withdrew into his private space and sat at the desk in the far corner. For a few minutes he just sat and relived the events of the afternoon. Inevitably his mind moved to thinking about the girls. For a while he brooded over how his intervention to stop the demonstrators might be viewed by Thelma. *They are her friends,* he thought glumly. *So she is not likely to go out with me now.*

But despite that he couldn't help hoping and he fantasized about various scenarios during which he would win her admiration and then her love. But then his gaze wandered to the model sailing ship under construction on the table. Reaching forward he drew the model closer and set to work. He carefully tied a piece of cotton to a pin protruding from the hull of the model. Then he picked up the tube of Tarzan's Grip, unscrewed the cap, took a gentle sniff; then dabbed a tiny blob of glue on the cotton knot. With deft fingers he replaced the cap on the glue tube, resisting the temptation to take another whiff. He was no glue-sniffer and was well aware of the dangers of such a practice, but for him the smell of model glue was a real pleasure!

Probably because it reminds me of all the enjoyment my models have given me, he mused. He checked that the glue was dry before trimming the loose end of the cotton thread. Then he gently placed the model down on the concrete floor and looked around.

They are a good collection, he thought with satisfaction.

His contemplation was interrupted by his mother's voice calling him upstairs for tea. Reluctantly he obeyed. Later that night, when he lay in bed, he again fantasized about girls. To his own annoyance he found it hard to hold a firm mental image of Thelma. Images of other girls seemed to slip into his fantasies: Joany from Year 10, Max's sister Cindy, and even little Margaret. He tried to push these last thoughts out because she was too young but they remained the most accurate and persistent, mainly because she was the only girl he had seen nude and been naked with. This had occurred several times, most recently when they were on a picnic at Kamerunga and he and she had gone swimming together with nothing on. It had been a mixture of dare, wholly normal adolescent curiosity and affectionate exploration.

He fell asleep with his mind full of a mixture of erotic fantasies and vague worries about what might happen at school the next day.

Chapter 4

SCHOOL

As he walked to school on Wednesday morning Graham experienced a mixture of emotions. Chief among them was tingling anticipation and anxiety about how Thelma might view him. *I think she knows I exist now,* he thought. But after him fighting her friends would that do him any good? Graham could only shrug and hope.

The next strongest emotion was worry about possible conflict with Edmonson and any of his friends. *He is in Year 10 and he and his mates could make my life pretty miserable,* Graham mused.

On arriving at the high school Graham was suitably cautious. He had experienced grief from older bullies before so was wary of just blundering into potential trouble. At each doorway and corner he paused and took a cautious peek before proceeding. To his relief he saw no sign of Edmonson. Nor could he see Jerry Denham, the Year 12 boy who had been with the demonstrators.

The first of his friends he met was Stephen. They went and sat in their usual spot and chatted about the incident on the destroyer. Graham was still a bit put out that Stephen had slipped away but did not want to risk the friendship by making accusations. *Steve won't want to get into trouble with his oldies,* he reckoned.

Next to wander by was Andrew Collins. Andrew stopped and said, "Hi Graham. I hear you got into a bit of trouble on the destroyer."

Graham nodded. He liked Andrew but was jealous of him, partly because he thought him better looking than himself but mainly because he was already a navy cadet. "That's right. Two of those demonstrators were trying to pull down the ensign and replace it with some peace flag," he explained.

Andrew grinned. "Good for you!" he said.

That made Graham feel better and they began to discuss the incident. As they talked Max joined them and then Peter. The friends discussed the fight and its aftermath. As they talked about this Graham spotted Edmonson in the distance. *There he is! I hope there is no trouble at school,* he thought. He had been in trouble too much already this year and had no desire to visit the Deputy Principal's office again.

Luckily Edmonson did not see him and walked on. Soon after that the bell for classes went and the friends stood up and began moving to their classrooms. As they walked Graham scanned the faces of the other students, hoping to see Thelma.

He did, but only after they reached the classroom. She was on the veranda busy digging books out of her school bag. Nerving himself, Graham approached her. Trying to sound very casual and relaxed, he said, "Hi Thelma!"

Her response was to look up and then give a half smile. "Hello!' she replied. But it was a very off-hand response and her smile was frozen and perfunctory. Before Graham could speak again she quickly moved away into the room. As she normally sat next to Janet Graham got no other chance to speak to her.

She at least said hello, he told himself hopefully. *She knows I exist.* But her response had hurt. In his heart he knew she had rejected his advance.

For the next hour Graham sat at his desk and gazed with hurt adoration at Thelma. His seat was in the back row over near the right of the room and she was one row in front, and to the left of him. Thus he could look at her without turning his head, or appearing to stare.

She is wonderful! he thought. For several minutes he admired the delicate lobe of her ear, the gentle curve of her throat, the sparkle of light on her hair, the shape of her neck (She's got a few freckles there. Hmm, never mind. I've got plenty myself). He then focused his adolescent boy's mind on the way her right breast strained at the cloth. An itch of desire pulsed through him.

"Kirk!"

Graham imagined himself at sea on his gunboat, rescuing Thelma from the clutches of Arab slavers. He had just put the gunboat alongside the Arab Dhow and is poised, pistol in hand to...

"Kirk!"

It was Mr Wilesmith, his teacher, a grumpy man in his 60s. He was bellowing now. Graham jerked back to reality. *What did the old coot say?* he wondered with a sense of rising alarm.

Mr Wilesmith—'Old Wily' to the kids—smiled and said mildly: "Ah! I see you have returned. Did you enjoy your trip?"

Graham blushed. "Yes sir," he replied, trying not to sound cheeky.

"Oh good! Where were you?"

"Persian Gulf sir, fighting Arab slave traders," Graham replied.

A titter of giggling ran round the room. Old Wily smiled but he had a kindly gleam in his eye. "Very interesting, but this is maths. Please attend to the problem."

"Yes sir," Graham said. He sighed. Nowadays it seemed he was always in trouble like that. *Old Wily is OK. He understands that a kid has to escape sometimes,* Graham thought. But some of the other teachers weren't that tolerant. What hurt Graham the most in this case was that Thelma had heard. The class knew him of old as a daydreamer and story teller so that did not bother him, but he did want her to think well of him. *I don't want her to think I am just a little kid,* he thought.

To his dismay she half turned to look and then quickly looked away. Graham got only a glimpse of her face and was left worrying that the expression he had seen on it was a sneer of contempt. *Oh I hope not! I must be more careful,* he told himself.

Graham tried to settle down to work, but maths was his weakest subject and he wrestled miserably with the maths problems for a while, in a fog as to what they were all about. His attention wandered again after 10 minutes and he started to sketch on his notebook. While Old Wily gave a detailed explanation of how to solve a problem Graham quietly drew. A new gunboat took shape on the page.

Maths ended and the German teacher arrived: the much feared Miss Hackenmeyer, an acid-tongued woman in her thirties whom Stephen unkindly said was once Hitler's mistress. The lesson began: conjugating verbs. Graham quickly lost interest and turned back to his drawing of the gunboat. Refinements were added to the picture: guns blazing; tracer pumping out of the Bofors; a JU87 Stuka dive-bomber crashing in flames with a very satisfying trail of black smoke behind it.

Stephen sat beside him, also drawing. He busied himself with making up a cartoon sequence on the pages of his notebook. On the bottom of each page he drew a tiny motorcycle and rider. On each succeeding page the motorcycle was drawn closer to a ramp, then on the ramp, then in the air, then crashing. By flicking the pages quickly with his thumb it gave the impression of movement as in a movie. When he was finished Stephen polished his glasses, nudged Graham and showed him. They both guffawed.

The result was inevitable. "You two boys will stay in at lunch time and copy out all of pages 56 and 57," snapped Miss Hackenmeyer.

Graham sighed. *Another lunch time detention! I always seem to be in trouble!* What really hurt was that he would not be able to see Thelma at lunch time. He was in the process of trying to pluck up courage to ask her for a date and had decided that first he should strike up a casual friendship. *If I hardly ever get a chance to see her that plan won't work,* he thought.

But he didn't stop drawing ships in class. He dreamed of ones that he might build and sketched rough plans for them. And when he and Stephen did get out at the latter half of the lunch break it wasn't Thelma that Graham met but Edmonson.

They almost collided at the corner of a building. Both stopped and then, as recognition came, Edmonson scowled. "You, you little turd! I should smash you!" he snarled. Then he reached out and grabbed Graham's shirt front. "You get in our way again and you'll be sorry!"

Graham stepped back and wrenched his shirt free. He opened his mouth to reply but could think of nothing to say. Edmonson then glanced at Stephen before shouldering Graham aside and continuing on his way.

Stephen pushed his glasses up his freckled nose and grinned. "I see your plan to convert the world to your point of view isn't working yet!" he jibed.

Graham could only snort and resume walking, pretending he wasn't upset or scared. A few seconds later they passed Janet and another girl.

Janet is Thelma's friend. I need her on side, Graham thought. After swallowing with anxiety he plucked up the courage to speak. "Hello Janet," he said.

Janet turned and looked at him, then curled her upper lip into a sneer, but made no reply. Graham flushed with embarrassment and kept on walking.

Stephen grinned again and said, "You'll have to polish your technique if you want to have a girl in every port!"

Graham scowled. "I don't want that!" he retorted.

Stephen laughed and teased him some more: "Fine words, but what will you do when some scrumptious tart calls out 'Hello sailor!'?"

Graham again made a face and did not reply. He was a bit hurt by Stephen's attitude and he told himself he would never go with girls like that. *Only with nice girls like...* An image of Margaret sprang to mind and he shook his head. *Like Thelma,* he told himself, deliberately conjuring up her image. Then an image of Cindy swirled provocatively into his mind and he experienced such a surge of lust that he knew he was a hypocrite. The knowledge was followed by more guilt at having such thoughts.

Stephen then hurt Graham's feeling again by swerving left. "Oh, there's Lorna. Hi Lorna! See ya Graham."

Graham was left standing, his emotions reeling from the triple blows to his self-esteem. With resentment and jealousy in his heart he watched Stephen walk over to Lorna, a bubbly, busty brunette in their class. Stephen grabbed her and gave her a kiss on the lips, in blatant defiance of the school rules. Lorna's response was to giggle and hug him back. Stephen then put an arm around her waist as they strolled off.

Stephen's easy manner and his obvious success with the girls really rankled with Graham. *How does he do it? He's an ugly bugger with those freckles and glasses and he's not as good looking as me. So what has he got?* Graham wondered.

Feeling quite dejected he went and sat on a bench seat under 'B' Block. For a few minutes he sat there, staring moodily into space and wondering how he could win with Thelma. Then he shrugged. *I'm probably not going to,* he decided.

A girl stopped in front of him and he found himself staring at a very nice pair of legs. Graham looked up. It was Joany. She smiled and said, "Hi Graham! You look like you've lost your last penny."

"Hello Joany. No. I just had a problem with one of the Year 10 boys," Graham replied. Even though she was years older Graham felt curiously at ease when talking to her. Then came an urgent rush of desire that quickly got him so aroused he physically squirmed and hoped nobody would notice.

"Which Year 10?" Joany asked, seating herself beside him.

"Edmonson," Graham replied, looking anxiously around and hoping that Thelma was not around.

"Why?"

Graham told her, describing the incident in detail. Joany listened intently and then put her hand on Graham's arm. "You will be all right. I don't think he will do anything at school," she said. She began to chatter about an incident with Miss Hackenmeyer, keeping her hand on his arm while she did. The upshot was Graham becoming even more aroused by her touch. He did not dare let on and nor was he game to stand up and walk away in case his condition was noticeable. So he sat there in pleasant arousal and secret embarrassment. It was a relief when the bell went to resume classes and she stood up and gave a cheery goodbye and left. He was able to relax and make his way to the classroom.

One result of the lunch time meeting with Joany was that Graham found his thoughts straying from Thelma onto her. *She is nice,* he decided. And he had enjoyed being touched by her and appreciated her friendship. *Maybe?* he thought, hotly aware that Thelma was not responding.

When the bell went for the end of classes Graham made his way outside to put his books in his bag. As he did he noted Thelma and Janet further along the veranda, both also packing their bags. At that moment Janet looked up and her eyes met his. A hostile look crossed her face and she said something to Thelma who glanced towards Graham. Then she quickly looked away but not before a look of annoyance had crossed her face. The two girls walked away in the opposite direction to the one Graham usually went.

For a few seconds he contemplated following them and putting everything to the test by asking Thelma outright for a date. But then he found the prospect of trying to do so with Janet present too daunting. Feeling sad and despising himself as a coward he turned and made his way downstairs and out to the street.

Head down as he walked along brooding Graham crossed the street and suddenly found his path blocked by three youths. He looked up and found himself staring into the hostile gaze of Edmonson.

Edmonson shoved Graham hard in the chest and snarled: "You got me into a lot of trouble you sneaking rat! My dad gave me a good hiding when I got home and that was your fault."

"No it wasn't. You were doing the wrong thing," Graham replied, his heart hammering his ribs hard with anxiety and his mouth going dry from fear.

"Wrong thing! What a moron! Anyway, you owe me and I'm gunna take it out of your hide," Edmonson threatened. He raised his fists and stepped forward.

Graham swallowed and gulped and then looked around for a way out. Edmonson was bigger and older and he had his two cronies Macnamara and Harvey with him. *How can I escape?* Graham thought.

Chapter 5

FEAR AND HOPE

Even as these thoughts raced through Graham's mind Edmonson swung a punch. Graham twisted away but not quickly enough. The blow took him on the left shoulder. He sprang back but behind him was a busy street and no escape until the traffic lights changed. All he could do was put up his own fists and try his best.

Another punch also missed his head but struck his chest. Graham was able to deflect a third punch and thanked his lucky stars that his father had taught him how to box. Edmonson swore and jumped forward again. Again Graham danced clear and received only a glancing blow.

Graham looked around but all he could see was a blur of cars and people on the other footpath. *Maybe a teacher will save me?* he hoped, knowing that teachers were on duty at the gate after school.

But none intervened and the next punch caught Graham hard on the forehead. He reeled back and fell on his buttocks. That hurt as well as it was on the concrete guttering. Tears of pain and then of mortification sprang to his eyes and mocking laughter rang in his ears.

Edmonson stepped forward and grabbed Graham's sleeve as he tried to get up. "Grab him you blokes so I can really teach him a lesson," he ordered.

Graham tried to break free. In desperation he swung at Edmonson but the blow was swept aside and in return another punch took him in the face. Then Graham's arm was seized by one of the jeering cronies. Edmonson's sneering face filled Graham's vision and then a punch drove into his stomach and he doubled up in pain. Before he could straighten up another took him in the side of the head, causing waves of dizziness.

There was a screech of rubber and through his pain-misted eyes

Graham noted that a bicycle had stopped right next to him. Shoes appeared and then he heard Stephen's voice. "Let's make it a fair fight," he yelled.

Graham looked up to see that Stephen was placing his glasses in his shirt pocket. He then put up his fists. Peter also appeared, his bike being flung onto the footpath. Edmonson let go of Graham and stepped back. So did his cronies. Stephen spoke firmly: "Let him go!"

To Graham's relief, Edmonson stepped back even further and lowered his fists. "He was just annoying us," he snarled. "So we were teaching him a little lesson."

"Crap!" Stephen retorted. "It was just payback for yesterday. Show some guts why don't you? Fight one-on-one, man-to-man."

"Mind your own business!" Edmonson replied, but he stepped back further as Peter ranged alongside Stephen.

"It is our business," Stephen answered. "He's our mate."

"Huh! Poor choice of mate, picking a weakling and a dobber!" Edmonson blustered.

"Oh yeah? So put 'em up and we will see who is a weakling?" Stephen replied.

Instead Edmonson turned and walked way, following his two cronies who had already retreated 20 paces. "You'll keep Kirk!" he called. "You won't always have your ugly mates around to protect you."

With that he and his cronies hurried away. Peter turned to Graham. "You OK mate?"

"Yeah, just a bit bruised," Graham replied. He straightened up with an effort and looked around. As he did his eyes met Thelma's. She and Janet were both standing on the other side of the street and the look on her face sent a chill of distress through Graham. *She saw that and she is laughing at me!* he thought.

That hurt. But then he noted the look of mocking malice on Janet's face and he felt even worse. Sadly he shook his head and looked away. Turning to Stephen he said, "Thanks mate. You saved my bacon then."

Stephen took out his glasses and began polishing them. "They are just gutless bullies," he replied casually. "They aren't game to fight when the odds are even."

Peter helped steady Graham and picked up his bag. "You had better watch out for them Graham," he said.

"I will. Thanks."

"If they give you any grief you let us know," Peter added.

"Thanks," Graham replied. He was very grateful to his friends and glowed inside because he had such good ones but at that moment he was feeling more battered emotionally than physically. *Thelma doesn't like me and Janet is an enemy,* he thought. Tears of rejection and self-pity welled up and he sniffled and struggled to hide them.

After thanking his friends again he quickly turned and hurried off homewards. Once there he went to his Ship Room and sat brooding, the misery welling up from time to time in bouts of depression and tears.

What can I do? he wondered. And there was the gnawing anxiety about what might happen at school the next day.

That night Graham lay awake for hours, his hopes and fears alternating. In a deliberate attempt to push concern about the bullies out of his mind he constructed fantasies about girls. To begin with these centred on Thelma. *I am sure she will like me,* he told himself. *If only I can get her away from that Janet.*

But when he imagined heroic battles to rescue Thelma her face and body kept changing. To his annoyance he images of Cindy kept slipping into the scenes. That made him feel disloyal to Thelma until he woke from a dream in which he had been doing things to a naked Margaret. That left him very aroused and very confused. When he tried to imagine Thelma again he felt guilty about Margaret.

She's just a little kid, he told himself. But that was no real help as he knew he wasn't being honest with himself. The real issue, he admitted, was that Margaret was still in Primary School and he did not want to be teased by his mates. *She is only a couple of years younger. In a few years time that will be quite normal,* he thought.

But he still tried to tell himself that it was Thelma he was in love with and he attempted to make her the focus of his thoughts. *When I get to school I will ask her for a date,* he told himself. Then niggling fear added the qualification that he would ask but only when she was alone.

As luck would have it Thelma was almost the first person he met when he got to school the next day—and she was alone. Graham swallowed and forced a smile. "Hi Thelma! How are you?" he said.

To his great relief Thelma gave a smile in return. "Ok thanks," she said. But she did not stop walking and as Graham was going in the opposite direction he could not summon up the courage to speak. So he just kept walking, berating himself for being a fool and a coward. *But at least she smiled and spoke to me,* he thought.

All through the morning lessons Graham admired her and imagined what he would say and then the romantic delights he hoped would follow. Determined to ask her during the first break he even worked hard in class and resisted Stephen's attempts at mischief.

When the lunch break came Graham did not go with his friends. On the excuse of going to the toilet he left Stephen and set off in the direction that Thelma had vanished in. To his frustration she was nowhere to be seen. Anxious to ask her while he had his courage up he hurried around the school looking for her.

Only to almost walk into Edmonson and his cronies!

They were walking towards him but were a whole building away. Graham spun on his heel and hurried back around the corner, not wanting them to see him too obviously flee. But fear was spurring him and as soon as he was out of sight he broke into a run.

Not wanting to be bashed or sent to the office for fighting Graham bolted. He dashed along the length of one building and then around the far end and across to the other side. Here he halted and peeked around the corner, fearful that Edmonson or his mates might have run along that side of the building to cut him off.

But they were nowhere in sight so Graham took the chance and dashed across the space to the next building and across the end of it. Again he halted and peeked around the corner. Then his heart leapt. Coming towards him, and on her own, was Thelma.

Now! he told himself. *Don't be a coward. Ask her.* So he casually strolled around the corner and smiled. Thelma saw him and gave him a smile in return.

"Hi Thelma. I was hoping to meet you," Graham said. Then he faltered as his courage seemed to ebb away. He licked his lips and knew his mouth had gone dry. He wiped sweaty palms on his shorts.

"Oh? Why?" she replied, giving a quizzical smile.

"Because I think you are really nice and I'd like to take you out," Graham managed to force out. By the time he was finished speaking his heart was hammering.

Thelma nodded but looked serious. "That's nice. Thank you, but not right now," she replied.

Graham's mind tried to grapple with the implications and he opened his mouth to reply. But before he could speak he was grabbed from behind and shoved hard against the brick wall.

A voice snarled in his ear, "Leave Thelma alone turd face!"

Graham's heart leapt and he jerked in fright. For an instant he thought it was Edmonson but then another face came into focus and he felt another spasm of fear. It was Jerry Denham, the Year 12!

Denham shoved him again. "Stay way from Thelma. Get out of here," he growled.

Graham stumbled past Thelma, burning with shame that she was watching his humiliation. But Denham had two other Year 12 boys with him and Graham did not dare stand up to them. But his pride was at stake too so he turned and mustered some courage and tried to look defiant, despite his insides quivering.

"I'll talk to who I like," he managed to reply. Thelma looked at him and gave a smile but he could not decide if it was amusement, scorn or sympathy on her face.

Denham took a step toward shim, his clenched fists on his hips. "Clear off you little Year 8 wart, or else!"

It was on the tip of Graham's tongue to point out that Thelma was only a Year 8 too but he managed to bite the words back. Tossing his head and attempting to regain some dignity he curled his lip and began walking away. *Speaking of cradle snatchers!* he thought, but wisely did not say.

There were students sitting under the next building and Graham burned with embarrassment and hoped they hadn't seen what had happened. To check he glanced at them—and his eyes met Joany's. She grinned back and as he got closer she called, "I thought it was the Year 10s that were giving you trouble. Now I see you've graduated to annoying Year 12s! Are you tired of living?"

Graham could only grin foolishly while he tried to think of something to say. *Did she see me getting knocked back by Thelma?* he wondered.

Joany pushed her friend along and indicated that Graham should sit beside her. The other girls all smirked and he blushed but did so. Joany at once put her hand on his arm. "Well, what was that all about?" she asked.

"Denham. He was one of the demonstrators at the wharf the other day," Graham said, hoping to lead the conversation away from Thelma.

"Oh was he? I wonder if he will be down there this afternoon?" Joany replied.

"Why would he be down the wharf this afternoon?" Graham queried. He was very conscious of Joany's nearness and her touch and that was causing his body to stir.

Joany pressed against him with her shoulder. "Because there's another warship coming in. British I think," she answered.

Graham was surprised and a little bit hurt. *How does she know about a warship coming to Cairns?* he wondered. His was the family with the maritime connections and he made an effort to know about such things but had heard nothing. Swallowing his dented pride he replied, "That should be interesting."

Joany nodded. "Mmmm! That's what I thought. Let's go and watch. It is due to berth at 4:00," she said.

That idea had instant appeal but then Graham remembered what his mother had said about telling her where he was going. For a moment he hesitated. But Joany was now holding his hand and he did not have the courage to admit to her he had to ask his mother. "OK," he said.

"See you at the bike racks after school then," she said, squeezing his hand and sending little electric pulses of desire through him.

But that gave him his out. "I will have to go home to get my bike," he replied. At that moment the bell for classes went and Joany sighed and stood up, still holding of his hand. "Oh drat! I don't want to go to Chemistry," she said.

"Who's your teacher?" Graham asked, not wanting to stand as he was now quite aroused.

"Miss McLeod," Joany replied. "Come on naughty boy, get to class or you will be in trouble." She gave an impish grin and hauled him to his feet. For a moment Graham thought she was going to kiss him and their bodies did touch but then she smiled and let go of his hand. "See you later," she said. Then she was walking away and waving.

Graham was quite overwhelmed. Then he remembered where he was and looked guiltily around. There was no sign of Thelma but several other girls were looking at him and doing some behind the hand whispering and giggling. *They can see I've got a horn,* he thought. Blushing furiously he turned and hurried off, willing the erect member to go down.

All through the next lessons Graham sat in a sort of confused daze.

He still thought he was in love with Thelma but understood that she had turned him down. Yet there was Joany, being very friendly and without any effort on his part! *Maybe I should ask Joany out?* he mused. *She would be good fun; and I wouldn't be disloyal to Thelma as she has turned me down.*

Reasoning thus and now filled with hopes of romantic adventures Graham endured the rest of the day. As soon as the last bell went he hurried from the room and placed his books in his bag.

Stephen came and stood beside him. "What's the rush?" he queried.

That gave Graham and spurt of conscience. *Steve and Pete don't know about the British warship,* he thought. *They might be interested.* "I am going to the wharf to see a British warship come in," he said.

Stephen pushed his glasses up his nose and raised his eyebrows. "What ship? When?" he asked.

"Don't know its name. It is due at 4:00 I was told," Graham answered. He did not want to disclose that it was Joany who had told him and who he was going with. *I don't want my mates teasing me,* he thought.

"Good idea. Let's find Pete and go," Stephen said.

As he said this Graham looked past him and saw Thelma and Janet. Janet had been bending down to pack her school bag but now she looked up and their eyes met. A frown crossed her face and she bent down and began whispering to Thelma.

I hope Janet didn't hear me, Graham thought. To put Stephen off he nodded and muttered, "Yes, but I have to go home and get my bike." To get away from Janet he turned and began walking towards the bike racks.

Stephen followed and began chattering about how they rarely got warning of warships coming anymore, "It is so that terrorists don't have time to plan attacks on them," he explained.

Downstairs they hurried to the bike racks and as they got closer Graham scanned for Joany. Stephen pointed. "There's Pete. Let's ask him," he said.

Graham looked and saw Peter unlocking his bike nearby. Then he saw Joany and got all flustered. "I have to go and get my bike. I'll meet you at the wharf," he hastened to say. Then he hurried over to Joany.

She gave him a big smile and began talking to him while she loaded her school bag into her bike's carrier. "Hi Graham. Glad you waited. I am really looking forward to this," she said.

Graham tried to act calm as he chatted to her but to his annoyance he noted Stephen and Peter glancing at him and obviously talking about them. *Bugger!* he thought. *I wanted to keep Joany secret.*

Worse still just talking to her was getting him aroused and he began to feel like he needed to squirm. It was a relief when she had unlocked her bike and begun wheeling it towards the school gate.

As they went through the gate Peter and then Stephen rode past out onto the footpath. Stephen looked back and smirked. "Don't forget you are supposed to be going to the wharf," he called.

Joany poked her tongue at him and yelled, "Mind your own business Stephen Bell! We will do what we like."

"Oooh! Watch out Graham. She's a hot one," Stephen called back.

Graham blushed but his mind raced. *How does Steve know Joany is hot?* he wondered. Then his pulse rate increased. *I might be in luck here.*

But, as his dad said, everything in life has a price and in this case the price was being embarrassed. *I hope Kylie and Margaret aren't at home,* he thought as he and Joany walked towards his home. They both went to a different school and Kylie often went to Margaret's after school.

As he turned into his street Graham studied his house. The front door was open which was good as it meant his mother was home but he could not tell if his sister and Margaret were as well. On reaching the front gate he saw there was no bicycle lying on the front lawn. *Good! Margaret isn't here,* he decided.

Turning to Joany he said, "Wait here while I tell my mum and get my bike."

That left him feeling a bit of a heel as he knew he was being both deceitful to his mother and bad mannered. Leaving Joany at the front gate he hurried upstairs and went through to the kitchen at the back. Luckily his mother was there. "Hi mum. I'm just going to the wharf to watch a British warship come in," he said.

"What warship? Who with?" his mother asked.

"Stephen and Peter and... and a few others," Graham answered.

"Don't you be late for tea," Mrs Kirk said.

"No mum." Thankful that the interrogation had not been prolonged Graham scurried down the back stairs and got his bike from under the house. Quickly he wheeled it to the front gate, wanting to be gone before his mother asked more questions or saw Joany.

Then Graham groaned. As he rounded the front of the house he saw that both Kylie and Margaret had just arrived. They were both eyeing Joany with hostile curiosity. As Graham pushed his bike through the gate Kylie snapped, "Where are you going Graham?"

"To the wharf to see a ship," he replied.

"Can we come?"

"You'd better ask mum," Graham replied. He was blushing he knew and the hurt look in Margaret's eyes seemed to bore into his consciousness. He quickly mounted his bike and began pedalling. Joany followed. Feeling hot and embarrassed Graham pedalled as fast as he could until he was around the next corner and out of sight of his sister and Margaret.

Joany called, "Hey, slow down!"

Feeling puffed and upset Graham did. Joany rode up alongside. "What's the rush?" she asked.

"Just didn't want my sister Kylie asking more questions," Graham answered. He shook his head. *Little sister will have gone racing up to mum to tell her I am going somewhere with a girl,* he thought. It would mean questions and trouble when he got home but he shrugged again as the delight soared. *But I am with a girl, one who wants to be with me.*

Hopeful that more good things would follow, he smiled at Joany and continued pedalling.

Chapter 6

"HELLO SAILOR!"

About 20 minutes later, Graham and Joany were cycling along the Esplanade past the RSL. Out to sea to their left the British warship was visible. It was heading into the Trinity Inlet along the shipping channel and already Graham could identify features on it.

A Type 23 frigate, he decided. "We will just make it in time," he told Joany.

As he pedalled along Graham breathed deeply and felt wonderful. Just looking around made him feel good. He loved living in Cairns and now he drank in the tropical scene of palm trees, the sea, the dark line of mangroves on the far side of the Inlet and the very distinctive line of jungle covered mountains beyond. He knew that those mountains were what sheltered the Inlet and Port of Cairns from the prevailing South East winds.

And I'm with a pretty girl who likes me, he thought happily as he eyed several attractive young women whom he surmised were European backpackers or tourists.

They were entering the tourist strip by this time and had to slow down because of the traffic. Impatience made Graham fret. *I want to be there when it berths,* he thought. Several worries occupied his mind as he dodged cars and pedestrian: Would the demonstrators be there? Would Thelma be there?

Part of his mind told him he should give up on Thelma and accept that he had a good chance with Joany. *Even if she is two years ahead of me at school,* he thought.

At the entrance to the bus station and car park Graham and Joany dismounted and locked their bikes together. They then made their way across to the shops and went through to the main wharf entrance. To Graham's surprise there were hardly any people there. At the doorway were two policemen but they made no attempt to stop the pair walking out onto the wharf.

Outside on the wharf Graham looked around, first to check on the frigate and then in the hope of seeing Thelma or his friends. He saw that there were only a dozen people standing at the edge of the wharf or behind a barricade along the wharf. There were a dozen uniformed police officers and a couple of TV cameramen. Stephen and Peter were there but there was no sign of Thelma or of any demonstrators. *Maybe they didn't get word of the ship coming in?* he decided.

The frigate was already at the end of the main shipping channel and a tug was moving to join it opposite the yacht marina. Graham stood and watched, his eyes flicking from the slowly moving warship to the long line of posts that marked the 9 nautical mile long shipping channel that extend right out from Trinity Inlet to the open sea. It was a piece of the ocean Graham knew well from voyages on his father's ships and from pleasure trips to Green Island.

His eyes took in the details of the ship and his memory confirmed it was indeed a Type 23 frigate. The ship had a black hull number edged in white but Graham had not memorized such details so he did not know its name until it got closer and he heard a man say: "HMS *Cumberland*."

It was only when the frigate was stopped directly opposite them and staring to turn that Graham realized that Joany was holding his hand. *When did she do that?* he wondered. But he didn't mind. It felt very nice. The skin was smooth and warm and sent delicious sensations up his arm and through his body. So did the feel of her hips and shoulders as she bumped against him. *This is nice. I might be in luck,* he told himself.

Then he noticed Stephen grinning at him and saying things to Peter. Peter looked around and also grinned. A flush of mixed embarrassment and pride washed through Graham and added to his heightened emotional state. Keeping a firm grip on Joany's hand he edged across to stand with his friends.

They began to discuss the ship as the tug nudged it in against the clear section of the wharf beyond the barricade. Joany pointed to the sailors lining the sides and superstructure. "They look nice. How many men are there on a ship like that?"

To his shame Graham did not know. "Not sure, a hundred or so I guess," he replied.

"Oh goody!" Joany muttered, leaving Graham puzzled. He went back to study the fine details of the frigate: its guns, missile launchers, radar scanners and other fittings. It all looked good to him and sparked his imagination. The fact that it was a British warship helped. His own Grandfather, now dead, had served as an officer on British ships way back in World War 2 and Graham was very proud of that. *He took part in all those really famous naval actions in the Mediterranean and Indian Ocean and South Pacific,* he thought. The fact that most of the history books and novels he read were by British authors also helped to make him a loyal supporter of the Royal Navy.

They were joined by Andrew Collins and his big sister Carmen and two other students Graham knew were Navy Cadets: Blake and Luke Karaku, a Torres Strait Islander. Greetings were exchanged and the ship's characteristics and role discussed

Joany letting go of his hand was the action that pulled his thoughts out of his daydreams. She still stood beside him, jiggling from one foot to the other and looking excited but she was focused on the ship. Graham shrugged and watched as the lines were thrown to the men waiting on the wharf and then the frigate was eased in to its berth.

Peter had learned that the frigate was in Australian waters after anti piracy patrols in the Indian Ocean and South China Sea. "It is here for some R & R and then an exercise off New South Wales," he explained.

"What's R & R?" Joany asked.

Peter looked at her. "Rest and Recreation," he explained.

Stephen sniggered. "The sailors call it rape and ruin," he added.

Joany gave him a look of distaste and said, "Don't be gross Stephen."

Graham glanced at Stephen and frowned. He was embarrassed that Stephen had used such words in the presence of a girl and regretted moving over to join his friends. The very notion of a male forcing another person to have sex he found repugnant and disgusting and he was sure Joany felt the same. Certainly Carmen gave him a sour look. To change the subject he began talking about the frigate's armament.

The frigate was secured and a gangway placed in position. Blasts of a whistle on the loudspeaker system called attention to a change and Graham was interested to note that the people on the upper deck all stood to attention and the union jack was broken out at the bow staff and the white ensign at the stern. At the same time the white ensign that had been flying from the mast was lowered. This little piece of naval ceremonial kept his attention so that he did not notice that Joany had moved away.

The sailors on deck were dismissed and an armed sentry moved into the bows and others took up station amidships at the top of the gangway and at the stern. These men were armed with short automatic weapons—SA80s, Peter said—and were dressed not in the white sailor's uniform but in dark blue trousers, light blue shirts and dark blue berets.

Stephen pointed at the guards. "Do they have real bullets in those guns do you reckon?" he asked.

Peter nodded. "You bet! Ever since the War on Terror they have been deadly serious with their security."

Stephen looked back and then pointed. "Here come some demonstrators. That might test them."

Graham looked and saw a dozen people carrying anti-war and anti-nuclear placards moving onto the wharf through the entrance. Among them were the scruffy youth he had grappled and also the rabble-rouser with the black beard and his busty blonde girlfriend. They were chanting and waving their signs but were not really aggressive. The police allowed them to advance to the barricade and then stopped them.

No sign of Thelma or Janet, Graham noted. He could not even see Janet's sister. To his relief there was no sign of Edmonson or Jerry Denham either. By then a stream of British sailors in uniform were hurrying down the gangway, each one saluting the white ensign as they did. *Going on leave?* he wondered.

The British sailors walked to the gap in the barricade and began making their way to the entrance past the watching people and demonstrators. They looked to be in a happy mood and just smiled at the slogan chanting group, all except one sailor who had an anti-nuclear sign waved in his face.

"No nuclear power! No nuclear weapons!" cried the demonstrator.

The sailor laughed and in a broad English country accent replied, "Nuclear! You've come to the wrong ship chum. This one's still steam driven or clockwork."

Graham admired that answer. *Nuclear power!* he thought with derision. *This ship is just a general purpose frigate for hunting submarines and the like.* He turned to watch the sailor leaving, and got a shock. Walking out through the entrance beside a sailor was Joany!

Graham gaped and then felt a flush of embarrassment. *I thought Joany came here to be with me!* he thought. Hotly aware of possible public humiliation he glanced around at his friends. None appeared to have noticed anything, so Graham decided to follow her. *Where is she going?* he wondered.

Making his way quickly through the rapidly growing crowd Graham headed for the exit. To frustrate his attempt to hurry were another group of sightseers, more demonstrators and the group of sailors still waiting to go in through the doorway.

It took Graham several irritating minutes to get through the doorway and past another group of people. Then he hurried along the arcade past the shops. *Where has Joany gone?* he wondered, horrible suspicions swirling in his mind.

And there she was—kissing a British sailor!

Graham was so astonished and hurt that he just came to a standstill and gaped. Joany and the sailor were just in the entrance to a shop and the man's mates were chaffing him good naturedly as they walked past. The sailor looked to be young and fit, perhaps nineteen or twenty, with dark hair. He was not only kissing Joany but running his hands over her body. And Joany was obviously not objecting as her arms were around his neck and she was responding. The details of the man's white square neck top seemed to leap into Graham's focus.

Then the sailor glanced at Graham and stooped kissing. Joany frowned and then turned her head. "Graham!" she said.

"Joany, what are you doing?" Graham asked, blushing with embarrassment and at the knowledge that he was probably making a fool of himself.

"Just saying hello to this sailor," Joany replied. "Welcoming him to Cairns."

The sailor looked from one to the other then said to Graham, "Is she your girlfriend?"

Graham did not know what to say. He wanted to say yes but could only shake his head and mumble, "No, she's just a friend."

The sailor looked at Joany and said, "You're still at school aren't you?"

Joany nodded and took her arms from around his neck. The sailor made a wry face. "How old are you?" he asked.

"Fifteen," Joany replied. She gave Graham a look that he could not interpret.

The sailor took his arms from around her waist. "Oh well, that was nice. Thanks, but you'd better run along with your boyfriend before you get into trouble," he said. With that he turned and hurried on along the arcade after his mates.

Joany gave Graham an accusing look. "You didn't have to follow me and spoil my fun!" she said.

His emotions swirling, Graham swallowed and found the courage to reply, "If you wanted a kiss I could have given you one."

At that Joany gave a wry smile. "Yes, but he is more experienced than you. And he will be gone tomorrow."

The implications hit Graham like stinging blows to his pride, but also puzzled him. "What do you mean?" he asked.

"Oh Graham!" Joany cried. "I just wanted a bit of safe experience, to learn what to do; and I didn't want a relationship." She must have seen the look that crossed his face because she reached forward and quite tenderly touched his cheek. "Oh you poor boy! I've been misleading you. I like you Graham, but I don't want a boyfriend."

By now Graham was so confused, embarrassed and upset he really just wanted to run away but he stood and nodded, tears prickling at his eyes and troubling his male pride.

Joany shook her head. "It's OK. You are good looking boy, and you are nice. You won't have any trouble getting a girlfriend."

"Thanks," Graham mumbled.

"Sorry Graham. I do like you but I have already been teased by my friends about talking to a boy from a lower year level," Joany added. "They are saying that you are my Toy Boy."

Another fierce pulse of shame swept through Graham at the thought of what the Year 9 girls might have said. He had heard the expression 'Toy Boy' and vaguely understood it to mean a younger male who was the friend of an older female, but he suspected it had worse connotations and blushed some more.

Joany put her hand on her arm and smiled. "It will be all right. We can still be friends, but not that way. Now, you go back and join your mates and I will go home," she said. With that she turned and walked quickly away.

Not wanting to face more emotional pressure Graham slowly followed her instead of returning to the wharf. He was careful not be seen lest she think he was checking up on her but he did worry that she might try to catch up with the sailor—or meet up with another. To his relief he saw her unlock her bicycle and pedal off in the direction of her home.

As he went to walk across the car park Graham saw Max and his big sister Cindy arrive. They had obviously been home because they had changed out of school uniform. Not wanting to speak to them at that moment Graham went into a shop and watched. To his surprise he saw Cindy speak to a passing British sailor and then stand talking to him. Max looked at his sister and then shook his head and hurried across the wharf entrance. To avoid him Graham went right into the shop and hid until Max had passed. When he came out there was no sign of either Cindy or the sailor. *She is a real flirt,* he thought.

He went to his bike and unlocked it and then rode home, his shame and anxiety growing at every minute. *Kylie might have told mum about Joany,* he worried.

She had. As soon as Graham went upstairs to the kitchen, Mrs Kirk raised one eyebrow. "Kylie tells me you were with some girl. Who was she?"

Graham shrugged. "Just a girl from school. Joany is her name."

"Is there anything between you? Should I know about her?" his mother asked, obviously annoyed.

This time Graham shook his head emphatically, images of Joany kissing the sailor filling his mind. "No mum. She is just a friend. She is in Year 10."

"Where is she now?"

"Gone home I suppose. She left the wharf before I did," Graham answered. To add to his defence he added: "We weren't the only ones there. Stephen and Peter were too, and Andrew Collins and his sister."

To change the topic he described the British frigate and how the wharf was partitioned off for security reasons. On hearing that his mother frowned. "Were those demonstrators there?"

"Some of them," Graham answered, silently cursing the verbal minefield he had walked into.

"Was there any trouble with them?"

"No mum. I just watched the ship come in and then came home," he answered.

To his relief he was allowed to go. To get his jangled feelings under control he took himself to the Ship Room and sat brooding. In his mind he kept hearing Joany's words and he could only shake his head and feel very immature. *He'll be gone tomorrow!* he told himself. The notion that girls might deliberately meet up with strangers like that just to experiment quite shocked him and left him wondering about just how life might be.

That night he brooded and indulged in a fit of the dejections rather than fantasizing about females. But he knew he was still interested in them and that he passionately desired to have a real girlfriend.

There was then the anxiety about being shamed at school the next day. He went there dreading being teased but to his relief none of his friends made any comment. He did see Joany once in the distance and she gave a friendly smile but he did not go over to talk to her, eyeing the other girls near her with some trepidation.

In class he sat and worried about himself and life. *Joany said I am good looking and that I should have no trouble getting a girl friend,* he thought. But there was Thelma and she had rejected him. And so had Ailsa. Into his mind swam an image of Margaret and that annoyed him. *She is too young!* Another image of Jocelyn in 8D came to taunt him. She had made big eyes and friendly overtures as few weeks earlier but he thought she was a silly, gawky creature. *And Cindy is in Year 10 as well,* he thought moodily.

The only positive was that the bullies seemed to have lost interest in him. When he accidentally encountered Edmonson and his mates at the Tuck Shop Edmonson just curled his lip and then ignored him.

Then, thankfully, it was Friday afternoon and the school week was over. This was Graham's favourite time of the week. His mother always brought home a collection of comics and chocolates and in the evening there was Scouts. Graham had been a cub scout for three years and a scout for two and he really enjoyed being part of the group. He particularly enjoyed the hikes and camping trips that the scout master organized.

And his friends were there. Graham was in the Crocodile Patrol with another friend, Roger. Peter was in the Platypus Patrol and Stephen and Max were Kookaburras.

As soon as he met Roger Graham said, "You should have been with us on Tuesday Roger. We spent a couple of hours on that destroyer that is in harbour."

Roger nodded: "I know. Peter has been telling me about it. He said you had a fight and got into trouble," he replied. Roger was a chubby kid with brown hair and brown eyes, replied. He was almost the same age as the other two but, because of a January birthday, was a whole year level lower at school. As a primary school kid he was only tolerated because the three had all been in the same Scout Troop for years.

"There was another warship in port on Thursday," Graham added. "We went to see that as well."

Roger looked a bit hurt. "You could have got me," he chided. Then he asked if anything happened.

For a moment Graham endured burning images of Joany kissing the British sailor but then he shook his head. "No, not really. There were a few demonstrators but the police kept everyone well away from the ship.

After that the conversation faltered and Graham found it a relief when Peter arrived. The Scout meeting then began. As usual there were games and learning activities but for the first time Graham found some of it a bit boring and he wondered if he was outgrowing scouts. This was partly because his thoughts kept wandering to girls.

How can I get a girlfriend? he fretted. His focus shifted back to Thelma. *She didn't actually say no. She said not now,* he rationalized. *So how can I get her to notice me and go out with me?*

Chapter 7

BATTLE OF THE RIVER PLATE

Saturday morning meant chores. There were bird cages to clean out, dogs to wash, the guinea pig hutch to be moved to a clean area of lawn, gardens to be weeded, rooms to be swept and tidied. All of this kept Graham, Kylie and big brother Alex busy for much of the morning. Only when they were done to her satisfaction did their mother relent and allow them to have morning tea. During all of this time Graham brooded about Thelma and about how he had probably ruined his chances. This led him into more daydreams during which he rescued Thelma from the clutches of pirates who had taken over the cruise liner she was on in the South China Sea.

After morning tea Graham retreated to the Ship Room. Here he sat and daydreamed some more while working slowly to rig one of the many model sailing ships he had been too lazy to do properly. After a while he began a game, moving ship models into position to fight a pretend battle.

"Hi Graham. How's tricks ?"

Graham looked up from where he was kneeling on the concrete. It was Max. Graham liked Max. He was almost his opposite in many ways. Max was olive skinned in contrast to Graham's freckles on a ruddy complexion. Max had dark hair while Graham's was fair. Brown eyes and blue eyes; an extrovert nature compared to a shy Graham, and a bubbling sense of mischief which often surfaced as practical jokes.

Max sat down beside Graham and glanced at the model ship he was pushing across the floor. He had seen them many times before so paid little attention to them. "Whatcha doin'?" he asked.

Graham indicated the line of six British warships closing in on a similar line of Spanish ones. "The British are attacking a Spanish treasure 'Flotta'," he explained. The British ships all had hulls painted Nelson-style: black hulls with broad white bands along them over the gun ports, which showed as a chequer pattern of black squares. The Spanish ships on the other hand were a blaze of bright colours with red and gold predominating.

Graham, being a romantic, had not allowed reality to stifle him. His Spanish ships were all 16th Century designs: galleons, caravels and oared galleys, plus a huge carrack. They had the red Crusader crosses on their sails and were festooned with flags and banners. Graham was well aware that the design of warships in the 18th Century had not varied much from one European country to another, but had felt this to be boring. So he had made his navies conform to different patterns for variety.

Thus the Spanish were the most colourful and least homogenous of the fleets. There was the golden galleon—*La Santisima Trinidad* with her sails of mauve and pink silk; and the smaller galleon: *Santa Anna* with blue trimmings to match the gold. The fleet had begun with a small model of one of Columbus's ships, the caravel *Nina*. The *Pinta* had followed, then the *Santa Maria*. There were two oared galleys rowed by slaves and armed with two huge cannons in their bows, inspired by the story in *Midshipman Hornblower*. Two schooners, which were Guarda Costas (needed so Captain Jenkins could have his ear cut off every time war seemed like a good idea), completed the Spanish fleet.

Graham also knew that sailors did not wear uniform in the 18th Century but found it too confusing to sort out who was who when the crews of two ships became involved in hand-to-hand fighting, so he insisted on national uniforms. Thus the British sailors all wore blue shirts and white trousers; the French wore all blue, the Americans all white, and pirates whatever they liked. The Spanish sailors all wore yellow shirts and red trousers and their officer had body armour made from aluminium foil, which looked most impressive.

Max watched the game for a while but soon became restless. "That was fun yesterday when we visited the frigate," he said.

"Yes it was. I wish we could go again today," Graham replied.

Max agreed, but both knew it was pointless. The ship was now at the naval base and was not open to the public. Max asked, "What are you doing this afternoon?"

"Nothing much, why?"

"I've got a video you might like. Dad got it this morning. It's called *The Battle of the River Plate*."

"What's it about?" Graham asked.

"It is about a naval battle during the Second World War—British against the Germans. Dad says it is a true story. Do you want to watch it?"

Graham nodded. "Yeah, all right. When?" he asked.

"After lunch?"

So after lunch Graham walked the three blocks along the street to Max's house. He liked going there. Max's mum was very nice and always put on good afternoon teas. And Max's dad was an interesting character. He worked as an accountant but Graham knew that many years ago he had been a commando and fought in Timor and Afghanistan, and that ensured Graham's respect. However the main reason for liking Max's house was Max's big sister Cindy. Graham secretly hoped to see her, remembering a scene the previous week when she had been out in the back yard in a skimpy bikini while she washed the car. *I might be lucky enough to see her like that today,* he thought.

But, to Graham's secret disappointment, Cindy wasn't home. The two boys sat in the lounge and watched the film on TV. Mr Pullford stopped with them for a few moments and commented: "This is a true story. You see that ship there, the cruiser *Achilles*? She is the actual ship that fought in the battle. After the Second World War the British made this movie about the battle; and they used the *Achilles* to play herself. There is another real ship in it later, the heavy cruiser HMS *Cumberland*. And the other two British cruisers are real World War 2 ships."

"What about the German ship?" Graham asked.

Max jeered. "It was sunk!" he said.

Max's father answered: "In the film an American heavy cruiser plays the part of the German pocket battleship *Admiral Graf Spee*."

They settled to watch the movie. Graham knew the outline of the story. He was a keen reader of naval history and his grandfather had been an officer on British ships during that war. A photo on the side table at home of Grandad in his naval uniform was a constant reminder, as was the photo of his father during the more recent operations to free Makassang.

The film was about the cruise of the German pocket battleship (Panzerkruezer) *Graf Spee* in 1939 in the South Atlantic and how she was finally caught and driven into Montevideo in Uruguay by three much smaller British warships: the 6" light cruisers *Ajax* and *Achilles* and the 8" heavy cruiser *Exeter*. Graham sat transfixed. He became wholly absorbed in the story, although at times the English period-slang and acting jarred on him a bit.

Max was less impressed. "Bit corny the way these guys talk," he commented as Commodore Harwood held a conference with his cruiser captains. Graham barely heard him. He just wished he was there as one of them. Just seeing the officers in their tropical white uniforms planning the action filled him with a deep yearning to be like them. When the action began he was totally absorbed in it. The images of the great ships wheeling over the blue sea, their guns belching fire and smoke gripped him and set his imagination racing.

When the movie was over he sat for a while in silent contemplation. Not so Max. He broke into animated talk. "Weren't those cruisers great to watch?"

"Yes," Graham agreed. "Especially the Colony-class with the three triple 6" turrets." They were, he decided, the very essence of good looking warships—real warships, with lots of guns. They had a balance to their design that he appreciated but could not put into words.

"You should make modern ship models, like those," Max said. "We could play with them then."

The idea sparked deep in Graham's brain. "Yes we could. In fact we could play now. There are a few modern ship models at home we could use. There is a plastic destroyer somewhere."

Max stood up. "Let's! Come on!" Max cried.

Graham wasn't so keen. He was still hoping for a glimpse of Cindy. Memories of her in that very skimpy bikini fired his youthful fantasies and he vaguely understood that the physical and emotional urges that he was experiencing were not entirely under his control. But she wasn't at home so all he could do was pretend he was enthusiastic and go with Max.

The two boys set off and were back at Graham's within 10 minutes. Graham ran upstairs and went to a toy box and began to rummage. Max chattered away excitedly about the movie. After a minute Graham extracted what he sought; a toy warship. It was a plastic destroyer about 30cm long and 4cm wide. The hull was a hollow shell which had once contained wheels, a sparking mechanism and a flywheel. It had originally been designed to be pushed along the floor. The details such as torpedo tubes and lifeboats were moulded as part of the hull but the three gun turrets turned (although 'B' Gun had lost its barrel). He held it up.

"How about this?"

Max sniffed and looked at it critically. "OK I suppose. But we need two ships to have a battle."

Graham was a bit hurt at Max's criticism but he wracked his brains: A second ship? Ah! Yes! He pointed down. "I've got an old ironclad downstairs. You could use that."

Max looked doubtful but followed Graham down to where the fleets of sailing ships still sailed in the ship room. In a corner, festooned with cobwebs and with a broken mast, was the model ironclad. This was also about 30cm long and at least 6 wide and nearly as high. It was painted a greasy dark grey and looked like a wreck.

Graham picked it up and blew at the dust and cobwebs. "It is a French ironclad from the days when ships still had sails as well as steam engines," he explained.

Max made a face. "So where are the sails?"

"I only ever rigged the lower masts and she got knocked over by the dogs one day," Graham answered. He plucked at the broken rigging and dusted more rubbish off. The model looked sad to say the least.

"What's its name?" Max asked, clearly unimpressed.

Graham felt foolish. "I can't remember."

Max shook his head. "It wouldn't have a chance against a modern destroyer. One torpedo and it would be blown out of the water. Are those all the guns it has got?" he said, pointing to a row of cannons poking out of gun ports along the side.

"Yes. But we could pretend she has really thick armour and that she has been re-armed with modern guns," he suggested.

"I suppose so," Max replied doubtfully.

"Look, I'll take her if you like and you have the destroyer," Graham offered. Now that the idea had been planted in his mind he badly wanted to try a modern naval battle. Max brightened up but looked suspicious: "How many guns has that Ironclad got?"

Graham counted them. There were ten on each side. "Twenty. We could say they are 4", the same as the destroyer."

"How thick is the armour?"

"That would have been 12"."

Max looked sceptical. "So I could never knock her out. It would take a battleship's gun to do that," he replied, adding, "Anyway it would have been centimetres. The French went metric back during the French Revolution and that was long before ironclad steamships were invented."

Graham was surprised Max was so knowledgeable but compromised. "You could hit her guns and her bridge; and torpedoes could damage the rudder and propellers."

"Ok. How do we decide when something is hit?" Max asked.

Graham knew from bitter experience, both with his big brother Alex, and from games against Max and Peter, that this was the crucial issue. For battles with HO scale soldiers they used dice.

"Same as we do for land battles," he suggested. We throw dice."

"OK. What are the odds?"

They haggled about this for 10 minutes and then went upstairs. By then Graham had more or less cleaned the ironclad and felt more content with his choice.

Max picked up the destroyer and examined it critically. "What's its name?" he asked.

Again Graham felt foolish and shrugged. "I don't think it ever had one," he said. "Call it whatever you like. You be the Germans."

Max immediately reacted. "No fear! You be the Germans. I'm the British."

"I am!"

"No you aren't. Didn't you say that was a French ironclad?"

Graham reluctantly conceded it was.

Max seized on this: "So you are the French and I am the British," he insisted.

"But they were allies in World War 2," Graham objected.

"Not all the time," Max pointed out. "My grandad fought the French in Syria. Some of them were on our side and some helped the Germans, after the blitzkrieg over-ran France."

Graham bit his lip. In the back of his memory floated something he had read about the British having to sink French ships in 1940 to stop the Germans getting them. He gave up the argument and wished he had paid more attention to what he read.

"OK. Let's get on with it. I will be a coast defence ship and you can raid the harbour," he suggested to Max.

Max liked this idea and took the destroyer out onto the front veranda. Graham placed the ironclad on the carpet and struggled to think of a suitable name.

The battle began. Max's destroyer steamed in at high speed and both sides 'opened fire' with lots of sound effects and shouting. The dice was thrown again and again until everything which could shoot had.

Max cheered loudly. "My front 4" gun has hit your second cannon," he cried.

"And three of my guns have hit you. That is a five. Your captain is dead. Your ship is out of control for one move," Graham answered.

They moved again. Max fired multi-barrel anti aircraft guns at close range and fired four torpedoes. One hit. Graham claimed to have knocked out two of Max's guns but it was hard to decide, even with the dice. They both got heated and excited.

The noise attracted Kylie and Margaret who had been in Kylie's room. The girls came and looked to see what the boys were doing. Graham gave Margaret a half-smile, half-scowl. At his age he did not like being found pushing a toy around the floor—and to be losing.

The boys moved their ships again. Max fired four more torpedoes. The dice rolled: a 6.

Max clenched both fists upwards. "Hit! You are sunk!" he cried.

Graham could not argue. He stood up and shook his head. "This is too one sided. We need more equal ships."

Max agreed. "Where can we get them from?"

"What about plastic kits?" Kylie suggested. Graham had several plastic kit models of modern ships; given to him as Christmas and birthday presents: HMS *King George V*, USS *Missouri* and the *Titanic*. He considered these for a moment, then picked one off the bookshelf beside his table.

After a moment's thought he shook his head. "No. The scale is too small. These are all 1:700 or 1:720," he said. "Besides, you can't buy other ships of the same scale to make a fleet."

"What do you mean?" Margaret asked, her brown eyes shining with interest—at Graham, not the ships.

He explained: "If we have battleships we need to have smaller ships to work with them as a team, destroyers to escort them and so on."

"Escort?" Margaret said doubtfully.

Graham was aware that the word had other meanings, some of them dubious regarding women. "No, not like that. An escorting warship protects other ships, by chasing submarines or using its anti aircraft guns and things like that," he explained.

Margaret brightened up. "Oh, I see. Don't they make plastic kits of them?" she asked.

"Yes they do, but they don't seem to build them to scale. If they make a model of a destroyer then it comes in a packet the same size as this battleship and is rarely the same scale. It is like these two." He picked up the 1:700 scale model of the battleship *King George V* and placed it beside the toy destroyer. They were the same length. "See. A real destroyer isn't even half as long as a battleship. It looks all wrong," he said.

Max agreed. "It looks silly."

Kylie frowned. "Couldn't you make your own models?" she asked. "You make sailing ships, why not modern ones?"

Why not indeed? thought Graham. So that night he began.

Chapter 8

THE GUNBOAT

After Max had gone home Graham sat and thought for a while. Then he went downstairs and rummaged in the large box which contained pieces of wood. These were mostly off-cuts from beams which he had picked up at building sites or from the bin at Manual Arts lessons. Most of the wood was soft pine and it was what Graham had been using to make the hulls of his sailing ship models.

Presented with the problem of making a model of a modern ship with a steel hull Graham was unsure of how to proceed but decided that similar methods would do as an experiment. Time was also a consideration as Max would be over again the next day and he needed the model completed by then.

It needs to be the same scale as the plastic destroyer, he decided. But he did not go and measure the destroyer to calculate this accurately. Instead he formed a rough idea in his mind. *A gunboat with a gun that can at least equal the destroyer in firepower,* he thought.

A nice clean piece of pine 17cm long, 6cm wide and 2cm thick caught his eye. He picked it up and dusted it. "This will do," he muttered. Without further delay he set to work. With a pencil he marked the curve of the bow and stern on both top and bottom of the piece of timber. The shaping was done by eye. Lacking a good saw Graham proceeded to hack and whittle away the unwanted wood using a large and very sharp sheath knife. This took about half an hour and left him sore in the hands and perspiring.

The rough hull was then securely fastened in a vice and Graham set to work with a wood rasp to smooth off the jagged edges left by the knife. This was easier work and also more satisfying as he could see the correct shape appearing before his eyes. When he was satisfied that both sides were as equal as his eyes could judge he picked up some coarse grained sand paper and set to work smoothing the rough timber surface. 5 minutes of this was enough. Fine grain sand paper was brought into use and the wood became pleasantly smooth to the touch.

"That is good enough," Graham muttered, feeling the timber for smoothness and nodding happily. He swept up the wood chips and sawdust and tidied the work bench, then carried the new hull upstairs. It was placed on his desk and a pencil used to rough out the deck plan.

While picturing the model in his mind, he muttered to himself, "A 4" gun here; and then the superstructure back to here. Then another gun at the back—an anti aircraft gun in one of those circular gun tubs. And some depth charges in racks on the stern. Hmmm... and two boats, one on each side,"

Graham happily mulled over various ideas, dimly aware that he wanted a ship from one of the World Wars of the 20th Century rather than a modern ship with missiles. In his mind's eye was a picture he had once seen of a British gunboat bombarding the Italians in Libya during World War 2. The memory of the picture helped his thinking although a niggle in his conscience told him he shouldn't be so lazy. *I should find the picture,* he told himself. But he didn't. *Near enough will do,* he decided.

But the memory gave him the idea for the gun mounting. He made that first. The gun was a piece of 2mm thick balsa wood 3cm long which he cut to shape with a razor blade. The blade had been snapped in two and was excellent for slicing the soft wood. The breech section was trimmed away from the barrel. The barrel was then roughly rounded by careful longitudinal slices. Sandpaper was used to transform the rough octagonal shape into a smooth cylindrical shape with a slight taper to it. A pin was pushed through the breech section at right angles. The pin was then pushed down through a small block of balsa about 3mm square to make the gun mount. A ball-point biro was then used to carefully indent a black hole into the front end of the gun barrel.

That is the bore, he told himself.

Satisfied with the result Graham went on to make the base of the gun mounting and then the gun shield. The base was a cardboard disc 2cm in diameter with a hole in the centre for the pin. A hole was driven in the top of the hull with a punch and the base glued over it. The gun was then glued in position on the base with Tarzan's Grip. While the glue dried Graham set to work on the gun shield. He tried to make this with balsa wood by cutting up flat 1mm thick sheeting. The sides and top were easy but the front gave him problems as it needed a hole for the gun barrel to poke through and he also tried to cut out tiny slits for the gun layers to look through. The thin balsa split twice before he produced a front he was happy with. The pieces were then glued together to make a box with no bottom and an open back.

By then it was tea time and Graham reluctantly left his desk to go and eat. As soon as he had eaten he hurried back to The Shipyard. The first thing he did was test whether the gun turned. With his finger he gave the barrel a gentle push and was happy when it rotated smoothly. He pondered how to make it also elevate and depress but decided that the result would not be worth the time and effort.

The gun shield was glued in place, being braced with blocks of wood and an eraser to hold it in position till the glue dried. A block of wood, another off-cut, 8cm long, 1.5cm high and 4cm wide, was selected from a shoebox full of such treasures. With a black pen Graham drew small doors and portholes along each side. This was the superstructure and was glued on just behind the gun.

Already the model looked like a warship to Graham and he smiled happily as he worked. A balsa bridge 6cm long, 3cm wide and 2mm thick was glued across the front of the superstructure. Thin cardboard sides 5mm high were glued to the ends and front of this. Several small square or oblong pieces of balsa were glued on to represent the boxes and lockers which Graham had noticed on real ships. A small signal lamp was added, made from a piece of cylindrical balsa 2mm in diameter and 2mm long glued on top of a 1mm thick, 7mm high post.

The funnel was made of cardboard glued in a cylinder. It was 4cm high and 2cm in diameter and had a black top coloured with a felt pen. Several more lockers and boxes were added around this. A mast made from a toothpick was glued on at the back of the bridge. Two lifeboats were made from 5mm balsa. They were sliced roughly to shape with a razor, then sanded smooth. Using a pen a canvas awning and safety ropes were marked on the top and around the sides. The boats were glued on either side of the superstructure.

By then Graham was mightily pleased with the result. This was increased when either Alex or Kylie looked in from time to time and their initial rude comments gave place to admitting that it did look like a warship. By the time the cardboard gun tub (3mm high and 4cm in diameter) and Bofors gun (made from a pin stuck in a block of balsa on a cardboard base, with a few short lengths of fuse wire for controls and tiny blocks of balsa for the ammo lockers) were added they had even admitted grudging admiration.

Kylie was the more gracious. "It is good Graham. It looks like a real gunboat. Are you going to paint it?"

That brought Graham to a mental halt. *Painting! I didn't think of that.* He knew that it was best to paint a model before it was assembled and wondered if he should bother. Then he shook his head. "I haven't got any grey paint."

"You could buy some on Monday," Kylie answered. Graham agreed. He had a shoe box, which held about twenty tiny tins of Humbrol model paint, but the colours were bright and suited the sailing ship models he had been making.

To finish the model Graham added two racks of depth charges, made from balsa. To do this he cut off a length of 2mm square balsa 15cm long. With the razor he sliced the edges to make it into an octagonal length. By holding it in one hand and rubbing it on a piece of sandpaper; both backwards and forwards, or rotating it he was able to make a long, smooth cylinder. From this he sliced eight 5mm lengths, each a depth charge. Four of these were glued on either side at the stern.

A few small squares of balsa were glued to the deck to represent hatchways or lockers. Tiny round lengths were glued in pairs to represent bollards and a cardboard breakwater was added to the focsle in front of the gun.

By then it was bed time. Graham lay down, well-pleased with his efforts, placing the model where he could see it from his bed. He fantasized about captaining a gunboat battling desperately against the enemy. The ship was close to the shore, giving gunfire support to a hard-pressed army unit. The decks were littered with used shell cases and strewn with dead and dying men. Blood ran across the deck. Steel splinters flew past. Graham was badly wounded, but bravely stayed at his post giving orders and directing the gun onto a new target, blood staining his white uniform. Grimly he held himself up, then slipped quietly off to sleep.

***

Sunday morning meant church. Graham and Kylie both happily went with their mother, but Alex usually refused. Graham was often rostered as one of the alter boys but this Sunday he was not. On arrival at the church Graham found his two best friends outside: Peter and Roger— and Margaret.

Kylie and Margaret paired off to talk so Graham joined his friends. A few minutes later the church bell rang and they made their way in. Roger's mother sat next to Mrs Kirk and the children all sat in the next pew. Graham tried to sit between Peter and Roger but, at the last moment Roger moved and Margaret ended up there. Graham wanted to scowl but managed to hide it.

I do like Margaret, he admitted to himself, *even if her open affection is a bit wearing.* There was also a feeling of shame at how he had treated her, and that was part of the problem. A few months earlier, when Graham was approaching puberty, he and Margaret had done some very intimate exploring of each other's bodies. After a few weeks of this they had reached a potentially dangerous stage in their experimentation and affection. The next step would have been very serious and they had pulled back from that. Afterwards both had been shy of each other and now the memories were a bit of a barrier in Graham's mind.

But she's a good kid, he thought. And that summed it up to him. *She is just a kid.* He imagined himself to be a mature man of the world. As such he needed a partner of similar maturity: like Thelma. All through the church service his mind kept straying to contemplate Thelma's virtues, and to fantasize about doing heroic things to win her affection. Afterwards he wasn't exactly rude to Margaret, but he did not pay her the attention she craved.

Outside the church after the service the boys discussed their plans for the day.

"What are you doing today?" Peter asked Graham.

"I am playing a ship game with Max this afternoon," he replied, mildly embarrassed by the disclosure.

"Oh yeah! What's that?"

Graham described the model ship he had made and how they had played the day before. It was only a variation on how he had played for years with his sailing ship models and plasticine people so Peter just nodded.

Roger was more interested but also had his own proposal. "I've just got some new HO scale model railway stuff, an engine and some carriages. Would you like to see it?"

All three of the boys had an electric train set and were interested in trains so they agreed to go to Roger's for the remainder of the morning. Parents were consulted and were happy with this suggestion. The boys set off at once, Graham noting a wistful look from Margaret cast in his direction.

They walked to Roger's house. It was a typical old high-set Queenslander with the downstairs area concreted over. It was similar in layout to Graham's house, with a carport, laundry, fernery and a pleasantly cool lounge area among huge pot plants. Half of the downstairs area was walled off to make a large storeroom and workshop.

In the centre of this Roger had laid out his HO scale railway. This comprised an oval track 3m x 2m nailed to a baseboard made of chipboard. There was a single passing loop. The baseboard had been roughly painted green with a road network added and a few model trees glued on. Sitting on the track were two trains. One was a mixed goods with a Hornby 0-4-0 British Great Western Railway Tank loco in front of a flat car, oil tank wagon, cattle wagon and a guards van. The other train, parked on the main line, was a passenger train comprising a black locomotive and three passenger coaches.

The boys crouched down to examine the so-called new acquisition, for a glance showed it was old and had seen hard usage. The paint on the rolling stock was chipped in many places and the details battered and scratched. The loco was an old English tender engine with a 2-6-0 wheel arrangement. It had originally been painted black but was so worn that the metal bodywork showed though as silver in many places. The coaches had once been chocolate and cream but were likewise tarnished. They all had bogie suspension.

"Where did you get them Roger?" Graham asked.

"From Aunty Iris up in Atherton. She said her Jack wouldn't be needing them anymore and they were just sitting in a box in her storeroom," Roger replied.

Peter unhooked the loco and picked it up to examine it more closely.

Graham placed a finger tip on a coach and rolled it gently along. He was pleasantly surprised at how smoothly it ran.

"These feel all right," he commented.

"They are," Roger replied enthusiastically. "They run really well. You watch." He unhooked one coach and gave it a sharp push. The coach rolled off around the oval, its tiny wheels humming almost inaudibly. It made it almost all the way around before running to a standstill.

Peter nodded. "Smooth as silk," he commented. He put the loco back on the tracks. "Show us how she runs Rog."

Roger was more than happy to. He switched on power to the transformer and backed the loco up to connect the coaches, then turned the controls to forward and sent the train humming around the oval. Graham was impressed. "It's good. It really goes well, doesn't it?"

They took turns to play with the train. Peter then suggested they try a race to see which engine was the faster.

Roger nodded. "OK, shunt all the coaches onto the siding."

They tried but two coaches would not fit.

"You've got too much rolling stock now Roger. You need another siding," Graham said.

"I've been thinking about that," Roger agreed. "I can easily fit another track around this baseboard."

"You could build a giant railway in this room," Graham said. "It could be a Train Room, like my Ship Room."

Roger nodded and looked around. "I suppose so. I'd have to ask Dad first."

Peter positioned the new black loco on the other side of the oval from the tank loco. Roger then turned on the power and the two engines began running. It was apparent within seconds that the newly aquired loco was by far the faster one. Its connecting rods moved as a silver blur and it caught the tank loco before it had even made one lap.

Next they placed the black loco just in front of the tank loco to see how many laps it would take for the black loco to catch up with the tank loco. That was just over two. Then the boys experimented with which loco was the stronger. Here at least the tank loco held up well. Both locos could haul all the wagons and coaches that Roger owned but the black loco was marginally faster.

Two hours passed happily. The boys then reluctantly parted to their respective homes for lunch. Graham was in a good mood and was really looking forward to the afternoon. His good temper even survived finding Margaret having lunch at his house. She said nice things about his new model, but Graham paid no attention to this. *She would say anything I did was nice,* he thought cynically.

Max did not appear till nearly 2pm. To Graham's surprise and delight Cindy came with him, looking very cool in a white cotton top and very short, very tight, white shorts which set off her honey coloured legs to perfection. She was so attractive Graham could hardly keep his gaze off her. Margaret had to struggle not to let her concern and jealousy show.

Graham produced the model gunboat. Max glanced at it and sniffed. Clearly he was unimpressed. This nettled Graham. Then Max asked: "What's her name?"

Graham went red with embarrassment. He had not thought of giving the gunboat a name. His mind raced as he groped in his memory for a suitable name. Names of famous ships flitted through his head: *Victory*, *Hood*, *Bismarck*, *Enterprise*, *Iron Duke*. Every one that came up he rejected as it seemed too grand, or too famous. At last he seized on one. "*Terrible*," he said.

Max made a face. "I know it is terrible, but what is its name?"

That hurt. Graham resented it and went red. He stubbornly repeated: "That is her name: HMS *Terrible*."

Max laughed and nodded. "Yeah OK. What about that grubby old French Ironclad? Is that in the game today?"

"Yes. She is my troop transport," Graham replied.

"What is her name then?"

Graham had at least remembered that. "*Gloire*. It means Glory."

Max laughed. "Won't be much of that today for you," he said. "Where is my destroyer?"

"Here. What are you going to call her?" Graham asked, hoping to catch Max out in the same way.

"*Devastator*," Max replied instantly.

It was such a good name Graham could only agree. "That is good. Now, what game will we play today?" he asked.

"You try to transport your troops across the room and I will try to stop them," Max suggested.

"What troops?"

"All those HO Scale ones you have," Max replied. Graham and Alex between them had hundreds of HO Scale plastic soldiers of various armies.

"They are the wrong scale," Graham objected.

"Doesn't matter! They will do for today," Max replied.

Graham moved to where his toys were stored in boxes. Cindy walked over and stood next to him so that her legs were right in front of his face. "Can I help?" she asked.

"Y... Yes. I suppose so," Graham answered, his eyes taking in the shape of her body, clearly outlined in the tight shorts. *Gosh she's got nice legs,* he thought. With an effort he tore his eyes away and hoped nobody had noticed. As he sorted HO soldiers and loaded them onto his ships with Cindy's help he cast a guilty glance at Margaret. She was sitting talking to Kylie and did not look happy.

Max was given an army of about fifty Australians. Graham loaded a similar number of Germans onto his two ships. All the while Cindy kept crouching near him, chattering away and asking questions. Graham was granted a wonderful opportunity to study her legs close up.

The game was played with the same rules as the previous day. Graham tried to claim that his gunboat had such a shallow draught that it could not be torpedoed, but Max refused to allow this. Dice were thrown, guns fired, torpedoes launched. The *Gloire* was quickly sunk and Graham was only able to rescue about twenty of the soldiers. But with his new gunboat he battled gamely on. She managed to hit the destroyer three times and damaged her guns and engines before she too was torpedoed.

A halt was called for afternoon tea. The children all trooped through to the kitchen and seated themselves on stools. Cindy contrived to sit beside Graham and several times her knee bumped his, making him look down at her thighs. He found himself marvelling at the smooth perfection of her skin.

Is she doing that deliberately? he wondered. Margaret obviously thought so, as she made a sour face when next it happened. Graham felt embarrassed, aroused and guilty all at once and was glad when they returned to the front veranda to continue playing.

Another game was played. This time Kylie and Margaret went off to Kylie's room, Margaret somewhat unwillingly. Cindy again helped Graham. Several times she bent over right in front of him and she crawled around in front of him so that her backside was very obvious. Graham could not help looking. *She's got a nice bum,* he thought, and became embarrassed again.

In the second game Graham again had his troop transport sunk by torpedo but managed to save 35 soldiers. Then his gunboat landed a hit on the destroyer's torpedo tubes and Max had to grudgingly admit she had been blown in half. Graham was jubilant. He was able to land what was left of his army and start the land battle. Here the gunboats main gun and the rapid fire Bofors both caused enemy casualties. In the excitement of the battle he lost all interest in Cindy.

In the end Graham was unable to win the land battle so both boys were happy. They sat back and contemplated the play area with satisfaction. Graham picked up the *Terrible* and admired her. He now thought she was his favourite ship.

Max was happy too. "That was good fun," Max said. "What about another game next weekend?"

"You bet! I will make another ship by then," Graham said.

"OK. See you then. Come on Cindy. Time we went home," Max said.

After they had gone Graham sat for quite a while and admired the model ships. He felt very happy.

Chapter 9

MONDAY

As he walked to school on Monday morning Graham experienced a mixture of emotions. High among them was concern about how Thelma might view him. *She knows I exist now and that I like her,* he thought. But would she go out with him? He could only hope.

Another strong concern was worry about Edmonson and his cronies. *I will try to avoid him,* Graham decided.

And then there was the sheer pleasure of thinking about making ship models and having battles with Max. By focusing on them he was able to push the other worries to the back of his consciousness so that he arrived at school in a positive frame of mind.

As usual Graham was suitably cautious. At each doorway and corner he paused and took a cautious peek before proceeding. To his relief he saw no sign of Edmonson.

Graham was able to reach his classroom without nay trouble. There he met Stephen who was chatting to Lorna. Seeing that stirred jealousy in Graham. *Why can't I get a girlfriend?* he wondered. *How does Steve just pick them up so easily?*

While they chatted on the veranda Thelma and Janet arrived. Janet gave Graham a sharp glance and Thelma appeared to completely ignore him but he felt sure she was aware of his presence. Then he looked out across the school yard and got two shocks in quick succession. First Edmonson walked across from 'B' Block to 'C' Block and then Cindy strolled by with a group of her friends. Luckily, Edmonson did not look in his direction and walked on.

Then Cindy reappeared and the sight of her gave Graham a lift. *She is very horny,* he thought. With difficulty he tried to follow the conversation with Stephen and Lorna while eyeing Cindy till she went into a classroom. Only then did he realize he was being disloyal to Thelma. *God I'm weak! I fall for every pretty girl I see,* he berated himself. He shook his head and thought, *There is no point in wasting time on girls who are older than me. I should concentrate on girls my own age—like Thelma.* But at the moment he thought this into view walked one of the Year 11 girls; the stunningly beautiful Anastasia. *Oh yes! Now she is nice to dream about,* he told himself. *She really sets the blood on fire! If only...* Then he grinned at his own hypocrisy.

Soon after that the bell for classes went and the friends moved to their classrooms. For the next hour Graham sat at his desk and gazed with hopeful adoration at Thelma. *She is so pretty!* he thought.

And then he was in trouble with the teacher for not focusing on his school work. Graham tried to make himself work, but the maths eluded his wandering mind. His attention wandered again after 10 minutes and he started to sketch on his notebook. While Old Wily gave a detailed explanation of how to solve that particular problem Graham quietly drew. His new gunboat took shape on the page.

During the breaks Graham stayed with his friends. He did not feel brave enough to try approaching Thelma and he still feared encountering Edmonson and his gang. So the day dragged, only lightened by the planning of model ships.

That afternoon Graham went home and started work on a second gunboat. For the hull he went and rummaged in the off-cuts box but could not find another piece of wood the same size. The nearest he could find was one 15cm long, 6cm wide and 3cm high—significantly broader in the beam ("Shorter and fatter," was how Kylie described it later).

Graham decided this would do and he set to work shaping the hull. That was all he got done that evening as he had homework and was busy reading a novel. He sanded the hull and placed it beside the *Terrible* on his desk before he went to bed. From his bed he could look at the models and fantasize. In his imagination he went back to rescuing Thelma but fell asleep before she could do more than give him a grateful kiss.

Next day at school Graham continued drawing ships. Once again he attracted unwelcome attention from Old Wily who came walking around the class to check on people's work. Old Wily picked up Graham's book and leafed through it.

"Hmm. Interested in ships then Graham?"

"Yes sir. I'm going to join the navy."

"The navy! You might find that a bit of a shock. You have to do what you are told there. Do you have any idea what it might be like?" Old Wily asked.

Graham nodded. "Yes sir. My dad's a ship's captain and I've been to sea lots of times," he replied.

"I know what your father does," Old Wily replied. "I have known him since we went to school together forty years ago. But going to sea with your dad might be a bit different to being under naval discipline."

"Oh, I dunno sir. My old man's pretty strict," Graham replied.

Old Wily smiled. "Captain Bligh you call him behind his back, so he tells me."

Graham blushed and was aghast. He did not know his father knew the children's nickname for him. "Yes sir," he replied, thinking, *I'd better watch what I say or Old Wily will tell dad—and then it'll be a dozen lashes at the gangway Mr Mate!*

Old Wily went on: "If you think the navy is what you want then you should get a taste of it by joining the Navy Cadets. That way you have more information on which to base your decision."

"Oh, I'm going to do that sir, as soon as I turn thirteen," Graham replied enthusiastically.

"When is that?"

"In a month's time sir, in August," Graham replied.

"Good. Now stop drawing and start doing maths. If you have any ambition to be an officer like your dad you will need to be good at that," Old Wily replied.

"Yes sir," Graham replied. He took his book back and settled to work. But not for long. Within 15 minutes his attention had wandered and was focused on his upcoming birthday. *I will have a big birthday party and invite Thelma,* he decided. That seemed like a brilliant idea so he fell to planning the party and quickly pencilled down a list of who he might invite.

Then another thought struck him, bringing the planning to a halt. *I suppose I'd better ask mum first.*

During German Graham managed to keep out of trouble and Geography he enjoyed so when morning break came he was free. In hopes of striking up a conversation with Thelma he quickly left the room and made a point of avoiding Stephen. But then he lost sight of Thelma in the milling crowd of students. Despite walking quickly around to all the usual places she frequented he could not find her. Feeling quite despondent he went to the toilet and then went looking again.

But it was not Thelma he met but Cindy. She smiled and waved and left her friends to join him. "How are you today?" she asked.

Graham could only nod and grin. To his own surprise he found he wanted to talk to her. As they talked his gaze drank in her beauty and he was almost mesmerized by her physical closeness. Suddenly he was filled with desire. To his delighted consternation he became quickly aroused. As they were both standing in a passageway under the school where many other students could see them he became anxious lest his condition be obvious. The surge of lust became so strong that he felt an urgent physical need to squirm.

Then his anxiety level shot up another notch when he saw Thelma and Janet approaching. To his relief they did not seem to notice him and walked past a few paces away. *I hope they don't think I like Cindy,* he thought. But then another thought came to him. *But I do like Cindy—and she seems to like me. Maybe I should stop trying to win on with Thelma and try her instead?*

At that moment the bell for classes went and Graham was left standing as Cindy gave him a cheery "See you later!" and walked off. Then he had the embarrassing problem of walking to class while hiding his arousal. This was so stressful that he quickly lost any desire and it was with relief he slumped into his desk ready for history. His arousal returned several times during the next lesson as he thought about Cindy. Then he became guilty because Thelma was in front of him and he felt he was being disloyal. *I am a real weakling,* he castigated himself. Once again he tried to think of a plan to attract Thelma's attention. *I will try asking her out again,* he told himself. *But only when the moment is right.*

Having decided this Graham sat and fretted, plotting and hoping for an opportunity. When lunch time came he set out to try to implement his plan. But once again he could not find Thelma anywhere and he ended up sitting with his friends.

Peter, Stephen, Max and Graham usually sat in the same place each day and there was nearly always something interesting to talk about.

When Graham joined them they were deep in discussion about model railways. They were discussing types of railways. This degenerated into an argument about which was best: old-fashioned, with steam locomotives; or modern, with diesel-electrics or electrics.

Graham favoured the steam engines. "They are real engines," he said. "They have a soul and seem to be a living thing, not just a smelly box on wheels."

The bell to go into classes ended the argument but they agreed to meet at Roger's after school. Graham and Stephen headed off. On the way Graham got another shock. Heading for the same room were Thelma and Janet but with them were Edmonson and Denham from Year 12. The group stopped, deep in animated discussion so Graham and Stephen continued on to the classroom. There was no way Graham would try to talk to her in those circumstances. *I don't want the embarrassment and the possible humiliation if she turns me down,* he thought.

Despite the setback Graham kept his attention on Thelma all afternoon, but she seemed unaware of him and he made no attempt to speak to her at the end of classes. After school Graham walked with Stephen and Peter over to Roger's house, which was only a block from the school.

Roger's mum welcomed them and gave them a large afternoon tea. Graham had known her all his life and was aware that she was glad that Roger had such good friends, because she often talked about kids getting involved with the wrong crowd and ending up in trouble.

Roger smiled. "My dad says we can build a big railway in the storeroom," he said enthusiastically. "He says he will help with the building and wiring and stuff but wants us to draw the plans."

"Can we help?" Stephen asked.

"If you like," Roger agreed.

Stephen nodded. "Will you let us run our trains on the layout?"

"Of course. That will really make it good," Roger agreed.

"What sort of railway is it to be?" Graham asked.

Roger wasn't so sure. The lunchtime discussion was re-kindled. It soon degenerated into an argument, about which type of model railway was best: steam engines; or modern, with diesel-electrics. Graham stuck to his defence of the steam engines, partly because his great grandad had driven steam engines on the Kuranda Railway, but also because he was a romantic at heart and they had more appeal. The debate fizzled out after a while with three against one in favour of steam.

The boys then went down to the storeroom, now to be the 'Train Room'. For a time they just looked around and considered the room's potential. Peter then asked: "How large is the room Roger? If you are going to plan this railway you need to know the dimensions."

"Don't know," Roger replied. "But we can soon find out."

A tape measure and ruler were produced. Peter said, "OK Graham, you and Roger measure the end wall. Steve and I will measure this wall."

The task was soon done and the dimensions noted: 9 metres long and 3 metres wide. The ceiling was not quite 3 metres up, and uneven, being the beams supporting the timber floor of the main living area.

Peter looked around with satisfaction. "You will be able to make a really good layout here Roger," he said.

"You blokes can help me," Roger said. "I would like us to do it as a team effort."

The others were a bit embarrassed by this statement and gruffly agreed, to hide their feelings. There was a short pause before Peter said, "Thanks Roger. That is a good idea. But what sort of railway is it to be?"

"Not diesels," Graham said.

"I know. We have agreed on that," Peter answered. "I meant what type of physical location will we try to create? Is it to be rural or city and so on?"

"English countryside would be nice," Roger said. "There are plenty of books available, and the engines and rolling stock are easy to get."

Stephen shook his head. "So are American stuff," he said. "We could build a Rocky Mountains layout with lots of tunnels and high trestle bridges."

Peter frowned. "I would like a big city layout," he said. "One with lots of sidings at a big marshalling yards, and spur lines running off into factories with lots of lights and machines in them."

"We need a port too," Graham added.

The others laughed. Peter grinned and said, "You just want to make another model ship."

"Yes I do," Graham replied. "But it would be easy to have a spur line to a wharf on the side of the layout."

They argued around in circles for a while; Roger wanting a castle and sleepy little village with cottages and a church and dairy cows in fields lined by hedges.

Stephen snorted scornfully. "You've been watching *Thomas the Tank Engine* too much," he said. He held out for an American Pike. Peter stuck to his idea of an industrial layout with a big steelworks and oil refinery. For a while it looked as though the idea would fall down for lack of agreement till Graham made another suggestion.

"I reckon we should build a North Queensland layout. We could have a small port, a coastal plain with cane farms and a sugar mill for industry then a mountain range all covered with jungle. The railway could go up it through lots of tunnels like the Kuranda Railway. On top we could make the Tablelands with farms—that would give us the dairy cattle—and even a sawmill; and possibly a branch line out into the dry country to the west to have beef cattle on a cattle station."

There was silence for a while as the others thought it over. Roger spoke first: "I like it! We could even make a model of the Barron Falls and the railway station at Kuranda."

"And the sugar mill would make a good model," Peter agreed. "We could add a second railway; with narrow gauge sugar trains running all over the place."

"A sugar mill would be a really good model," Stephen said enthusiastically. "We could use N-gauge track for the sugar trains."

So it was agreed to try to make a North Queensland layout. Peter said, "Everyone go home and draw up plans and sketches of what they reckon the layout should be. Try to make it so that it can be done in sections so we can play on it as soon as possible while we work on other sections."

Graham walked home full of ideas and sat for hours that night sketching what he thought the layout should be like. One consequence was that he did not do his homework. Another was that he did almost nothing on his gunboat. The only real movement in ship construction was to decide, on the basis of looking up a book that had photos of the British gunboats *Aphis*, *Gnat* and *Ladybird* bombarding Italian-held Bardia in Libya in 1941, that this new gunboat should have a larger gun: 6", the same calibre that the real ones had carried. But he didn't like the names. So while he made the larger gun he puzzled over what to call the new ship.

Terror he liked, but she had been a 15" Monitor, and he had no picture of her to give him any idea of her design. He thought *Ladybird* too sissy for a warship; and the other two insects too tame. So he opted for *Tarantula*.

Feeling content with his progress he took himself off to bed, to dream of wooing Thelma.

Chapter 10

TENSION ALL WEEK

O n Wednesday morning over breakfast Graham broached with his mother the idea of a birthday party. She had no objection and turned to the calendar to select a suitable date. Graham's birthday was on August the 4th, a Thursday, so the logical choices were the Friday evening, or Saturday.

"Not Friday mum. That is Scouts. I would rather have it on the Saturday night."

"Aren't you going to enrol in the Navy Cadets on the Saturday?" his mother asked.

"Yes mum," Graham replied.

"Will that be too much in one day?"

"No mum. It will be fine," Graham insisted.

So it was agreed. Graham set off for school with his head so full of exciting and interesting things that there was little room for schoolwork. On the top of his mind was planning for the party. *It will be the best birthday party I have ever had,* he decided. A key element in making it so was his plan to invite Thelma. *But I will also need to invite some of her friends,* he thought. *Hmmm. Which ones?* That was a problem and he only wrote down Janet before deciding to leave the final choice until later. During the day he continued making a list of people to invite, interrupting this to jot down ideas for party games.

Graham also spent some of the day sketching plans for the model railway layout. At lunchtime he showed these to the others and this led to a lot of discussion. While they were talking Max joined them and the plans were passed to him for his opinion. He studied them and said, "I like this idea of the railway up the mountain but won't it limit the types of engines and rolling stock you can use? I mean, unless the curves are very gentle, it will all have to be short wheel base stuff; tank engines and four-wheeled wagons. You won't be able to have any big engines."

"We could," Roger said. "It wouldn't matter."

"Yes it would," Stephen disagreed. "It wouldn't be authentic."

Peter clicked his fingers: "I know. We can have it so that the port on the coastal plain is on the main railway from Cairns to Brisbane. That way we could have big freight trains and even an express pass through."

Stephen laughed. "Fair go Pete! This is the Queensland Railways we are talking about here. Express!"

Graham spoke up, remembering a model train he had seen at the show two years before: "We could make a model of the *Sunlander* by repainting some coaches."

"I thought we agreed no diesels?" Peter asked.

"Yes, well, anyway, we could have a big passenger train," Graham said.

Peter agreed. "And the main line could pass out of sight under the mountains; then loop around to bring the same train back from the direction it vanished in."

"Good idea Pete!" Graham said. "We could have storage tracks and passing loops hidden under the mountains for all the main line rolling stock when it wasn't needed."

Roger frowned. "That will mean access from the back or underneath," he said.

So the plans for the model railway progressed. Max listened for a while, then turned to Graham and asked, "Are you still coming over to my place on Saturday arvo with your ships?"

"Sure," Graham replied. "I have nearly finished another gunboat."

"What's her name?"

"*Tarantula*," Graham replied.

"Is she the same as the other one?"

"Pretty much," Graham replied. But he was careful not to mention that the new gunboat had a 6" gun. *That is a secret*, he told himself, by way of rationalizing his deceit.

That conversation made Graham realize how little he had made of the second gunboat, so that afternoon after school he hurried home and settled down to construction. He used almost the same techniques and design as the previous model but added a few more boxes and lockers to the deck and superstructure. Because he was basically repeating the same plan he was able to make things a lot faster and slightly better, with the result that the model was almost completed by the time he went to bed.

Somehow Thelma had been pushed out of his mind for most of the day. It was only when he was at last in bed that he turned his thoughts to her. He began to conjure up a romantic fantasy involving her, but drifted off to sleep long before it had progressed very far.

Thursday brought new challenges and problems. Graham resolved to strike up a conversation with Thelma. *Then I will ask her for a date,* he told himself. But there was no chance to do that before school and none in class. At the start of the morning break Thelma and Janet hurried away so quickly that Graham was left behind. Then he had to disengage from a conversation with Stephen. Only by saying he needed to go to the toilet was he able to do this.

Once outside Graham did go to the toilet and then he hurried around looking for Thelma. This time he did find her but when he did he got a nasty shock. She was in a huddle with Janet, Edmonson and Jerry Denham. For a few moments Graham surreptitiously studied the group. *She looks very matey with Denham,* he thought. That was a depressing notion. *How can I compete with a Year 12?* he worried.

Feeling quite dejected Graham wandered off. Not wanting to be with his friends while he was in such a mood he walked down to the school oval.

That afternoon after the last class Graham hurried downstairs and took up a position where he could observe Thelma leaving without being seen himself. To his disappointment she did not appear. *She must have gone already,* he decided as he strolled dejectedly back through the school.

As he did he encountered students in army camouflage uniforms. They were army cadets, the school having a cadet unit run by his History teacher, Mr Conkey. For a few minutes Graham stood and watched the army cadets but it was only a casual interest as in his own mind he was already superior to them. *I am going to be navy cadet,* he told himself. Feeling better he made his way home and set to work to complete his second gunboat model.

Thursday came and went with no chance for Graham to talk to Thelma on her own. Instead he stayed with his friends to avoid Edmonson and the other bullies. The talk was all about the model railway plans and the broad outline was agreed on. Detailed planing was then begun.

Friday was a busy day. During the lunch time Graham followed Thelma into the library with the intention of striking up a casual conversation. But as he watched her talking to Janet and another girl his courage evaporated. He turned to the bookshelves so that she would not suspect he was watching her. In doing so his eye caught sight of a large book on warships. It was one he had never seen before. He pulled it out and began to leaf through the pages. The book was full of excellent photos and large drawings of ships. He became engrossed to the extent that, when he remembered Thelma 15 minutes later and looked up, she was nowhere to be seen.

After school Graham hurried home to enjoy the usual treats of comics and chocolate. In the evening was Scouts.

Graham really enjoyed Scouts that evening. He was one of those selected to be leaders and he was promoted to be the assistant Patrol Leader of the Crocodile Patrol. To add to the pleasure of the event Peter was made second of the Platypus patrol and Stephen of the Kookaburras. The only sour note was seeing Max looking resentful and unhappy at not being promoted. The promotion really lifted Graham's spirits and made him feel better about himself.

In between coming home and Scouts Graham found no time for model building, so it was not until he had completed his Saturday morning chores at home that he had time to settle to finish his gunboat. The *Tarantula* received her finishing touches by 11am. Graham then sat for a while admiring the model and pushing it around the table.

After that he began to prepare to go to Max's. Downstairs he found a cardboard carton and in this he carefully packed both model gunboats, plus the plastic destroyer, the *Gloire* and the packets of HO scale soldiers. That task completed Graham found he still had time on his hands. He took the three ships out and lined them up on his desk.

A destroyer, that's what I need, he thought, looking at the plastic model. *I wonder...?* Curiosity took him down to the off-cuts box. Yes. There was a piece of wood almost exactly the same size as the plastic model, only a little wider. It was 30cm long, 6cm wide and 2cm thick. A shorter piece of the same thickness 15cm long gave him the idea of using that to build up the raised focsle of the typical World War 2 destroyer. A few small blocks for superstructure were also dug out.

The next problem was how to shape the hull when it was in two pieces. Graham decided to fasten them together. He found some wood glue and liberally applied it, then placed the two pieces together and proceeded to nail them as well. That done he marked out the rough shape of the bows with a pencil and went upstairs for lunch.

After lunch he repacked the completed models in the carton and set off for Max's, confident that his new gunboat would tip the balance in his favour.

Chapter 11

MAX'S HOUSE

Max lived three blocks along in the same street. His house was also old, but of a different design. To start with, it was low block. Secondly, it had an open front veranda and a porch at the rear. A short flight of four steps led up between ornate concrete arms to the carved wooden railings of the veranda. Through the front door was a large lounge dining room. On the left were two bedrooms: a large one, Mr and Mrs Pullford's bedroom; and a smaller one, currently in use as Mr Pullford's office. On the right were two more bedrooms, Cindy's and Max's.

From the rear of the dining room two doors opened into the back of the house. The one on the left led into the kitchen and pantry. The door on the right led down a short corridor past Cindy's bedroom to a bathroom. From the corridor a door opened to the back lawn. Here there was an L-shaped concrete porch or patio with a veranda roof over it. Beyond was the back lawn, with a fenced off swimming pool on the right and a timber and corrugated iron garage on the left. The driveway to the garage led in along that side of the house.

Outside the door to the corridor which led past the bathroom was an extension added to the house later; a toilet (installed when the house had been converted to sewerage), and a laundry. These made up the arm of the 'L'. The back patio was the favourite play area for the boys and it was to here that Graham was conducted when he arrived.

"What will we play?" Graham asked.

Max pointed across the back lawn. "Why don't you try to get your fleet to try to sail from the coconut palm near the garage to land your army on the concrete here? The grass is the ocean and the concrete is the land."

"OK, but I am not the Germans. I am the British," Graham replied.

"No you aren't. I am," Max insisted. This began a furious argument which led to both boys getting heated and obstinate. In the middle of it Mr Pullford came out of the toilet and said in passing: "Why don't you both compromise? Make up two fictional countries and call them some other name; like the Lilliputians or Slobovians or something?"

The boys considered this reluctantly but it made sense. Max spoke first: "All right. My ships belong to Hibernia. Get it? Hi- bern- ians."

Graham laughed. That was the name on the front of the house and he knew it was the ancient Roman name for somewhere like Ireland. He cast around for a suitable name for his own fictional nation. One name that sprang to mind was Trojans, as he had not long before seen a movie about Helen of Troy and had been very impressed by the Trojan's blue and gold armour.

"Mine are the Trojans," he said.

Max laughed. "More like Troglodytes!" he replied.

Graham wasn't quite sure what a troglodyte was except that they were some sort of subterranean people. Rather than admit ignorance he compromised. "That's right, they are. When the Trojans were defeated some of the survivors fled into underground tunnels and evolved into half Trojan, half Troglodytes. They are Trogolites; Trogs for short."

Max laughed again: "Trogs! Bullfrogs you mean!"

The teasing made Graham obstinately stick to his decision. Ignoring Max's jibes about toads he carried his ships over to the back of the garage after handing over half the soldiers and the plastic destroyer to Max.

"How far can we move each turn?" he asked.

"1 ruler for every 5 knots," Max replied.

That led to another delay. The relative speeds of the ships were then debated. Graham wanted to know why Max wanted the speeds to be just ruler lengths. "Real ships can go at 31 knots and 33 knots and so on."

"I know they can but we need to keep it simple," Max insisted. "So we will agree on jumps of 5 knots in speed. How fast could those gunboats go?"

Graham did not know so he guessed. "About 15 knots."

"So that is 3 rulers. The destroyer can do 35 knots, which is 7 rulers," Max said.

That sounded a lot so Graham tried to argue this down to 30 knots but

Max carried his point. The speed of the old *Gloire* was set at a miserable 5 knots. Then Graham raised another point.

"How far can the guns fire?"

"Something simple," Max replied. "After all, if we calculated their range according to scale they would be lobbing shells into the next block. Let's go for 1 metre per inch of calibre."

Graham considered this for a moment. The absurdity of mixing old Imperial inches with metric measure did not bother him as all the models had gun calibres measured in inches in the reference books. Because the Americans still used feet and inches both boys were familiar with the measurement.

Thinking to gain an advantage and expecting resistance to the idea, Graham said, "OK, but the main gun on the *Tarantula* is a 6"."

"Fine," Max replied, somewhat to Graham's surprise.

The basic rules agreed on, the game began. Graham loaded his soldiers onto the *Gloire* and set sail from behind the shed. He sent the two gunboats out ahead and as soon as he could he opened fire with his 6" gun on Max's army, which was spread right along the beach in ones and twos. To his surprise, the destroyer stayed back out of range. Max steamed it to the far corner of the laundry.

To push his ships forward across the grass Graham knelt down. Max did likewise. Then he stood and went out of sight behind the laundry. Curious to know why, Graham looked up—and was horrified.

Into view was slid a large model warship made of wood. It was, Max explained, a cruiser. Graham looked at it in dismay. Max had obviously made it in secret. The hull was about half a metre long, of unpainted wood, with the bows cut to a V by a saw. The superstructure was made of wood blocks glued on and it had two cardboard funnels and two masts. But what mattered most of all was that she had three gun turrets for the main armament. These were small blocks of balsa wood about 3cm x 4cm with a nail driven down through them so that they revolved. The gun barrels were nails pushed into the face of the turrets, but Graham could not argue that they did not look like guns. They did!

"6" guns," Max added. "Nine of them."

Graham counted. There were three in each turret. Three turrets: two forward and one aft. He was so dismayed he just felt like giving up there and then. "That's not fair!" he cried.

Max grinned. "Yes it is! All's fair in love and war."

"I can't fight that," Graham said.

"You can try," Max said.

Graham gritted his teeth and did try. He sailed both gunboats towards the cruiser, but it could do 30 knots (a figure he did not dispute), and Max was able to pull back out of range of Graham's 4" gunboat while he pounded the new *Tarantula* to metaphorical pieces. Then he closed in and sank the 4" gunboat from just outside its gun range. The troop transport was only saved by fleeing ignominiously back behind the garage.

Max looked very happy. "What about another game?" he asked.

"No. I haven't got a chance against your cruiser," Graham replied. He was so upset he was on the edge of tears.

"All right. I'll tell you what. You can have your destroyer back and I will just have the cruiser," Max suggested.

After some persuasion Graham accepted this. The cruiser was slid back out of sight and Graham sat and considered his tactics. This time he moved the gunboats and the destroyer to meet the cruiser while the troop transport headed for the beach. Max's cruiser came out to fight and the dice flew hot and fast.

This time it was a lot more even. The destroyer was able to get close enough to launch a torpedo (after another heated discussion about torpedo ranges). The *Tarantula* also got in some 6" hits before being overwhelmed. Even the 4" of the *Terrible* managed to score two hits before she was sunk. Graham then noted that the sides of Max's cruiser were lined with secondary armament: little blocks of wood with small nails in them. "4" guns," Max explained.

Again Graham did not dispute that. Images of the British cruisers in the movie told him only too clearly that Max was right and also suggested where the idea for it had come from. *Why didn't I think of that?* he thought.

"What about another game?" Max asked.

"OK," Graham agreed. "But only if I can hide my ships before you come sailing out, and you aren't allowed to walk around looking for them. Pretend it was night and the sun is just coming up."

"What about radar?" Max asked. "I would know where they had gone."

"This is before radar was invented," Graham replied firmly.

Max agreed to this and took his cruiser off behind the laundry while Graham hid his ships. While he was doing this Cindy arrived home. She had been to her regular Saturday afternoon netball match. Graham was kneeling near the laundry door moving his 4" gunboat when she walked out of the back door. He looked up as she greeted him cheerfully.

"Are these your models?" she asked in a friendly way.

"Yes," Graham replied, eyeing her short sports dress and her long and shapely legs with interest. He explained the game and Cindy nodded, then went into the laundry. To Graham's surprise she stood there and peeled off her netball uniform and threw it into the washing machine. That left her just wearing her underwear. Graham was embarrassed and did not know where to look when she walked back out. She seemed to think nothing of this and went off into the bathroom.

By then Max was getting impatient and called out. Graham assured him he was ready and the battle was resumed. This time it was hot and furious and close range. The destroyer managed to torpedo the cruiser and halve its speed, but not sink it; and the 6" gunboat knocked out two turrets before being sunk.

As the game went on, Cindy came out of the bathroom after having had a shower. She stood in the back doorway to watch them while she dried her hair. Graham was astounded to see that she wore only a towel wrapped around her; and that this did not quite cover her at either top or bottom! He goggled and looked away, then peeked again, flushing hot with embarrassment and desire.

Cindy then turned and walked off to her room. As she went along the short corridor away from him Graham glanced after her and was rewarded with a glimpse of the bottom of her buttocks. The sight made him become instantly aroused. The surge of desire was so strong it amazed him and he was disturbed at how his body reacted.

After the battle was over Cindy came out, dressed in skirt and top, to call the two boys in for afternoon tea. Both had had enough by then and were happy to go inside for cordial and pumpkin scones with honey. Cindy sat with them and her nearness caused him to become quickly aroused.

To take his mind off her, Graham turned the conversation back to model ships. "I enjoyed that Max. Will we have another battle some other day?"

"Yes, if you like. What about tomorrow?"

Graham made a face. "Sorry. Not tomorrow. We have church in the morning, and after lunch we will be going down to the wharf to meet dad. He is due back then," he replied. His father had been on a voyage around to Normanton and had been away a month. In reality, Graham wasn't really looking forward to his father coming back. He respected his dad enormously, and was very proud of him, but he was also somewhat afraid of him. Graham saw his father as a hard man: hard working and strict, with little time for his youngest son's romantic notions. Love was not a word that sprang to mind to describe the relationship.

At 4pm Graham walked home carrying his models in the carton. All the way his thoughts alternated between images of Cindy wearing only a towel and the notion that he needed a cruiser to beat Max. As soon as he got there he rushed to the off-cuts box and rummaged through it.

"Ah! I thought I saw a piece the right size!" he said. He lifted out a length of soft pine half a metre long, 6cm wide and 3cm thick. It was almost the same dimensions as Max's cruiser. Anxious to have the model ready when they next met he carried the piece of wood upstairs and sat at his desk to draw sketch plans which he then pencilled onto the piece of timber.

As Graham worked on this his eye caught the partly completed destroyer. He picked up the hull and examined it, then placed it aside. *No. I will build a cruiser to match Max's first. Then I will finish the destroyer,* he decided. But another model destroyer seemed like a good idea.

After tea he went downstairs and hacked and rasped at the block of pine until a bow and stern had taken shape and it had been rasped and sanded so that it looked like a ship's hull. That was all he got done that night but he went to bed fired with plans to build more ships after flicking through the pages of several books showing photos of cruisers.

***

Sunday church was a bit of an ordeal for Graham. He and Roger were rostered as alter boys. In the past, Graham had been proud to do this, but this time he felt very self-conscious in his vestments. The reason was his awareness of Cindy in the congregation. Max rarely came to church, but Cindy often did. Graham was now hotly tormented by memories of her wearing nothing but a towel. He became very aroused and this led to a surge of guilt and embarrassment. *Thank heavens the vestments hide it!* he thought.

Then guilt assailed him and he prayed earnestly to be forgiven for having such lascivious thoughts in God's House. When he recited the bit about 'the sinful desires of the flesh' he felt quite uneasy.

After church Graham had to hurry home, so had no time to visit Roger's to study his plans for the projected model railway. Morning tea and a change of clothes and the family piled into the car and drove to the wharf at Portsmith. Mrs Kirk had been in contact with the Captain Kirk's ship *Malita*, by radio, so knew his expected time of arrival.

While waiting for the ship Graham sauntered along to the dry dock and peered through the fence at a naval Patrol Boat which was in for repairs. The sights, sounds and smells of the place were wonderful to his nostrils. Hungrily he watched a young sub lieutenant giving instructions to a rating before vanishing through a doorway. *That'll be me in a few years time,* Graham told himself.

The toot of a ship's siren sounded from the entrance to Smiths Creek. Graham ran out to the end of a jetty to look. Yes. It was his dad's ship. The *Malita* was a 250 ton coaster with a raised focsle, well deck and raised poop. The superstructure was on the poop, cabins and galley on the poop deck level and the wheelhouse and boats on the next deck up. A blue painted funnel was positioned behind the wheelhouse. At the break of the focsle was a sturdy mast and derrick for cargo handling. The hull was painted black with red boot topping, but she looked the worse for wear, with paint flaked off and streaks of rust in places.

The little ship came steadily up the deep mangrove inlet, her bows cleaving the murky green water. Graham could see his father on the bridge beside the man at the wheel. He waved and started running back to the wharf. His father didn't wave back but Alan Marshal, the Mate, did.

By the time Graham had reached the wharf the ship had turned, nosed in, and the first mooring line had been heaved ashore. Alex took it and placed it over a bollard. The ship was then eased in and Graham took the stern line when it was thrown onto the wharf. The thick, bristly rope hurt his hands and it was heavy but he struggled with it till he had dragged it back to the nominated bollard and placed it securely over it. The gangway was then lifted into position by Freddy the Engineer and old Carl the Cook.

The kids rushed aboard, followed by Mrs Kirk. They greeted the crew and went scampering up to the bridge. Their father greeted them there, Kylie with a kiss and a hug, and the two boys with a gruff handshake. As always when going on board Graham was struck by the smells: the tang of salt, reek of diesel, paint and grease and the odd, musty odours.

For a time he stood in the wheelhouse and fingered the wheel and engine controls. His father's binoculars caught his eye and he hung them around his neck and went out onto the wing of the bridge. For 10 minutes he studied the shipping tied up along the creek and imagined himself as a captain. Then he was ashamed of himself because he wished to be the captain of a smart new warship, not a grubby old coaster. He did not want to admit that he secretly felt the *Malita* to be an inferior vessel.

After about an hour the family drove home. Once there Graham's father did exactly what Graham had thought he would: had a shower and lay down to sleep. Apparently he and the mate had been on 'watch and watch' for the last five days and he was worn out.

As it was only mid-afternoon Graham toyed with going to Max's but his mother vetoed this. Instead he sat down at his desk and set to work on his new model cruiser. A length of pine was glued on to make up the main part of the superstructure. Another block was added for the bridge structure and a smaller one aft for the secondary control position.

Cardboard was cut and rolled to make three large funnels, similar to those on the County-class heavy cruisers of the 1930s. This decision was prompted by a photo of the 2nd HMAS *Australia* in an encyclopaedia. Then an image floated into his mind from the movie *Battle of the River Plate. The HMS Cumberland had three funnels too,* he thought. Then more recent memories caused him to pucker his lips in sourness: the frigate HMS *Cumberland* berthing at the wharf and Joany kissing the British sailor.

Graham shook his head and tried to tell himself it hadn't hurt. Then he concentrated on the model. The funnels were glued in place. *She needs secondary armament,* he thought, remembering Max's cruiser firing hers.

So a secondary armament of six 4" guns was added to each side in semi-circular cardboard barbettes, the gun barrels being pieces of cylindrical balsa wood about 3cm long. That idea came from another old photo. The effect was very pleasing to Graham and he was even more content when he added four anti-aircraft guns in circular tubs, six balsa boats and a variety of lockers and boxes. *Now the main armament,* Graham thought. *Max's cruiser had 6" guns but both the Australia and Cumberland had eight 8". Will I give her 8" guns?* he wondered.

For a minute or so he studied the model and only then did he realise that he had miscalculated—and badly. *I haven't left any room at the front for two main armament turrets!* he thought. As the realization of his mistake swept over him he felt hot shame and then a searing flash of anger at himself. For a minute or so he contemplated throwing the model in the bin and starting again. But then the sobering realization that there was possibly no other piece of timber of a suitable size to make another hull stopped him. *I will have to try to fix this one up. Oh, what a bloody fool I am! I should have drawn some plans and measured things better,* he told himself. So he decided to salvage what he could from the disaster.

There is room for one turret at the front but the only place I can fit a third turret is aft, he thought unhappily. *That will mean one gun turret forward and two aft. They will all tease me and say my ship is too scared to fight and is built for running away!*

For a time he contemplated tearing off all the bridge works and funnels but then simply gave up. Feeling depressed and angry he got up and went off to find something else to do. His mother saw him moping around and called on him to help her in the garden. He wasn't interested but did so.

Dinner that night was a bit of a trial. Graham had not been looking forward to it because whenever his father was home he questioned them in detail on their doings in his absence; and particularly about their performance and behaviour at school. When the time came Graham gave what he hoped were satisfactory answers and was relieved to escape from the table, even if it was only to the washing up.

Later that evening he reluctantly sat down to do some homework. While he worked he eyed the half finished cruiser and wondered what to do with it. He also picked up the hull of the destroyer and studied that. When he had done enough time at his homework to satisfy his father he set to work on the destroyer.

This time he was more careful to measure where things were to fit on the deck and marked them carefully with a pencil. Construction then proceed: a block of wood for the main superstructure and a smaller one on top for the bridge; a block aft for the superstructure there, then a cardboard funnel, raked back and with a black cap to it. Two gun turrets with twin 4.5" guns were added to the front, one superimposed behind the other; and a third to the stern.

To plan this ship Graham had a photo in a book and also a war comic with an N-class ship of the 1940s which very much took his fancy. He went to bed considerably happier, with the destroyer half completed.

Chapter 12

ANOTHER SURPRISE

School the next week was average for Graham. He sat in class and admired Thelma and wondered how he could impress her enough to agree to go out with him. He drew ships on his notebook. At lunch time he eyed Thelma from afar, talked to his friends, or looked at pictures of ships in the library. And he got into trouble.

He and Stephen began playing a game of Battleships of the simple kind where each ruled up a page of their notebook into a grid with numbers along the top and letters down the side; then distributed their ships without the other seeing where they were marked on the page. While hiding their own page from the other player they took turns at calling a map reference to a particular square. If there was an enemy ship in that square on the other player's map then it was hit and sunk.

Inevitably the two boys became engrossed in their game and this attracted the attention of Old Wily. The writing of lines resulted. Undeterred the two boys started another game the next day, this time being more careful not to be observed. Once again caution slipped as the battle developed. Graham sank Stephen's battleship and was chortling with excitement when he realized Old Wily was standing beside him. Lunchtime detention and extra work resulted.

Bewailing the fact that he would not be able to talk to Thelma, Graham sat beside Stephen in the classroom and wrote out a page of the textbook. All the while he sulked and felt rebellious and resentful.

As the boys worked, their Geography and History teacher, Mr Conkey, appeared in the doorway. Graham liked Mr Conkey, who was a chubby and cheerful man, and whose main claim to fame, in Graham's eyes, was that he was the captain of the school's army cadet unit.

"What are you two in trouble for?" Mr Conkey asked.

"Playing Battleships sir," Graham replied.

"Battleships eh? Show me."

Graham opened his pad at the page where the splotches of the half finished battle showed. Mr Conkey nodded. "Yes, that is one way to play it, but there are better ways."

"How is that sir?" Graham asked, his interest dissolving his surliness.

"You need three players," Mr Conkey explained. "You draw two large grid maps with identical numbers and each player puts their fleet on one half of it. You need to agree beforehand on things like how many squares you can see, how many squares each ship type can move, and how far they can fire. You arrange it so that the two maps are side by side but with a divider or screen so that the players cannot see each other's fleet."

So far the game sounded the same as what they had been playing so Graham asked: "What does the third player do sir?"

"He is the 'Adjudicator'. Both sides move at the same time. They can rub out where they marked a ship and redraw it in another square. The adjudicator then looks at both maps and checks what each player can see. If ships can see each other he marks them on the other map with a letter, like 'B' for battleship. Then both sides fire if they are in range, using a dice to decide if ships are hit or damaged."

This sounded much more interesting to Graham. *This is a better idea. The ships can be moved*, he thought.

Mr Conkey went on: "There are two good things about this form of the game. Firstly, it introduces some sort of tactics and does away with much of the pot luck of the simple version. Secondly, you get that thrill of not knowing what the enemy has got, or where it is, until it appears."

"Did you play that way sir?" Stephen asked.

Mr Conkey nodded. "Yes. When I was at university we had a little group that would battle for hours. We developed a fairly complex set of rules I remember."

"Have you still got them sir? Could we see them?" Graham asked.

"They will be at home in the storeroom somewhere," Mr Conkey replied. "I will have a look. But only if you promise me you won't play it in class time."

"Yes sir. Please sir," Graham answered. The game sounded interesting and he badly wanted to see it.

For him the rest of the day went well. After school he stopped in at Roger's and studied Roger's plans for the model railway. Afternoon tea was offered and after that Graham walked home and set to work on his model destroyer. A set of four torpedo tubes was added behind the funnel, two racks of depth charges on the stern, and two anti-aircraft guns on sponsons out from the superstructure. He supported these with two uprights and two diagonals made of thin wire which were glued in place and was very pleased with the result.

While he worked the problem of a name nagged at him so he hauled out several books and leafed through them. At last one appealed to him; a World War 2 British destroyer named HMS *Grenade*. Happy with that he went back to work on small details before he was called to tea.

With his father home Graham had to spend two hours in the evening doing homework, so did not get back to the model until just before bedtime. Even so he was very pleased with it, the pleasure increased when his father came out to his room and looked at the model.

Capt Kirk studied it then said, "Making a destroyer, eh son? She looks pretty good. What's her name?"

"HMS *Grenade* Dad. She is a World War 2 ship."

"Yes, I can see that. Are you going to paint her?"

"Aw, I suppose so. But I need her for Saturday," Graham replied.

"What happens then?"

Graham explained his game with Max. His father nodded. "Pity I won't be here. I am off on Friday."

"Where to Dad?"

"New Guinea. Load of machinery and building supplies to Lae," his father replied. "Anyway, let me know who wins won't you?"

"Yes Dad."

Graham went to bed happy, both the new models positioned on his desk so he could see their silhouettes against the light from the streetlight outside. In his imagination he had no trouble thinking of them as real ships steaming at full speed towards the enemy.

Next day during History Graham was told by Mr Conkey to stay at the end of the lesson. Mr Conkey pointed to a plastic carry box on his desk. "I dug out that game I was talking about yesterday," he explained.

So Graham, Peter and Stephen stayed when the lesson finished. It was morning break and normally Graham would have rushed out to try to talk to Thelma but he was very keen to see what the game was like. From the carry box Mr Conkey unpacked some large cardboard maps drawn up with grids on them. He laid these on his table.

"As you can see we marked in some land as well. The islands gave it more tactical interest and the harbours added to the fun. We had rules for submarines and mines as well in this game. Because the moves were adjudicated by the third person it was possible to move these and to spring some real surprises. We often tried to send a minelayer in during the night to lay a minefield off the enemy's harbour."

"What about radar sir?" Peter asked.

"Oh, we ruled that out. We set the game before radar was invented to keep it fairly simple," Mr Conkey replied. He then placed several small metal containers on the table and opened one. Onto the table he poured dozens of small balsa tokens. Most were only about 2cm long and 5mm wide. They were all coloured green and had large letters marked on them to indicate what they were.

Graham picked one up and inspected it. The token was only a bit over a centimetre long, 2mm wide and 1mm thick. It had a sharp bow and the letter 'T' on it.

"Torpedo Boat," Mr Conkey explained. "And this was a battleship." He picked up a much larger piece 3cm long, one centimetre wide and 5mm thick. It was shaped to have a sharp point at both ends. A 'B' was marked in the centre.

Stephen reached forward and raked through the tokens. "There are a lot of tokens sir," he said.

"Not really. This is two identical fleets remember. There has to be a duplicate ship for the adjudicator to place on the other player's map if it is seen. There is a 'Red' fleet in this other tin, for the second player to use."

Graham studied the tokens: cruisers with square sterns, destroyers with a cut-away deck to indicate the raised focsle common to that type, submarines, minesweepers, minelayers, even oil tankers and troopships. "We could make tokens like this easily," he said.

Stephen picked a token up to examine it. "Did you have aircraft carriers sir?" he asked.

"No. Too hard to keep track of all the planes," Mr Conkey replied.

"Are those the rules sir?" Peter asked, indicating a wad of notepaper.

"Yes they are. You can have a look but I want them back thanks."

Peter picked them up. "Can we photocopy them sir?" he asked.

"Yes, I suppose so."

"Thanks sir. Come on Steve, let's go to the library and do it," Peter said.

Mr Conkey shook his head. "At lunch time. You won't have time now before the bell goes," he said.

The game was packed away and the rules loaned to Peter. The boys thanked the teacher and walked off excitedly discussing the game and when they might play it. It obviously wasn't suitable for playing in class. At lunchtime Peter photocopied the rules and returned them to Mr Conkey. Each boy got a copy and Graham devoted his afternoon classes to reading them. This at least kept him out of trouble as he was quiet and not disruptive.

That afternoon he completed the model destroyer by adding some ship's boats and masts and other small details like searchlights, signal lamps and lockers. He then contemplated his cruiser.

I suppose I'd better make the best of a bad job and finish it, he thought. *After all I need it on Saturday.*

Having decided he was faced with the problem of what size guns for the main armament. His initial thoughts had been to outgun Max by giving the cruiser 8" guns but again he hesitated. *The County-class were much bigger ships and this is only the same size as Max's. Maybe I'd better not.* At the back of his mind was the fact that the HMS *Exeter*, which had taken part in the Battle of the River Plate had been a small heavy cruiser with only six 8" guns. *The big heavy cruisers had eight 8" guns,* he told himself. A few minutes of leafing through reference books soon confirmed that the *Exeter* had indeed had only six main guns. *I could do it,* he thought.

Again Graham studied the available deck space and was still faced with the problem of not having enough room forward for two turrets. Then he shook his head. *Max might get angry if I do. I will just match his cruiser.* So he opted for nine 6" guns in three turrets.

He worked on the cruiser till tea time, making balsa gun turrets which rotated on pins driven through them. Balsa gun barrels were sanded to shape and glued on the front of each turret. The gun turrets at least made the model look like a warship and Graham's spirits rose somewhat.

While washing up after tea his mother asked him if he had decided who was attending his birthday party. "You had better make your mind up so you can send out invitations," she said. "People need a few weeks warning. You wouldn't want to be disappointed by finding someone you really want to be there had already made other arrangements."

That idea sent Graham into a lather of worry. He went to his desk and collected pen and paper. Quickly he wrote Thelma on the sheet. Then he added Peter, Stephen and Roger. Max's name went next and that prompted him to consider whether Cindy should also be asked. He sucked his pen for a moment, then jotted her name down.

His mother came and sat on his bed and studied the list. "What about your brother and sister?" she chided. Graham blushed. He had forgotten them. He added Alex and Kylie.

"Are you going to ask Margaret?" his mother asked. Graham didn't really want to but could not bring himself to say no so he wrote her name down also. Then he chewed the end of his pencil. Who else should he ask? After a moments thought he wrote down Janet. *I can't ask Thelma and not her best friend,* he decided.

His mind ranged over the people in his class and he added the names of two more girls: Rowena and Louise.

His mother smiled but shook her head. "You can't just invite girls," she said.

Graham blushed. He did not want his mother to know that he was now very interested in girls. After some thought he wrote down three boys names: Wayne, George and Michael. Then he thought of Andrew Collins and put his name down as well. He wasn't sure if he knew Andrew well enough but decided it was worth a try. Then he added Andrew's sister, Carmen.

The images of two more girls popped into his mind: Rhonda, the sultry blackhead, and Dawn, the busty blonde. They were added to the list along with another boy: Chris.

"How many is that?" his mother asked. Graham counted them.

"Nineteen mum; twenty counting me."

"Hmmm. Ten boys and ten girls. That should be fine. I think that is enough. Any more will become unmanageable. Now, you had better get to work and write some invitations."

Graham spent the rest of the evening cutting up white card, drawing ships on the front and writing an invitation composed by his mother on the inside. The bundle of invitations was then placed in his school bag and he prepared himself for bed.

Once in bed Graham began to day dream. He started off fantasizing about rescuing Thelma again but found his thoughts straying to other girls who were invited to the party. Finally he focused on Cindy. That conjured up images of her wearing only a towel and the memory caused him to become aroused. This was quite normal for him but he was worried about it. Recently he had seemed to be much hornier than usual and he was concerned because he seemed to have no control over when or where it happened.

While lying there he wondered what it might be like to have some of the experiences the older boys were always boasting about. Having almost 'done it' with Margaret he was fascinated by a desire to really try it. Driving this urge was not only his physical desire but also a gnawing concern to find out if he was normal. *Will I be able to?* he worried. Because he had reached the stage where he felt the need for physical relief almost every day, he knew that part of his body worked well but he was deeply anxious that he not fail when he was with a female.

That led him to heated memories of being with Cindy and to speculation whether she might be persuaded to try it.

The next day at school started off in a very ordinary way, but in Period 3 Graham made a smart comment parodying Mr Wilesmith which made the class all laugh. To his delight Thelma turned and grinned at him and laughed too. The joke cost him some lines to write but he felt that they were worth it.

At morning break, as he went down the steps he was surprised when Thelma turned and said to him, "That was funny Graham. Do it again."

Graham repeated his impersonation of Old Wily and Thelma giggled again. Even Janet smiled. Somehow Graham managed to strike up a conversation and they stood talking while they ate their morning snack. *Thelma has got lovely hazel eyes,* Graham noticed. He tried very hard to impress her, clowning and saying silly things. Only when he returned to class later did he remember that he had the invitations to the party in his bag.

That thought brought him out in a cold sweat. *How do I hand them out without being obvious, or without offending the people who aren't invited?* he fretted. He decided the relaxed approach was the best and just dug them out and started to pass them to the people named on the envelope. Feeling deeply anxious he walked over to Thelma's desk and held out the invitation.

"What's this?" she asked.

"I... I... I'm having a birthday," Graham stammered.

Thelma took the invitation and he turned at once to Janet, fearful that Thelma might see how concerned he was. Janet took the envelope but did not smile. As Graham handed one to Michael he saw Thelma open hers. She read it and smiled. "Ooh! A party! Thank you Graham. I like parties. Who else is coming?"

Graham turned and indicated half the class with a sweep of his hand. Thelma's eyes danced and that made his spirits soar. She asked: "Will there be party games?"

Graham was stunned. Party games! He had not thought about what they would actually do at the party. "Yes," he mumbled.

"Oooh goody! What games?"

"What would you like to play?" Graham answered, stalling for time while the names of various games he had heard of flitted through his mind.

Stephen grinned. "Pass the parcel!" he called. That caused a ripple of laughter and Graham blushed.

Louise joined in: "We will definitely have to play Sardines and Postman's Knock."

Graham had heard of them but wasn't quite sure how they were played. But he was aware that they were games that teenagers played that somehow involved kissing and cuddling together in dark corners and he badly wanted to do that. The others added a few more games to play and Graham tried to remember them all. As he listened he wondered how he could find out all about them without people realizing he was ignorant, or innocent. He did not want to be ridiculed.

The arrival of the teacher ended the discussion but Graham set to work to jot down a list of games. Once he had six he re-arranged them into a rough program. His mind went off into a fantasy of playing a game where he had to kiss Thelma and where they would then have to hide in the dark. One result was that he became aroused. Another was that Miss Hackenmeyer singled him out for not paying attention.

"Stand up and speak up boy!" she said.

Graham broke into a cold sweat. That was the last thing he wanted to do but he was terrified of her so reluctantly did so, leaning forward on his desk to try to hide the front of his shorts. As he stood there he was aflame with embarrassment and painfully aware that every eye in the room was on him. It seemed to his heated mind that Thelma's gaze was focused on his problem. But the shame only lasted a few minutes. When Miss Hackenmeyer had finished her tirade he was no longer aroused and he slumped into his seat feeling wrung out.

Lunch time Graham spent walking around finding people to give them their invitations to his party. He found it a highly embarrassing experience as he feared a rebuff each time; and wondered whose feelings he was hurting by not inviting them. But at last the chore was done without suffering any direct rejection and his spirits rose.

That afternoon after school he worked on his model cruiser; and once again had the problem of deciding on a name for her. To help him with this he looked in books which had pictures of cruisers from the period. Most seemed to be named after towns or cities. *That isn't very inspiring,* he thought.

In the end he could not decide on a name so he settled to working on the model instead. After tea he again worked on homework and then went to find his HO scale electric locomotive, a British Great Western Railway King-class 4-6-0. Roger had asked to see it with the idea of using it on the planned model railway. Graham had not played with his electric train in over a year and found the loco badly needed cleaning. The task kept him busily occupied till bed time.

Next day at school Graham was pleasantly surprised to be greeted as soon as he arrived by Rowena (in his mind the most beautiful girl in the class). She gave him a big smile and said, "Thank you for the invitation to your party Graham. Mum says I am allowed to attend. I'm really looking forward to it."

That made his day. Later, when Thelma also said that she would attend his party he was so happy he felt like singing aloud. Several others also said they would be able to attend. The day passed happily without any clashes with the teachers. That afternoon when he got home Graham completed the model cruiser by adding various small details.

He immediately began construction of a second cruiser. His intention was to correct the design fault in the first one by putting two turrets at the front and one at the stern. *And to outmatch Max in case he has made another cruiser,* he thought.

Friday came and with it a farewell to his father. Capt Kirk said a gruff goodbye to the two boys, shaking hands with them. He kissed Kylie and hugged their mother, then went down to the car. The children went to school while their mother drove their father to the wharf. It was a familiar event for them and the family rule was stiff upper lips and no emotional gush over partings.

At school Graham received more acceptances for his party: Janet, Rhonda, Dawn, Wayne and George. These made him feel even happier. He already knew that his best friends would be there so the party now looked viable in numbers at least. Hoping to make it a real success he bent his thoughts again to the program.

Again the day passed without incident. Graham felt a mounting sense of excitement as the day wore on. This was added to when Max checked that he would be over to play model ships on Saturday afternoon.

"Yes, Max, I'll be there," Graham assured him cheerfully.

"Have you finished that new destroyer?" Max asked.

"Yes I have. You will be in trouble this time, even with your cruiser," Graham replied confidently.

"We'll see," Max said with a grin.

Chapter 13

THE NAVAL ARMS RACE

Saturday morning was taken up by chores for Graham. The lawn had to be mowed, gardens weeded, the dog washed, guinea pig hutch cleared out and his bedroom tidied up and vacuumed. This gave him little time to work on the second cruiser, or to think about the coming game. In fact his thoughts were as much concentrated on Cindy as on warships.

It was with pleasurable excitement that he set out after lunch with his models carefully placed on a sheet of plywood. He would have liked to catch Max by surprise by suddenly producing his cruiser the way Max had done the previous week but he had no chance to do that. On arrival at Max's the new destroyer and cruiser were at once inspected by Max.

Graham watched Max's face anxiously to detect any hint of a sneer at his workmanship, but was heartened by the comparison with Max's cruiser. His own was obviously superior in quality. Worry over what Max might say when he noticed that two of the turrets were at the stern then became the dominant emotion. But Max's thrust, when it came, was quite unexpected.

"What's her name?" Max asked. Graham silently cursed himself. Fool! He had forgotten to decide. Names jumbled in his brain as he tried not to look or sound flustered. One came to the surface and he grabbed at it, lest hesitation betray the fact he had not named the ship.

"HMS *Contagious*," he said.

"Contagious!" Max cried. "What is it; some sort of disease?"

Graham felt his cheeks burn as he realized that was not the word that he had been after; but stubbornness then came into play. Not for anything would he now admit that he meant *Courageous*.

"That's right. *Contagious*. And those are 6" guns."

"Contagious!" Max cried. Then he burst out laughing. Graham flamed with shame but stuck to his decision. Max chuckled and made another verbal stab. "She should fly a yellow flag to show you have an infectious disease on board. Contagious! Haw, haw, haw!"

Gritting his teeth to hide his hurt and to keep his temper Graham endured the teasing. In an attempt to divert the taunts he asked, "What is the game today?"

"I thought we might try the same as last week," Max said. "You try to land your army and my fleet try to stop them."

Max's cruiser was placed on the lawn over near the coconut tree and his army on the concrete porch. Graham looked at the setup suspiciously. Max seemed too relaxed and not at all fazed by the fact that Graham had an extra destroyer and a cruiser equal to his. Graham walked to the corner of the laundry and looked around. Nothing lurked there.

Max laughed again. "Don't be so suspicious," he said. "Just get your fleet over to the shed and put them in quarantine." He began to laugh again. Graham felt his temper rise but did as he was told. The game began.

This time Max rushed in with his cruiser, trying to sink the troop transport. Graham turned the transport back and tried to block the cruiser with his five ships. The game was fast and furious for 10 minutes, at the end of which Max's cruiser had been so badly battered that its main guns were all out of action and its speed cut by two thirds. Graham had lost a gunboat and a destroyer and his cruiser had lost its forward turret.

As soon as Max's cruiser began to withdraw Graham started to chase her. *I am winning,* he thought. So he walked over to his transport and turned her round to head it for the enemy coast. No sooner had he done this than Max walked past and around to the back of the garage. Graham became instantly suspicious—and had his suspicions stunningly confirmed.

Into view slid a huge model ship, all turrets and funnels.

"A battleship," Max revealed with pride. "Ten 11" guns and armour 24" thick."

Graham stared at the model battleship with dismay. It was roughly constructed from a large plank of wood about 75cm long, 10cm wide and 4cm thick. The bows were just sawn off with no pretence at a smooth curve and the stern was just sawn off square. The superstructure was made of wood blocks glued or nailed on and the turrets were wood blocks with nails driven into the face to represent gun barrels. A nail through their centre allowed the turrets to rotate. The battleship had three big cardboard funnels and a row of ten 6" guns along the side of the superstructure as secondary armament. A few balsa boats and minor detail had been added.

The workmanship was poor but the overall effect was impressive, if only from sheer size. Graham swallowed and counted the guns: Four main armament turrets, two forward and two aft, with three guns in the lower turret and two in the super-firing turret. 11" guns! And armour 24" thick! *How can I hope to fight that monster?* he wondered. For a minute or so he stood there feeling angry and defeated. Mostly he was angry with himself. *If I could build more ships so could Max. I should have known!* he berated himself.

"Well?" Max demanded, "Are you still playing or not?"

"How can I hope to beat that?" Graham cried angrily.

"You can try."

Graham felt like just going home but a spark of stubborn pride made him stay. Yes, he could try. Better to go down fighting than to crawl away like a dingo!

The battle was resumed. Graham strove to get his cruiser and surviving destroyer within torpedo range. In this he nearly succeeded, causing Max to turn and run. The battleship then hammered Graham's ships from way out of range until all were sunk. In spite of being beaten Graham enjoyed himself. It had been a good game.

"Another game?" Max asked.

"Yes, all right," Graham agreed.

"You defend this time. Put your army on the porch and I will attack," Max suggested.

Graham agreed to this. He carefully hid groups of HO scale soldiers behind things like chair legs which he was confident Max would accept as being proof against the battleship's guns. When he was ready he called Max and the game started.

As they played, what Graham had been secretly hoping for happened—Cindy arrived home from netball. She walked through her door out to the laundry next to where Graham was kneeling on the lawn.

"Hello Graham. Who's winning?" she asked.

"Max. He's built a battleship and I can't get close enough to hit it," Graham replied looking up. Cindy stood close to him and her tanned legs were right in front of his face. His eyes travelled up to where they vanished under her short skirt, then up to meet hers. These were brown and danced with amusement.

Cindy nodded. "He's been working on it all week," she said as she went into the laundry.

From across the yard Max called, "Stop magging and move." Graham did, but half his attention was focused on Cindy who proceeded to strip off her sports dress. This was tossed into the washing machine and Cindy came back out in her bra and panties. She only had small breasts, Graham noted, but her body was nicely shaped and he began to breathe fast and harden up.

Cindy stopped and crouched down to look at Graham's new destroyer.

"Did you make that?" she asked. Graham nodded. She leaned forward so that her body almost touched his and picked the model up. "It's good Graham. Much better than Max's."

"I made a cruiser too," Graham said. He was getting hot and flustered as he became aroused and knew he was staring at her. She smiled at him and bent to the cruiser. Max called across the lawn: "Stop showing off Cindy and let us get on with our game. Graham doesn't want to peer up your fanny."

At that moment Max's mother called from the kitchen door. "Max! Don't you say crude things like that! Cindy! And you go and get some clothes on miss!"

Cindy stood up and ran into the bathroom. From there she looked back around the door and grinned, suppressing a giggle. Then she closed the door and Graham heard the shower start. Graham stayed crouched over his model, aflame with embarrassment. The game was resumed. Graham battled hard but he was distracted by thoughts of Cindy and the hope that when she came out of the bathroom she might wear a towel in the way she had the previous week.

Instead he was granted an even better surprise. When the bathroom door opened Cindy looked out, checking both directions. Then she grinned at Graham, lights of mischief dancing in her eyes. She stepped out totally nude and walked off along the passage way to her room. Graham gaped and his heart pounded furiously.

Max snorted and said, "Never mind her. She's always running around in the nuddy. She's a real show-off."

Graham was speechless. He kept glancing along the corridor hoping for another glimpse but when Cindy came out she was dressed in jeans and T-shirt. She sat down to examine Graham's model cruiser and made smart comments to Max while the boys played. Graham found her presence very unsettling.

After being defeated a second time by the battleship Graham declined another game. The three were called in to have afternoon tea, following which they sat and watched TV for a while. Graham found he was constantly looking at Cindy and she kept smiling at him. The memory of her nude form made him very aroused and he squirmed to hide the fact and was glad they were sitting.

Max turned to him. "Will we play again tomorrow?" he asked.

"OK. I've got a second cruiser under construction. I will try to finish it," Graham replied. He didn't really care about playing but he did want to see more of Cindy!

"What time?" Max asked.

"In the afternoon. I have to go to church in the morning," Graham replied. Max sneered. He did not go to church much and claimed not to believe. Graham blushed but lacked the courage to argue about it.

At home again Graham set to work on his second cruiser. This model he called HMS *Warrior* because of its similarity to a World War 1 armoured cruiser. He armed her with three turrets and an assortment of secondary and tertiary armament. But her most distinctive feature was the four tall funnels. Graham was aware that the model was an odd amalgamation of ideas and the thought niggled in his brain that perhaps, if he made scale models of real cruisers, it might produce better results. The idea appealed, but promised to be a lot of work, so he continued adding detail to the model he was building.

All the while he worked he was aroused. It lasted for hours and he wondered if it would ever go down; not that he minded. It felt very nice. It was just that he did not want his mother, or Kylie or Alex to notice it. At the same time he was nagged by the thought that he would not be able to defeat Max, even with another cruiser.

Shaking his head gloomily Graham muttered, "He's probably hard at work on a second battleship." Sitting there after he had completed the cruiser—a real rush job devoid of fine details—he flicked through a book on ships, hoping for inspiration.

"Maybe I should build some Torpedo Boats," he mused. Then he clicked his fingers. "No, better still, I'll build a submarine! That will stop him in his tracks."

Seized with this new idea Graham rushed down to the storeroom and found a piece of wood 20cm long and about 2cm square. He set to work with knife, rasp and sandpaper and soon had the hull shape of a submarine. This was carried upstairs and placed on the desk. It did not look very impressive. With the intention of improving the model he studied it for a time.

I wonder if it would look better painted?

He decided it would. Old newspaper was placed on the desk in case of spillage and a tin of Humbrol opened. Within 10 minutes the job was complete and the brush cleaned. The hull was now a glistening black. *I will add a light grey conning tower,* he decided.

But he had no light grey paint. Pale blue was the closest. "That will have to do. It is the sort of colour the Trogs would use," he told himself. A piece of balsa 5mm thick x 2cm x 2cm was rounded fore and aft and painted blue. Shipbuilding then ground to a halt. He could not glue the conning tower on until the paint dried; and he had used gloss paint which would take several hours.

"While I wait I will make a second sub," he said. So he went down to the storeroom again and rummaged for a second piece of timber the same size which he remembered seeing. As he searched his eye fell on a plank nearly a metre long. It was an old piece of 4x2 and was slightly bigger than the plank Max had used to build his battleship.

I can build a battleship too! And I will give it bigger guns than his, Graham decided. Inspired by this idea he dragged out the baulk and dusted it down. For a while he wrestled with cutting the bow to shape before his mother called him up for supper.

"Bedtime," she said. "The shipyards will have to close for the night."

"But Mum! I need a battleship to beat Max," Graham said. He explained what had happened. Alex was no help. He just jeered. Kylie was more sympathetic but wasn't really interested in ships.

For a long time after he was sent to bed, Graham lay awake and planned his new fleet. The silhouette of the *Warrior* gave him inspiration. Then his thoughts wandered and he became hot and excited over Cindy. For over an hour he tried to imagine what it might be like to do it.

His torments of the flesh continued next day as Cindy was also at church. Graham was not an alter boy but was still hot and ashamed as he was quite unable to prevent himself becoming aroused almost from the moment he saw Cindy. It became a trial just to sit with his hands on his lap to hide it. He was very anxious that his mother not become aware of his condition. Confessing his sins before Communion only seemed to make him more aware and more aroused but thankfully it subsided before he had to go out to the altar rail. Through it all he barely noticed Margaret, who sat next to Kylie and kept smiling her worried little smile at him.

After church Graham hurried home. He glued the conning tower on the sub, which he christened 'S 1', then decided it needed a deck gun, in keeping with submarines of the period. A balsa gun was added to the fore casing. Then he set to work on the second submarine, working as fast as he could. However time ran out and he had to leave her half completed.

Once again he loaded his fleet onto the piece of plywood. The models now constituted an awkward load and it was an effort to carry them the three blocks to Max's. On the way Graham had to stop several times and was sweating when he arrived. He contrived to hide his new submarine among the shrubbery at the front steps before going up and ringing the doorbell.

Max opened the door. "Come in. Gee! That new cruiser looks good. What is her name?"

Graham told him. This time Max did not ridicule it. Instead he produced a large plastic cargo ship of the type made for little kids to play with in the bathtub. It was bright green. "This is my transport ship," Max explained. "I've loaded my army ready to invade." He opened a hatch cover to reveal a collection of toy tanks and armoured cars of various scales.

"They are the wrong scale," Graham pointed out.

"Doesn't matter! They will do," Max replied.

The boys went through to the back. Graham noted that the garage doors were open. "Where are your parents?" he asked.

"Gone to the markets," Max replied.

"What about Cindy?"

"Over at the Freeman's I think. Never mind her, what game will we play?" Max said.

"I will defend again," Graham said. He looked around, wondering if Max had another horrible surprise to spring on him. Max agreed and carried his transport over to the shed. Graham began deploying his army and fleet, wondering how he could get the sub without Max noticing. Finally he waited till Max carried his battleship over behind the garage, then did a quick dash through the house. As he returned to the back door he placed the sub in a corner. Max appeared not to notice.

The game began. Once again the battleship kept back out of range and started to pound Graham's ships to bits before they could close the range. At that stage Graham threw a dice.

"You've just been torpedoed," he said, seeing a 6 come up.

"Oh yeah? What by?" Max sneered, indicating the two destroyers, which were clearly too far away.

"A submarine," Graham answered.

"Submarine! What submarine?" Max jeered.

Graham stood up and walked to the doorway and produced the sub. It was placed on the lawn within range of the battleship. For a minute Max stared at it. Then he swore and said, "That's not fair! How can you prove that it was there?"

"I measured the moves. Starting here, at 1 ruler per move that is about where it would be," Graham replied. He felt very pleased to have sprung the surprise on Max but was worried by the anger of his reaction.

"I still say it's not fair," Max insisted. "You should have told me you had one. In the real world I would have known if the enemy navy had subs."

"And I would have known if they had battleships or cruisers," Graham retorted. Through his mind ran Max's comment about 'All's fair in love and war' but he did not use it. *Max is upset enough as it is,* he decided.

"Stick it up your bum!" Max cried. To Graham's astonishment he appeared to be about to cry.

There was a tense silence. Graham wondered what to do to smooth over the situation. "Do you want to keep playing?" he asked.

Max shook his head. "No. I can't win. I haven't got any anti-sub vessels," he replied.

"What if I give you the plastic destroyer and we start again?" Graham suggested. "And I will start my sub on the surface to begin with."

Max considered this then nodded. "All right. But it takes two dice throws; one to get a hit, then a second to see what damage the torpedo did."

"That's fine by me," Graham agreed.

So the game was restarted. Graham enjoyed it immensely as it was much more even. He managed to sink the cruiser and damage the battleship before the sub was sunk by the plastic destroyer. By then one of his cruisers was sunk and the other damaged and the destroyer had blown up. Max got his army ashore and they battled on land for half an hour. In the end Max won, but only just.

"Want to play again?" Graham asked.

"Yeah OK, but only if I can have a sub too," Max said.

"Where will you get one?" Graham asked.

"I just remembered; I've got a plastic one in the toy box." Max went into the house and returned a few minutes later with a toy plastic submarine about 30cm long. It was the sort that had a battery powered motor and which actually dived when in a pool or bathtub.

"It isn't the right scale," Graham said. The thought of an enemy sub made him very uneasy.

"Doesn't matter. It will be under water," Max replied.

"Does it really work?" Graham asked, watching Max fiddle with the propeller of the toy.

"I think so. It used to," Max replied. "The batteries are probably flat though." He tried to turn the motor on but got no response. "It used to dive really well. Would you like to see it? I know where there are some spare batteries."

"Yeah, all right."

Max led the way into the house and found batteries in the kitchen. These were inserted and the switch pushed across. The motor burst into buzzing life, the tiny propeller whirring round at great speed.

Max pointed to the toy. "You watch, the rudder turns from side to side and the diving planes go up and down," Max said. Graham watched with fascination as the control surfaces moved slowly. Max grinned and said, "Let's try her out in the pool. She is really good there."

He led the way out to the small swimming pool. This was about 7 metres long and 5 metres wide and varied in depth from 1 metre to 3 metres. Max rummaged around in a box and produced some goggles and a face mask.

"Here. I use these when I am playing frogmen." He handed Graham the goggles. Then he proceeded to strip off. Graham was both surprised and embarrassed. He had often seen Max without any clothes on, skinny dipping at Freshwater Creek or Kamerunga but now he felt quite anxious. It always amazed him how casual Max was about it, as though he thought it the most natural thing in the world.

"What about the neighbours?" Graham said, glancing anxiously over his shoulder.

Max shook his head. "They can't see the pool because of that high fence," he replied. Holding the toy submarine he stepped into the pool. "Brrr! Bloody cold. I need a bit of hot in here," he said with a grin. Seating himself on the step he proceeded to adjust the controls on the toy. Graham felt mildly embarrassed, but also ashamed to admit to himself that he was somewhat interested.

Max started the submarine's motor and then gently placed it in the water. The toy sub buzzed around, bumping the sides until it submerged. It nosed its way along the bottom and then surfaced after a lap of the pool. Laughing happily Max stepped into deeper water, putting his facemask under the surface to watch the sub's progress.

"Use your goggles Graham. It looks really good," Max cried.

Graham did not want to as it would mean he would be looking at Max's nakedness but he complied. With his heart beating with anxiety he knelt beside the pool and put his head over the side. It was an experience that made him feel quite uncomfortable and he blushed with embarrassment.

Max did not help by standing up in the shallows. Seeing Max's nakedness made Graham very self-conscious and for a moment he wondered if Max might be 'one of those people his father had warned him about'.

Max turned and beckoned. "Hop in Graham and have a go,"

"I haven't got any bathers, and I don't want to get my shorts wet," Graham replied.

Max curled his lip. "Huh! You can swim in the nuddy."

"I'd rather not," Graham replied, going red with embarrassment.

"Why not? Are you shy? Do you think I will laugh at you?" Max asked.

"What if your parents come home?" he asked.

"They aren't due back for hours. Don't be a scaredy cat! Get in!"

"What about Cindy?" Graham asked anxiously.

Max shook his head. "She's at netball. Come on, aren't you game?"

Graham had no answer. Reluctantly, but stung by the dare, he took of his clothes. Hotly aware that Max was looking at him Graham self-consciously stepped in. To add to his embarrassment he quickly developed an erection. *I hope Max doesn't get the wrong idea,* he thought. To hide himself he knelt down and placed his face in the water. He stayed that way while watching the sub buzzing around and around.

"It's good isn't it?" Max asked.

Graham looked up and nodded. At that moment Cindy appeared around the corner of the laundry. She stopped at the gateway in the pool safety fence. She appeared to be nude and was holding a towel in front of her. Graham could see bare flesh right down her side and on down her thighs to her legs.

"What's this then?" she asked in surprise.

Max stood up and pointed to the toy. "We are testing our submarine," he replied. To Graham's surprise he made no attempt to cover himself from his sister. She looked down at his penis and curled her lip, then said, "That's not a submarine. That's just a little dick."

Graham went red but Max just laughed. "No it's not. That is my torpedo," he replied.

Cindy laughed. "Huh! You won't sink any ships with that! Now go away so I can have a swim."

Max picked up the submarine and stepped up out of the water. Graham flamed with embarrassment and desire. He remained crouched in the water, covering himself with his hands. His heart hammered frantically. A red mist seemed to form in his mind. To his mingled dismay and delight, Cindy looked down and said, "Don't be shy Graham. Hop out please."

Graham was struck speechless. He wanted to; but he was terribly afraid. His mind seemed to split into the part that wanted to and the part saying no. He heard his voice answer, saying, "I don't want to offend you." He actually meant: 'don't want to get into trouble', but was too afraid to admit that. Burning memories of her seeing him naked a few weeks before added to his confusion. And her mischievous smirk didn't help.

Cindy shook her head. "You won't. I see Maxy all the time."

Now anxious to get dressed and out of there Graham stood up, blood surging and pounding in his skull. Cindy suddenly took the towel away from her front and handed it to him. "Here, use this one," she said, her eyes flicking down to where Graham was now trying to cover himself with one hand. Graham was so surprised that he just stood and stared at the lovely vision of her nude form until Max sniggered and made a rude comment.

With a conscious effort Graham turned his back and began to dry himself. Behind him Cindy bent down to test the water. Then she stepped in. Graham was terribly torn, wanting to look but ashamed to do so. Almost overcome by a mix of emotions including desire and fear Graham towelled himself. Then, driven by urgent curiosity, he risked a glance at Cindy as he bent to pick up his shorts. He was rewarded with a delightful side view of her. The image set his pulses racing. *She is really beautiful!* he thought.

At that moment a car drove across the back yard and into the garage.

Cindy looked that way. "Mum and dad are home!" she cried. "Quick! Get dressed and get out of here!" Before the first surge of panic had washed through Graham she straightened up. Grabbing the towel from Max she pushed past them and fled through the gate towards her room, leaving the two boys in a state close to panic.

Chapter 14

LIFE'S MYSTERIES

Graham felt a surge of pure fear. Dropping the towel he grabbed his shorts and tried to pull them on, even though he was still dripping wet. But his haste was his undoing and his foot caught in the wet cloth. As he struggled to free it his eyes were fixed on Cindy as she ran naked across the lawn and around the corner of the laundry.

Max snatched up his clothes. "No time for dress. Bathroom!" he cried. Grabbing his clothes and the toy submarine he followed Cindy. Graham's mind raced and he knew he only had seconds to escape before Max's parents got out of the car and reached the doorway to the garage. For a fleeting moment he considered running away along the side of the house but he instantly rejected that as the neighbours or people out on the street might see him. So he snatched up the towel and his shirt and, holding them across his front, ran after Max, heart hammering with fear.

As he raced the 10 paces to the corner of the laundry Graham kept glancing at the garage door, dreading being caught in such an embarrassing situation. But he made the corner unseen and was around it in a flash. Gasping with concern he scurried through the back door and into the bathroom behind Max.

Max spun round and slammed the door, then quickly turned on the taps and shoved in the plug. "We will pretend we are playing with the sub," he said.

Graham felt so scared he thought he was going to be sick. He quickly dried himself and then pulled on his shorts and zipped them up. Quickly hauling on his shirt he knelt beside the bathtub and tried to button it up. But he was shaking so much with fear that his fingers were all thumbs and he became very anxious. Max pulled on his shorts and placed the toy submarine back in the water. Turning its motor on he watched it butting its way around the tub. Max then finished dressing. He grinned and said, "That was close."

Graham gave a sickly grin in reply. He felt terribly guilty and had lost all desire. With his heart pounding with anxiety and reaction he reached out and turned the sub around. There were voices outside; Max's mum and dad. *They will skin me alive if they find out!* he thought. From outside he heard Cindy speak to them. There was a tap on the door and Max's mum looked in.

"Are you boys dressed? Good. Come and have some afternoon tea when you have finished playing. And don't splash any more water on the floor," she said.

"Yes Mum," Max replied. As the door closed, Max grinned again and winked.

Graham swallowed. He was trembling with emotion. "Sorry Max," he said.

"What for?"

"Being rude to your sister."

Max curled his lip and laughed. "Forget it! Cindy has been seeing me without clothes ever since I was a baby. She doesn't mind. I told you; she is a real little nudist. She likes to show off. I often see her with nothing on."

Graham was astounded. He was also intensely interested and felt a sudden rush of desire. But the subject so embarrassed him he was speechless for a few moments. Then he said, "That must be nice."

Max just shrugged and said, "They are funny things girls. I don't understand them. Come and have afternoon tea."

Graham did not really want to be in the same room as Cindy's parents but he could not see any way to avoid it without being impolite so he followed Max out to the dining room. Cindy was there with Max's parents. Now she wore a short denim dress and a T-shirt. On her face was an impish grin and to Graham she looked very sexy. As soon as he saw her Graham felt a surge of desire, despite being very scared. He tried not to blush or look guilty but had trouble acting casual, as though nothing had been going on.

It seemed however that the parents did not suspect anything so Graham sat and accepted a glass of cordial and some cake. As he lifted the glass to his mouth his eyes met Cindy's and she gave him a mischievous smile. It made his blood pound and he felt his heart lurch.

Both parents soon went off to do various things, leaving the three children alone. Max asked, "Are we going to play Battleships again?"

"If you like," Graham replied. "What about after school?"

"Aw yeah, I suppose so. Where, your place or mine?"

"What about mine?" Graham suggested. "I've got the Ship Room. We could clear a space there or play out on the lawn." He thought that it might be safer to be away from temptations over Cindy.

Max nodded. "That'll be OK for a change," he replied.

"Can I come too?" Cindy asked. Again she gave her wicked grin.

Graham hesitated. "I suppose so," he agreed.

Max laughed and said, "Only if you promise to behave yourself."

Cindy made a face. "Spoil sport! I wanted to see some more torpedoes."

Graham blushed fiercely at the innuendo, while simultaneously experiencing a surge of lust which left him trembling. He was astonished at the strength of his own reaction and could hardly think straight or speak.

When he had calmed down a bit he managed to get himself under control. "I'd better be going home," he said. He stood up and went to collect his ships, burning with embarrassment because he still partly aroused. While he loaded his ships onto the sheet of plywood he tried to hide this. As he left the room he walked quickly, hotly aware that Cindy seemed to be watching, a knowing smirk on her face. To escape her stare he fled. Walking down the street was an ordeal, as he felt sure everyone would notice and snigger. But he met no-one, and as far as he could tell, no-one even looked at him. Once at home he slipped into the Ship Room and waited until his body returned to normal.

But not his mind. For the rest of the afternoon and evening he was assailed by waves of lust and guilt. His thoughts kept returning to the scene at Max's pool and he remained aroused until it hurt. Thoughts of what sex might be like began to slip into his fevered mind and he started to construct wishful fantasies which included Cindy. It was all very stressful and left him feeling both guilty and hopeful. To divert his mind he settled to planning his model battleship.

One of the books he had was an old encyclopaedia of his fathers. In it was a picture of Britain's last battleship, HMS *Vanguard*. Graham decided he liked the look of her, and the name. But he wasn't sure if Max would accept the armament of 15" guns. Remembering Max's strong reaction to the submarine Graham decided to only put 12" guns on his model. *That is only 1" bigger than Max's battleship has*, he reasoned. *He should accept that. After all, my ship will be a bit bigger than his.*

So he set to work to draw a rough plan. This allowed for four main armament turrets; two forward and two aft. Then he considered how many guns to put in each. The *Vanguard* had twin mountings giving a total of eight big guns but Max had put ten barrels on his. Graham decided that he would do the same: 10 x 12". *I suppose I can mount them in the same layout as Max's?* he thought. *That means that the guns would be arranged 3-2---2-3.* But somehow it did not seem right. Niggling at the back of his memory were things he had read about battleships.

That sent him to his father's library again and he found a book on battleships of the World Wars. This included many good photos but also diagrams of each class of ship. That was even better. A few minutes flicking over the pages showed him that no British battleship of World War 1 had three guns in a turret. The only British ships he could find with three guns per turret were the *Nelson* and *Rodney*, both built in the 1920s and famous for their actions in World War 2. For a few minutes Graham considered making the model into one of them, but then he shook his head. "No, they both had 16" guns and Max will really get upset if I do that," he told himself.

He resumed scanning the pages. For a while he lingered over the Austro-Hungarian battleships of the Viribus Unitus-class with their four triple turrets of 12" guns but again decided Max would be angered by that. Next Graham looked at French battleships with 10 x 12" guns but they were like the old British Dreadnought-class with two of the turrets set on either beam. Then he discovered the Italian ships of the Cavour- and Andria Doria-classes with their 12 x 12" guns in a 3-2-3-2-3 layout, the middle turret being set up amidships. They made him think hard. So did the Russian Dreadnoughts but he did not like the way two of their turrets were in among the superstructure and funnels. *That must have really restricted their fire ahead and astern,* he mused.

American ships of the Nevada-class with a 3-2-2-3 layout caught his interest but they had 14" guns so he rejected them. That sent him back to leafing through the pages of British ships. He really liked the King George V-class ships of World War 2 with their 10 x 14 guns set out

4-2-4 but knew Max would get upset if he made one of them. The same argument applied to the R-class and Queen Elizabeth-class with their 8 x 15" guns. Then the Orion-class, Iron Duke-class and King George V-class of World War 1 caught his attention. They had 10 x 12" guns but in five turrets: 2-2-2-2-2. The centre turret was in among the superstructure but they looked like a nice design.

"That will do," Graham muttered. He went to work with rubber and pencil and redrew his deck plan to fit five turrets. The result was more crowded and chunkier than he liked but seemed to fit so he accepted it.

For secondary armament he adopted the World War 1 design of putting the smaller guns along the side in barbettes. Twelve 6" guns seemed a good number so these were sketched on. Some small anti aircraft guns were also included.

With the main features decided on, Graham set to work. On the roughly shaped hull he sketched where the gun turrets and superstructure would go. The wood was then rasped and sandpapered again and a block of soft pine glued down as the main part of the superstructure.

By then it was tea time and Graham was absorbed by the life of the family and unable to return to The Shipyard until nearly 8pm. Before he went to bed two hours later he added a large block of wood to represent the bridge structure at the front, and a smaller block behind, plus several smaller blocks. He then hid the pieces in case Max did come over the next day.

In bed again he was assailed by hot thoughts of Cindy. He writhed with frustration and lay awake for hours fantasizing. Several times he became conscious that it was Cindy who was dominating his thoughts, not Thelma. But after brief periods of guilt he found his imagination again gripped by heated thoughts of Cindy.

One result of this was that he was tired and short tempered at school the next day. Another was that he felt very guilty when he saw Thelma. *I hardly thought of her all weekend!* he realized. This guilt was sharpened when she approached him and said that she would be attending his party. That made him very happy, but also added some stress. Now the party had to be good. The problem of party games resurfaced.

In class another issue was raised. All of the class studied a foreign language: either Indonesian, Japanese, German or French. Graham and Stephen had both opted for German. Thelma and Janet learned French.

Before they went to language class, Old Wily, who was their Form Teacher, read from a notice.

"There is going to be a French naval ship visiting port on Thursday next week. The school is going to organize a trip to visit it. This is mainly for those students who are studying French but they wish to know if any others are interested."

Graham's ears instantly pricked up. A warship! He was gripped by a strong desire to go. His hand went up at once. As soon as Old Wily had counted how many wanted to go Graham asked, "Excuse me sir. Do you know what type of ship it is?"

"I think it is a destroyer," Old Wily replied, "But I'm not sure."

Another destroyer! Graham thought. *That should be good.*

"What's its name sir?" Janet asked.

"Her name," Old Wily replied. "Ships are feminine gender. I'm sorry I don't know."

Janet frowned. "Why are ships feminine, sir?" she asked.

"Just the way the language developed," Old Wily answered.

Stephen called across to Janet, "Hey Janet, are you going to go down and demonstrate against this ship too?"

Janet turned and eyed him coldly. "All warships are bad. But we haven't thought about that yet."

Graham burned at those words. He wanted to defend the navy, to point out its long history and why he believed it was important to have one, but he did not quite know how to word this. Nor did he want to offend Thelma.

David then surprised Graham by saying, "We shouldn't go sir."

"Why not David?"

"Because the French let off nuclear weapons out in the South Pacific; and they also oppress the native peoples in the islands."

"What islands?" Thelma asked, her cheeks showing red.

"New Caledonia and out around Tahiti," David replied.

Thelma frowned. "Where's New Caledonia?"

"Out on the other side of the Coral Sea. It is a big island and it is closer to Cairns than Brisbane is," David replied.

"Oh it is not!" Thelma retorted.

Old Wily nodded. "Yes it is. Sorry. Check your Atlas." Graham stared at Thelma in amazement. *How could she not know that?* he wondered.

David continued. "And the French deny the local people freedom."

"They do not!" Thelma cried.

"They do so!" David insisted.

A fierce argument began. Old Wily quelled this. "Stop arguing! None of you seems to have the facts. What you all need to do is get some proper information and then you can form an opinion."

"Can we have a debate sir?" David asked.

Old Wily nodded. "Yes, good idea. We need two teams: the 'for' and the 'against'. Who would like to take part?"

Janet put her hand up. "What is the topic sir?" she asked.

"That France has no right to be in the South Pacific," said Old Wily.

"Oh they have so sir! They have as much right as us," Thelma said.

"They do not," Graham said. He spoke before he realized what he was doing but he was nettled because only a month ago he had given a morning talk on the French Foreign Legion and Janet had accused them of just being a bunch of criminals and thugs. To support his case Graham added: "The French use their Foreign Legion to guard their Nuclear Base at Mururoa Atoll; and also to keep control of the native people by brute force. They are Europeans and should go back to Europe and leave the islands to their own native people."

"You are a European too," Michael said. "There are a lot of Aboriginal people who probably think we should all go back to Europe too."

"I was born here," Graham replied hotly.

Old Wily again stopped them. "That will do. We seem to have two teams. In the 'for' team; that is that the French should stay, we have Michael, Thelma and Janet. In the 'against' team we have David and Graham; and we need one more."

"Me sir," said Louise. She was a freckly blonde with a cheerful grin.

"Thank you," Old Wily said. "Now, we will have the debate on Wednesday morning. That will give you all time to assemble some facts so you aren't just waffling hot air. And we will do some research during Social Studies so that the whole class knows something about what territories the French actually own and what they are like. Now go to your foreign language classes."

Graham left the room feeling he had made a serious mistake. The last thing he wanted to do was argue with Thelma; and now he was pitted against her in a debate! He wondered how he could escape from the task but no easy answer came to mind. No-one else wanted to swap and take his place. Knowing that Old Wily expected a high standard when it came to getting the facts right, Graham devoted his lunchtime to study in the library.

This had the unexpected advantage that Thelma and Janet were also there, and wanted the same books. This allowed Graham to be close to Thelma and to speak to her and he was relieved to find that she seemed friendly enough. But as he came out of the library, Graham received another shock. Outside he met Cindy. To his surprise, she smiled and fell into step with him. She struck up a conversation. It was ordinary enough, just "How are you?" and so on, but it was enough to get Graham's mind and body going. It was at the end that she really stunned him. She said, "Do you mind if I come over to see your model ships this afternoon?"

Graham was actually embarrassed by the request. He was very self-conscious about people knowing about his hobby in case they thought he was still just a little kid. This applied even more to such a big girl as Cindy but he could not think of any reason why not. "Yeah, OK," he replied.

As he walked along Graham noted several people look at him and Cindy and that made him feel better. *She is a pretty girl,* he told himself, *and very desirable!*

That boosted his ego and he kept glancing at her in a sort of wonder. After they had parted at the door to her classroom he could not get her out of his mind. That caused him more guilt and he told himself he was weak and disloyal to Thelma. But he also knew that he was now fascinated by Cindy and what she potentially promised.

After school Graham met Max and Cindy. The trio walked home together. Max's house was their first port of call to collect his ship models. Carrying a couple each the trio walked the three blocks to Graham's. On arrival they went in and Graham found they had the place to themselves.

"Where's your mum?" Max asked as they drank glasses of cordial.

"She's at work. She won't be home till after 5 o'clock," Graham said.

"What about your brother and sister?" Cindy asked.

"Alex will be with his mates and Kylie has gone to Margaret's," Graham replied. He suddenly had a wicked thought as he looked at Cindy. She met his eye and appeared to telepathically communicate because she said, "What are we going to do then?"

Max sniffed. "We came here to play Battleships."

Cindy pulled a face but made no more hints. So after afternoon tea they made their way down to the Ship Room and looked at the sailing ship models. It was quickly decided that there wasn't enough space there so they proceeded to play on the side lawn. To do this they crawled around on the grass, pushing the models.

Once again Max's battleship was the war winner. That made Graham even more determined to complete his as quickly as he could—and to make it better. It also made him glad that he had hidden the pieces so that Max did not see them when they went up to the front veranda to talk after the game.

Graham was anxious to know how quickly he needed to have his new battleship in service so he asked when they were playing again. Max frowned and wrinkled his brow. "Can't be tomorrow. And I have soccer practice on Wednesday afternoon. Maybe Thursday," he said.

"What about next weekend?" Graham asked.

Max shook his head. "Nope. We are going away to visit relations in Tully," he replied.

Graham badly wanted to know if the 'we' included Cindy but did not dare ask, lest he betray his interest. All he could do was look at her and raise an eyebrow but she just smiled and did not answer.

While they talked, Cindy lay on Graham's bed. That allowed him to admire her legs and to look at her face. She seemed to spend a lot of time looking at him and she smiled a lot. *She is acting as though she likes me,* Graham thought. But he could only shake his head in doubt. *Nah! She is in Year 10. She wouldn't be interested in a Year 8!*

But as Cindy and Max were leaving, Cindy waited till Max was out of earshot and whispered, "I really like you Graham. Can I come over again tomorrow afternoon?"

Chapter 15

CINDY SMILES

Graham spent much of the evening in a haze of euphoria. *Cindy likes me!* he thought in amazement. In his mind he replayed every memory of her. His body had a part to play as well. Without any conscious thought he kept getting aroused. He seemed to have no control over it at all and found it very embarrassing. All he could do was keep out of everyone's way, particularly Kylie's. So he sat at his desk and worked on the model battleship. He decided to make the funnels next. From a piece of thick cardboard he cut out two pieces each 7cm x 15cm. These were rolled and then glued to make two tubes with a diameter of about 4cm. Using a black felt pen Graham coloured in a black band around the top of each funnel. The funnels were then glued onto the main superstructure.

A study of battleship photos gave him another idea and he set to work to make two searchlight platforms. Each on comprised a piece of 2mm thick balsa measuring 2cm x 1.5cm. One edge was rounded to fit the curve of the funnel. On the opposite edge the corners were rounded. Then a thin cardboard rail 5mm high was glued around the outside edge. The piece was then glued onto the side of the funnel half way up. Several small blocks of cardboard to represent lockers were added.

For the searchlights Graham made two small cylinders of balsa, each 5mm in length and 5mm in diameter. One end of the cylinder was rounded slightly by rubbing with sandpaper. On the other end Graham glued two 5mm circles of aluminium foil. The circles were cut from the thin aluminium foil from the top of Milo tins. A short pin was pushed through the top of the searchlight and then through a smaller cylinder of balsa which was the mounting. Two tiny slivers of balsa were glued on top of the searchlight on either side of the pinhead to represent the sights.

The whole assembly was then stuck into the platform, and to finish it all off Graham made two tiny ladders out of cardboard. This was done by using a black biro to rule two lines 4cm long and 2mm apart. Between these parallel lines he then drew crosspieces. He then cut the ladder out with scissors and glued it to the side of the funnel so that it led up from the deck to the platform.

The model looked so good that Graham sat for quite a while just admiring at it from different angles. *This is going to be a good model,* he thought. The knowledge that Max would not be home on the next weekend helped. *I have time to make the model properly,* he told himself. But thinking about playing games with Max led to thinking about Cindy.

That night in bed his fantasies took on a whole new dimension. Cindy dominated all his thoughts and this pushed Thelma into the shade. *Thelma is a good girl. I love her and adore her. She must not to be exposed to any base lust (well... not yet anyway; or at least only a little),* he told himself. Cindy on the other hand appeared to be an altogether different type of girl and he felt no guilt at fantasizing about her.

At school the next day Graham was itching to see Cindy and he spent most of his time walking around looking for her. When his friends asked him what he was doing he found he was too inhibited to even mention her. But the memory of her nude form kept plaguing him in the form of a series of involuntary erections at the most inconvenient times. These were made worse when he finally saw Cindy in the distance. She was with a group of her Year 10 friends. He wanted to talk to her but was too scared to approach her while she was with all the other girls.

Remembering Joany's comment about younger boys and shame he bit his lip. *Cindy is three years older and will not want to be seen with a mere Year 8,* he thought. But oh! How he wanted to be with her!

His chance came by accident at morning break as he walked along under the school. Cindy appeared from the other direction on her own.

"Hi Graham," she said with a smile.

Heartened by her apparently friendly greeting Graham replied, with hammering heart: "H... h... hello Cindy. Er... um... er Cindy..."

She stopped and looked at him, one eyebrow raised quizzically. "Yes?"

"I... er... Yesterday afternoon. I... I was really glad you were there," Graham stammered. He blushed furiously and began to become aroused.

To his relief she smiled. "I liked it too. I think you are very nice."

After licking dry lips, Graham managed to say, "Would you like to... to... er... to come over to my place?"

Her face dimpled into a mischievous grin. "Yes, I told you I would, but only as long as you promise not to tell anyone."

"I promise," Graham blurted out.

"Not to any of your mates, no boasting," she said. "And definitely not to Maxy."

"No. I won't. I promise."

"Good. When?"

To Graham's annoyance one of Cindy's friends came along and stood next to her. Graham glanced at her and felt very inhibited. After licking dry lips he managed to say, "What about this afternoon straight after school?"

"Yes, all right," Cindy replied.

Graham's heart leapt. Blood began to surge in his veins. "I... I'll see you then," he stammered. His heart hammered fast at his own daring but he was unable to continue in the presence of the other girl.

Graham could not believe his ears. It seemed too good to be true. A real girl—saying she liked him! He did not know what to say. By then he was very aroused and that was causing him severe embarrassment so he mumbled thanks and fled to hide himself in the library.

In class he could hardly think straight and his arousal would not go away for more than a few minutes. Graham even found he did not want Thelma to look at him. He sat hunched forward, hoping no-one, including Stephen beside him, would notice.

During the afternoon lessons Graham could think only of meeting Cindy. Heated fantasies formed in his brain and he became so aroused it eventually hurt. He also began to fret, worrying that either Kylie or Alex might be at home and spoil the opportunity.

After school Graham waited outside the front door for a while to see if he could speak to Cindy to check that she really was coming over. But he saw no sign of her. Feeling very anxious he walked quickly home. At every step he seemed to imagine the worst: that she would not turn up, that they would get caught and be in terrible trouble.

But as he turned the corner into his street he saw her bicycle leaning against the front fence. *She is there!* he thought. His heart leapt and his body began to heat up with excited anticipation. With high hopes he hurried the last hundred yards. Cindy was sitting on the front steps and gave him a smile and a little wave as he got closer. He waved back and smiled but his face felt like it was made of plastic and he felt suddenly awkward.

As he opened the gate, Graham was suddenly overcome with shyness and anxiety. "Hi!" he said. "Do you want some afternoon tea?"

"Better not. I have to be home soon," Cindy replied.

"Just bring your bike inside in case someone pinches it," Graham suggested. He was quite unsure of what to say next or of how to proceed. Suddenly it was all a bit too real and grown up and he knew he was scared.

Cindy nodded and went out to get it. As she did she blushed and also looked shy. She laid the bike on the front lawn and the pair stood looking at each other. Graham's mind was in ferment. *What do I do now?* he wondered. *What do I say?* It all seemed a little bit cold-blooded and his feelings became even more mixed. *Where do I suggest we go?* he wondered. Upstairs came to mind but there were beds there and he thought that she might be upset if he made too blatant a suggestion.

"Will we go to the Ship Room?" he suggested.

Cindy hesitated then nodded. "OK."

They walked around to the Ship Room and went in. By then Graham's heart was hammering furiously and he was more scared than aroused. He did not want to do the wrong thing in terms of being the great lover—and nor did he really want to do the wrong thing in terms of morals and the law. But equally he really did want to experience Cindy's female charms!

Torn as he was he led her to the far corner. There they stopped and looked at each other, both breathing fast and both obviously anxious. After standing looking at her for an embarrassing minute, Graham licked his dry lips and plucked up his courage to say, "Can I have a kiss please?"

Cindy blushed and became all shy. But she smiled and nodded then said, "If you want."

But Graham was no expert at kissing. His entire experience to date had been a few pecks. Scorching memories of Joany kissing the British sailor and of saying he had more experience added to his anxiety. Cindy stepped closer and they very tentatively held hands. Now Graham became even more anxious and he licked his lips again. Her eyes seemed to go out of focus and he summoned up what courage was left and leaned forward. She leaned forward as well and their lips came together. It felt nice, but also not right. It was a clash of dry skin, teeth and noses. Both drew apart and licked their lips and they tried again. Graham had to think about which side to turn his face to avoid her nose. This time it was better and it was immediately obvious to Graham that Cindy knew how to kiss.

Wonderful scents and tastes flooded Graham's consciousness and he felt his passions stir. *This is nice,* he thought as he kissed again. As they did she put her arms around his neck and their bodies came together. Graham could feel her breasts pressing against him and his own arms went around her waist. He became very aroused and pulled away so that Cindy would not feel it and be put off. But to his delighted surprise she kept holding him tightly, pressing her body against his. *She must be able to feel it,* he thought, his anxiety returning.

She obviously could. She rubbed her body against him and murmured, "Ooh! That feels nice!"

That sent Graham's mind into a riot of speculation and hope. He kissed her more determinedly and, greatly daring, pressed himself hard against her. Her response was to wriggle and murmur with obvious pleasure. *Heavens, this is good!* he thought.

Then a noise attracted his attention. He looked up and felt an instant spurt of fright and frustration. It was Alex. He had come through the front gate and was wheeling his bike along the side lawn. Graham at once disentangled himself. "Quick, pretend we are playing," he hissed, his heart now hammering from anxiety.

He quickly walked over to where Napoleon's army was marching across the concrete in a 5 metre long column. "You start moving that army this way," he hissed, pointing to the nearby Lucranian army. Seething with annoyance he knelt and picked up the front cavalry scout and shifted him half a metre towards the border of France.

Cindy looked annoyed and did some under-the-breath muttering but complied and did as she was asked. She crouched beside the green-coated army of plasticine soldiers and began shifting them one at a time towards Graham.

They were only just in time. By then Alex had walked in under the car port and placed his bike against the paling wall. He saw them at once and stopped. "Oh, it's you," he said to Cindy. "I wondered whose bike it was. What are you two doing?" he asked.

"Just playing," Graham replied, hoping that his voice sounded normal but thinking it was a hoarse croak. His whole body still felt as though it was on fire and he knew he was blushing.

Alex laughed and then winked. "Just playing eh? Playing what?" he said in a voice laden with sarcasm.

Graham blushed some more and knew he shouldn't. His mind raced, struggling to come up with a sensible answer that wasn't a direct lie. But Cindy answered instead. "You keep your dirty thoughts to yourself Alex Kirk!" she snapped.

Alex stepped back from her anger. "OK, just joking! But it does look a bit suspicious."

Cindy snorted and then said, "I am just helping Graham until Maxy arrives."

Alex nodded. "OK. But Max won't be coming. I saw him riding off towards town."

"Oh! OK. Then I suppose I had better go home. You can take over here Alex," Cindy answered.

Graham wanted neither of those things to happen but he could not think of any sensible option so he muttered 'yes' and nodded. To his relief Alex shook his head. "Not me. I've got better things to do."

With that he walked away. Graham and Cindy both stood up and looked at each other. Cindy made a wry face and said, "I had better go home. No more fun today."

That was real disappointment to Graham but he could only nod. "What about tomorrow then?" he asked.

To his delight Cindy nodded. "OK. That was real nice. You are getting to be a real good kisser."

With that she turned and walked out and Graham could only follow her. At the front she gave another wry grin and Graham could see she was annoyed. He felt very frustrated himself but could only hope for more. After she had gone he made his way up to his room and resumed work on his battleship.

***

That afternoon and evening Graham added the secondary armament to his battleship. He did this by the same method he had used for his first cruiser, by placing the guns along each side in barbettes. To do this he first glued six small balsa blocks, each 1cm long x 5mm square, evenly spaced along the sides of the superstructure. Then he cut a long piece of 3mm square balsa which he cut into lengths of 3cm. Through one end of each of these he pushed a short pin at right angles. At the same end he measured 1cm and carefully cut in for a tiny bit all around. He then used a craft knife to trim slivers of wood off the remaining 2cm, cutting back from the other end as far as the cut. Once this was done he used sandpaper to round this to look like a gun barrel. By pushing a black biro into the end he made the gun muzzle.

The pin was then pushed down into one of the blocks of balsa. As he completed each one and stuck it on Graham felt better. *My battleship is no longer helpless. She has guns and can fight off some enemies,* he thought.

Next he cut pieces of cardboard 3cm x 1.5cm and marked out a rectangle 2.5cm x 5mm on each one. This smaller rectangle was cut out by using the craft knife. This left a window. The cardboard was then bent into a curved shape and glued at both ends to the superstructure and at the bottom to the main deck. Thus the armoured barbette was made. A small semi-circle of cardboard covered the top.

It was only after he had started that Graham bothered to look at a photo and then he noted (to his annoyance) that on the real ships the secondary armament were along the side of the hull. As he had begun placing them along the side of the superstructure and resting on the main deck he felt quite silly.

"I shouldn't rush into things," he muttered. Presented with the choice of pulling them all off or of hoping no-one else noticed he opted for the latter.

By the time all twelve barbettes had been glued in place Graham had all but forgotten this as the end result looked very good to him. *Looks like the real ones,* he decided as he crouched to view the rows of guns from various angles.

Having completed the secondary armament really pleased Graham. "My battleship now has twelve 6" guns, and funnels and engines and so she can steam and fight. She has as many guns as a light cruiser so I will use her if I have to," he told himself. But he didn't want to unless he absolutely had to. "Better to keep her a surprise," he muttered. So the battleship was slid out of sight under his bed.

But it was not Battleships he fantasized about when he lay in bed—it was Cindy. He became very aroused and very hopeful. *She likes me and she says she is coming over again!*

So all day on Friday Graham was excited. He was aroused so often and so long that it became painful. During the day he saw Cindy several times in the distance and each time she gave him a cheerful grin. That sign of promise kept his hopes high. His big concern was whether Alex or Kylie might be at home after school and he did not dare ask either lest they become suspicious.

After school he hurried home, walking as quickly as he could. As he rounded the corner into his street he looked at his house in eager anticipation. But there was no bicycle leaning on the fence and he felt a sharp stab of disappointment. When he got there he looked around but there was no sign of her. For a few minutes he walked around the house in frustration.

Then he shrugged and went to the kitchen to have afternoon tea. After eating two biscuits and drinking a glass of cordial he went to his table. "I may as well work on my battleship," he muttered.

The next parts of the model he planned to work on were the main armament gun turrets. Still squirming with frustration and half aroused he sat and began measuring and cutting rectangles of 6mm thick balsa. He was just slicing off the third one when he heard the front gate open. Turning in his chair, he looked down the front steps and felt his heart leap. It was Cindy.

"Hello. I was starting to think you weren't coming," he said as he got up to meet her.

Cindy grinned. "I thought it might be better if I took my bike home first. Then if Max comes by he won't know I am here."

What a good idea! Graham thought. He told her so, then led her through to the kitchen for some refreshments. By then he was fully aroused and his heart was hammering with anticipation. He could hardly wait before suggesting they go down to the Ship Room again. To his relief Cindy nodded. "That's why I'm here," she said. She gulped down the last of the cordial and put the cup down, then followed Graham down the back stairs.

Without any more preliminaries they began kissing. It was at once apparent to Graham that Cindy was feeling excited as well and that made him both more aroused but also slightly scared. But he wanted to kiss her and relished every second. He also badly wanted to touch her but was afraid to ask. Instead he began to slowly move his hand over her clothing, first at the back and then on her sides. The whole time they kept their bodies pressed together and he enjoyed that as well.

After a time he leaned back and managed to slide his hand around from her left hip onto her stomach. This brought his fingers to just under her left breast and there they seemed to freeze with the paralysis of fear. A minute went by before she kissed him again and then leaned back and said, "You can if you want."

Graham was astounded—and scared. He knew he had to act. *Do something you weakling or she will despise you,* he told himself. The concept of being a man flitted in the back of his thoughts. But he knew he was afraid. The fear was as much about making it obvious he was inexperienced as about getting into trouble for doing something so naughty.

She must have sensed this as she gave a gentle hug and said, "It's all right. I want you to."

"I... I'm not quite sure..." he stammered.

"Would you like me to show you?" she asked.

Graham could only nod, his arousal pounding in his skull and his fingers twitching in anticipation. For him the next 10 minutes were heaven as Cindy coached him in the gentle art of giving a girl pleasure with his hands. Graham found himself trembling and thrilled in a way he had never thought possible.

Then she moved his thoughts to a higher level of pleasure by saying, "Of course it's even nicer when you don't have any clothes on."

Graham was almost stunned speechless. "W... would you like that?" he asked.

Cindy nodded and his hopes went up even more. But there was an anxious pause. They stepped apart, both breathing fast and perspiring slightly. Graham badly wanted to do that but now he was frightened and he had to keep wiping sweaty palms on his shorts. "Me too?" he croaked.

"Yes please. I want to learn what boys are like," Cindy replied. That was incredibly exciting to Graham but also very frightening. Cindy then stepped back and in a decisive gesture pulled her dress up over her head and tossed it on the floor. Seeing her in bra and panties got

Graham breathing even faster. She stood and let him look for a minute, then reached behind her back and unclipped her bra. Then she got all shy and hesitated. For another minute they stood looking at each other, both panting with anxiety before she peeled it off and stood straight for him to look at.

Oh yes! Graham thought as he studied her. To his juvenile mind she looked just perfect. He stepped forward and put his arms around her, instinctively not touching her too soon. Instead he kissed her and caressed her back. The feel of his hands on her silken smooth skin was a wonder and a delight and he shuddered with pleasure and suppressed passion. Cindy sighed and shivered with obvious pleasure.

Cindy did the prompting. "Well, show me," she said.

But fear still held Graham. "Promise you won't tell anyone or complain," he croaked, his heart pounding and his throat dry.

"I won't," Cindy replied. "I'm not like that."

Somewhat reassured and now driven by an intense urge, Graham fumbled at the buttons of his shirt. He was astonished to find that his fingers were trembling and he had trouble undoing them. He took the shirt off and then started to undo his shorts. As he did he kept looking around and listening in case someone came. He was now very scared but very excited. Cindy just stood and watched as he slid down his shorts. He gulped and summoned up the courage to peel off his underpants, to stand erect before her, his heart hammering furiously. He found it the most stimulating thrill.

Seeing Cindy's eyes widen with interest added to his excitement and he stood defiantly aroused while she stared with rapt attention. She bent forward and studied it minutely while Graham stood in embarrassed pride. For a few minutes she touched him and experimented, causing him to squirm and pulsate. This made her giggle so she did it again. Graham sighed and shivered with the sheer pleasure of it. He felt his urges mounting and reached forward to grip her. She looked into his eyes and he could see she was panting. Her pupils were dilated and her lips slightly parted.

"You are beautiful," Graham croaked, aware at the back of his mind that he was skating onto very thin ice indeed. *She is under age you fool!* the back of his mind whispered. "Jail bait," his dad had called them in a father-and-son talk the year before.

But he was so gripped by lust that he lifted her up and stepped forward to kiss her again. This time they were both on fire and their bodies rubbed and pressed at each others. As they kissed and explored with their hands, Graham's vision seemed to blur and the blood pounded in his skull.

But when his desire urged him to go further, Cindy moaned, "No," and stepped back. Her face looked drawn and flushed, but scared.

"I'd like to," Graham said, half shocked at his own daring.

"No, not yet," she groaned again. She pushed him away.

Graham felt a fierce urge to do it, succeeded by a wave of shame and fear as he realized what he had been doing. With an effort of will he let her go and stepped back. "Sorry," he muttered. "I was just losing control."

"I'm sorry too," Cindy said. "It is my fault for leading you on. Thank you for being kind. I am just interested in how boy's bodies work."

"Can I touch you too?" he croaked.

Cindy nodded and murmured yes. "But hands only," she added. They came together again and kissed and then began using their hands to pleasure each other.

Oh this is heaven! Graham thought as Cindy helped him to reach a climax.

Voices!

Graham snatched his hands away and stepped back. Movement at the front steps caught his eye. He felt a wave of shock. "Alex and Maxy!" he gasped.

Chapter 16

WILL I?

G raham stared at Cindy in alarm. She looked frightened and annoyed. Hastily she snatched up her bra. In the process it caught on the mast of a sailing ship, snapping some of the cotton rigging and spilling tiny plasticine crew members onto the concrete. Graham was torn between asking her to be more careful and telling her to hurry up. An instinct cautioned him against rebuking her for not being careful.

His mouth dry with fear and his heart hammering furiously Graham tugged on his shorts and began pulling on his shirt. Anticipatory shame caused him to burn with embarrassment and his fingers fumbled with the shirt buttons. Cindy pulled on her knickers.

Then, to Graham's intense relief, Alex went up the front steps, followed by Max. Instantly Graham's mind formed a plan. "Quick, follow me!" he hissed.

But Cindy didn't. Instead she began to put the bra on. Graham had never seen this done and despite his fear watched with fascination. By then he could hear the footsteps of the two boys passing overhead and he broke into a fever of impatience. "Hurry! Hurry!" he hissed.

"I'm going as fast as I can!" Cindy snapped back.

"But we need to get out of here," Graham replied, his eyes shifting to the back stairs.

Cindy snorted with annoyance as she dressed. "If I run out here half undressed it will tell everyone what we have been up to. At least with my clothes on we can pretend we are just playing."

That made sense to Graham but he moved to the door, ready to run. Cindy picked up her dress and quickly pulled it over her head and wriggled into it. As she tugged it into position, she moved to follow.

"Where are we going?" she whispered.

Graham didn't wait. He pointed and went out into the carport and across to the laundry. Cindy followed. Directly opposite the back stairs was a large opening where the underneath had not been completely enclosed. Both of them went through this onto the east side lawn even as Graham glimpsed feet descending the back stairs.

A moment of indecision held Graham. *If I run left and try to go through the front gate they can see us through the palings if they go into the Ship Room. But if they go out onto the back yard they will see us if we go right,* he thought. Where were the boys most likely to go? Graham decided the Ship Room and began running to his right beside the laundry and kitchen. By then all of Alex's legs were visible and his body was coming into view.

But almost at once Graham wondered if he had made a mistake. In the back yard 10 metres away was the guinea pig cage. That was often a popular destination, particularly for Kylie and Margaret. *I hope they don't come this way,* he thought.

He continued to run, Cindy close on his heels. They went past the guinea pig cage and in among the rows of vegetable gardens that took up much of the back yard. By then Graham was in a state of high anxiety and excitement. He knew that both of them would now be visible to anyone who came out onto the west side lawn or to the back of the laundry.

A glance behind showed no sign of either boy so Graham kept running. After swerving through the gate to a fenced off area that had once been a fowl run, he led Cindy past the big mango tree to the back fence. There was a gate and he came to a puffing stop when he reached it.

As he opened the gate, which led out into a grassy laneway 25m wide, Graham asked, "Where will we go now?"

Cindy slipped past him through the gate and looked anxiously back. She shook her head. "Nowhere. I'm going home. I don't want Maxy to see me."

"Aw, but... I was just starting to enjoy that," Graham muttered.

"So was I, but I am not in the mood now," Cindy replied.

Graham bit his lip and tried to think of a counter argument. Unable to do so, he said, "Can we meet again tomorrow then?"

Cindy shook her head. "Sorry, no. Maxy and I are going away for the weekend to visit relations in Tully."

"What about Sunday afternoon?"

"Doubt it. It would depend what time we get home and then I would need an excuse to sneak away," Cindy replied.

Graham could see the problems in trying to organize that. He said, "What about Monday then?"

To his relief Cindy nodded and said, "Yes." Then she set off at a fast walk along the lane.

Graham watched her go but she did not look back or wave. By now he was sure that he was in love with her and he urgently wanted to be with her. It was only after she had turned the corner and was no longer visible that he thought of Thelma. That gave him a shock and he suddenly despised himself.

"God I am a weakling!" he muttered. Then the heated memories if fondling Cindy and of being kissed by her swamped his mind and seemed to wash out all images of Thelma. For a few minutes he stood there, tcrn in his emotions and feeling doubly guilty. He knew he was being disloyal to the image of Thelma and he also knew that he was fired with desire to do physical things with Cindy that he knew were illegal and immoral.

But they were also enormous fun! And he had to admit he even enjoyed the excitement of nearly being caught. The memories of the frantic scramble to get dressed and the dash to get away made him grin. Then he realized he needed an alibi so that he could convincingly go and meet Alex and Max.

The guinea pigs, he thought. So he went out into the lane and pulled up several large handfuls of succulent guinea grass. With these as his excuse for being out the back he made his way inside, closing the gate behind him. As he walked through to the fowl run gate his eyes scanned the back of the house and side lawns but there was no sign of the boys. He reached the guinea pigs unseen.

They were glad to see him and noting the eager way they came to him sniffing and nibbling at the grass made him feel guilty. *I have been neglecting you little fellows,* he thought. He tried to rationalize this by telling himself he was not as attached to these guinea pigs as the ones that had been killed by the savage dog a few months earlier.

That memory made him feel awful. Not only had there been the trauma of trying to stop the dog killing the pets but it had attacked Kylie and he had used a fence paling to save her. In the process he had hit it on the head. The blow had killed the animal and that made him feel much worse as he really loved dogs. The traumatic memories now returned and he stood there trembling slightly.

Alex's voice pulled him out of them. "Oh, there you are Wart!"

Graham looked up and saw Alex and Max at the back entrance to the laundry. Suddenly Graham felt relieved and was glad he had his props. He held the other handful of grass in for the guinea pigs. "I'm just giving them some fresh grass," he said.

Alex nodded. "Good. Now, we want to play so come and join us."

Phew! They didn't see us! Graham thought. He said, "OK, come and help me move the cage to a fresh bit of lawn first."

They did that and then Graham was used to adjudicate a map battle between Alex and Max. They used the rules given them by Mr Conkey and each had an identical fleet of five battleships, five cruisers, five destroyers and five submarines. Graham thought it an oddly unbalanced fleet but was still interested. Just watching the pair play gave him a good insight into their mental processes. It confirmed his thoughts that his big brother was more brawn than brain. *Alex made lots of mistakes,* he thought afterwards.

After Max had gone Graham resumed work on the turrets for his new battleship. He cut out five rectangles of balsa, each 6mm thick and measuring 6cm x 4cm. A study of a photo showed him that the turrets on the Iron Duke-class ships were not rectangles. They had curved sides which sloped slightly inwards towards the top. This shape was achieved by shaving with a craft knife and by using his small wood rasp and then sandpaper. The end products looked quite good to him.

A black biro was used to mark where each gun barrel was to be glued on. Next he made five circular mountings from balsa, each 4mm thick and 4cm in diameter. These were glued in position on the deck or superstructure of the model. By pushing pins down through the turrets and on into the mountings each turret was added to the model. The pins allowed the turrets to rotate and Graham spent a few minutes turning them and imagining the guns firing. *It is going to be a good model,* he thought.

Kylie and Margaret arrived soon after that and he had to talk to them for a few minutes. Then his mother came home and she had the usual Friday collection of comics and chocolates. Reading kept Graham happy until tea time. Margaret said goodbye and rode off on her bike and the children were fussed at to have their baths and to get ready for Scouts and Guides.

Scouts was fun. Best of all Max acted quite normal so Graham felt sure that Cindy had not been seen and that their secret was safe. But he did feel guilty about not thinking of Thelma more.

That night, when he lay in his bed, Graham did try to fantasize about Thelma. It was easy enough to begin with. He made himself the hero—a naval officer on a gunboat up a crocodile infested river in Papua a hundred years earlier, tasked with rescuing a missionary and his lovely daughter (Thelma) from the cannibals. But once he had fought off the first wave of imaginary savages and was holding Thelma it all became difficult. Instead of her face his mind kept filling with images of Cindy.

Try as he might he could not stop thinking about Cindy and he realized that he was smitten by her. *Maybe I am in love with Cindy?* he rationalized. The heated memories kept him awake far into the night and left him yearning urgently for more experiences with her.

Because Cindy was away, Graham found Saturday a boring and very frustrating day. Thinking about Cindy just got him aroused and edgy. There were also chores: cleaning the bird cages, feeding the fish, moving the guinea pig cage, washing the dog, sweeping his room.

Graham also worked on the gun barrels for his battleship model. He was not sure want size to make them and tried to visualize the guns on Max's model. In the end he decided that making them 6cm long would be about right. In fact he found he had to make two of them slightly shorter. The guns of the centre turret ('Q' according to the British system of naming them from bow to stern as A, B, Q, X, Y) were just too long to fit into the available space. They needed about 2mm trimmed off them.

To make the gun barrels he sliced a long length of 4mm x 4mm balsa. This was then cut into 6cm lengths with a craft knife. By carefully longitudinal slicing he shaved off the edges to make each one roughly octagonal. Having chosen the muzzle end of each piece Graham measured 2cm from the other end and then made a shallow cut right around that. He then carefully shaved in from the muzzle end to the shallow cut so that the front end of the gun barrel was slightly smaller than the back end. By gently rubbing with sandpaper he was then able to make the whole barrel round and also slightly tapered.

The end result looked very good to him. The muzzle was made by pushing the end of a black ball point pen into the centre of that end. Feeling particularly pleased with the result Graham glued them on to the turrets using craft glue. To hold the ends of the barrels up while the glue dried he rested them on pencils.

Seeing the battleship with its main armament complete gave Graham a real sense of achievement. This was almost immediately tempered by two breakages. When he tried to turn a turret, he pushed sideways against the gun barrels with a finger. The turret turned but in the process the gun barrels broke at the point where they were glued on.

I need a better way of doing this, Graham thought. But he just glued them back on and resolved to always turn the turrets by gripping them, not by pushing at the guns.

***

Sunday was another frustrating day. At church he had to put up with Margaret—and with his conscience. When the minister read about 'Sinful desires of the flesh' Graham again squirmed inside and felt very guilty. It also came to him that he was potentially harming Cindy by trying to persuade her to do sinful things. But just thinking about the sinful things gave him even stronger desires to do them!

For a while he contemplated the whole moral issue of sex both before and after marriage. He knew that the church did not approve of people who were not married having sex but he was also aware that a lot of it went on. Adultery he understood and despised. *That is not about sex, it is about the betrayal of trust,* he thought. But he could also see that the more fanatical, fundamentalist 'wowser' religions did not take that view.

If I do anything really serious with Cindy then I could be doomed to hell, Graham thought. *And so would she.*

That was the theology, but somehow he did not believe it and did not want to. But it niggled at his conscience all the same, making him feel very anxious and uncomfortable. Then he decided that he would not really go to hell forever just because he was naughty with Cindy; or with any other girls.

Surely God isn't that cruel and unjust? he thought. *Anyway, a few days of pleasure and excitement with Cindy are worth a few weeks or even months in hell as punishment!*

During the remainder of the day Graham stayed at home and either read or worked on his model battleship. After studying photos of the *Iron Duke* he added small sighting ports and range finders to the gun turrets and then added more bridge platforms and a main range finder to the superstructure. By the time these were done the model really did look like a battleship. Then there was the problem of the name. When he had started making the model Graham had the name *Vanguard* in mind. He had found that there was a *Vanguard* of the *Dreadnought* type in World War 1. But it had a different turret layout and when he read that it blew up at Scapa Flow in 1917, probably because of faulty cordite, he decided that he would call his new ship *Iron Duke*.

But much of the day was taken up by fantasizing about Cindy and by planning where they could meet without danger of being disturbed. Once again it was a very aroused and frustrated boy who lay awake for hours in his bed, tortured by the urgent needs of his body and the conflicts with his conscience.

But the physical desire won. Along with it was a deep fascination with the physiology of it all. Graham really wanted to know how girls were made and how their bodies worked but was too afraid and embarrassed to go to a library or to ask an adult. So lack of accurate knowledge also tormented him. He was dimly aware that his fevered imaginings were not quite right and that bothered him.

Monday came at last and he hurried eagerly to school so as to make arrangements with Cindy. But the first girl he met was Thelma. He gave her a smile and she returned it with a faint movement of the lips. That was a double jolt. *Do I love her?* he wondered. He was conscious that she did not even seem to like him but he did not want to put that into words. And where did Cindy fit into all that?

Graham became quickly aware that his physical urges were winning over his conscience and will power. His body seemed to take control and he became very aroused just thinking about Cindy. But he did not see her during the morning so school was more of a drag and boring torment than usual.

All afternoon in class the impending tryst was all Graham could think about. He was aroused nearly all afternoon and was quite sore as a result. He also got into trouble from Old Wily for inattention. The teacher reminded Graham that he had to perform at the debate about the French on Wednesday. The prospect sent Graham into a lather of concern and he made an effort to learn some facts.

It wasn't until the end of the school day that he got a chance to speak to Cindy. By then he was in a real ferment of urgent desire and anxiety. As soon as the class was dismissed after the last lesson he hurried to the bike racks and that was where he saw her. The moment he did he started to get aroused again and he found his heart fluttering with anxiety. *I wonder will she want to be with me?* he thought. Plucking up his courage he began making his way through the throng towards her.

As he did she looked around and saw him. Her face lit up in a smile and his fears evaporated.

"Hi Cindy! Are we still meeting this afternoon?" he asked.

"If you still want to," Cindy replied.

"I'd love to," Graham admitted, his heart racing with excitement.

"Do you want to do it?" Cindy asked.

The bluntness of the question quite stunned Graham. All he could do was nod. Cindy gave an anxious smile then said, "Promise you won't tell, not your brother or your mates."

Graham's heart leapt. He nodded vigorously. "I won't," he replied. Blood began to surge in his veins as the implications of what she had said sank in. Then another worrying thought came to him and he stammered in anxious embarrassment: "What if there is someone home?"

Her face dimpled into a mischievous grin. "I have thought about that. I will go home and change. You go home. If your brother or sister are home then stay inside at your desk. If they aren't home then sit out on your front steps. I will walk past to check. If they aren't home I will come in."

Graham nodded. He was now so excited and aroused his mouth had gone quiet dry and his throat felt constricted. Cindy took her bike and headed off and Graham went the other way. So aroused and excited was he that he ran almost all the way home. As he approached his house his heart was pounding in anticipation and fear. *Oh! I hope no-body is home!*

But once he arrived home Graham found Kylie and Margaret there. That sent him into a tailspin of worry in case Cindy arrived. He tried to act nonchalant and wandered through to the kitchen to get some afternoon tea. While he was there he heard girl's voices at the front. Cindy!

In something of a flap Graham walked quickly back to the front door.

Cindy was talking to Kylie and Margaret. As he appeared she looked at him and said, "Hi Graham. I just wondered if Maxy was here?"

Graham swallowed. "No... No he isn't. I think he said he was going to the bike shop."

"Oh I see. Thanks. Oh well, see you tomorrow," she said. She turned and went down the steps leaving Graham in a quandary as to whether he should somehow sneak away and follow her to her house; or whether she actually meant tomorrow. In the end he decided it would look odd if he went out so he sat at his desk, pretending he was happy instead of being all frustrated and disappointed. In a real grump he set to work on the model battleship.

After a while his mood lightened as he became absorbed in the problem of making some anti-aircraft guns. He was aware that the original *Iron Duke* was built before World War 1, when aircraft were not a problem, but one book he had looked at mentioned that she was still in service as a gunnery training ship and then as a decoy battleship, made up to look like a KGV-class. By then she did have AA guns so he went ahead and added six Bofors type guns to the superstructure. These were the same as the AA guns on his gunboats and they did not revolve but they still looked good. When they were in place he smiled. *The model really looks like a battleship now!* he thought. He admired it from several angles then went to have his bath.

During that he thought about Cindy again and fantasized she was in there with him. That was both very enjoyable and very frustrating and he was quite short tempered during the evening. *We need another place to meet,* he thought. For quite a while he pondered this and at last came up with a solution. Through his mind flitted memories of him and Margaret playing naughty nude games the previous year in the swamp at Centennial Lakes and up in the Bamboo Patch on Edge Hill. Then he thought of other bits of bush closer to home.

But would Cindy go along with it? That was the worry.

The next day at school Graham went through the same anxieties and agonies of decision. Was it Thelma he loved; or Cindy? Was it love? Or was it lust? In class he studied Thelma and found he still worshipped her. *She is so nice, so pretty, so pure,* he thought.

But his tormented body urgently wanted to be with Cindy so at lunch time he sought her out. When he found her she was with a group of girls but he caught her eye and she nodded and a few minutes later detached herself from the group and wandered over to where he was.

As she approached, Graham smiled. "Hi Cindy! Do you still want to meet this afternoon?" he asked, his throat dry with fear and lust.

To his dismay she shook her head. "Sorry, I have to go home. Mum has booked me in at the dentists and she is picking me up at 4 o'clock."

Graham's hopes crashed and his whole body felt like it would burst with frustration. "Oh! When can we meet then?" he asked.

"Have to be tomorrow," Cindy replied.

"OK," Graham agreed, now feeling a desperate anxiety.

"Yes, but not at your place," Cindy replied.

Graham nodded. "I agree. I've been thinking about that. What about the bush behind our Scout Den? There is a nice little clearing there."

Cindy looked doubtful but finally nodded. "Yes, all right. I will meet you there straight after school."

"I'll meet you there then?"

Cindy nodded. "OK, but bring something to lie on," she replied.

Graham smiled and felt his pulses race as desire surged. For the rest of the afternoon lessons he was so aroused he fidgeted continually and was unable to think straight.

As soon as he was dismissed after last period Graham hurried out and made his way to the Scout Den. This was built amid a strip of bush land between the railway and a swampy drain. Along the edge of the drain were patches of thick scrub, clumps of trees and a thicket of tall grass. He walked into the front yard of the Scout Den and felt very conspicuous. There were several houses nearby and he knew he could be seen from them. Knowing he was planning something both immoral and illegal sent his heart rate shooting up his mouth went dry.

Hoping to find a good place Graham went to the side of the building and poked around among the trees and long grass to find the best area. There were numerous tracks made by the Scouts and the local kids and he knew them all. But his memory had failed him and the place he thought best wasn't as good as he had remembered. Through gaps in the long grass he could get glimpses of houses on both sides of the railway and swamp.

"It will have to do," he muttered as he returned to the side of the Scout Den.

Only as he walked out to the street did Graham realize the full implications of what he wanted Cindy to do. It was scary adult stuff and against the law. But it was also enormously exciting and he felt a driving urge to do it. He knew he was frightened.

Will I be game if she still wants to do it? he wondered. *Will I do it?*

Chapter 17

HEATED WORDS

Graham walked home slowly, his emotions and mind in turmoil. Most of all he was gripped by the possibility of him and Cindy doing it. *She asked me if I wanted to,* he thought. But that bothered and frightened him and he kept wondering if he could. All the arguments and ideas he had heard swirled in his head. Deep anxieties like whether he could physically do it or whether he would fail at the crucial moment rose to gnaw at him. There were also the concepts of being a man, of being game, of being good enough. On top of that were all the right and wrong issues and religious theories.

Added to them all was anxiety lest he somehow be found out and get into trouble. Fear and desire warred in him to make him very edgy. He found he was ashamed of himself and did not want to look his sister or mother in the eye and he burned with shame when he lied about where he had been, saying he had been at Roger's. It was all very sobering and he knew he was glimpsing the hard realities of life. Thinking about it made him sad.

To divert his thoughts he settled to working on his model battleship, even though half of his mind now derided the idea of toys and models and little kid stuff that was now behind him. This time he made the ship's boats for his battleship. There were eight of these: two motor launches 5cm long, four lifeboats 4cm long and two smaller boats. They were made from 6mm thick balsa and were first cut out as rectangles. The ends were then cut roughly with a craft knife—a V at the bow and a smaller taper at the stern. He then curved and smoothed the balsa with his tiny rasp and with sandpaper. A black biro was used to mark a waterline on each motor launch and then he coloured the area below the waterline with a black permanent felt pen. He knew that paint would have looked better but was impatient and was satisfied with the result.

For the lifeboats he used the pen to make a scalloped line around the top about 1mm down from the top to represent the canvas cover and then used the pen to make little semi-circular loops all the way around to represent the ropes hung on the sides for survivors to cling to. They looked quite good. The two smallest boats he did not put covers on. Instead he used the pen to mark out seats. *Thwarts are their proper name,* he reminded himself. Next he coloured the spaces between them black. That looked good enough so he then glued the boats to small pieces of balsa on the sides of the superstructure above the secondary armament and on the aft superstructure.

During the evening he forced himself to do some homework. Mostly this was preparation for the debate about the French which was to happen the next day. *I wish I'd never got involved,* he muttered, still wondering how he could take part without damaging his position in Thelma's eyes.

After he went to bed his mind and body stayed in turmoil over what he and Cindy had been doing and he had a lot of trouble dropping off to sleep. Even before he did he had wrestled with his conscience and decided that they should not do it. *It is wrong. If Cindy is a virgin and I take that from her then she might live to bitterly regret it. She might meet a man who wants to marry a virgin and that could spoil everything. I don't want to harm her like that,* he reasoned.

There were also the other fears: of making her pregnant and of all the problems of a baby; of parents finding out and of getting into trouble with the law and ending up in court or in a juvenile detention centre; or even of catching some horrible disease. He had enough knowledge to be aware of sexually transmitted diseases and HIV and AIDS and the images they conjured up made him shudder with revulsion.

On Wednesday morning it was a very confused and anxious boy who made preparations to go to school. But it wasn't as easy as he thought. In the light of day his fears seemed to evaporate as the possible event came closer and his young body surged with hormones. He found he was fearfully aroused, so much so he had to avoid his sister and mother as much as he could.

The anticipation got him so excited he found he was trembling and he squirmed and fidgeted. Nor did packing his school bag help.

He remembered Cindy's comment about bringing something to lie on so he snuck a towel from the cupboard into his bag. But that sort of cold-blooded preparation just seemed to make the moral issue worse. Somehow it made it feel sordid and sneaky, which he knew it was.

There was also the problem of the debate. It was to be held that afternoon and Graham did not feel up to it. In class he could hardly think straight. Over and over in his mind he argued with himself over the rights and wrongs of it. Finally he made a decision. *I really want to do this, but it is wrong. I will wait till I am older (he was going to say married but the urgent desires of his body made him doubt if he could wait that long!). I will tell her no.*

Having made that decision Graham tried to clear his mind for the debate. This was not helped by seeing Thelma and by him knowing he had been very unfaithful to her the day before. Several times during the morning he had to argue with himself as his physical desire began to wrestle with his decision. But in the end he made his mind up. *We must not do it,* he told himself.

So at lunch time he went looking for Cindy to say this to her. But when he found her she was with friends and he had no chance to talk to her alone. Nor did she seem to take any hints to come away on her own. She just smiled and winked, sending his body into overdrive and his emotions into turmoil. *There will be time to talk her out of it this afternoon,* he reasoned. So he retreated to join his friends and to act as though everything was normal.

The afternoon lessons were a torment. His body caused him pain and his conscience bothered him. The conflict of physical desires with moral values resulted in genuine mental anguish for him. He was lucky to get through the lessons without getting into trouble from the teachers for inattention. There was also the class debate about the French in the Pacific.

The debate began as soon as the class was settled. Old Wily called the two teams to the front and they were seated facing the class on either side of the room.

"Now," said Old Wily, "let's make sure everyone is clear on the topic. The issue being debated is: 'That France has no right to be in the South Pacific'. That means that the team who are for the topic are against the French. Is everyone quite clear?"

The class chorused that they were. Graham nervously studied his notes and glanced repeatedly across at Thelma. She appeared cool and calm.

George opened the debate for the 'For' team. He gave a short history of European exploration and colonization in the South Pacific, laying heavy stress on the negative aspects such as introduced diseases, destruction of traditional lifestyles and the use of force to maintain control.

Janet was the leader of the opposing team. She countered with a barrage of facts about all the positive aspects of European Imperialism; and, in particular, the great benefits of Gallic culture which had flowed from it. She spoke extremely well and with real spirit and that made Graham even more nervous.

Then it was his turn. His theme was the French use of force to maintain their rule. He gave a history of the unhappy troubles in New Caledonia. He produced a large sketch map of New Caledonia and talked about the Kanak uprisings, of the poor types of colonists the French had introduced, such as when the islands were used as the dumping ground for French convicts. He laboured the point that the French had flown in thousands of soldiers every time there was a plebiscite on Independence.

"All the soldiers, being French citizens, can of course vote. So the pro-France lobby always win. It has been French government policy to encourage French people to settle in the islands so that now the indigenous people are outnumbered in their own homelands."

"Sounds a lot like Australia." Michael observed dryly.

Graham ignored the dig and went on to point out that the French had thousands of troops based on islands that were just as close to Cairns as Brisbane was. "And they always have a squadron of warships in the area. This includes, from time to time, nuclear powered submarines. These warships often visit Australia, yet for some peculiar reason they attract almost no protest, while the visit of any British or American warship invariably raises a storm of objections from the peace protesters."

It was a sore point with Graham. To him it smacked of some sort of anti-British or anti-American prejudice, rather than anti-nuclear, and the apparent hypocrisy rankled. He knew he should not labour the point so much but it burned him up. He was aware that Janet was giving him a hard look and that Thelma looked unhappy but he kept on until the 5 minute bell rang.

Thelma then took the floor. She spoke very fluently and with real emotion which surprised Graham. She brought up arguments he had not even thought about, and directly refuted several of his claims. But, it seemed to Graham, she was trying to make much out of little and after a while she dried up and began to repeat parts of her argument, then shifted to arguing on general principles that people should be free to live where they choose and to be governed how they choose.

Louise went next. She dealt with the issue of French nuclear weapons testing, and she did it with fire. Graham was astounded. He was not aware that Louise could speak that well, or that she was strongly moved by anything. She launched heavy attacks, some of which were a bit dated. She mentioned contaminated seas and radio-active fish and natives dying painful deaths. She talked about the time when the French did nuclear tests in the atmosphere and the radio-active fallout had even been deposited in North Queensland.

"On us, that is, or on our parents before we were born. So much radio-active fallout came down that it was measured in the milk from the Atherton Tablelands. Pregnant women were advised not to drink milk, because of the fear of genetic mutations. We all know what terrible mutations exposure to radioactivity can cause," she said fiercely.

Stephen butted in: "That explains a few people in this class then." The joke drew a gust of laughter from the class.

"You shut up Stephen Bell!" Louise snapped. "It is no laughing matter. The radiation has caused terrible deformities and birth defects among the Polynesians, although the French deny this. They say it is perfectly safe the way they test their weapons. My question to them is this: If it is so safe, why don't they test their nuclear bombs in France? Or in the Mediterranean Sea?."

This brought a murmur of agreement from the class. Louise certainly had them on side and that cheered Graham up. Only then did it dawn on him that perhaps he would rather Thelma's team won than his own.

Michael spoke last. He had trouble putting up a convincing argument as he clearly believed much of what Louise had said, but he struggled on about economic developments and cultural links and how the South Pacific territories were part of France and that the Polynesians were brown Frenchmen. The performance raised Graham's hopes again that his team would win.

Then it was time to sum up. Janet took the floor. She flabbergasted the audience by agreeing with the 'For' team on almost everything. "I agree completely with Louise about the nuclear weapons," she said. "There should be no nuclear weapons in the world, and certainly none at all in our part of it. The French should stop testing and take their disgusting weapons away."

The class cheered this and Graham found himself applauding. Janet held up her hand and went on: "I also agree with Graham about the French warships and soldiers. We should protest at the visits of their ships; and we shall!" She shouted this, holding a clenched fist aloft.

This was a bit too real for most of the class and most kept an embarrassed silence. Janet went on: "But the point I don't agree with Graham about is the warships and the soldiers. The world would be a better place if there were no warships or soldiers. We should be able to settle our disagreements by peaceful negotiations and discussions. All the millions and billions of dollars spent on arms could be used to make the world a better place. We should protest against all warships, not just nuclear armed or powered ones!"

Graham burned as he listened. He itched to rebut her arguments and thought angrily of all the things he would say. He began making hasty notes. It was George's turn then and he did a very polished summing-up, thanking the opposition for shooting themselves in the foot by supporting his team.

Janet sprang up and shouted: "Never mind this silly debate. I am talking about real issues. We must work for peace. We must make sacrifices and struggle against the forces of war and darkness. We should scrap all warships and disband the armies and navies."

George faltered. Old Wily called on Janet to sit. Somewhat flustered George resumed, pointing out how France denied the natives their right to self-determination. But the debate had been sidetracked.

Janet kept interjecting. "Scrap all the warships! Ship the Foreign Legion back to France and stick them in jail. The world doesn't need navies or armies. It needs love and understanding."

"But warships often provide useful services, like rescue," Graham pointed out.

"That can be done by a civilian Rescue Organization," Thelma said, "Like the Coast Guard."

"But the US Coast Guard has ships which carry guns and anti-submarine weapons," Graham countered.

Thelma shook her head. "Only because it also does police and customs jobs. They don't have to be armed. We have a civilian Emergency Services Organization. We don't need any warships," she retorted.

Graham saw little red spots in her cheeks and her eyes glinted but he was stung, and hurt. "And what happens if we are attacked by someone like Napoleon, or Adolf Hitler? What do we do if Indonesia is taken over by Moslem Fundamentalists, or by a military dictator?"

"The world unites against them with peaceful, non-violent sanctions," Thelma replied hotly.

Graham could not help himself. In his anger he snorted then cried, "Sanctions! What rot! They have never worked."

Old Wily stepped forward. "That is enough. We are getting off the topic. End it now thank you."

The two teams subsided muttering into their seats. Graham bit his lip and mentally kicked himself. *How could I be so stupid?* he thought *To argue with Thelma and make her an enemy!*

Old Wily declared that the 'Fors' had won the debate but it gave Graham no pleasure. He wondered yet again what strategy he could use to win Thelma's affection.

The debaters were sent back to their seats. Old Wily then said, "Now, the debate has reminded me. Who has returned permission forms for the visit to the French destroyer tomorrow?"

Graham had his and handed it in. He was very keen to go now. To his surprise Janet and Thelma also handed back permission forms.

"I didn't think you would be interested," Graham said to Janet.

"We are very interested," Janet replied, her eyes flashing.

"You aren't going to cause trouble by protesting are you?" Graham asked suspiciously.

"We will do what is right," Janet replied enigmatically.

Graham returned to his seat wondering just what she meant by that. Stephen nudged him. "You did well mate. Made those sheilas bite."

"Umm. Thanks," Graham replied. That idea made him more unhappy. That had not been his aim at all. He sat in class and brooded after that, casting occasional wistful glances at Thelma. Knowing that he had been so unfaithful to his love for her the previous day; added to the impending problem of trying to say no to Cindy after school put him into a real state of emotional upheaval. *But I must say no,* he told himself in an attempt to bolster his weakening resolve.

Balanced against the knowledge that he might really get to do it with a girl if he wanted to, his decision seemed a flimsy thing!

***

As soon as classes were over Graham carried out the same plan as the previous day, hurrying to the Scout Den. He half-hoped that there might be people there to save him having to make excuses or to argue but there weren't. He checked the clearing and found it as he had left it, mosquitoes and all.

A few minutes later Cindy arrived on her bike. She was wearing a sports dress which showed off her legs to good effect. The sight got him speculating and aroused and he had to battle against this to stiffen his wavering resolve.

Her bike was wheeled into the long grass. As she dropped the bike Cindy said, "Did you remember a towel?"

"Yes. Er. Cindy I..." Graham stammered, unsure how to tell her.

She did not seem to hear and from a bag she pulled out another. "Good. I brought one too. Where do we go?" she said.

Graham led the way along the short track into the line of trees beside the drain. Once they were in the clearing Cindy looked around and Graham could tell she wasn't impressed. "It's a bit public," she said, indicating the houses they could glimpse through the trees.

They stood and eyed each other apprehensively for a minute or so. "Are you ready?" Cindy asked.

Graham nodded, quite unable to speak from a combination of urgent desire and fear.

Cindy spread her towel on the flattened grass. "Put yours here beside it," she instructed.

That threw Graham off-balance. "Er... do you think this is a good idea?" he managed to croak.

"Apart from the bloody mozzies, yes," Cindy replied, smacking a mosquito on her leg. Then she bent over to adjust the towel and Graham was all but lost when he saw her bare bum.

Battling with surging desire he swallowed to moisten his throat. "I...
I... don't think we should," he managed to stammer.

Cindy straightened up and took the towel from him. Looking him
earnestly in the eye, she said, "Are you scared?"

Graham could only nod. She nodded as well and then smiled. "It will
be all right. We can help each other." She spread his towel beside hers.

"But... but you might..." He was going to say get hurt but she shook
her head and interrupted. "I won't get pregnant if that is what you are
worried about. It is the wrong time of the month. I checked."

Graham had read just enough to understand that and blushed. "But..."

Cindy stood up and shook her head. "Relax! You said you wanted
to and now I want to try it too." With that she reached down to the hem
of her dress and lifted it up. In one sweeping motion she peeled it off to
reveal that she wore no underwear. Graham goggled at her nude form
and felt himself become aroused. He had to struggle even harder for
self-control as physical desire battled with his fears and sense of right
and wrong.

When he said nothing she smiled, and said, "Do you like me?"

Graham could only nod and pant. His heart rate shot right up and he
became fearfully aroused.

Into his mind flashed another old saying of his father's. He had
cautioned him that: *A standing prick has no conscience*. Now Graham
knew what he meant. He felt a driving urge just to do it. It took all of his
willpower to shake his head and mutter, "No!"

Cindy frowned. "Don't you want to?"

Graham licked dry lips and plucked up the courage to repeat
himself. "No."

"But yesterday you said you did," Cindy snapped. "What's wrong?
Don't you like me?"

"I like you very much; and I care for you. I don't want to hurt you,"
Graham managed.

Cindy looked hurt, then irritably slapped at a mosquito that was
biting her left buttock. "Why not then?"

"Because it is wrong. We are too young and I don't want to get you
to do anything you might regret," Graham said.

"Oh piffle! You mean all that religious crap? Or are you just a
coward? Are you scared of getting into trouble?" she demanded. She

stood facing him hands on hips and stark naked so that his eyes were continually drawn to her charms. In the face of such temptation he felt himself weakening but he clung to his argument.

"No," he croaked.

"No what? No, you aren't a coward; or no you won't do it?" she cried angrily.

"Both," he said.

"Then stuff you!" Cindy shouted. Angrily she turned her back and snatched up her dress. She was shaking so much she had trouble pulling it on and Graham could only stand and burn with shame and embarrassment while she dressed. She tugged the dress into shape and then bent to snatch up the towel, casting him a venomous look as she did.

"Cindy! It's not like that," he said.

"Stick it up your jumper!" she yelled. "I thought you were more of a man. Well little boy, go back and play with your silly model ships! I will find a real man to teach me."

Graham was shocked and he burned at the insults. He was also appalled at her comments. "Cindy don't!" he said.

But she ignored him and picked up her bike. A few seconds later she was pedalling out of the front yard. Graham was left feeling both enormously relieved and greatly hurt. *Oh I hope she doesn't!* he thought. Tears came and he sobbed for a while. The mosquitoes finally drove him out of the grass but he was still too upset to want to be seen in public so he waited at the back of the Scout Den.

Then he got an even bigger shock—a police car was turning into the driveway! It drove in and stopped! *Oh my God! The police! Has she told on me?* he wondered.

Two hard-faced constables came around the corner and looked at him. "What are you doing here kid?" one of them demanded.

"This is my Scout Den," Graham answered. Inside he turned to water and his knees felt weak.

"It might be, but I wanted to know what you were doing here? Are you up to mischief?"

Graham's mind raced and his mouth went dry from fear. He knew that the law was very strong against under-age sex. He decided that the best answer might be a version of the truth. "I came here to be out of sight because I am upset," he answered.

The policeman stared hard at his face. "I can see you've been crying. Why? What's wrong?"

"My... my (sniff) girlfriend just... (sniff) b... broke up with (sniff) me!" Graham sobbed. He tried to hold back the tears but couldn't.

"I see. A lady phoned us saying there were two kids here; a boy and a girl. You are a bit young to be having woman trouble aren't you? How old are you?"

"Nearly... th... (sniff) thirteen," Graham answered.

The policeman nodded. "Much too young."

"Th... that...(sniff) that's what I told her," Graham sobbed. *If they know I may as well tell the truth,* he reasoned.

But the two policemen just laughed and the other one said, "Never mind son. Plenty more fish in the sea. Now get going and don't come here except for Scouts."

They turned and walked away and Graham followed them, puzzled and miserable. *Am I in trouble or not?* he wondered.

He wasn't. The policemen got back into their car and drove off leaving him upset and confused. Sadly he made his way home. Seeing the police had been a terrible shock. It had seemed like the wrath of God being instantly visited upon him. Then another thought came to him. *If I had said yes then they would have arrived while we were doing it. Then we would both have been in terrible trouble.*

Picturing that scene brought him out in a cold sweat and made him doubly glad that he had been brave enough to say no. *I did the right thing,* he told himself. But Oh! How he still yearned to try it!

At home Graham made a point of avoiding his mother as he felt sure she would be able to tell there was something wrong. The easiest way for him to do this was to work on his model battleship so, even though he did not feel like making models at all, he sat himself at his desk.

After a while his mood lightened as he became absorbed in the problem of putting the masts and rigging on the model. Here his vast experience with sailing ship models came to his aid. To make the lower masts he used bamboo skewers, cut to suitable lengths. The forward lower mast he made into a tripod. The photos showed this but also into his mind came two dramatic quotations he had read. One of them was from Warren Tute's book *The Admiral* when he had described the reaction of Admiral Graf von Spee when he sighted tripod masts in Port Stanley as the German cruiser squadron he led approached the Falkland Islands in December 1914.

"Some officers on the *Gneisenau* thought they could see the tell tale tripod masts of capital ships... it was not for another half-hour that the appalling truth revealed itself to the Germans and immediate flight began," Graham quoted, imagining the scene and wishing he had been present on one of the British battlecruisers.

The other quote had been in C. S. Forester's novel *Brown on Resolution* when the captain of the fleeing fictional German cruiser *Zeithen* saw the tripod masts of a British Dreadnought battlecruiser on the horizon and knew, "There was death in that insignificant little speck."

Graham sat and pondered what it might have been like. *I think I would have been brave enough,* he thought. But then he remembered Cindy's scathing words and they scorched him. *Am I really a coward? Was it because I have no guts that I wouldn't do it?* he agonized. For quite a few minutes he replayed the scene and tried to remember every word. It so upset him that tears came and he had to blink these back to hide them from Kylie as she went past. Once again he bent over a model as a refuge from anyone noticing how unhappy he was.

Up on the tripod mast Graham glued four cardboard triangles and on top of that a balsa platform. Underneath he glued on a yardarm. On top of the platform he added two balsa blocks to represent the spotting top and range finder. A thin upper mast of balsa coloured black was then glued above the top.

The second mast on the aft superstructure block was merely a thin upright. To this he added only a gaff. He then used thin black thread to add some rigging; from the top of the forward mast to the end of each yardarm and down to the superstructure where it was glued. The loose ends were then trimmed off with a craft knife. These represented the signal halyards and he contemplated making tiny coloured flags out of paper to attach to them. A second thread ran from the main mast head to the end of the gaff and then down to the superstructure. This thread supported the gaff and also gave a halyard to glue the white ensign to.

When that was done Graham sat back and looked at the model with satisfaction. For the first time in hours he smiled. The model really looked like a battleship now! He admired it from several angles then flicked over the pages of the book he was using for ideas. His eyes settled on a large colour picture of the last HMS *Vanguard*. It was one of his favourites and he really enjoyed looking at it for inspiration.

Prominent in the picture was a naval fighter aircraft; a single-engine, propeller driven type. It was racing across the foreground of the picture, just above the waves.

A plane. Big ships used to carry them, he mused, remembering the scene in T*he Battle of the River Plate* when one of the British cruisers had launched a float plane from a catapult. That made Graham re-examine his plans. *Could I fit on a plane?*

He decided that he could, if he placed a catapult athwartships just abaft the second funnel. *But should I?* he wondered. His reading told him that the *Iron Duke* actually did carry planes but from platforms on top of B and X turrets. *They were only Sopwith Camels or Pups,* he thought. After a few minutes he decided that it would be all right to add a catapult for a single-engine, low wing monoplane.

That is how she might have been for World War 2, he reasoned. The next half hour was taken up with constructing a balsa catapult, which he placed on top of Q turret. The catapult consisted of two pieces of balsa glued across the top of the superstructure. On the sides of each piece Graham drew a criss-cross of black lines to represent the latticework frame. This slightly overhung Q turret on each side.

There was then the ordeal of pretending everything was normal during the evening meal, bath time, TV watching and so on. For once Graham did his homework without being prompted and he managed to stay out of trouble. But he was terribly torn as he crept miserably into bed. There he lay awake, tormented by doubts about his courage and by his physical urges. He even began to wonder if he could make it up to Cindy.

Finally, he slipped into a troubled sleep.

Chapter 18

ANOTHER LESSON IN LIFE

Graham stared up at the superstructure of the French destroyer. The pamphlet in his hand said she was FNS *Montcalm*, a C70-class ship of 4170 tonnes full load; 139 metres long, 14 metres broad and with a draught of 5.7 metres. The destroyer was armed with missiles, guns and torpedoes. From where he stood at the bottom of the gangway Graham could clearly see the Crotale Surface to Air Missile launcher on the superstructure abaft the funnel. The 100mm main gun was also just visible, but he had to look to find one of the two 20mm guns. It was hidden away among a jumble of fittings and boxes just behind the bridge. He presumed there was a matching one on the other side. The Surface to Surface and Anti sub missile launchers and torpedo tubes were not obvious to him.

Stephen nudged him. "This thing's got two helicopters on it."

Graham had already noted the flat helicopter deck at the stern with the square box-shaped superstructure forward of it which must be the hangar. "I know," he replied.

Peter waved a pamphlet he had just been handed by a French sailor. "It doesn't go very fast," he commented. "Only 30 knots. That's no faster than ships a hundred years ago."

Graham nodded. "Mr Conkey said something about that the other day; that ship speeds had plateaued a long time ago. He said that in the age of the jet fighter and the guided missiles the speed of the ship wasn't all that important, except to get from one area to another. It's their electronics that matter."

"This thing has got two lots of engines," Stephen said. "Two gas turbines and two diesels."

"That is normal," Graham replied. He felt himself to be very much the resident expert on matters naval and tried to act that way.

Behind him Cindy spoke up. "Two hundred and sixteen men. Now that sounds hopeful!" The girls with her giggled. Graham frowned and was not amused. Nor could he bring himself to face Cindy. Instead he burned with a mixture of frustrated dejection, humiliation, regret and lust. He had only seen her briefly that day as they got on the bus and when their eyes had met she had scowled and looked away. Now he wondered if she was deliberately taunting him. *I still did the right thing though,* he told himself. But it still hurt!

Stephen tapped Graham's arm and pointed along the wharf. "There's your anti-French protest."

Thankful for the distraction from his jangled thoughts Graham looked through the milling throng of students. Near the bow of the ship stood five people holding placards, which read: Stop Nuclear Testing! and Ban nuclear weapons! Two policemen stood nearby. Graham recognized the same people who had been at the previous demonstration and the term he had heard, 'Professional demonstrators', flashed through his mind.

Their leader, he noted, was the same skinny, bearded man but this time he had no megaphone. Beside him stood two girls. One was his girl friend, the big blonde. The other girl with the black hair stood on the leader's other side.

Stephen called to Janet: "Hey Janet, is that your sister?"

Janet nodded: "Yes it is." She stepped out of line and waved. "Hi Danielle! Hi Paula!"

The girls smiled and waved back. The bearded man ignored her.

Peter looked around. "No TV cameras today," he observed. Graham nodded. That just increased his sense of grievance.

After a security check with metal detectors the long line of students began to move. There were two hundred of them and most were in a holiday mood. They started filing up the gangway with much calling out and giggling, a few teachers intermingled to maintain law and order. Graham tore his eyes from Thelma, who was just ahead of him, to study the French sailors.

Matelots is what they are called, he remembered. He found it interesting to see the different uniforms: the blue and white striped jersey and the white tops with a collar scarf similar to those worn by Australian seamen in their dress whites, but with a different cut and different badges. But it was the white sailor cap with its bright red woollen pom pom on top which was the most distinctive item. As always Graham was surprised at how pale-skinned and clean the ship's company were, from living much of their working life inside in air conditioning.

As he walked up the gangway Graham noted the eyes of the French sailors. They were openly appraising the girls, one by one. The girls knew it and mostly played up to it, although a few looked embarrassed or annoyed. Graham felt resentment stir. *Bloody Frogs! Ogling our girls,* he thought. Then he went back to studying the ship, in between ogling the girls himself.

Cindy stopped beside him as they moved slowly along the crowded main deck. She was very excited and was looking at every Frenchmen she passed. Just once she met Graham's eyes and she half-sneered, half-smirked before looking away.

Graham shook his head. *What a bloody flirt! At least Thelma won't behave like that.*

The students were not given any choice about which way to go. The route was marked and sailors stood to usher them past the roped-off and guarded out-of-bounds areas. But it was still very interesting. There seemed to Graham to be lots of places open to visit that had not been possible on the Australian ship. The route took them forward to the focsle, past the 100mm gun in its mounting. Graham had a good look at this and touched the grey steel as he passed. Then, with ship modelling in mind, he studied the arrangement of anchor chains, capstans and hatchways on the focsle itself.

A mooring rope led down to the wharf through a fairlead. Graham looked over to see how far down it was. He noted that the five demonstrators still stood on the wharf with the two policemen. He shrugged. They weren't causing any disturbance. He turned his attention back to the ship, looking up over the main gun to the bridge and radars.

His friends took his interest as natural and stayed with him as the less interested students flowed past. Cindy and her friends vanished, still flirting with every sailor they met. Thelma and Janet also moved slowly and seemed to be looking carefully at everything, which surprised Graham. They even struck up a conversation in halting French with two young French ratings.

Graham was jealous, but only a little. *The girls are actually trying out their French,* he told himself. *And obviously with limited results,* he decided, judging by the good-humoured laughter of the two men.

Peter was the only one in Graham's group who learned French and he acted as their interpreter whenever they had a technical question to ask.

The route led across to the other side. Graham was really enjoying the visit by then. He stood and gripped the rail, inhaling the medley of sea smells: salt water, mud, paint, diesel; and rotting god-knows-what. He looked out over the water of the inlet and then up at the superstructure. For long minutes he swept his vision slowly over the array of masts, rotating radars, aerials and grey steel. They passed the outlet of a forced draft fan and the hot, oily stench engulfed them briefly. Graham loved the way the whole ship throbbed as engines and machines worked. It made it feel alive.

Thelma, Janet and Louise were still just ahead of him with the two young ratings showing them around. Graham and his friends stayed with them. The ratings opened a steel watertight door and led them inside. Graham followed and was surprised and intrigued to find that they were in an accommodation area. Several other groups of students were also there, being shown around by ratings.

Graham felt a bit embarrassed as it was the living space of the crew and there were men sitting and lying around, reading, writing letters and playing cards, many just in shorts and sandals. The ratings seemed to take it in good part and grinned good naturedly and tried to answer the questions in schoolroom French.

The guides then led them along a narrow passage way. Ahead a door slid aside and out stepped a sailor wearing only a towel. He had obviously just had a shower. The two guides said something to him and he grinned and chattered back then stopped and slid the door open as the girls reached it. He pointed in and grinned.

The girls peered in and then shrieked. Graham was close behind and looked in as well. It was a shower. Several naked men stood there washing themselves. At the girl's squeals they turned to look. The man nearest the door turned and grinned as his mates called to him. Graham saw that the sailor had what appeared to be a very long penis. With a flourish he waggled it at the girls and they shrieked again.

Graham was embarrassed and jealous. He did not want Thelma to see such things—yet she looked again as the ratings all laughed and the man waved it at her. Graham noted that most of the girls, while red with embarrassment, were laughing or only pretending to be shocked, their excited eyes and giggling suggesting they weren't offended.

The girls moved on past the door and the grinning matelot in the towel, but more girls, attracted by the shrieks, came along the corridor, wanting to know what was going on. The door was slid open for them as well and those girls shrieked as well. Graham blushed and walked quickly away.

More shrieks and more girls. The boys mostly tried to pretend they weren't interested or, like Graham, were stony faced. Then a teacher's voice; Miss Boyland's, sounded, telling the girls to get back out with the others. There was a mass scampering of giggling girls, which swept Graham and his friends out onto the main deck once more.

There Graham got another shock. Behind some lockers and gear beside the funnel were Cindy and a girlfriend with two young matelots. One of the French sailors was standing very close to Cindy and had his arm around her. He had his hand firmly on her bum. She was staring up into his eyes and smiling in a way Graham knew only too well. He experienced a sharp stab of hurt and jealousy but did not know what to do.

At that moment Miss Boyland arrived and she spoke very sharply to Cindy and her friend, telling them to behave. Cindy gave her a sulky and rebellious look in return and reluctantly moved on. The matelot winked and said something in French to Cindy. Miss Boyland snapped back at him fluently in the same language. Graham could not understand what she said, but he could guess. The young matelot who had been touching Cindy stepped back and looked abashed, but his friend grinned and winked at Miss Boyland and said something which made her snort and blush. She moved on after Cindy and her friend, ushering them on.

Graham's group, still with its two guides, went up a steel ladder to the next deck and along past the boats and the 20mm guns to the bridge. To Graham's chagrin the two young matelots were giving a lot of attention to Thelma and Louise, and they appeared to be returning it. Janet appeared to have frozen them out, but still kept asking questions.

The bridge was interesting. Graham looked carefully over all the controls and stroked the captain's chair, then peered in turn with everyone else into the repeater screen of the navigation radar. He wanted to visit the control centre but that was not allowed. An armed guard blocked access. But seeing the matelot's sub-machine gun and knowing it was almost certainly loaded with real bullets was still a good thrill. The group ended up on the roof of the bridge beside the mast and various aerials and antennae.

Graham leaned over the rail and slowly scanned the length of the ship, noting details and soaking up the atmosphere. As he did he noted the flow of students around the decks below and waved to some. Already students were leaving the ship and a check of his watch told Graham that their visit was more than half over. He looked aft to check what else he wanted to see. As he did he noted Cindy and her friend go down the gangway to the wharf; and just behind them the same two young matelots.

At least Graham thought they were the same two. He could not be sure at that distance. With a catch in his heart he watched as they went across the wharf and into the shops beyond. *They shouldn't be going in there,* he thought. *They are supposed to stay with the group and come back to school.*

A horrible thought crossed Graham's mind, fuelled by that humiliating memory of Joany and the British sailor, but he thrust it aside. *No, Cindy is too young. She is only fifteen. She wouldn't really do anything.*

But then he remembered her comments from the previous afternoon and the thought kept niggling insidiously. The emotional confusion was made worse by the fact that near him was Thelma, and she had even spoken to him from time to time.

The group made its way down another steel ladder and aft past the funnel to the anti-aircraft missile launcher, then down through a hatchway to the hangar deck to look at the helicopters. But by then the worms of jealousy and morality in Graham's brain had robbed him of any interest or pleasure in the warship. *What is Cindy doing? Why had she left the wharf area? Oh, I hope she isn't doing anything silly,* he worried.

The mental anguish increased until he found he just had to know. He excused himself to Peter with a mumble about the toilet and slipped away. Elbowing his way past slower students he made his way to the aft gangway. On the way he passed a torpedo tube, barely noticing it. So concerned was he that he almost ran down the gangway and across to the doorway leading to the shops, only to be pulled up by Old Wily.

"Where are you off to Graham?"

"Toilet sir," Graham lied, and blushed. By then he was quite upset and agitated. Old Wily nodded so Graham strode on. Once through the door he was confronted by several shopping arcades full of touristy type shops. He sped through these with his mind in ferment wondering where Cindy and the others might go and fearing he would not find them. Within a minute he was out at the car park where busses waited to ferry the students back to school. There was no sign of Cindy there, and, because several teachers stood there talking, Graham did not think they had gone that way.

They will have gone out to that park at the back, he decided. He almost ran through the arcades again, dodging around tourists and shoppers, to arrive panting at a side door. Beyond was a small park with flourishing flower gardens to obscure the view and provide privacy.

Now, where will they have gone?

Suspicion about their intentions made Graham swerve to the right and follow a path which led to the back of the ornamental garden where it butted against the rear of some office buildings. He walked quickly along, breathing fast and feeling worried and upset.

And there they were! In a small pergola which gave plenty of privacy. And they were kissing! No, they were more than kissing. Graham's stomach turned over as his mind registered what he saw. The matelot was sitting on the bench with Cindy sitting astride him. They were locked in a passionate embrace and Graham had no doubt that they were 'doing it'. Graham's mind boggled and then jealous misery swirled.

For a moment he stood and gaped in fascinated horror. The matelot saw him and glared. Cindy became aware and looked around, her eyes glassy and apparently out of focus. Then she turned back to the French sailor and kissed him passionately on the lips, her arms around his neck

She has let him do that! Graham thought incredulously. It was all too obvious that she had, that she wasn't struggling to escape, only writhing with enjoyment. Cindy again looked at Graham and this time she recognized him and cried his name in a strangled sort of voice, but she didn't stop. The matelot said something sharply to him in French.

Graham knew he was telling him to clear out, but all he could do was stand and stare, shocked and sick at heart. Then Cindy turned again and gasped: "Go away Graham. Go away, and please don't say anything!"

Feeling stunned, Graham turned and walked away, wondering if he was going to be sick. He felt somehow dirty and unclean; and immensely saddened; and knew with a deeper insight, that he was also a hypocrite. The sailor was doing exactly what he had wanted to do not 24 hours earlier. He was deeply hurt and furiously jealous.

For the next 10 minutes Graham stood on the back porch of the shopping complex, fidgeting and torn up by emotions that were too complex to clearly identify. He was also fearfully aroused. Half his mind wanted to run away, the other half kept him there, unable to leave, as though he had to endure every last detail. The most horrible thought was that perhaps Cindy might be doing it for money, as he had heard some girls did. That notion made him feel even sicker.

Then Cindy's friend appeared. She was with another matelot and looked all hot and flushed. The matelot kissed her and squeezed her buttocks and she clung to him and cried. Graham looked away, aroused, upset, and fiercely jealous.

He saw by his watch that it was time to head back to the busses or they would be missed. *Then there will be trouble as the teachers will be marking rolls and be counting us on,* he thought.

Determined to try to save Cindy, or at least keep her out of trouble, Graham summoned up his courage and walked back along the path. The second matelot stopped kissing Cindy's friend and said something to her. She looked at Graham who blushed, then stammered: "We... It's... It's time to get on the bus. You'd better go."

The girl was very embarrassed but also very hostile. She nodded and called out: "Hey Cindy, you'd better come."

"We are," Cindy called back. As the double meaning struck him Graham felt so nauseous he wanted to vomit. The girl went crimson. The sailor with her said something in French and she struggled to answer it. Then Cindy appeared, adjusting her school uniform, the matelot following and straightening his collar.

Cindy met Graham's eye defiantly. There was an awkward pause as the pair halted facing him. The matelot eyed Graham and asked Cindy a question. Graham did not know what he said but he let her hand go.

"The busses," Graham croaked. "We have to go."

Cindy nodded and explained to the sailor. He shrugged and answered her, then spoke to his friend. The two then said goodbye to the girls and walked off along a path leading to the street. Cindy again met Graham's eye, her whole face guilty defiance.

"Don't you say anything Graham."

"I won't," Graham replied.

"Not to anyone! Not to your mates or to my brother," Cindy added. Then she stunned him by saying, "I'll let you do it with me if you promise not to tell."

For several seconds Graham could only stand and stare, unable to believe what he had heard. Then the ugly notion crossed his mind that she was trying to bribe or blackmail him into silence. Fear was swiftly followed by anger that his word was being doubted.

"I said I won't!" he snapped.

They eyed each other for what seemed like minutes but must have only been seconds. More terrible thoughts squirmed in Graham's mind. Then, to his own shame, he found himself tempted by her offer. But he instantly rejected the idea. That ugly word 'blackmail' screamed in his mind and turned the whole incident into something even more sordid. He just repeated: "I won't tell, don't worry."

Then Graham thought Cindy was going to burst into tears but she steadied her breathing. She was obviously deeply embarrassed. *Or is she just ashamed that she was seen?* he wondered.

Cindy met his eyes and held them for several seconds then shook her head. "Let's go," she said.

The three of them walked back to the shops and through the arcade in silence. Graham was too overwhelmed for speech. He was also intrigued at how Cindy could apparently act quite normally and appear so bored after doing such a thing. He had presumed it would somehow show.

As they came out into the open at the car park Graham realized he should have thought ahead. It was obvious they were late. The busses were all loaded with students and teachers were anxiously checking rolls. Their arrival was noted; and not just by the teachers. With a feeling of sinking despair Graham saw Thelma looking at him through the window of a bus.

Old Wily called them over. "Where have you people been?"

Graham could only blush and stammer. Cindy answered, cool as you please. "Just looking at the shops sir, sorry."

"Get on the bus."

They climbed aboard and Graham found he had to sit next to Cindy because it was the last seat left. As he sat down his eyes met Thelma's along the length of the bus. His stomach turned over and he wondered how he could retrieve the situation. The bus started up. Graham glanced at Cindy but she said nothing and ignored him, staring out of the window. All the way back to school Graham wanted to ask her why, but could not pluck up the courage to speak.

Finally, as the bus pulled up, Cindy turned to him. "Please don't tell on me Graham. I'm sorry. I didn't mean to hurt you."

"I won't say anything," Graham replied, blushing furiously. He hesitated then asked: "But why Cindy? Why?"

Cindy shrugged. "Because all my friends have done it and I wanted to see what it was like. I was curious."

Graham was puzzled as well as hurt. "But... but... why didn't you let me?"

"Because you said no. And because you'll still be here tomorrow and he won't. His ship will sail and I won't ever see him again," Cindy replied.

Graham was flabbergasted. While they filed off the bus he could not say more but his mind raced in a turmoil. Did Cindy mean that she done what she had knowing that the sailor wouldn't bother her again; whereas he would?

He put this to her. She shrugged and nodded. "Yes, that's partly right. Mostly I just wanted to see what it was like. It doesn't mean anything. I am just learning; and he knew what he was doing."

"And I don't?"

"No, not yet."

Cindy turned and walked away. Graham stood, shaking his head sadly as he mulled over this new lesson in life.

Chapter 19

MAX IS UNHAPPY

After school Graham walked home deeply distressed. All he could think about was what he had seen Cindy doing with the French sailor. He kept shaking his head in disbelief. The memory made him feel a mixture of disgust and jealousy. Knowing he was a hypocrite about it did not help. As well he agonized over the religious aspect, of her having sex but not being married. *I wish she hadn't done that. I should have stopped her,* he agonized. The idea came to him that it was his fault. *I was the one trying to lead her astray. If I hadn't been suggesting it maybe she wouldn't have?* he thought. Guilt began to swirl in him like sour bile.

When he got home he lay on his bed and brooded on the affair, pretending to read a book. His mother noted his mood as soon as she came home.

"How was the visit to the French ship?" she asked.

"Oh, OK mum. Interesting," Graham replied, trying to appear normal. He sat up and met her eyes.

"So what is the matter?"

Graham swallowed. He could not possibly tell her; but nor could he lie to her. After a pause he shrugged: "Just something someone did mum."

"Are you in trouble?"

"No mum. It wasn't me. I'm all right. I'd rather not talk about it. In fact I won't tell you."

Mrs Kirk raised her eyebrows. To Graham's relief she answered, "OK. What do you want for tea?"

Graham told her, then went to his desk and sat down. Absentmindedly he toyed with his half completed model battleship, turning the turrets without really seeing them while his mind's eye replayed the sordid scene in the gardens. As he did he accidentally broke one of the balsa gun barrels.

"Damn!" Annoyed with himself he reached for the glue and bent to fix it. After a few minutes his attention shifted to the model. He began working on it as a way of taking his mind off things. In this he was only partly successful but it kept him busy till bed time, by when he had added a host of small details such as breakwaters and capstans on the focsle and signal lights on the bridge.

The model now really looked like a battleship and he was pleased with it, but filled with doubts about whether he wanted to go to Max's to play. *If I do I will have to see Cindy. What will I say to her? How can I go?* But he knew he would go—wanted to go.

His problems were many. His mind kept churning over the moral arguments and he knew that Cindy had done one of those things that were irrevocable, that no amount of wishing or regretting could reverse. *She will have to live with that for the rest of her life,* he thought sadly. That got him thinking about when he had said no and he was simultaneously glad and filled with regrets.

Did I say no because I was strong and moral or did I say no because I am a coward who didn't have the guts to be a man? he agonized.

What added to his anguish was the knowledge that he was still filled with urgent lust and several times he considered Cindy's offer. But that just filled him with self-loathing and he became truly upset. To his annoyance the erotic images and desire came flooding back a few minutes later.

The problem of what to say to Max had to be faced the next morning as Graham met him on the way to school.

"Hi!" Max called cheerfully. "Are we playing Battleships this weekend?"

"If you want to," Graham replied, blushing with guilt. *Does Max know? Does he have any idea?* Graham wondered. From his attitude Graham decided that he did not.

Max nodded and smiled. "Fine. Your place or mine?" he asked.

"What about mine for a change?" Graham asked. *That will keep me away from Cindy,* Graham thought. But that notion just added to his doubts about his courage and convictions.

Max was happy with this. "That'll be OK. After lunch tomorrow then?"

So it was agreed. The boys walked in the front entrance at school and met Stephen just inside. Stephen said, "G'day Max. G'day Graham. Where did you get to yesterday afternoon?"

Graham went red and started to sweat. "When?"

"On that Frog ship. We were all looking at the helicopter and you tcok off like a rocket down the gangway and off the wharf," Stephen replied.

Graham blushed again. He shook his head, unable to think of a lie he was prepared to tell. Stephen grinned and said, "Look at the colour of him! It has to be a girl. Who was she Graham?"

Graham refused to say. He tried to change the subject. Another twist was added when Peter said, "We didn't notice but Thelma did. She was quite worried you would get into trouble."

Thelma! Graham had quite forgotten her. Feeling both guilty and embarrassed, he shook his head again. There was an awkward pause. The arrival of Roger provided an opportunity to change the subject, to Graham's relief.

In class Graham looked at Thelma and wondered. Had she really noticed him leave? *I doubt that she even knows I exist!* he thought bitterly. Then another worrying thought crossed his mind: had Thelma seen who he was following? He decided that was improbable. Cindy had left the wharf before he had started down the gangplank. *But she did see me come back with Cindy to get on the bus,* he remembered. The thought made him feel sick with concern.

Next he was tested by meeting Cindy during morning break. They almost ran into each other at a corner. Both stopped and stared at each other. "H... hello Cindy." Graham stammered, knowing he was blushing furiously.

Cindy grunted and pushed past him. That hurt Graham even mcre. He wanted to call out to her but could not think of what to say—and did not want to risk another even more public snub. He shrugged unhappily as she strode away. *Women! They are certainly a puzzle,* he told himself.

After school Graham went home and worked on his model. Scouts that night were not enjoyable because Max was there. The mere sight of him nagged at Graham's guilty conscience. Peter, Stephen and Roger just shrugged. They knew that he sometimes went into a fit of the dejections, usually over some girl.

***

Saturday morning was taken up with chores. Then Graham did some last minute work on his battleship. This included making the tiny model aircraft. This was a Supermarine Seafire made of balsa. It was only 4cm from nose to tail, with a 5cm wingspan. Rather than trying to paint it he coloured it with felt pens and made tiny red, white and blue roundels of paper which he cut out with scissors and glued on. Then he held the finished product at arms length and decided it looked quite good.

Max arrived just after 1pm. To Graham's mingled relief and disappointment Cindy was not with him. Max carried a large carton in which he had stacked all his models and toys. The boys moved downstairs, agreeing to play on the lawn beside the house. Max unpacked his models and Graham saw that he had made another destroyer. The workmanship was a marked improvement and quite excited Graham's jealousy. He picked it up and inspected it.

"What's her name?" he asked.

"HMAS *Anzac*," Max replied. "Dad helped me get the scale right."

"She is really good Max," Graham replied. He admired the sets of quintuple torpedo tubes. These even rotated on their mounting.

Max then asked: "What surprises have you got this time?"

"You'll see. Let's start," Graham said with a grin.

But before they had begun visitors arrived: Peter and Stephen. They were most interested in the game. Graham asked: "What are you blokes doing?"

"Nothing. Just riding around," Stephen answered. They sat down on the back steps to watch. Peter carefully examined the models. Graham anxiously watched his face while he looked at his. He was very sensitive to criticism of his hobby. The game began and the two friends were called on to help move ships; Peter to help Max and Stephen to help Graham.

Graham had to move his battleship into view almost at once as Max's monster started blasting his cruisers at half the length of the yard. Max's eyes narrowed and he walked over to look at the model. He looked a bit strained.

"What it is?" he asked.

"A battleship of course," Graham replied. "HMS *Iron Duke*."

Max studied the model and made a face. "How big are the guns?"

"They're 12"," Graham said matter-of-fact. Max made another face and counted them.

"They should be only 11"," Max said at last.

"Why? The real *Iron Duke* had 13.5" guns," Graham replied with some defiance.

"What about the armour?"

"24" on the side and 12" on the turrets," Graham replied. He could sense that Max was greatly unhappy but, just as stubbornly, wasn't going to back down.

"That's not fair," Max said.

Stephen cut in with: "All's fair in love and war!"

Max bristled. Graham said, "She is bigger than your battleship. That is why I reckoned she could have bigger guns and thicker armour."

Max went and got his model and placed it beside Graham's. There was no doubt; Graham's was bigger. He said, "I told you mine was longer."

Stephen laughed and made a play on the double meaning: "Don't skite Graham! How do you know yours is longer than Max's? What have you two been up to?"

Images of being naked in the pool with Max flooded Graham's mind and he blushed crimson. He swore silently. Sometimes Stephen could be very crude and irritating.

Peter tried to arbitrate: "I can see why they used to have all those treaties once to limit the number and size of real battleships," he said.

"Are you going to play?" Graham asked anxiously. He did not want to hurt or offend Max.

Max shrugged. "Yeah, OK," he agreed. "But only if you don't have any submarines."

"Yes, all right," Graham agreed. So the game began. Graham won the first battle, largely because of his battleship's bigger guns. Max was not happy. The boys agreed to a second game, with Max to hide his ships before the start, to allow his destroyer a chance to get closer.

At the start of the second game Graham launched his Seafire from the battleship and flew it around the yard searching. As soon as Max saw it he got angry. "No planes! That isn't fair! How can I hide if you have a plane?" he cried.

"But the real ships carried planes," Graham answered. He had discovered Max's destroyer hidden in a garden bed.

Max wouldn't have it. "Our game is before planes and radar."

Graham got annoyed. "No it isn't! We didn't agree on when this battle is."

Peter stepped forward. "Maybe you should agree," he suggested.

Max shook his head. "I'm not playing anymore!" he cried.

"Don't then!" Graham snapped back.

"Calm down you two," Peter said. "You can settle this without having anyone spit their dummy."

"I'm not spitting my dummy!" flared Max.

Peter spread his hands. "I didn't say you were," he answered soothingly. "Look. Stop the game until you can agree on the details. Where are your rules?"

Graham indicated a crumpled sheet of paper with a few dice scores marked on them.

Peter read it and nodded. "We can improve on this. If we use percentage dice instead of ordinary six-sided dice we can have a greater range of results."

"Percentage dice?" Graham asked.

Peter explained: "Two ten-sided dice, one for tens and one for ones. I've got some at home. Do you want me to bring them over next time?"

"If there is a next time," Max sniffed.

Peter nodded and said, "Fair go Max. I'd like to play this game too, if you'll let me."

That was a new idea to both of them. They looked at Stephen but he shook his head. "Not me. I'm too busy now. I will help play if you want but I don't have time to make even more models. I'm tied up with a model aircraft competition with 'Willy Willy' Williams at the moment."

The boys sat down and began serious negotiations. Out of this came the decision that they would set their game back during early World War 2 to eliminate jets, infra-red sights, guided missiles and nuclear weapons.

"What about radar? It had been invented then," Graham pointed out.

"We will just ignore that. So no radar, but we can have aircraft and tanks," Peter said.

"What about subs?" Graham asked.

Peter nodded. "Yeah, and subs."

"No!" Max snapped.

"You can have them too," Peter pointed out.

It took some argument but Max finally agreed. Peter then introduced another technical problem. "What scale are you working to?"

Graham felt foolish. "None in particular," he replied.

"We need to agree on a scale," Peter insisted. "Let's measure these models and see what they are."

This was done and the measurements compared to the dimensions of real ships in the reference books. Peter kept going "Hmmm." while he did calculations. "OK, do we want to work in metric or in Imperial measurements?"

"What are Imperial measurements?" Graham asked.

Stephen sneered. "Boy! Didn't you pay close attention in primary school!" he commented. Graham blushed.

Peter answered: "Feet and inches and all that stuff."

"What does it matter?" Max asked.

"Well most of the reference books are in old Imperial measurements, feet and inches. And anything from America still is," Peter explained.

"Feet and inches then," Graham answered. He had no desire to do mathematical conversions. Max agreed.

Peter did some more calculations. "OK, it looks like the best scale will be about 1:240. That is, 1 inch equals 20 feet. If we use that then planes will be about the size of the one Graham has made and these ships will be fine."

Graham liked that idea. "What about a really big ship? What about the battlecruiser *Hood* or the Japanese battleship *Yamato*?" he asked.

Peter checked a reference book and then did a sum and held his arms apart. "They would be about this long, a bit over a metre."

Graham's imagination was fired by this. He had seen a picture of the famous *Hood* in one of his dad's books. To him she appeared to be the most beautiful ship ever made. He resolved to make a model of her. *And she will have 15" guns!* he thought.

The boys then argued over rules for the next hour till it was time for Max to go home.

"Are we playing tomorrow?" Graham asked as Max stood up.

"All right. But it will have to be at my place," Max replied. Graham had to agree to this. He had no possible excuse he could think of. But he wasn't looking forward to seeing Cindy again. Max took his leave. Stephen went as well, leaving Peter and Graham to continue the discussion.

Peter looked at the flag on Graham's battleship. "What countries will we have?" he asked.

"Well, I wanted to be the British, but so did Max, so we agreed to be the Hiburnians and the Trogs," Graham explained.

"Trogs?"

"Descended from the ancient Trojans, who gave them courage; and the Troglodytes who gave them strength and cunning," Graham answered.

Peter gave a good natured laugh. "I like it. OK, I will think of some country to be. What about other real countries, like Germany or Japan?"

"You can be them if you like."

"Not me," Peter replied.

The friends discussed the game for another hour before Peter had to go home. Graham felt really excited. Now it would be real fun! He flicked through his reference books of ships looking for ideas on what to build next. *I need something to surprise Max again,* he thought. An idea flickered, then seized him. An aircraft carrier! That would get him.

Graham rushed downstairs to the wood box and rummaged through the off-cuts. The best that he could find was a piece 40cm long by 10cm wide by 5cm high. *It will have to do,* he decided, thinking of how little time he had to get this new model finished. He seized a saw and set to work.

To shape the bow he merely cut off two triangular pieces, making no attempt to round the curve. The stern was left square. After a perfunctory effort at smoothing the wood with a rasp and sandpaper Graham carried it up to his work bench. He did not draw any plans and, apart from measuring the block of wood, made no calculations. In his mind an aircraft carrier was just the flight deck and the planes.

To make the flight deck he found a sheet of grey cardboard. It was not long enough which meant that he would have to join two pieces to get the right length. That did not trouble him. He was aware that the flight deck on most aircraft carriers overhung the hull but he did not know by how much. To make sure he added 1cm to the dimensions all round. With ruler and pen he marked out the shape of the deck. Scissors were then used to cut out the two pieces of cardboard which he then glued end to end on top of the block of wood. The front end of the flight deck he rolled down as he could see something like this in the photos of ships.

Already he was pleased with her. *HMS* Glorious, he decided. He knew that the real *Glorious* had looked different but was not going to be bothered with such trifles. He liked the name.

Next came the superstructure. A block of wood 6cm x 3cm wide x 2cm high was glued on the starboard side amidships. On top of this he added a balsa bridge and wheelhouse, then several small balsa lockers and protrusions to represent all the many small platforms and decks the real ships seemed to have. A cardboard funnel, short bamboo mast and balsa signalling lamp completed the superstructure.

By then it was tea time and he had to stop. Alex came in and admired the model and while they ate tea Graham described their game and how Peter was going to play.

"What about me?" Alex asked. "Can I play too?"

"If you like," Graham replied. "You can be the Germans or Italians and attack everyone."

"Pigs bum! They were the enemy," Alex replied. A fierce argument began which was only quelled by their mother.

The evening was spent adding details to the aircraft carrier and making planes for it. A 3" gun in a mounting was placed on the flight deck in front of the bridge and two batteries of three 40mm anti-aircraft guns were glued on either side of the flight deck. Low cardboard walls were placed around these to separate them from the actual working area of the flight deck. The AA guns were just a thin sliver of bamboo for the barrel glued at a 45-degree angle on a small piece of balsa. From a distance they looked quite effective.

The planes were made in the same way as the Seafire on the battleship: a balsa fuselage cut to shape by a razor blade, thin balsa wings and cardboard tail and tail planes. Graham made them all by eye and only rejected a couple which did not look quite right. Paper markings were added. In all he made six Seafires. These were arranged on the flight deck and for the next 10 minutes he was lost in a private game while he refuelled, re-armed and intercepted imaginary enemy planes.

"Torpedo bombers attacking!" he muttered excitedly, dimly aware that those types of planes once existed and were deadly to ships.

He flew off two fighters around the room making aeroplane and machine gun noises. As he did, Alex came in and at once entered the game, picking up a HO scale model of a Spitfire off the shelf and starting to dive at the carrier.

Graham stepped forward shaking his head. "You can't use that," he said. "It is British, and this is a British carrier."

"I thought you were the Trolls," Alex replied, continuing his dive. Graham swept in with the two tiny Seafires.

"Trogs," he corrected, then made stuttering multiple machine gun noises. "Anyway, that plane is the wrong scale."

"It's just a big one," Alex replied. Graham insisted it was not in the game. Then he insisted he had shot it down. "Anyway, I am beating off some torpedo bombers which are attacking."

"What torpedo bombers?" Alex asked, looking around.

"Pretend ones. I haven't made any yet."

Alex laughed and landed the plastic model back on the shelf. "Then I will make some. Give me some balsa."

"Use your own!"

"I haven't got any of that thin stuff left," Alex replied. Knowing that he was only an intermittent model builder Graham grudgingly agreed, aware that he needed an opponent to make the game really exciting. When Alex had gone back to his own room he returned to his desk.

"Torpedo bombers. Yes, I need some strike planes on the carrier. Now, what will I have?" he muttered. He opened the reference books and histories. The most obvious British plane from World War 2 was the Fairy Swordfish; but that was a biplane and looked like it might be very hard to make on such a tiny scale. He also noted that carriers had dive bombers as well.

He decided to make three torpedo planes and three dive bombers. For the torpedo bomber he selected the Fairy Barracuda, hoping that the others would not say it was too modern since it only came into use later in World War 2. The dive bomber was the Blackburn Skua. Both were fairly easy to make. He made no attempt to put on wheels or propellers. The cockpits he marked on the balsa with a black pen. For the three torpedo bombers he made small balsa torpedoes, which had red warheads on the front, coloured with felt pen. When these were glued under the planes the aircraft tipped over on one wing. That did not look very satisfactory so he then added two tiny balsa undercarriage legs.

When the planes were finished Graham stood back and admired the result. He could easily ignore the rough shaped hull of the carrier as it was no longer obvious, being half hidden by the flight deck. In any case the eye was drawn to the flight deck and planes. Content with his handiwork he played quietly for half an hour, launching strikes against the plastic destroyer, which he now considered unworthy to be in his fleet, being a bought toy, not a proper scratch-built model.

But the darkness after bedtime brought guilty and arousing thoughts creeping back. Memories of Cindy caused him a mixture of intense lust and deep revulsion. Knowing he was a hypocrite did not help and guilt of a different kind took its place.

Graham's guilty conscience struck him with full force at church next morning. Graham and Roger were rostered as altar boys and from that vantage point he could scan the whole church. Cindy was there, sitting next to her mother and looking the picture of beautiful innocence— except when their eyes briefly met and hers glinted. Whether it was with tears or regret or hate Graham could not decide but it left him feeling very upset. During the confession he felt wracked with guilt and it came to him that he should do it properly. *I should do a proper confession to Father George,* he thought.

It took him some effort to summon up the courage to mention this to Father George when they were briefly alone in the vestry after the service. Father George looked at him in surprise and raised an eyebrow. "Confession Graham? Is it urgent? Yes, you look upset. All right, what about tomorrow afternoon after school?"

Graham could only nod he was so choked up with emotion. After hastily changing he wiped his face and hurried out to join his family. With an effort he acted normally and even managed to laugh at one of Max's jokes. But inside he felt disgusted and very guilty.

On Sunday, after lunch, he and Alex walked along to Max's, carrying all the models in two cardboard cartons. This was necessary to hide the carrier, and to stop the wind blowing the planes off. Peter was already there, talking to Max in the lounge room. Graham looked around for Cindy, but to his relief, she was not in sight. He did not dare ask where she was. There was no way he was going to indicate that he was interested in her.

"What have you got there?" Max asked as Graham put down the large carton he was carrying. Graham extracted the aircraft carrier.

A horrified expression crossed Max's face. "A carrier! That's not fair!" he cried.

"Why not? We agreed we could have planes, and they had carriers then," Graham answered.

"We don't have any rules to deal with planes," Max answered.

"Let's make some up then," Peter put in. Max did not want to but was prevailed on to accept some rules. These were quite simple: AA guns had a ten percent chance of knocking a plane down if it flew within 3 paces of them (40mm guns) or 5 paces (3" or 4"). The planes were assessed at having a 25% chance of hitting a battleship with a torpedo but had to launch within 2 metres.

"20% chance of a hit on cruisers, 15% on destroyers, 10% on gunboats and 5% on subs and torpedo boats," Peter said.

"We haven't got any torpedo boats," Graham pointed out.

"I have," Max said. He brought out four new models. They were all 15cm long, 1cm high and 2cm wide. Each torpedo boat had two 40mm guns; one forward and one aft, four balsa torpedo tubes; two either side, a small block for the bridge, some lockers and hatch covers and a stubby mast. They looked good as a set and Graham was struck with envy.

"How fast?" he asked.

"40 knots," Max replied. That did not please Graham, but when he disputed it Max produced an old book with this information in it. A photo of a torpedo boat at full speed, throwing up a huge bow wave of white spray, was the clinching argument.

After some discussion the boys moved to the back yard. Peter and Max were the defenders. Their army of HO Scale soldiers was deployed on the back porch. The ships were positioned and the game began. Graham began with air strikes on Max's battleship. He lost all three torpedo bombers but sank the battleship, much to Max's anger and dismay. One fighter plane was also lost. Then Graham launched the three dive bombers at Max's torpedo boats which were racing across the lawn towards his fleet.

Two were shot down and they did not hit any of the torpedo boats. Graham claimed the dice were rigged and became even angrier when he tried to strafe the torpedo boats with his fighters and Max objected.

"Torpedo boats were only made of plywood," Graham pointed out. "Machine guns could punch right through."

"No they couldn't," Peter replied, "Their bullets could."

"Don't be smart Pete. You know what I mean," Graham snapped.

It was decided that the fighters could attack the torpedo boats and Graham made another attack and sank all four, for the loss of four fighters. He then made a strike against Max's destroyer which he sank, but for the loss of his last dive bomber. Max got very upset and Graham thought he was going to burst into tears.

Graham's battleship was then moved forward into range and started hitting Max's cruiser. Max got more upset and angry. He scattered marbles on the lawn. "There is a minefield there. Your battleship is sunk!"

"How did the mines get there? Where is your minelayer?" Graham countered.

"We put them there before the battle," Max replied.

"You still need a minelayer," Graham insisted.

Peter interjected: "We used the destroyer."

Graham could only scowl, but knew that some destroyers had been used for mine laying, although the technicalities of how were not clear to him. He withdrew his battleship with so-called 'damage to her engines which halved her speed'. He then used his other ships to batter Max's surviving ships to burning wrecks. Then he used all his ship's guns to pound the HO Scale defending army to bits before he landed his own

Peter had brought some HO Scale soldiers of his own and battled hard to stop Graham. Max sat and sulked. Graham tried to ignore this. He said, "These HO Scale soldiers are no good. We need things that are the same scale as the ships."

"How could we make soldiers that small?" Peter asked.

Graham did not know. He shrugged and said, "Maybe we could just fight with tanks and things?"

They briefly discussed this but could not agree. The battle went on, ending in a victory for Graham. He felt very pleased with himself.

Max wasn't happy. "It isn't fair," he insisted. "We need some way to keep the two sides equal."

"We could use the method Mr Conkey used in his game," Peter suggested, "Have prices for things and each player have the same amount of money to buy things. Then we could structure our navy the way we wanted."

"But you might buy five battleships while Graham gets fifty submarines," Max objected.

"Or five hundred planes," Graham added.

"So what?" Peter replied. "Once we have it we can't change, and after a while we will know roughly what the other side has."

"How would we get more?" Max asked.

"By an income," Peter said. "Perhaps once a month we could all get the same income in marks or points, so we could buy new things."

"I like that idea," Graham said.

"It sounds fair," Alex agreed.

Reluctantly Max agreed too. "I suppose so; but how will we know what things cost?"

"We will have to do some research I suppose," Peter said. "Then we can agree on a price list."

There was some dispute over the practicality of this but Peter said, "If we can't find what the real prices were we will just agree among ourselves. That will be fair."

Graham agreed; "OK. I like that idea. When do we play again?"

"Next Saturday?" Peter asked.

Graham hesitated. "I am going along to the Navy Cadets next Saturday to find out about joining."

"Naval cadets!" Max cried. "What do they do? Peer at their navels?"

"Very funny!" Graham sneered. He went red and felt his temper rise.

"So when then?" Peter asked.

"Saturday morning after morning tea," Alex suggested.

"We have chores," Graham reminded him.

"They can be done in a couple of hours if put our backs into it," Alex answered. Graham nodded, and so it was agreed.

Chapter 20

LITTLE WARS

A t school on Monday, Graham's mind was in turmoil. Half of it was anguishing over his personal life and guilt over Cindy (and guilt over still having frequent lustful thoughts about her!); and half filled with ideas about the new game of Battleships. These so dominated his thoughts that he paid little attention to teachers, his friends or even Thelma. He spent the day hoping yet fearing to meet Cindy but he only saw her in the distance several times and had no chance to speak to her. During lessons he sat and brooded or sketched plans for the game or made up draft copies of rules they could use to play with. The more he thought about it, the more rules seemed to be required, if only to prevent future disagreements and unpleasantness.

He was also pleased to have several more people tell him they would be coming to his birthday party, now only two weeks away. Somehow he managed to keep out of trouble with the teachers and even did some of the class work. At little lunch and lunch time he stuck with his friends and got them to discuss some of the game rules, although it soon became obvious Stephen wasn't really interested and that Peter preferred not to talk about the game at school.

As the afternoon lessons dragged on Graham became more and more apprehensive about the impending confession. He began to regret having arranged it and wondered how he could get out of it. *I could just not go,* he told himself. But that made him feel bad. *Father George will wonder and I will despise myself as a coward,* he thought.

The memory of what he and Cindy had done and might have done and of what she and the French sailor had actually done churned in him in a mixture of disgust and lust that left him physically sick and trembling.

At one stage he found himself sweating and panting for breath and he felt so ill he thought of putting his hand up to ask the teacher if he could go to the sick room. But he was also aroused and decided to wait. In the end, he stayed in class, turning over and over in his mind what excuse he might say.

After school Graham walked slowly to the rectory. All the way he battled with himself over whether to go ahead with the confession or not. When he got there he hesitated at the gate and felt utterly wretched. Then Cindy's scornful questioning of his courage came to him. He bit his lip and shook his head, then pushed the gate open while muttering, "In you go. Don't be a coward!"

Father George was waiting for him and showed him in to his office. "Would you like a cup of tea Graham?" he asked as he ushered Graham to a chair.

"No thank you Father," Graham muttered. He sat down and burned with shame.

Father George gave him a kindly smile then said, "We can do this the Catholic way with me out of sight if you prefer."

Graham shook his head. Instinctively he knew he needed to see the man's eyes. "This will be fine Father."

"Well, take your time and tell me your problem in your own way, although it's hard to imagine what a young person like you could have done wrong," Father George commented.

At that Graham nearly burst into tears and when he tried to speak he found he was all choked up. But after a few minutes of gentle coaxing he loosened up and started to talk. "I did something with a girl Father, and she did something worse and I think it is my fault. But I won't tell you who she is."

"I would not expect you to and nor will I ask who she is," Father George replied. "But I will pray for her soul and for her forgiveness. Now go on."

For the next 20 minutes Graham haltingly told the priest the outline of what he had done. Father George listened and then said, "Well, it sounds to me very much like you are a perfectly normal young lad who is curious about girls and who has done a little bit of naughty exploring. But there is very little sin in any of that. It is just a normal part of growing up I think, so don't get too upset. As long as you don't do anything more serious that could harm the girl's reputation or cause her physical problems like babies that is. You didn't, did you?"

A tearful Graham shook his head. "No Father. But she did, with someone else and I think it is my fault."

"Why is it your fault? Did you force her? Is she younger and you convinced her it wasn't wrong?"

"No, she is two years older," Graham sobbed.

"So how is it your doing?"

"Be... because... because I asked her to and... (sniff) and sh... she said that (sniff) sh... she would like to t... t... try it."

Father George frowned. "But you just said you didn't do anything."

"No, but I wanted to and we started. Then I stopped and said no because it was wrong. She got very angry with me."

Father George nodded. "Women do when they make such an offer and then get rejected. It makes them feel humiliated and cheap—and I suspect frustrated as well."

Graham nodded. "She said she would find someone else to do it with," he explained.

"So she did this with some other person. How do you know she did? Were you there?"

Graham did not know how to answer for a second but finally nodded. "Y... yes but (sniff) I didn't know sh... sh... she was going to do that. I just came along l... later and saw th... th... them."

Father George shook his head. "And you feel guilty because you think you put the idea in this girl's head?"

"Yes!" sobbed Graham.

"Oh you poor boy! Are you in love with this girl?"

"No Father. I just like her," Graham replied.

"Well, it seems to me that you are not responsible. If she is older and if she did it with someone else then your share of any guilt is quite minor. If you care for her and try to persuade her to behave that is probably the best you can do, but don't torture yourself over things that are not within your control. Now, let me grant you absolution and give you a blessing. Please kneel."

Graham knelt and Father George placed his hand on his head while he prayed. As he did Graham stopped crying and he felt as though a heavy load had been lifted from his shoulders. At the end of the blessing

Father George said, "You are good boy Graham and a brave one to face up to this the way you have. Now go home and try to think of a way to help the girl without getting too involved."

Graham nodded, too wrung out with emotion to speak. Feeling enormously relieved he hurried out and down the stairs. He then walked quickly home, hoping he would not have to lie to hide the fact that he had been to see Father George.

***

At home he was relieved to find that neither Alex nor Kylie had noticed his late arrival so he settled immediately to his desk. The germ of an idea had been niggling at him all afternoon and he wanted to try an experiment. This was to construct a model tank on the same scale as the ships and aircraft. He dug out a reference book which gave him the basic dimensions of a real tank. Then he converted this to their game model scale of 1:240.

The results of his calculations surprised him. A real tank 7 metres long and 3 metres wide would only be 3cm long and 12mm wide. *Oh well, if that is it, then that is it!* He shrugged and pulled a piece of 5mm balsa sheet over and measured out those dimensions. Then he used half a razor to slice the piece off. Next he puzzled over how to make the wheels and caterpillar tracks at such a tiny scale. He decided they could not possibly work and that cardboard and paper were probably the best materials.

Using a paper punch he punched a dozen small circular pieces of cardboard out of a sheet. These he glued to the sides of the tank so that they just protruded below the bottom of the hull. Thin strips of paper with the track pieces drawn on in black ink were then glued around the wheels and the ends glued together on top. To hide the join a piece of cardboard slightly larger than the hull was glued on top of the hull. This gave mudguards. Next the drivers slit and hatch were marked on in black ink at the front and the engine covers and exhausts at the back.

A small piece of wafer thin balsa was glued on top of the hull and then a turret was pinned on, the pin having been cut off short by a pair of shears. The turret was sliced from 3mm balsa sheet and Graham gave it a distinct taper towards the front. A main gun made from a thin piece of balsa 2.5mm long was inserted into a hole in the front of the turret and glued in place. A hatch was then drawn on top of the turret and a tiny piece of fuse wire 4mm long pushed in beside the main gun to represent the co-axial machine gun.

To Graham the finished product looked most realistic. It was somewhat larger than he had planned but still looked about right. The tank did not match any real tank but he liked it. It looked powerful and workmanlike. But he was aware that it had taken a lot of work, over an hour, just to make one tank.

"It isn't a British tank," he muttered. "So it had better be a Trog tank." That raised a problem. What were the Trog markings and what was their national flag? By a mental process which associated 'Trog' with 'Frog' he decided to make the flag similar to the French tricolor but substituting dark green for red. He took out felt pens and drew a green, white and blue tricolor. This looked all right, so he tried drawing roundels to glue on the tank.

He tried both colour combinations: Blue in the centre and green as the outside circle, and vice-versa, but did not like either one. So he made a green dot and put blue dashes either side, roughly similar to the arrangement of US aircraft markings. That looked all right. Next he tried a blue dot and green dashes and thought that looked even better. Using the felt pen he marked this on both sides of the tank.

The new Trog tank was just doing its first tryout around the tabletop when Alex arrived home. He looked at it and made a few disparaging remarks before walking through to his room. Graham heard a humming noise which he recognized as Alex imitating an aircraft engine. Alex re-appeared. In the fingers of each hand he held a tiny aircraft made to their game scale. Both were twin-engine and had wings made of aluminium foil taken from the top of Milo tins.

Before Graham could react Alex had executed two dive bombing passes. "Got ya! Your tank has been blown to bits by bombs," Alex cried.

"No it isn't. You've got to throw a dice," Graham said.

"Poop little brother! If I say it is blown up it is," Alex retorted.

A heated argument ensued over what the odds should be for a dive bomber to knock out a tank, and what chance the tank had of knocking out a plane with its pintle mounted machine gun. Alex bent to study the model tank.

"It hasn't got a machine gun on top," he snorted.

Graham had to concede it did not. "It is too hard to make at that scale; but real tanks have them so we will pretend it has one."

Alex conceded this. He flew off with his two planes while Graham found the percentage dice. Alex then returned and made more attacks. It took him two runs before he got a score that knocked the tank out. Graham failed to hit either plane. Alex chuckled and flew off back to his room.

The air raid was serious food for thought. What had Alex made in the secrecy of his room? A spy mission seemed called for so Graham sauntered along to the door way of Alex's room. Alex was busy cutting balsa at his desk as Graham came in. He at once covered what he was doing and called out: "Get out of here you little bugger. We shoot spies."

Graham tried to pretend that he was just dropping in to discuss something else but Alex was not bluffed. He got up and pushed Graham back out of the room. All Graham got to see were at least four more planes of the same type in process of construction.

"And you keep out of my room you little wart," Alex threatened. "If I find you've been sneaking in I'll pulp you."

Graham retired to the enclosed veranda that he was using as his 'bedroom'. *Hmmm. If he is building planes I must have them too.* For a moment he contemplated using the aircraft off his aircraft carrier, but discarded the idea, *They are British and Alex will dispute whether they would help the Trogs. I had better build a Trog air force.*

Construction started immediately. Using 3mm balsa he cut out five fuselages and drew cockpits and markings on them. Without thinking about it he matched his brother's air force by also making twin engine bombers, although his had thin balsa wings with square tips and the engines mounted below the wings so they looked quite different. Only then did he realize that he needed some fighter planes as Alex mounted another raid, ignoring their mother's call to tea, to roar in and bomb his ships and tanks with six bombers carried on a piece of cardboard.

After tea Graham set to work to make five single engine fighters. He made these in the same way but gave them rounded wing tips for variety. Alex kept coming in to see what he was up to, necessitating frequent hiding under a sheet of cardboard but before bedtime he had them completed. He immediately mounted his own raid on Alex's bedroom: five bombers escorted by five fighters.

The raid resulted in a lively and rowdy battle which Kylie objected to as she was trying to do her homework. The boys ignored this and flew round and round with loud sound effects and much laughter and shouting. Graham went to bed well pleased that he had trounced the Alexians well and truly. The two squadrons of Trog aircraft spent the night lined up on his desk top, guarded by the tank.

These were the first things Graham saw when he woke up in the morning. It gave him another idea. *I need a proper airfield with hangars and anti-aircraft guns and so on.* The planning of this took up most of his day, and got him extra work at lunch time for inattention in class. As soon as school was over he rushed home and set to work.

To his surprise Alex also came home early instead of playing sport with his mates. Both then tried to spy on the other, resulting in a lot of pushing, shoving and wrestling; contests usually won by Alex due to his greater aggressiveness and superior size and strength. Kylie came home with Margaret and both girls watched each bout with some disdain, the veranda being the usual scene of combat. In between annoying each other both boys worked on models.

Graham constructed five cardboard hangars, which he then painted with brown and green camouflage. He also cut up some old mosquito net and painted that for camouflage nets. Plasticine was used to construct blast bays for his aircraft. During this Alex made two raids. The first was by his six bombers on their own, resulting in five of them being shot down by Graham's fighters, for the loss of one fighter and four bombers parked on the airfield (his desk top). During the second raid Alex brought along six brand new single engine fighters, which he claimed were superior in speed and performance to Graham's.

By then it was time for bath and tea. Margaret said goodbye and went home and Graham tried to sneak another look into Alex's room. After tea both boys ignored their mother's instructions to do their homework and settled back at their desks to continue the war.

Graham set to work with razor and balsa to make five 40mm Bofors guns. These were placed around the airfield in plasticine gun pits and helped to down two bombers from Alex's next raid. But by then Alex had twelve of the silver winged fighters and swept Graham's defending aircraft from the sky before the bombers appeared. His new airfield was bombed to smithereens!

In retaliation Graham tried a counter raid on Alex's room. He got in the door with his planes and the fighters began to battle but there was no sign of Alex's bombers on his desk.

"Where are your bombers?" Graham demanded, circling with his own bombers looking for a target.

"In concrete tunnels underground," Alex claimed.

Graham fumed. Why hadn't he thought of that? "Where are the tunnel entrances?" he asked.

"Camouflaged so they blend into the mountainside," Alex replied with a smirk.

The best that Graham could do was pretend to bomb the wall beside the desk and claim that he had caused a landslide which sealed the tunnel entrances. Alex refuted this and used his superior strength in fighters to shoot down every single one of Graham's planes. Graham retired to the veranda feeling as though he had not planned things very well. That rankled as he considered himself to be smarter than Alex.

I need a better strategy, he mused as he lay in bed. More planes would be part of the answer but how to deal with those tunnels? *A commando raid perhaps?* He drifted off to sleep dreaming of how his heroic Marine Commandos would find the tunnel entrances and sneak in, to utterly destroy the enemy fortress.

School on Wednesday was a repeat of the previous days. Graham hardly noticed the lessons or Thelma and had accepted the fact that Cindy was not going to speak to him. To take his mind off her he sat in class and plotted how to defeat Alex. During the breaks he retailed the story of the war to his friends. Max and Peter both listened with interest and he was asked to show then the tank and aircraft.

That afternoon after school Max and Peter went home with him. Alex was not there because he had joined the school's army cadet unit and was at the weekly two hour training parade. The subject of cadets was a hotly contested one with Graham's declared intention to be a navy cadet being well known. With Alex away Graham did not want to waste the opportunity, but had to spend time talking to his friends.

Peter questioned him at length on the rules he and Alex had been playing by. Both wrote them down and made several suggestions to improve them. They also admired the tanks and aircraft and declared the airfield to look beaut. That made Graham feel good but he fretted at not being able to get on with construction. During the day he had decided on his new strategy; he would not raid with commandos, he would invade with an army. *To do that I need more tanks,* he decided.

A mass-production assembly line was set up to make five more tanks. (Why five? He didn't know. It just seemed a Trog sort of number.) In the process he gave up making the tracks so carefully and just drew them and the wheels on the sides with pen. This speeded up the production process remarkably so that by the time Alex came home Graham had six tanks and another five fighter planes.

As soon as Alex had gone to his room the invasion was begun. Graham lined the six tiny tanks up on the floor and placed five fighters with them as top cover. He began moving the tanks a ruler length at a time towards the door of the lounge room. Just as the first tank reached the doorway Alex returned from changing. He took one look and objected.

"The lounge room and dining room are both sea," he declared emphatically. "You have to use ships to get an army to my country."

Graham disputed this but Alex was adamant. Stalemate ensued, not helped by sarcastic and rude comments from Max and Peter. Finally Graham conceded that the two rooms were indeed sea, reckoning that he had the naval power to transport an invasion fleet. Alex's room opened off the side of the dining room so there was no other way to get there.

Graham went and started laying out his model ships but this caused another dispute. Alex pointed at the *Iron Duke* and said, "That is a British ship. The British won't help the Trogs. They will side with the poor little nation being attacked, in this case me."

Peter and Max laughed at the idea of Alex being a poor little defenceless nation and Graham advanced the legalistic claim that Alex had started the war by making an unprovoked air attack on his country. The dispute grew heated but Peter and Max both sided with Alex: The British would not help the Trogs. Graham was secretly pleased that they had conceded that his ships were indeed British but was stumped for naval power.

He pointed to the grey plastic destroyer. "That is a Trog ship, not a British one; and those two subs are also Trogolitian."

In the back of his mind was something he had once read; a quote by some British Admiral many years before about submarines being: "Unfair, underhand, and damned un-English!" so he was happy to swap them over to the Trogs, who were obviously a lesser breed with substantially lower morals.

Alex accepted this division of the fleet but then pointed out that none of those vessels had any cranes or deck space for transporting tanks. Graham had to concede he was right. Both brothers knew too much about loading heavy cargoes onto ships to dispute something so obvious.

So the land invasion was halted at the beach and the air war resumed. Peter helped Graham and Max helped Alex. The result was another defeat for Graham, with all his planes destroyed, his airfield plastered yet again, half his new tanks knocked out and even his destroyer damaged.

After his friends had gone home and Alex left for the bathroom Graham set to work on an idea that had instantly sprung to mind when Alex had pointed out that none of his Trog ships could carry tanks. He would build a Tank Landing Ship, a barge. As his father actually owned a real one, now used to transport cargo around Cape York Peninsula, Graham was intimately familiar with such vessels. It had once been a naval Landing Craft Heavy but was now just a merchant ship named the *Wewak*; bought third hand from a firm in New Guinea that had gone bust. At present it was under contract to an oil company moving stores in the Timor Sea.

A flat piece of 3mm thick balsa 3cm wide and 12cm long was used as the bottom of the landing barge. Sides of 3mm thick balsa 2cm high were glued on either side of the hull base and another piece across the stern. The side pieces were longer at the top so that the top of the bow sloped outwards. A bow ramp of balsa was attached at the bottom by a strip of cloth which acted as a hinge. The ramp was held up by a piece of bent wire which could be moved aside. A block of 1cm balsa was glued in the stern section to represent the armoured wheelhouse. Doors and vision slits were drawn on this with ink.

Graham was pleased with his new LCM and loaded his tanks in. He found he could just fit two tanks side by side but only two one behind the other, a total of four tanks. *I should have measured it better,* he thought with annoyance. He picked the model up and looked at it from various angles.

"It would look better with a few more details," he muttered. A history book showing photos of World War 2 amphibious assaults was referred to. The first thing which struck him was that all the landing craft in the photos had large numbers on the bows. This led to the decision to paint the model grey and to add numbers in white paint. Paint, brushes and thinner were quickly laid out on a sheet of old newspaper and within 10 minutes the model was painted. It was then slid under his bed to dry away from prying enemy eyes.

By then it was bath time and tea time. After tea Graham returned to his desk and began making a second landing barge. This time he measured it so that it was 15cm long and was able to carry six tanks at once. The model was constructed in about half an hour. This time some small details were added. Alex kept nosing in but Graham managed to keep the work hidden. The smell of the paint was his main worry.

By the time the second model was ready to paint the first was dry. This was because he was using a matt paint, rather than a gloss. With a very fine brush Graham added the marking 'L 1' to the bow of the first barge. The number did not look very good so before he painted it on the other bow he marked it out with a pen first. That gave a more satisfactory result.

Having painted the second LCM Graham then considered his invading army. "I will need infantry, tanks, artillery and trucks to move supplies," he told himself. Infantry were a problem. He could not think of any way to make tiny men at such a small size. Finally he just stopped worrying about them. Instead he made a small truck.

This was made from a piece of 1mm thick balsa 1cm wide and 3cm long on top of which he glued two small blocks of balsa to represent the engine and cab. Doors, windows and headlights were marked on by pen. Wheels were a problem. He tried making them from a long cylinder of 3mm balsa coloured black with an oil pen from which he sliced 1mm thick wheels. These were glued underneath but were prone to break off. He also added cardboard sides to the tray and contemplated how to put a canopy on the back.

In the end he left the truck open. Trog markings were put on the sides and it was added to a drawer out of sight. The next experiment was to make a field gun. This was not a success. The gun had so many fiddly bits: wheels, trails and seats and so on that he gave up in disgust.

"I will use the tank's guns," he said to himself. Another truck was constructed, this time with a paper canopy glued on the back. Even without wheels it looked good enough so he left the wheels off. Next he made an ambulance with a red cross drawn on the white paper canopy. Only then did he consider that it might have been a good idea to paint or colour the tanks and trucks some camouflage colour like khaki or green.

"Too late," he said, and shrugged. "I will paint the British and Australian vehicles."

Next he made a small jeep, then a petrol tanker, followed by a radio truck with small wire aerials sticking out of the block of balsa on the back, and a tow truck with a small wire crane on it.

Satisfied that he had his army ready he painted L 2 on the bows of the second LCM and loaded all the vehicles aboard. They looked very warlike he thought happily as he admired them.

At that point Alex launched another air raid which blew up two of the tanks, three of the bombers and damaged the destroyer for the loss of five Alexian bombers and four fighters. Graham attempted a return raid but was met half way by six new Alexian fighters, obviously the night's new work for Alex. These fighter planes were twin tail boom, twin engine types like the American P38 Lightning and Alex insisted they were so fast that Graham's could not catch them. A book settled the resulting argument. Alex held it out and pointed to the statistics:

"Look, your planes look like Hurricanes and they could only do about 350 miles per hour. The Lightning could do over 400."

Graham struggled to refute this. "But didn't the Lightning come into service late in World War 2? And aren't we playing early in World War 2?"

Alex read the fine print in the book: "It says here that the Lightning first flew in 1939."

"Yes, but when did it go into action?" Graham countered.

"It says here that a P-38 shot down a Focke Wolf Condor near Iceland in December 1941," Alex read.

That clinched the argument. Graham had to accept them, but fell back to disputing the air combat odds for the dice throws. It was to no avail. The entire Trog air force was again shot out of the sky. He went to bed nursing secret hopes for his invasion fleet, hidden under his bed.

Chapter 21

THE GAME DEVELOPS

On Friday at school, Graham made an attempt to speak to Cindy. His motives were not very honourable: He was feeling extremely horny and had hopes she might be induced to meet him secretly. She dashed these instantly by just snubbing his greeting and walking off. The rejection hurt and made him feel doubly guilty.

A second blow to his hopes was delivered almost at once when he saw Thelma talking to Jerry Denham. *How can I compete with a Year 12!* he thought miserably. Feeling very depressed Graham went off to class and comforted himself by planning his invasion of Alexia.

The day passed quickly enough that way. Meetings with Max and Peter at little lunch and lunch time confirmed the times for them to play. After school Graham could enjoy his usual end of week comics and chocolate, then work in the ship yards (The armament factory?). An added incentive to get to work at his desk was the knowledge that Alex, having read his comics, was also working at something in his room.

"And it won't be homework!" Graham muttered as he passed the doorway a second time trying to sneak a view.

Frustrated in his spying attempts he returned to his own desk and decided he needed more tanks so he set about making another five for the Trogs. These were made to the same plans as the first five, the original Number 1 being designated the HQ tank.

At that stage the Alexians mounted another air raid which totally defeated the Trogs, although for the loss of seven planes. Graham grumbled and pondered his strategy. *At least Alex hasn't seen the landing barges and the tanks,* he consoled himself. But air defence appeared to be a higher priority so he set to work to make an air defence battery. This comprised another jeep, a second radio truck, an ammunition truck and four trucks with balsa and wire 40mm AA guns mounted on them.

By then it was bath time and tea time after which the two boys headed off to Scouts. As usual Graham enjoyed Scouts but half his mind was on building a larger ship to carry his tanks; and on the need to be able to give his army gunfire support as it landed. His reading had told him that much. He walked home from Scouts with Max, at least as far as his house. The whole time they were walking Graham was worried that Max might say something about Cindy but this fear soon evaporated. It was apparent from Max's conversation that Cindy had made no mention of anything to Max.

Next morning, by 10am, Max and Peter had both arrived at Graham's house. Graham had been busy with his chores so had not had time to build anything extra, but nor had Alex, so he wasn't worried. Max brought with him his ships and a cardboard box. Graham eyed this with intense curiosity but Max would not reveal its contents. The decision was to first play a naval battle out on the lawn. Graham was not allowed to include his Trog ships, which he hotly disputed. So he was deprived of his two submarines. Max, on the other hand, now extracted a model sub from the cardboard box. Graham was not amused. Max and submarines were not something he wanted to be reminded about just then.

Alex joined in with two motor torpedo boats made of balsa. They were 10cm long and only mounted two tubes but they were still a real nuisance when added to Max's four larger torpedo boats. The resulting battle was hard fought and resulted in both fleets losing all but their battleships which were both deemed to be badly damaged. The game lasted over an hour and they all enjoyed it immensely, particularly Skip the dog, who kept running around them and sniffing the ships. Graham accepted the result as a draw and recovered all his ships, repairing a few minor damages as he did.

The boys then went upstairs and Graham insisted they play the invasion of Alexia. This was agreed to and Alex and Max retired to Alex's room while Peter helped Graham. By agreement they waited till Alex and Max launched the Alexian air force in an air raid on Graham's airfield. Graham deployed his new air defence troop to support the airfield AA guns, and sent up all his fighters. While this battle raged Peter flew the five twin-engine bombers around to try to bomb Alex's airfield.

The decoy plan was successful but the overall strategy was not. Peter got the five bombers to their target intact but found nothing to bomb. After cratering the runway, he flew back and encountered the surviving Alexian fighters, which had annihilated Graham's fighters. The result was disaster for the bombers.

Peter was disheartened but Graham was not. He now moved out his landing barges and destroyer and set sail across the lounge room floor. Alex and Max immediately launched air raids with their surviving three bombers and four fighters and managed to sink one LCM and to badly damage the destroyer, but for the loss of the three bombers. Graham's surviving landing barge reached the door to Alex's room and disgorged its load of six tanks.

"Go back and load up the other six tanks Pete," Graham instructed, "Then the anti-aircraft troop."

While Peter did this Graham advanced across the floor with his tanks, only to be fired on by some tanks of Alex's. These were also made of balsa and were about the same size as Graham's but they were not as well made. They had a squarish hull with a square turret in the centre. Their guns were small nails pushed in. A quick count revealed ten of them.

The dice rattled repeatedly and when the smoke cleared Graham had only two tanks left and Alex had five. Graham moved his surviving tanks across the floor seeking cover but was unable to reach any in time. There was another round of firing and all of his tanks were destroyed, while Alex still had three left.

Peter kept the barge moving and, despite two air attacks which he was powerless to beat off managed to load the next six tanks. Graham was sure he now had the game in hand. The LCM was able to cross the lounge room. Alex moved his remaining tanks to open fire as soon as the tanks were unloaded and the land battle resumed.

Three of Graham's tanks were hit on the first move. In return he knocked out two of Alex's. It looked a sure thing but then Alex retaliated with his three fighter planes, claiming they were now armed with rockets and cannon. This led to a sharp dispute which Peter arbitrated. The result was that one of Graham's tanks was considered knocked out. Then the tanks fired at each other and Alex was left with none while Graham had one.

With this sole survivor he began an advance across the floor under continual attack by the three planes. He managed to down two of them but on a third attack his last tank was hit.

"Go back and bring the Anti Aircraft unit Pete," he ordered, determined to push the battle to the limit.

The barge set out on another trip. All the way it was under constant attack from the surviving plane. By then the boys were nearly beside themselves with excitement and both Kylie and Mrs Kirk came to look. Kylie curled her lip and turned her nose up. The dice rattled as the fighter came in with small bombs. A hit! The barge was declared damaged.

"It can still sail. We will repair it," Graham cried.

But his mother shook her head. "No. That is enough," she said. "Come and have lunch you boys."

Reluctantly Graham agreed. They tidied up the battlefield at his mother's insistence then trooped through to the kitchen. As scones and honey were consumed Mrs Kirk said, "Graham, don't forget you are going to the navy cadets in an hour."

Graham had forgotten. He felt a sudden surge of excitement. Navy Cadets! Only one week to go!

***

After lunch, the boys sat around the veranda and talked about their game. Peter returned to the idea of having agreed amounts of money and standard price lists for things. Graham agreed with the idea but could see problems.

"What if you haven't actually made a model of something? How could you play with it?" he asked.

"You couldn't. We can only use the models we have made."

"What about little things, like planes and tanks?" Max asked. "Could we just bring out more to play with when we lose one?"

"If you had that written down somewhere on a budget to show that is what you spent your money on," Peter conceded, "But you couldn't pretend there were more taking part in any particular battle than you had models of."

"In that case you could just bring on a replacement the moment you lost one," objected Alex.

"What's wrong with that? That is what real armies do," Peter said.

Graham supported Peter: "I think it would be all right as long the replacement always came onto the game at the same place, and in the next move."

This was agreed to, but then another problem raised its head. Max said, "I can see all that but how do we know how much things cost?"

"We can find out from books," Peter answered.

"So how much did a battleship cost, say compared to a heavy bomber with four engines?" Alex asked.

Peter shook his head. "I don't know. We will have to do some research," he replied.

Max then raised another point: "What about differences between things, like between a Spitfire and a Messerschmitt ME 109?"

Peter shook his head: "That would make it too complex. What we could do is have a series of standard types. For example a 1939 Mk 1 Spitfire might be equal exactly to the 1939 version of the ME 109, but the 1940 version of both would be better."

"Could we do that with tanks?" Graham asked, dimly aware that there were huge differences between types of tanks.

"I think we could come up with some standard types without too much trouble," Peter answered.

"We need to," Max added, "Or we will be arguing all the time instead of playing."

"Can we do that with ships?" Graham asked. "I mean, how do we determine things like thickness of armour on battleships, or the different prices of battleships with say ten 14" guns as compared to eight 15" or nine 16"?"

"We can do it. It just means more prices on the list," Peter insisted.

Alex shrugged. "So what are the prices to be? Let's start making up this list," he said.

"Where do we start?" Max asked.

"Smallest item," Graham said, "With the jeep or the small gun. They should be the basic cost."

"What about infantry?" Alex asked.

"No infantry. Too hard at our model scale," Peter answered.

This was accepted. Graham put forward the first suggestion: "The jeep should be the basic unit. A truck could cost twice as much."

"We could find out the actual prices," Max objected.

"No," Peter said emphatically. "The system must be simple. If was say that a jeep is 1 point and a truck is 2, an armoured car 3 or 4 and a tank 5 or 6, then we have a simple system."

"Why not use dollars?" Alex asked.

Peter shook his head. "Because we have to compare different countries at different times so a point or mark system is better."

"Not marks," Max said. "That could be confusing with planes or tanks that came in different models, you know, a Matilda Mk I and a Matilda Mk II and so on."

"Yes. Points it is," Peter stated. This was agreed to. They started offering suggestions but Peter stopped them. "There is no point in this. We need facts to work on. I've got some old books at home that I think have some of the info we need in them so I will go home and make some notes. When will we meet again?"

"What about tomorrow after church?" Graham suggested.

This was agreed to. Graham then said, "I'm going to the navy cadets now. Does anyone want to come with me?"

"Navy Cadets!" Max sneered. "Watch out for homos."

Graham scowled. He had heard all the jokes about sailors many times before and was not amused. The others took their leave and he changed, then wheeled out his bike and set off.

About 20 minutes later, he parked his bike against the fence at the Navy Cadet's training depot: TS *Endeavour*. Inside he could see several cadets in uniform sitting apparently tying knots. Four others were working on cleaning a boat. Graham hesitated, overcome with shyness. For nearly 10 minutes he stood there, trying to pluck up the courage to go in.

"Hello Graham," called a voice. It took Graham a moment to recognize Andrew Collins from his own class in his cadet uniform. "What are you doing?" Andrew asked.

Graham liked Andrew. He was the same age, height, build and colouring, even to the blue eyes and fair hair. "I wanted to get an application form to join," he replied.

"Come in. I'll take you to the XO," Andrew offered.

Graham gratefully accepted. Feeling very self-conscious he followed Andrew inside and was led over to where a lieutenant with a beard sat at a desk. Andrew saluted and said, "Excuse me sir. This is Graham Kirk and he would like to join."

"Thank you Recruit Collins. You may go," the officer replied. Graham wanted Andrew to stay but he saluted again, about turned, and marched away to where four other cadets were working a signalling lamp. The lieutenant looked Graham up and down, with obvious approval.

"How old are you lad?"

"Thirteen next week sir," Graham answered. He was sweating with nervousness in case he was not allowed to join for some reason.

"Have you got any serious medical problem; like epilepsy, asthma or heart trouble?"

"No sir."

"What about hearing and eyes?"

"All right I think sir," Graham replied. He knew his left eye was a bit off but hoped it wasn't critical.

"Have you ever been in trouble with the police? Have you been in court?"

"No sir," Graham replied. He was shocked by the question and blushed bright red when he remembered Cindy. His father's advice about under-age girls again raced across his consciousness. It had never occurred to him that he could be excluded from the navy if he had done something wrong.

The officer asked him a few more questions and was evidently pleased when Graham told him who and what his father was, and that his own ambition was to be a naval officer.

"That's good young feller. Now, here is the enrolment form. You must take that home and get you parents to sign it, here," he pointed to the bottom of the form.

Graham was dismayed. "Both parents sir? My dad is away at sea."

"No, one will do, but another adult must witness their signature, in that box there," replied the lieutenant. Next he handed Graham a medical form and a Next-of-Kin form. "You need to see a doctor. Not a proper medical, just a check-up to let us know if there is any medical condition we need to take account of for safety," the officer said. He then went on: "You know Andrew Collins do you?"

"Yes sir. He is in the same year as me at school, and his big sister is my sister's guide leader," Graham replied.

"Carmen? Yes, she is a good hand. OK young Kirk, bring those forms back all filled in and signed next Saturday and we will enrol you. Here is a program of the unit's parades during the year, and an information sheet for your parents to read. Are there any questions?"

"When will I get a uniform sir?" Graham asked anxiously.

"After you have been with us a month and we are sure you are reliable; and you are sure you want to stay," the lieutenant replied.

A whole month! Graham tried to hide his disappointment. "Yes sir, thank you sir."

He made his way outside and sat down in the shade to read the papers through. He was pleased to note that the unit had camps scheduled for the June school holidays and again in September, as well as on a number of weekends.

After checking the paperwork Graham watched through the fence for a while before riding home to place the papers before his mother.

To his irritation she did not immediately sign them but sat and carefully read them first, from time to time going "Hmm" and compressing her lips in a way that signified doubt or disapproval. Again Graham was concerned. It had never occurred to him that his mother might be against him joining the navy cadets. She had never hinted at it. It was certainly food for thought. He was sure that his father approved though. He was often making statements to him and Alex like: "What you young tearaways need is a few years in the bloody army. That would soon straighten out your ideas."

After reading the papers carefully Graham's mother questioned him at length about what he knew about the navy cadets, what they did and who was in it. Graham could not tell her some of the answers and felt quite ashamed. Then she said, "You realize that this might mean you have to leave the Scouts? You might find that being in both takes up too much of your time and that your schoolwork might suffer."

That was another shock. Graham had never considered such a thing. He enjoyed Scouts so much that the idea gave him real pain.

"It will be all right mum," he insisted.

"Hmm. You don't know that. I am sure there will be times when both organizations have things on at the same time and that will cause friction. Then you will have to choose."

"Yes mum." Graham was confident he could solve such a minor problem, in the unlikely event of it occurring. Schoolwork he just mentally brushed aside.

His mother looked thoughtful. "All right, I will think about this," she said, further worrying him. He had expected her to sign the forms instantly. Instead she scooped the papers up and placed them on top of the fridge. "Now, do you want some afternoon tea?"

Graham did. Fruit drink and scones with honey were consumed before he went out to his desk and sat down. After a while his creative juices started to flow and he began making more tanks for the game. Only when he was in the middle of this task did it occur to him that the reason for his defeat in the battle that morning was not lack of tanks. *I had more than Alex,* he pondered, *but I just did not have them all on the battlefield when I needed them.*

The real problem he deduced was lack of sea transport to get them all there faster. *More Tank Landing Ships, that's what I need,* he decided. He studied his two model LCMs and concluded he needed a bigger ship. That sent him to the reference books in his father's bookshelves. Pictures of large Landing Ship, Tanks showed him what he wanted. He also noted the even bigger Landing Ship Docks which carried smaller landing craft in a well deck taking up most of the stern. He resolved to make both, starting with an LST which could carry at least ten tanks at once.

It will have guns on it too, he said, studying the photos showing the real ones cluttered with AA guns, life rafts and other equipment. After some thought he started drawing plans to scale in an old sketch pad. He used the real LSTs dimensions and converted them to the model scale.

The result was the plan of an LST which was 25cm long, 5cm wide and had two decks: the tank deck below and a vehicle deck above. As planned it could carry eighteen tanks in three rows of six, plus about thirty trucks or jeeps. It was to have four AA guns, two forward and two aft.

Graham set to work on it at once. The base of the hull, which was to form the tank deck and engine room, was cut out of 3mm thick balsa sheet. A square stern 2cm high was glued across and then two solid sides, also of 3mm balsa sheet. The sides only extended forward to where the hull began to curve in to form the bows. The vehicle deck was then cut out, again from 3mm balsa.

At that stage Graham paused to consider how the trucks on the vehicle deck were to get on and off and realized there had to be a lift or ramp. He opted for a ramp. To fit this in he had to cut out a section of deck 2cm wide and 5cm long. The vehicle deck was then glued on, thus forming a box which was open at the front and at the ramp. To shape the curve of the bow he cut out sides from some white cardboard sheet. It took a bit of trial and error and one discarded attempt before he got the piece the correct fit. A mirror image copy was then traced and cut out. The actual bow doors were cut off, to be placed on later. Both side pieces were then glued on.

Another thought caused a pause. The bow was to be ship-shaped, but there had to be a flat ramp which lowered from inside. Graham realized he had not measured this carefully. Worse still he realized it would have been better to have put the ramp in before he put on the cardboard sides.

"It would have been easier to paint too," he muttered, annoyed with himself for lack of foresight.

The bow ramp was made from 1mm balsa with cardboard stuck to it and tiny pieces of cloth for hinges. It took him 10 minutes of juggling and swearing and much use of tweezers to position the ramp inside. Experiment showed that it could be raised and lowered and that restored his morale. Already he felt that the unpainted box could be classed as an LST.

Having learnt his lesson Graham cut out thin cardboard sides for the superstructure, drew doors and portholes on it and bent it to fit. A bridge deck was cut from balsa with sponsons for the AA gun tubs. The wheelhouse was then cut from thin cardboard, the windows being carefully cut out with a razor. A cardboard funnel was easy to make, as was a cardboard screen to go around the front of the bridge, and cardboard sides for the gun tubs. Two gun tubs were made from balsa and cardboard for the bow and these were placed up on small blocks of balsa to raise them above the focsle sides. To get to these Graham drew tiny ladders on thin cardboard and cut them out.

When all these pieces had been made he set to work and painted the lot dark grey. This took over an hour and left him with a table which he could not use because it was covered with drying parts. Happy with his progress he lay down to read, the smell of glue and drying paint providing an enjoyable aroma. That night he slept very soundly.

Chapter 22

STONEFISH ?

On Sunday morning, Graham went to church with his mother and sister. He found it an uncomfortable experience because Cindy sat directly behind him with her parents and Max. To add to his torment, the theme of the sermon was on promiscuity and adultery. Every few moments while Father George talked Graham experienced waves of hot and cold. Sweat prickled and guilt coursed through him, made worse by the fact that, in thinking about his sins, he became aroused, making him feel even more guilty.

It was a relief to get outside and to talk to Roger. From the way Roger spoke Graham sensed that he was feeling a bit neglected and jealous. The primary cause of this was the Battleships game. Roger had not been invited to join; and Peter and Max were so much involved that they had no time for model railways. This resentment became even more obvious when Roger asked: "What are you doing before lunch?"

"Peter and Max are coming over to my place to talk about our Battleship game rules," Graham replied. He paused, then added: "You can come too if you like."

"No thanks," Roger replied. There was an awkward pause. Graham thought hard and suggested he come over to Roger's after lunch. Roger said no to this. He was going with his mum to visit an aunty.

Back at home Graham had half an hour to work on his LST before Max arrived. The paint was dry so he was able to glue the superstructure on. That really made it look like a model of an LST. He started work on the details: the AA guns and life rafts and so on but had to stop and hide it all when Max arrived. Peter pedalled up soon after and the three boys called Alex out of his room to join them.

Peter had a folder full of notes he had written on the prices of things. Graham was quite astounded. Most of the prices were in Pounds Sterling and Peter was careful to point out that the value of the money had changed a lot over time due to inflation. Graham vaguely understood this and was content to let Peter handle the intricacies of it all.

The prices of basic items were quite different from what he had expected. The item which first met his eye, and which he then used as a bench mark for everything else, was the cost of the last British battleship, HMS *Vanguard*. It had cost about £9,000,000. The HMS *King George V* of 1940 had cost £8,000,000 and the *Rodney* and *Nelson* of the 1920s had cost £7,000,000.

The next ships on Peter's table of prices were cruisers and these were a real contrast. The HMAS *Canberra*, built in the 1920s, of 10,000 tons and with 8 x 8" guns cost only about £1,000,000 while the Town-class built in the late 1930s, of similar displacement but with 12 x 6" guns cost £2,500,000.

"Why is that do you think?" he asked.

"Better ships all round probably," Peter suggested, "And they had things like radar and all that sort of stuff."

Graham kept reading. He noted that the large Tribal-class destroyers of the 1930s cost about £350 000. That made him do some calculations. *Hmm. For the price of one KGV-class battleship they could have bought twenty-two more destroyers. I wonder which would have been more use?* That led him to consider why they had gone ahead to build the battleships. This puzzle he then voiced aloud. Max suggested that they probably thought the battleships a better investment.

Peter put forward the idea that the weather in the North Atlantic may have had some bearing on the decision. "I read several books which mentioned that sometimes the weather got too bad for the destroyers. If the Germans had a battleship and the British had had none in those circumstances then the Germans stood a much better chance of winning."

"I suppose so," Graham conceded. He tried to imagine the North Atlantic in a storm, comparing it to the usually mild Coral Sea that he was familiar with.

The boys worked happily for an hour compiling a list of points costs for various items. Copies were made as they did so that they all had a list. They were then interrupted by a knock on the door. It was Andrew

Collins and another Navy Cadet: Arthur Blake, a cheerful lad with a freckly face and mop of black curly hair. He was in another Year 8 class.

"Hello. Can we come in and see these ship models you have been talking about?" Andrew asked.

"If you like," Graham replied. He went red with embarrassment and said defensively: "They aren't much to look at really."

"That's OK. Blake is interested in them and so am I," Andrew replied. The two naval cadets were led to the Ship Room and shown the model sailing ships.

Blake was enthralled. "I say! These are great!" he cried. He knelt down to examine them and asked a dozen questions on technical details of modelling. Graham was both gratified and embarrassed.

Andrew asked: "Where are your modern ships you have been playing this Battleships game with?"

"Upstairs. I'll get them," Graham answered. He went even redder because he was ashamed of the poor workmanship of most of them. For that reason he brought down the best destroyer first, then the battleship and aircraft carrier, then the LSMs and tanks. The boys seemed to be impressed and studied them with obvious interest.

Andrew asked: "Where do you play this game, on a map or here?"

"Out on the lawn or on the floor upstairs," Graham answered. "That is one reason why we don't put on too many details. They tend to get broken off out on the grass."

"You should play it in here," Andrew suggested. "That way they wouldn't get damaged as much."

Graham had not considered the idea. His initial reaction was negative: "I would have to pack away all my sailing ships," he replied.

Max looked around the Ship Room. "It is a good idea though," he added. "You already have countries and islands marked here."

Graham had to concede he did have but was still negative about the idea.

Blake then asked: "Do any of these models float?"

Peter laughed. "Only upside down," he answered.

Graham shook his head. "No, they are not designed to. They are all waterline models and are made to push around the floor," he answered.

Blake nodded, but appeared unimpressed. He said, "You should see the model ships our Training Officer, Sub Lt Sheldon, makes. He builds powered models which float. They have electric motors and are radio controlled."

"What sort are they?" Graham asked. He was peeved and jealous.

"One is a model of a patrol boat; and he has just completed a model of an FFG 7-class frigate," Blake replied. He held his hands wide apart. "It is about this long."

"What does he make them of?" Max asked.

"Plastic I think."

"You mean they are plastic kits?" Graham asked, his mouth beginning a sneer to show his contempt for anyone who did not scratch build.

Blake shook his head. "No. He makes all the pieces himself. The hull is some sort of fibreglass casting I think," he replied.

Graham flushed but tried to pretend he was not impressed. "Was he the officer I met yesterday?"

"No, that was Lt Ryan, the XO," Andrew replied. "You will like Sub Lt Sheldon. He is great. He really plans things well. He is an expert at sailing too."

"What are you doing this afternoon?" Blake asked. "Sub Lt Sheldon is going to show us his new model. You could come and watch if you like."

"Where?" Peter asked.

"Down at the Yacht Club," Andrew answered. "That is where we are going now."

"What time?" Peter asked.

"3 o'clock," Andrew answered.

Peter grinned. "That's not very nautical," he jibed. "Don't you mean 'six bells in the afternoon watch'?"

Andrew made a face and obviously did a calculation before answering. "Yes it is. 1500 hours if you prefer."

Peter nodded and said, "I'll come. Is anyone else coming with me?"

"I will," Graham replied. He was genuinely curious. Then he hesitated. "I'll just let mum know," he added.

Quickly he hurried through to the kitchen. "Mum, we are going to the wharf," he said. As a policy he did not ask permission.

Mrs Kirk looked up from her baking and raised her eyebrows. "You aren't going to get into trouble at some warship are you?"

Graham shook his head. "No mum, just to look at radio controlled models. Bye!"

Hats and bicycles were collected and the boys set off for the Esplanade. At the Yacht Club they found a dozen people working on various types of sailing boats. Three navy cadets in dark blue long trousers and long sleeved shirts were busy rigging a Corsair under the supervision of a bearded Petty Officer. Several others, including Carmen Collins, sat in the shade. Sub Lt Sheldon was there with his model. It was in the back of a station wagon and he lifted it out when asked by Andrew if the boys could look at it. The model was painted grey and black and was nearly 2 metres long.

As Sub Lt Sheldon laid the model carefully on the concrete he met Graham's eyes. "Hello. What's your name?"

"Graham Kirk sir," Graham answered. Embarrassed at being singled out he blushed bright red.

Andrew added: "Graham is going to join up sir. He got the application forms last Saturday."

"Oh good." Sub Lt Sheldon smiled and indicated Peter and Max. "What about your friends; are they interested?"

"No thanks sir," Peter replied. "I prefer to keep my feet dry."

"We came to see your model sail sir," Andrew said. "Are we too late?"

"Well, I have just given her a test run but I suppose I can give her another go," Sub Lt Sheldon replied. He went back to his car and collected some equipment. While he did Graham and the others bent to examine the model. Graham was impressed—and jealous. It was good. The hull and superstructure had a very professional finish to them. The lower hull in particular looked shiny and sleek. As always, when confronted by superior workmanship, Graham felt a wave of insecurity and inferiority which made him wonder if he was good at anything. *I don't know why I bother,* he thought. *I could never make a model as good as this.*

Sub Lt Sheldon knelt to insert batteries and to adjust the steering mechanism under the quarter deck. "It is the HMAS *Adelaide*," he explained. "She was an FFG 7-class guided missile frigate. Do you boys know much about ships?"

"A bit sir," Graham answered shyly. He did not want to boast and then be caught out by this officer.

Andrew laughed. "Graham is being very modest sir. His dad owns ships and he and his friends here have lots of models."

"Oh yes? What ships?"

Graham blushed again. "A coaster named the *Malita* sir, and an old Tank Landing Ship named the *Wewak*."

"Oh yes. I've seen them often," Sub Lt Sheldon replied. "What sort of models do you make?"

That made Graham blush again. He described his models in a deprecating way. In spite of that Sub Lt Sheldon said, "They sound very interesting. I'd like to see them if I may?"

"Yes sir," Graham replied. He squirmed inside and broke into a sweat, sure that the officer would sneer and laugh when he saw them.

Sub Lt Sheldon lifted his model and carefully placed it in the water. It bobbed up and down on the small waves which swept into the oblong hythe of the Yacht Club. This was a rectangular area about 50 metres long and 25 metres wide, with timber quays on either side of it and a shelving, sandy beach at the shore end. The seaward side opened out onto Trinity Inlet.

They waited till a sail boat had been launched and had made its way out of the enclosure before Sub Lt Sheldon picked up a radio control unit and clicked it on. He looked anxiously out at the Inlet and made a face. "Bit rough out there. We will keep her inside I think."

He clicked a switch and the gun turret on the model rotated and the gun barrel went up and down. Another switch set the radar scanner rotating. Still another made the missile launcher rotate and elevate. Graham was enthralled. *It is a marvellous model,* he thought enviously. At the press of a button the model started to move forward, pitching in the waves. The tiny propeller was visible whirring around underneath as she drew away.

Sub Lt Sheldon made the model sail across the enclosure on a curving course. When she was near the other side he brought her to a standstill by reversing the thrust of the propeller. Then he made the model turn on the spot before bringing her surging back across at full speed. The model threw up a fine clear bow wave as she came and Graham was even more envious.

They waited while a yacht came in and was beached. Then the model was sent for a circular run, with much stopping and starting. At times waves larger than the average set it rolling wildly but the model obviously had excellent stability as it stayed right side up and kept on going.

"Can we have a go sir?" Blake asked.

"Yes, if you are careful. Keep her inside the enclosure," Sub Lt Sheldon replied. He handed the radio control unit to Blake and pointed to the various buttons. Graham watched with twitching fingers. He badly wanted to have a go too but was scared to ask.

Blake sent the frigate racing across the enclosure then stopped her just in time so that she just bumped the other side. She was reversed, turned and set on a curving course with radar, gun and missiles all rotating.

"Doesn't she look good! She's a beaut model sir," Blake said.

Andrew stepped forward. "My go now," he said.

"In a minute," Blake said, holding the control unit clear of Andrew's reach.

Sub Lt Sheldon said, "Give Andrew a go, then these other boys if they like."

"Yes sir," Blake replied, but he kept holding the control unit. He sent the model racing around in a tight curve which made her lean over, then straightened her out.

Andrew held out his hand. "Give me a go before you flatten the battery Blake," he said.

Blake side-stepped quickly and laughed, then held the control unit away from Andrew. Max made a grab for it and Blake swung it back. "No you don't you... Oops! Ooh bugger!"

The control unit slipped from his fingers and fell into the water. For a moment it floated, then sank, leaving a stream of bubbles behind it. Graham sprang forward and knelt down but he was too late. It eluded his grasping fingers. The water wasn't deep and they could see the unit sitting on the bottom. Graham did not hesitate. He was only wearing old shorts and a shirt. He jumped in and dived the 2 metres to the bottom In a moment the control unit was in his hand and he surfaced. He held it up and Andrew took it and passed it to Sub Lt Sheldon. Peter leaned down and gave Graham a hand up.

As he climbed dripping onto the quay Graham looked around for the model. It was heading out through the entrance of the yacht basin at full speed!

Sub Lt Sheldon tried to get the control unit to work but it was instantly obvious that the water had shorted the electronics. The boys all ran out to the end of the quay to watch. The model frigate kept on going out into the Inlet. The waves were only a light chop of about 10cms or

20cms in height but to the model they were like huge storm waves. It drove hard into them and began to pitch and roll. Waves began to break over its focsle and Graham expected it to simply sink, or to roll over.

Graham watched intently as the model butted through the waves. By then it was at least 100 metres out in the inlet and still going strong. He saw it was turning slowly, helped by the waves which were battering it from the starboard bow.

Blake waved his arms in frustration. "If only we had a boat!"

"Or if one would come along," Peter added. They looked up and down the Inlet. Usually it was busy with small craft of all description but just at that moment nothing was moving on the water anywhere near them.

"It is turning," Max cried. "It is heading back towards the wharf."

They watched intently. Yes, no doubt about it. The model was following a curving course which would bring it back in to the shore somewhere upstream.

"She must have a touch of starboard rudder," Sub Lt Sheldon said.

"Come on!" Andrew called. "We will catch her when she comes inshore again." He set off at a run followed by the other boys. Graham ran close behind Andrew. Their route took them out through the entrance to the Yacht Club and across to the Green Island Ferry Terminal. They raced out onto the wharf there. A glance showed the model still heading inshore and apparently aiming for the Cruise Terminal at the old main city wharves. They ran through into the gardens next to the ferry terminal.

As he ran past the place where Cindy and the French matelot had misbehaved behind a garden bed Graham had a series of searing flashbacks and he shook his head at the pain of them. Max was close behind him and Graham wondered if he knew. The thought spurred him on to run faster. They raced into the tourist complex on the old wharves and through the arcades until they were on the main wharf.

Andrew stopped on the edge of the wharf and looked over. There was no sign of the model but a middle-aged couple who were obviously tourists were staring down.

Andrew approached them. "Excuse me. Did you see a model ship?"

The man, clad in a Hawaiian shirt and chequered shorts, answered with an American accent: "We surely did son. It steamed right in under where we are standing."

"Oh no! What will we do now?" Andrew cried.

Graham leaned over to look. "Climb under the wharf and have a look," he answered. From having been on wharves most of his life he was very familiar with them and knew they had ladders for people like maintenance workers to climb down. He ran along the wharf to the nearest one and looked down. The ladder was old, rusty, brown steel. It led down the side of a barnacle encrusted piling to vanish in the swirling, dark green water 10 metres down.

Without hesitation Graham turned and gripped the ladder. He began climbing down it.

Peter ran to the top of the ladder. "You be careful," he called.

"Don't fall in," Andrew added. "There are sharks in there."

Max laughed and said, "No there aren't! The crocs have eaten them all!"

They all laughed and leaned over to watch as Graham continued his descent. He knew what to expect but still found it frightening and forbidding. Underneath the wharf were rows of thick concrete pilings. From the high tide level down the pilings were covered with slime and marine growths. The outgoing tide was gurgling around the pilings; clearly showing the speed of the current. Graham knew that the water depth alongside was about 15 metres, even at low tide. He also knew that large aquatic creatures were reputed to lurk under the wharves, notably sharks and giant gropers. Bobbing at the end of rope painters tied to the ladder were two flat pontoons and a dinghy.

From near the bottom of the ladder Graham looked down into the murky green water. Several tiny fish flitted across a band of sunlight. The thought of what might be in that water made him shiver and hesitate. Only a month earlier a kid had been sitting on a pontoon just down near the Yacht Club fishing. He had dangled his foot in the water and a giant groper had risen to snap off three of his toes. Graham bit his lip and nerved himself to go lower and to move across onto one of the pontoons. He needed to do this to get out of the sunlight. It was very dark under the wharf and it took a few moments for his eyes to adjust. The shore under the wharf was a mass of slimy black mud which extended up to a concrete retaining wall. The whole place was gloomy and unpleasant. And it stank.

Under the wharf were thick concrete beams running out from the shore. These were on top of the pilings. As well there were pipes of various sizes—for water, fuel and so on. Graham reached up and gripped on of the beams for support and moved further under the wharf, his eyes peering into the shadows. A careful scrutiny revealed what he sought. The model was aground on the mud right at the back of the wharf.

"I can see it," he shouted to Andrew who had followed him down the ladder. "It is back there. I think I can reach it."

Andrew stuck his head in under the wharf and looked. "We need a boat."

"I'll use this dinghy here," Graham said.

"Has it got any oars?" Andrew asked.

Graham looked. He could see none. He shook his head and answered: "No. It will be all right. I will push myself along. Go back up and tell them what I am doing."

"Don't be silly Graham. We will run back to the Yacht Club and get one. Petty Officer Evans is there with a corsair. You just keep and eye on the model."

Andrew climbed back up the ladder. Graham stayed where he was and studied the arrangement of pilings and bracing under the wharf. *How will they get a sailing boat under here? They will have to lower the mast and pole it along.* he thought. It looked difficult. Again he studied the arrangement and decided he could get all the way to the model. *I will use the dinghy. It isn't that far,* he decided.

Graham stepped down into the small dinghy and untied the painter. The dinghy, an aluminium one which had once been painted yellow, was half full of water. Graham ignored this and reached up for the overhead beam. To reach it he found he had to stand almost on tip-toe. He set off, pushing the boat along under the beam and almost at once regretted his decision as the current from the outgoing tide was stronger than he had anticipated and he had trouble keeping his footing. When he reached the next piling he reached across to grasp it, and quickly drew his hand back. The piling was wet and slimy and covered with barnacles. A barnacle had sliced deep into his hand. Blood welled out, to trickle down his arm and drip on his feet and body.

As he pushed across to the next piling his eyes searched the black water for any sign of some marine monster which might suddenly lunge at him. The boat felt very unsteady and he slipped twice; getting more scratches from barnacles in his haste. *Slow down silly,* he told himself. *Or you will slip in.*

He tried to tell himself he wasn't scared but his heart hammered fast and he knew he was. He now regretted having started and knew that common sense said go back but stubbornness made him go on. Carefully he crossed another span. By now he was right in under the wharf and it was quite dark and gloomy.

"One more span to go," he muttered. With an effort he calmed himself. It looked a long way back to the ladder and sunlight. After taking a deep breath he set off on the crossing. He pushed hard and the dingy slid across the 5 metres of water to the next piling. Here Graham had another dilemma. The model had run its nose onto the black mud of the shore about 3 metres upstream from the piling. He could not reach the wharf overhead and there was nothing for him to grip.

I will have to push off and try to reach her, he reasoned. *Anyway, I can always paddle with my hands.* He measured the distance and braced himself, then pushed. The dinghy surged up against the current. Graham moved nimbly forward into the bows and knelt down. The dinghy did not quite reach the model before it slowed to a stop. Graham reached out, realizing at the same moment that the tide had taken a grip on the boat and it was starting to spin and drift downstream. His grasping fingers just brushed the model. In a last effort to reach it he stretched right out, just as the stern of the boat struck the piling. Too late he tried to shift his balance.

Splash!

Graham fell headfirst into the water. Even over that second of time he experienced a rush of pure terror. As he surfaced he was already lashing out into a swimming stroke. Driven by imagined marine horrors he clawed at the boat. It slid away on the current and he was unable to catch it. At that moment his struggling feet encountered slimy, cold ooze—the mud bottom. Urged on by fear he changed direction and swam up onto the mud. The dinghy drifted downstream out of sight.

The mud was pitch black, glutinous, foul smelling. A litter of rubbish and green slime marked the high tide level. The mud was so soft that Graham could only flounder on the lower part, most of his body still in the water. There was no way he could haul himself up the slope. Dismayed he looked fearfully around.

"Stop splashing," he told himself. "That is what attracts the predators." With an effort of will he lay still, eyes questing the dark surface for signs of a swirl that might warn of an attack. He tried to haul himself higher but gave up when he had sunk almost to his waist in the mud and was still only a metre from the water. *A croc can just slide up that and grab me,* he thought, his hair standing on end. For the first time he understood the concept of blood freezing. He stopped squirming and lay still.

Only then did he notice the model ship. It was only 3 metres away and was rocking on the waves as they lapped up onto the mud. The model's bow was embedded in the mud and its propeller was still turning, pushing it firmly ashore.

"Oh well. That is why I am here," Graham told himself. He forced himself to move, slithering and floundering across to the model. It took an effort to stand upright as his legs sank into the ooze right to his crutch and that brought the water up to his waist. Once he was steady he washed his hands, then gently gripped the model and pulled it clear. He turned it round, wondering what he should do with it. After a moments thought he let it go.

They will catch it more easily out in the open water than under here, he reasoned. *The batteries are going flat so it won't go far.*

He pushed the model clear and watched as it headed down the lane between the rows of piles towards the open water. Without any fuss the model sailed out into the sunlight and kept going. Only then did Graham turn his mind to his own predicament. *Now, what is the best way to get out of here?*

The policy of lying motionless on the mud till someone realized he was missing and came to rescue him did not appeal. *The longer I stay here the more likely I am that something with teeth will swim along looking for lunch,* he thought. Besides, his pride was also at stake. He contemplated swimming out to the ladder which he could just see. It looked a very long way and he doubted if he could make himself do it. The thought of his feet dangling down into that murk and of being grabbed by something was almost more than he could bear.

That only left drifting or slithering along the mud for 50 metres to the end of the wharf. Awareness of the rusting iron, broken glass and barnacles he was likely to encounter on this journey made him hesitate, conscious as he was of the blood still seeping from his cuts.

Blood! That will bring the sharks. I'd better get going, he told himself.

Graham started to move but within metres realized it was going to be a horrible ordeal. He slipped and fell, coating himself in mud. *I am splashing so much I may as well swim out and be done with it,* he thought ruefully. With this in mind he paused to get his breath and once again studied the route to the ladder, wondering if the could somehow climb up to the pipes under the wharf. Movement out on the Inlet caught his eye. A sail boat. He recognized it as the Navy Cadet corsair. It was heading away from him out into mid-channel, presumably in pursuit of the model.

I hope they come back for me, he thought.

He lay and watched, his heart beat slowing as he calmed himself. Then a splashing noise attracted his attention and set his heart racing again. He looked fearfully round, then relaxed. It was a boat. The boat had two people in it and was moving towards him underneath the wharf from the far end.

Graham was so sure the boat was coming to get him that he did not cry out. He just lay still, not moving in case he attracted a croc or groper. As the boat came closer he saw that it had two men in it and that it was powered by a small outboard engine which puttered rather than purred.

The boat stopped a few metres away and one of the men gripped an overhead beam. Graham was just about to call out when he heard one of the men say: "Do you reckon the cops will look under here?"

That was so unusual that Graham closed his mouth and lay flat on the mud. He could just see the men and recognized one as the bearded rabble-rouser who had led the two demonstrations against visiting warships: the thin, bearded man in his twenties. The other man looked to be middle-aged, had a paunch, grey hair and was half bald.

The middle-aged man said in reply: "For sure. They will certainly look under here for boats."

"So you don't think we can hide the canoes here then?" the thin one asked.

The middle-aged man looked around, his gaze sweeping over Graham who tensed but did not move. The man said, "No. They will be too obvious. There is nowhere to hide them. You will have to start the canoes from somewhere else. This could be the place to put the stonefish. They won't suspect that."

Graham's mind raced. These were demonstrators planning another demo. *There must be another warship coming to visit,* he reasoned. *But 'Stonefish'—what was that?*

The thin man looked around, his gaze skimming over Graham. "Has the stonefish arrived yet?"

The other man shook his head. "Not yet, but we hope to get it here in time."

The thin man shook his head. "I don't agree with using the Stonefish; particularly not here."

"Well my orders are to use it," the middle-aged man replied. With that he opened the throttle and the dinghy spluttered on past where Graham lay, the noise of its motor drowning out the thin man's reply.

Concerned and puzzled by what he had heard Graham made no attempt to attract the men's attention but instead lay still until the dinghy had passed out of sight upstream under the wharf. *Stonefish?* He shrugged and turned his thoughts to his own predicament. A consideration of the chances and relative effort made him decide to swim.

To keep the splashing to a minimum he slid slowly into the water and struck out with a breast stroke. Fear forced a sort of sob from him as he started but once he was swimming he moved fast. He kept close to the pilings in the hope they might give him some protection. It was just as he had feared. His feet struck down into a colder layer of water at each stroke and his scalp crawled with fear at the thought of them being grabbed by massive jaws. He found he had difficulty breathing and the current was faster and stronger than he had anticipated, forcing him over against the pilings.

The distance was only about 20 metres but seemed a hundred. Once he started Graham found he had no option but to keep on swimming; out into the deeper water. Panic began to build up and he increased his stroke. His gaze riveted on the ladder and he forced himself to swim as fast as he possibly could. Between the current and his mental turmoil the ladder never seemed to get any closer but he made it at last.

With a gasp of relief he grasped the rungs and scrambled up out of the water. Only when he was well clear did he stop. For a minute all he could do was cling to the ladder. Fear washed through him and he shook from head to toe. His breath came in rasping gasps. For a while his eyes went out of focus and dots danced before them. He heard voices and looked up.

A row of heads was leaning over the edge to look down at him. He recognized Peter and Max.

Max pointed and shouted: "It's the monster from the Black Lagoon!" The others all laughed. Graham gave a feeble grin, then shivered. He looked around. The corsair was heading towards them with Sub Lt Sheldon and Andrew on board.

"Did they get the model?" Graham croaked.

"Yes," Peter replied.

"Good." Graham took a deep breath and began climbing slowly up.

Chapter 23

13TH BIRTHDAY

As Graham reached the top of the ladder and climbed onto the wharf he was met by Peter, Max, Blake and Carmen Collins. Carmen at once grabbed his wrist and held it.

"You've cut your hands," she cried.

Graham shrugged. "It's nothing. Just a few scratches."

Carmen shook her head. "Scratches be blowed! This one is a real gash. It probably needs stitching. Come with me and we will wash it properly before it becomes infected."

As they started walking along the wharf Peter asked: "What happened to you?"

"Fell in," Graham answered shortly. He did not want to talk about it.

"What ever will your mother say?" Carmen asked, indicating his mud streaked clothes and skin.

Again Graham shrugged. "Nothing much. She is used to us coming home like this," he said; which was quite true. Mrs Kirk had long ago given up making a fuss over dirty clothes or grubby boys. To divert the subject he asked: "Did they get the model?"

"Yes they did. It's in the corsair," Carmen replied, indicating the sailing boat which was now sailing parallel to them.

Graham realized he must now ask them to try to retrieve the dinghy. He did not want to be considered a thief. He bit his lip in shame then called out, explaining the problem. Sub Lt Sheldon waved and the corsair set off down channel in search.

Back at the Yacht Club Graham had his cuts thoroughly washed, then dabbed with antiseptic and covered with band aids. By then most of the bleeding had stopped. What worried him most was the look Sub Lt

Sheldon gave him, and what he said. The corsair came in a few minutes after they arrived, the missing dinghy in tow.

Sub Lt Sheldon climbed ashore and his model was passed up. He placed it in his car then came over to where Graham was being doctored. "That wasn't very wise young Kirk. Thank you for getting the model but it is not worth risking your life for. We would have retrieved it without you giving the crocodiles some lunch. Don't do anything silly like that again please."

"Yes sir," Graham replied. He felt very small and very silly.

Sub Lt Sheldon then cheered him up by asking: "Are you still coming along to join next Saturday?"

Graham lifted his head. "Yes sir. I turn thirteen on Thursday."

"Having a party?"

"Yes sir," Graham replied. He met Andrew's eye.

Andrew grinned and said, "Carmen and I are going sir, so we will make it a good one."

Peter nodded. "We are going too," he added.

The party then became the topic of conversation, especially the games to be played and who else was going. Blake looked a bit peeved at being left out but Graham did not feel like inviting him at this late stage.

Graham had to explain again what had happened under the wharf and that made him feel foolish and he blushed furiously. And for no reason he could articulate he made no mention of the two men or their stonefish. The others laughed and the corsair set off to return the dinghy to its mooring.

Afterwards Graham, Peter and Max returned to Graham's house. Graham did not want his mother to see him all covered with mud so they placed their bikes just inside the gate and he did a quick reconnaissance. Luckily his mother was down in the vegetable garden at the back of the house.

"Go up and get me some clean clothes," Graham instructed. Max and Peter went upstairs and Graham went into the laundry. He peeled off the muddy clothes and stood at the wash tubs while he very self-consciously tried to scrub the worst of the mud off. When he had scrubbed off as much as he easily could Graham wrapped an old towel around himself and did another quick recce to check no-one might see him from next door then scuttled up the back steps.

At the top he almost collided with Kylie and Margaret. Graham bolted into the bathroom, very aware of Margaret's wide eyes and evident interest.

Kylie was more used to her brothers and just sniffed and said, "Graham! You look an absolute sight. Talk about black and white!"

Inside the bathroom Graham looked down at himself and saw what she meant. His arms, legs and head were plastered with black mud but his body was almost completely white where his clothes had been. He laughed aloud and stepped into the shower.

Later the boys sat around and discussed their game and its rules until it was time for the other boys to go home. In the evening Graham had to explain how he got the cuts and his mother redressed one of them on his left hand. By then it had begun to sting and the antiseptic she used brought tears of pain to his eyes. To help relax he went to his table and continued work on his model LST.

Small details such as the AA guns, Carley floats and deck fittings like bollards and fairleads (made from short lengths of wire bent to shape) were manufactured. These were painted grey as well and then left to dry. While he worked Graham dreamed of the party to come. It had become an integral part of his plan to win Thelma's affection and he fantasized about what might happen.

The following morning his mother made him uncover all the small cuts and scratches. These were then scrubbed and washed with more disinfectant, then re-covered with band aids or bandages. Several had clearly become infected and itched and stung. Graham hated the fuss but recognized its necessity.

He went off to school in a good mood. *Only three days to my birthday and six to the party,* he thought happily. But at school he received a rude shock. Almost the first people he saw were Thelma and Janet—talking to Jerry Denham and Edmonson! Graham stopped and watched from a distance. The four were deep in conversation and he did not have the courage to go over and talk to the girls. Instead he wandered around to where he and his mates usually sat.

Max, Peter and Roger were there. They were joined by Andrew and Blake. In the distance Graham could still see Thelma, Janet, Denham and Edmonson. As he watched they were joined by a Year 10 boy nicknamed Peabrain. His real name was Pendorski or something like it and he was one of those odious kids who was not only a geek but looked it—short hair cut, glasses, always did his homework, and always got top marks.

What on earth can they be discussing? Graham wondered. He could not imagine Janet or Thelma being attracted to Peabrain. Then he remembered. *Denham and Edmonson are demonstrators. Those men yesterday were talking about planning a demo. There must be another ship coming.*

Graham turned to Andrew and asked him if he knew if one was coming in.

Andrew nodded. "The only thing I know about is one of our Landing Craft; an LCH named HMAS *Tarakan*. She is due here sometime next week. The CO said we would be getting a trip on her for a day."

That was interesting news and excited Graham but did not answer his real question. Landing Craft of the RAN were frequent visitors to Cairns and he could not imagine the anti-war, anti-nuclear demonstrators making a fuss about something so small and mundane. Still, it was another thing to look forward to.

In class that day Graham made an effort to work and to behave himself. He smiled at Thelma when he met her eyes and, to his surprise, she smiled back. That sent his spirits soaring. The day went by in a flash after that.

After school Graham went over to Roger's and they talked and planned the model railway. Roger and his father had begun work already. The rough plan was chalked out on the concrete floor and some of the framework had been assembled and was waiting a coat of varnish to weather proof it.

"So that it won't warp in the changes in humidity," Roger explained. Graham was shown the large track plans and was impressed. So far only the main line, main station, and the line up the mountains to the Tablelands had been planned. The return loops and storage sidings under the mountains were only partly planned. Seeing the plans and the work under way Graham became interested once again. He was also reminded that he had a ship to complete. When he went home he glued on the details he had made then added the new LST to his fleet.

Alex had been busy too. Graham peeked into his room as he passed. Alex was not there, but on the table, in various states of completion, were another twenty tanks and a dozen trucks for the Alexian army.

I'd better increase the size of my army too, if my invasion is to succeed, Graham told himself. He returned to his desk and began the secret manufacture of a second regiment of eleven tanks. To differentiate these from the first regiment he added tiny yellow markers to the top of the turrets. They looked very pleasing when completed and all lined up.

School on Tuesday passed without incident. After school both Peter and Max came home with him. As soon as afternoon tea was over Max opened his school bag and took out a large tin which had once contained Christmas Chocolates. Onto the floor at the far end of the veranda he emptied about fifty tanks, plus dozens of trucks and several guns. Graham stared at them with interest and amazement. They were all painted grey, and all had a black cross on them.

"Germans!" Max said. "And they are invading your country of Trogo-whatever."

Germans!

Graham raced to his table and opened the drawer. His first regiment of tanks was deployed, along with the AA guns. "You need ships to invade," he cried, as Max began moving the tanks forward across the floor. There looked to be an awful lot of them to Graham.

Max shook his head. "No I don't. Germany has a land border with the Trogs," he replied. Peter was appealed to, but agreed with Max. A chalk line was drawn on the floor.

Graham dug out his new 2nd Regt as well but was plainly outnumbered. He then began mounting a series of air raids. Max opened another box and took out four small ME 109 fighters. They were made of balsa, with cardboard wings. They were coloured dark green and had yellow noses and black crosses as markings. They looked good and soon proved to be formidable opposition in the air.

The battle raged until all of Max's planes were down, plus half of Graham's. He then turned his air power on the advancing German armour. Excitement mounted as the German Panzer force continued to advance and the two tank forces started firing at each other. By then Max had lost nearly half his tanks to air attack. The dice flew quickly and excitement mounted. Tank after tank was knocked out on both sides. Alex came to watch.

Graham saw that he was loosing. He had only three tanks left and the Germans had a dozen. He launched more air attacks until he had lost the last of his Trog planes. By then he had no tanks or guns left and the Germans had four tanks still advancing. In desperation he started using the guns from his destroyer which was tied up in harbour. Max accepted this but simply hid his tanks behind cover and reached into his bag again.

Out came a model U-boat. Graham protested, but was over-ruled. His harbour had no defences: no booms or nets. Max's sub fired torpedo after torpedo and sank all of Graham's ships. He became desperate. Going to the far end of the veranda he picked up planes from the deck of the British carrier HMS *Glorious*.

"Britain is coming to the Trogs aid," he said. "In answer to the unprovoked aggression by the Germans."

Max said no, but this time Peter and Alex both sided with Graham and said that there were historical precedents for it. So Graham launched a massive air strike with the twelve carrier planes and blew up all of Max's tanks.

It had been a good battle and they all enjoyed it. Graham was a bit peeved that his new regiment of tanks were no longer a secret. *I will have to make another regiment,* he thought. Then he realized he probably needed more than one, if Max already had fifty German tanks and Alex over thirty.

That night he made another eleven Trog tanks, this time with a dark blue regimental badge. He also decided he had better make the British Expeditionary Force, to give him an army to come to the aid of the Trogs. He drew the plans for a Matilda tank then carefully made one. He painted it dark green. Three tucks, one with a canvas canopy, plus an ambulance, were added: *for proper logistical support because they will be a long way from home.* These were also painted dark green.

Inspired by this Graham next made three Spitfires for the RAF. These were also of balsa construction and he took particular care to make them accurately. They were painted green and brown camouflage and tiny plastic cockpits added. Markings of coloured paper were glued on. Graham held up the best of the finished planes and admired it from every direction.

"This is the Biggles squadron," he told himself. "And this one is Biggles' plane."

The Spitfire squadron obviously needed hangars and supporting vehicles so he set to work to make cardboard hangars and two jeeps, three covered trucks, a petrol tanker, a radio truck and an ambulance, all painted dark blue and with tiny RAF roundels on the sides. It was a very pleased boy who took himself to bed after that effort.

Wednesday passed quickly as Graham behaved in class. He devoted his spare thoughts to planning more developments for the game. One problem that had been nagging at him was the problem of the playing area. His veranda and Max's back patio had definite limitations. He experimented with various maps of the veranda to try to divide it up between Britain, the Trogs and the Germans and found it very constricted and crowded. This led his thought back to the idea he had initially rejected, of using the downstairs Ship Room for the new game.

I hardly ever play with the sailing ships or plasticine people any more, he told himself.

So, as soon as he got home, he went down to the Ship Room and studied the situation. His real problem was that he had great nostalgia for his sailing ships and little people but had to concede they were not played with much. He also noted that many of the plasticine people had become very soiled by dust and dirt on the concrete floor. Indeed some had become so dirty that it was hard to tell what the original colour of their clothes had been.

"I can clean these models up," he said, "And I can always take them out and play with them if I want to."

That decided he walked around the room considering where the various countries might go. The coastline and borders of several were already marked out in chalk but they weren't in their correct geographical relationship to each other. He had an odd-shaped Britain, which had a huge harbour in the south coast for the fleet to tie up. Nearby was France, but it only had good harbours on its Atlantic coast. It butted onto various other countries, some fictional, like Lucrania, and others real, such as Spain and Prussia. A huge rock nearly a metre high was placed on a peninsula on the Spanish coast. It represented the Rock of Gibraltar.

But Africa was not south of Spain, rather west of it. Graham shrugged. It would have to do. Beyond that on the other side of a narrow Atlantic was a collection of islands which represented the Caribbean, with North America north of them.

"I suppose we can redraw all this," he muttered. He stood contemplating how the area might be divided equally between four players. As he did his mind wandered back to when he had stood there with Cindy. That got his imagination going and he soon became excited and started to fantasize. For a while he enjoyed the experience, but then shame and guilt crept in and he bit his lip with regret. *I am partly responsible for her bad behaviour,* he thought. *So it is my responsibility to try to save her.*

At that moment Alex arrived home with Max so Graham went upstairs to talk to them. He found that they had gone into Alex's room and when he knocked on the door Alex told him to bugger off in no uncertain terms. He and Max were obviously plotting some mischief so Graham went to his desk and sat considering what he needed next for the game.

More Trog fighter planes, he decided. He only had five and Alex had eighteen. Work was begun to construct another five, to the same design as before. Max came out to see what he was doing but Graham was able to hide his work in his desk drawer in time.

Later Max chatted to him before going home and that left Graham feeling even more guilty and ashamed, and doubly so because he found he was still aroused by thoughts of Cindy.

I am so weak! he told himself

At tea that night his mother posed another problem Graham had not thought about. "This party you are having on Saturday night. Where are you going to play the games?" she asked.

"Upstairs here I suppose mum," he answered.

Mrs Kirk pursed her lips. "What about cleaning out your ship room," she suggested. "It is time it had a good sweep out anyway."

Graham nodded. That fitted in with what he had been considering anyway. "OK mum. I will clean it out," he agreed. "We are thinking of using it for our new game anyway."

"That will be a good idea," she said, "I am getting a bit sick of stepping over model ships all over the house."

Kylie nodded. "I agree," she added, "I don't like all the noise when you boys play your silly war games upstairs."

"They aren't silly!" Graham replied.

"They are!" Kylie retorted. "All war is stupid."

Graham shrugged. It was an old argument. "So are girls."

"Huh! So where would you be without us?" Kylie snapped.

"We'd get by," Graham replied.

Kylie snorted. "You wouldn't even exist. It is women who have the babies," she pointed out sarcastically.

"Good luck to 'em," Graham replied.

Mrs Kirk turned on them. "That will do you two," she said. "Stop arguing and do the washing up."

***

Later, after he had done his homework, Graham settled to finishing the five new Trog fighters. Then he decided he needed another Trog warship. *Something to provide naval gunfire support to the landing barges,* he thought. He decided that another gunboat, similar to the *Tarantula*, was what he needed. He began construction of it, humming happily while he listened to the radio. *Tomorrow is my birthday and I will be thirteen. I will be able to join the navy cadets.*

Then he began to daydream about saving Thelma from smugglers. After a while this turned to heated images of Cindy. Happily fantasizing he dropped off to sleep.

Graham woke early and happy the following morning. While he was rubbing his eyes Kylie came out onto the veranda. She carried a present.

"Good morning Graham. Happy birthday!"

Graham sat up and took the present. "Thanks Sis."

Kylie leaned over and kissed him on the cheek. As she did Alex came out onto the veranda. "Good morning wart. Happy birthday! Get out of bed, you slug," he ordered.

So saying Alex grabbed at the sheets and pulled hard.

"No!" Graham cried, hanging on tightly. "Leave me Alex. Stop it please. I'm trying to open Kylie's present," Graham pleaded.

"No chance," Alex laughed. He snatched the present out of Graham's hand and tossed it to Kylie. Then he used both hands to haul on the bedclothes again and this time pulled Graham right out of bed and onto the floor. At that moment their mother also came onto the veranda.

Mrs Kirk shook her head in disapproval. "Stop that Alex!"

Reluctantly Alex stopped pulling. Their mother just shook her head. She said, "You others go to the kitchen till Graham is ready."

She ushered the others out and followed them. Graham untangled himself and quickly dressed, then he made his way to the kitchen. Alex still thought it a big joke but Kylie just smiled and again offered him the present. Graham thanked her and sat to unwrap it.

"Oh thanks Kylie! This is just what I need," he cried delightedly. It was a box containing a dozen tins of Humbrol model paint, plus four brushes of varying size and a bottle of thinner to clean the brushes with.

Alex then offered his present. It was a bundle of balsa sheets, each a metre long. There were sheets of 1mm thickness, 2mm, 5mm and 1cm. "Thanks Alex. These will be very useful. Now I can beat you in our game."

"Some hope!" Alex snorted.

The present from his mother was something quite different, but something he had always wanted: a face mask, flippers and snorkel. He hugged her and said thanks. She then offered the present from his father. This was a huge book called *British Battleships of World War 2*. It had hundreds of pages and was full of photos and detailed plans and diagrams. Graham could hardly put it down to eat his breakfast. Afterwards he sat at his desk and began reading it. His mother had to shoo him off to school. He slid the massive volume into his school bag and took it with him.

At school he showed the book to Peter and Stephen. Peter was very interested. Roger came along but only glanced casually at the book. He opened his bag and took out a present. "Here Graham. Happy birthday!"

"Thanks Roger," Graham replied. He unwrapped the present to find it was a 1:700 scale plastic kit model of the British aircraft carrier HMS *Victorious*. Graham studied the plans carefully. He did not really want plastic kits, considering them to be beneath his dignity as a real model builder. But he was pleased that Roger had remembered and had given him something appropriate.

Peter smiled. "I'll give you my present at your party on Saturday."

"Me too," Stephen added.

Max and Cindy came along at that moment. To Graham's relief and pleasure Cindy gave him a smile. Max asked: "Who owns this book?"

"Graham's birthday," Peter explained.

Max nodded. "Oh yeah. It's your party on Saturday isn't it?"

"Yes. Are you still coming?" Graham asked.

"You bet. I suppose I'd better buy you a present. What would you like?" Max asked.

Graham shrugged. His eyes met Cindy's. She smiled and said, "I'm still coming too. What would you like me to give you Graham?"

Graham's mind raced. He couldn't decide if she was being nice or whether she was indulging in malicious teasing. There certainly appeared to be the hint of mischief in her smile and in the glint in her eyes. He struggled to frame a suitable smart remark but Stephen beat him to it. "I know what he'd like," he said with a snicker.

Cindy shook her head and replied: "He's too young for that."

Graham blushed bright red. Stephen smirked. Peter looked embarrassed. Max said sharply: "So are you!"

"Mind your own business!" Cindy snapped back.

Graham was now all embarrassed and worried. *Does Max know what Cindy did?* he wondered. Hot memories caused a surge of arousal, guilt and shame.

Cindy added to this when she turned to him and said, "Tell me later what you want Graham. I will try to give it to you."

Scowling at Max and then Stephen she turned and walked away, leaving Graham feeling excited and in turmoil. What had she meant by that? *Am I back in her good books?* he wondered hopefully. That was followed by more guilt and anger at his own weakness.

In class Graham showed his new book to several others and tried to read from it. This led to Old Wily spotting it, with the resulting interrogation as to why he wasn't doing his school work.

"It's my birthday sir," Graham replied.

Old Wily raised an eyebrow. "So? How old are you Graham?"

"Thirteen sir. Now I'm old enough to join the navy cadets."

"Fine. Now put the book away and do some work."

"Yes sir." Graham did as he was told. He looked around and met Thelma's eye. She smiled and his heart leapt. He smiled back. *She must like me! Maybe there is hope.*

After school Graham went straight home. He looked at his presents then settled to read the book on battleships. He was engrossed in this when Kylie arrived home with Margaret. Margaret came over to Graham with her hands behind her back.

"Hello Graham. Happy birthday," she said. Shyly she held out a present. Graham sat up and took it from her with a smile and thanks. "Oh!" she gasped; then leaned forward and put her arms around his neck and gave him a fumbling kiss on the cheek. Before Graham could react she fled into the house.

Graham sighed. *Poor kid!* He did like her, but she was too young—two years too young. Besides, how could she compare with Thelma, or with what Cindy might be going to offer him? His mind raced off into fantasies again and only returned to the study of battleships with difficulty. A cold shower helped.

The evening was spent reading and looking at the presents. When bed time came around Graham was reluctant to put down his new book. It was crammed with fascinating technicalities as well as detailed pictures. Already he had visions of making new battleship models that would be masterpieces of their kind. Between dreams of model ships and fantasies about Cindy he slipped into a pleasant sleep.

***

Friday was a fairly stressful day. Graham's mother reminded him in the morning that she had booked him in at the doctor's for his medical check-up after school. "3:30 at Dr Sword's," she said. Thinking about that got Graham quite anxious. *I hope there is nothing wrong so I can join the navy cadets,* he thought. The worry nagged at him all day. But apart from that most of the day passed in a whirl. All Graham could think of all day was the fact that he was thirteen and that he could join the navy cadets the next day. *If I pass the medical that is,* he thought.

As soon as school was over Graham hurried to the doctor's surgery. His mother met him there and sat with him in the waiting room. Even at his age Graham had enough experience of doctor's waiting rooms to have brought a book. In this case it was on battleships and it kept him happily engrossed until his name was called. He found that all to the good because he was more nervous than he cared to admit.

At length a nurse took him into another room and measured his height, chest expansion and weight, a process he found somewhat embarrassing. She then made some notes and left him.

Over 10 more minutes dragged by before the doctor appeared. He gave Graham a friendly smile and seated himself at his desk. Dr Sword had been the family doctor for years and was a grey-headed old gentleman. Graham had often been treated by him for various cuts and fevers but this was different. He hoped that the worst of the embarrassment was over but remembered stories from other boys and that kept him anxious. The other boys were right: there was more shame to come.

The doctor took his pulse, listened to his heart beat with a stethoscope, measured his blood pressure and had him stand up. Then he had Graham bend and kneel and jump to check that his limbs and joints were all working normally. That got Graham all hot and flustered again. Prancing up and down in his underpants in front of a middle-aged man he found very stressful. He found he was perspiring and felt uncomfortable and vulnerable.

But there was worse to come. The doctor asked him to turn around, pull his pants down and then bend over. While the doctor examined him from behind Graham could only burn with humiliation. Then he had to face the doctor and the man reached forward and gently gripped his testicles and felt them, then ordered him to cough.

"To check for hernias," he explained.

Graham had no idea what a hernia was so could only blush with embarrassment and obey. He found it a real relief to be told to pull his pants up.

The doctor then picked up a book and flicked through it. The pages were covered with patterns of coloured dots and he instructed Graham to tell him what he saw. Mostly Graham saw numbers and said so. The doctor nodded and said, "Colour vision is normal." The doctor then put the book down and looked closely into his eyes with a magnifying gadget. He then pointed to an eye chart on the wall. "Can you read the bottom line of that?" he asked.

Graham looked and read the letters. The doctor nodded and then said, "Cover your left eye. Now read the line above that."

Graham did so with no difficulty. The doctor made a note and then said, "Now, cover your right eye and read the next line up."

Graham covered his right eye and looked at the chart. To his dismay he found most of the letters on it fuzzy. Biting his lip with anxiety he read the line. Only after he had finished and could use both eyes did Graham see that he had got a couple wrong.

The doctor made a note and frowned. "That wasn't too good. You might need to have your eyes checked by an optometrist."

"Are they good enough?" Graham asked anxiously.

"For the navy cadets, yes. But I recommend that you have them checked by an eye specialist."

Graham bit his lip and felt his stomach lurch. It was something he did not want to think about. After the doctor was finished and Graham was dressed the doctor called Graham's mother in. "He's in excellent shape mostly, just a bit of a problem with his left eye. I recommend that you get him checked by a specialist."

Hearing that again sent a chill of dread through Graham. His mother nodded and they booked an appointment. Because the eye specialist was in such demand this was not for another six weeks. Graham was then handed his ANC Medical Form with the doctor's stamp and signature.

As they walked out to the car Graham's mother put her hand on his shoulder. "It will be all right Graham," she said.

Graham could only nod. *I hope so,* he thought.

At home there were the usual comics and chocolates before Graham lay down to read his book on battleships. Feeling happier now that the ordeal of the doctor was over he relaxed. In the evening he went to Scouts. That was good fun, except that it made Graham remember what his mother had said about probably having to choose between them and the navy cadets. In Graham's own mind this was no choice at all; and he was confident he would somehow manage both.

Chapter 24

NAVY CADETS

On Saturday morning Graham was awake early. As soon as he woke up he tingled with excitement. Today was the great day. First he was going to join the navy cadets, then he had his party. Vivid pictures of what the party was going to be like crowded his brain, to be pushed aside by nagging worries over whether people would come, or, more specifically, whether Glenys would come.

And Cindy, he thought. That was a whole new level of concern. He hoped she wouldn't, just to save any embarrassment. Yet, perversely he itched to see her and was then ashamed by the series of lustful and arousing thoughts which followed.

Straight after breakfast he went down to the Ship Room. As usual when at home he wore only a pair of old shorts. After a few moments thought he began picking up the model sailing ships and moving them onto an old table in the corner or onto the shelves in the small storeroom. This was a slow process as he looked carefully at each one, noting many things requiring cleaning or repair.

Once all the ships were picked up he went around with plastic butter boxes and picked up all the plasticine soldiers. Each box was labelled using a waterproof felt pen to show the contents.

While Graham worked his mother looked in from time to time. "You will have to sweep this place out, then hose it and scrub it," she said.

Then Alex put his head in while Graham was sweeping and made rude comments and told him to get on with it.

"Help me Alex," Graham asked.

"Pig's bum! It's your party. See you later," Alex replied as he left hurriedly. Kylie was no better. She said she had important shopping to do and also departed at speed. Graham finished the sweeping feeling quite grumpy. Then he hosed the concrete and ran a bass broom over it. That seemed to make it worse so he hosed it again. Lacking a squeegee he mopped up the worst of the water and was quite pleased with the result. The concrete felt smooth and clean to his bare feet.

Next he set up the step ladder and began pinning up streamers and party balloons. As he worked he remembered being there with Cindy and that got him fantasizing. As a result he became very aroused. He was in the midst of this when Margaret suddenly walked in.

"Hello Graham. Can I help?" Margaret asked.

"If you like," Graham replied. "You can blow up these balloons and pass them to me."

Margaret nodded and moved to the box of balloons. Graham's heart pounded and he hoped his aroused state was not obvious. He waited till Margaret seemed to be busy, then stepped down and moved the ladder along, hotly aware of his physical condition. His heart hammered and he licked dry lips. Taking the end of another streamer and a pin he climbed up the step ladder, keeping his back to Margaret. He then reached up to pin the streamer to the overhead beam.

As he pushed in the pin Margaret walked over to stand beside him. "Here's a balloon Graham," she said, holding it up for him. Graham took it, all the while willing his body to relax.

Margaret met his eyes with an anxious little smile and said, "You blow up the balloons and I will pin them up. You've got bigger lungs than me."

Graham did not like blowing up balloons as he had an unreasonable fear of them bursting and of his eyes being damaged but he agreed. Margaret took his place on the ladder and he moved to the bench. After a while the effort of blowing the balloons up helped his body to return to normal. Margaret chattered happily away as they worked. Graham found her company enjoyable and he was able to relax mentally as well.

By lunch time the two of them had transformed the Ship Room into a party setting. Chairs and small tables were arranged in groups around the sides. Streamers, balloons and ferns festooned the place giving it a cheery, festive atmosphere.

"There! That is a marked improvement. It was a gloomy, dirty place before," Margaret said as they surveyed their handiwork.

Graham had to agree. "It looks great Marg. Thanks very much. You've been a big help."

"What will we do now?" Margaret asked.

"I'm going to have a bath, then lunch," Graham replied, indicating his grimy arms and legs.

"That's a good idea. Can I have a bath too?" Margaret asked.

"If you like," Graham replied. Turning he led the way upstairs. He pushed open the bathroom door and was surprised when Margaret followed him in. "I'm going to have a bath," he reminded her.

"I know, you said so. So am I," Margaret replied.

Graham's mind raced. "With me?"

"Yes, if you don't mind."

Graham could barely believe his ears. "But... but I'm a boy."

At that Margaret smiled and went red. "I know. I've seen you before."

"But I don't want to offend you or be rude."

"We've had baths together before," Margaret reminded him. That was true. When they were younger he had often had a bath with Kylie and Margaret both in the tub with him. They had even bathed together a few months earlier. The memory made Graham flame with a mixture of embarrassment and desire. The embarrassment was because his mother had found them and both had been scolded for being naughty.

"But I'm a big boy now," Graham said, struggling with various urges, not least the desire to be nude with a girl.

"I know. I saw," Margaret said.

Graham went red and felt blood surging in his veins. He gave up the struggle, thinking that if he did what he liked then she might stop chasing him. He put in the plug and turned on the taps. While he did this Margaret peeled off her clothes. She stood watching him, nude and apparently relaxed.

Graham felt the blood pounding in his ears. To him she appeared as a creature of wonder but he could not help comparing her to Cindy. And thinking of Cindy did not help as that just got him even more aroused. He swallowed and unbuttoned his shirt. Her eyes followed his every move, making him feel very self-conscious.

"Don't watch me," he said. "I'm shy."

Her face dimpled into a grin and she stepped into the bath and began splashing the water around and mixing the hot and cold to the right temperature. Graham hesitated then took off his shorts and underpants. Burning with desire and excitement he stepped into the bath behind her and sat down. He began splashing water over himself, feeling as though he was on fire. Margaret looked over her shoulder and said, "Scrub my back please."

Graham did as he was bidden. He found the feel of her skin very arousing and he had to restrain himself. Again he compared her to Cindy and that got him even more aroused and confused. Guilt began to bother him. *She is too young!* he thought. But it was very nice! To further confuse him he sensed that he could do anything he liked and Margaret would let him. But he also knew that he actually cared for her so much there was no way he would do anything to harm her.

After a while Margaret said, "Your go. Turn around." Graham did so and Margaret knelt behind him and rubbed his back. It felt very nice and he would have been happy if she had kept doing it all afternoon.

At that moment the bathroom door opened behind them. It was Graham's mother. Graham hastily covered himself and fierce embarrassment coursed through him. His mother stopped at the door and said, "I wondered where you two were. You'd better hop out Margaret. You are getting too old to be taking baths together now."

Margaret blushed bright pink and nodded. "Yes Mrs Kirk," she replied in a croaky whisper. Tears started and she went on, "I'm sorry Mrs Kirk. Don't go mad at Graham. It was my idea."

Mrs Kirk pursed her lips into a wry smile. "Hmm! I doubt that. But come out and we will talk about it. Now, both you children hop out and come and have lunch," she said. Then she closed the door and went away.

Margaret climbed out of the bath. "I'm sorry," she sobbed. "Will you be in trouble?"

"I don't know," Graham replied. "I don't think so. But mum is right. I'm a big boy now and you are too young."

Margaret grabbed a towel and began drying herself. Graham crouched in the bath and found he was torn between lust and shame. "You'd better go," he said.

Margaret quickly dried herself, sobbing quietly all the while. Graham stayed in the bath, his eyes averted and his heart pounding with desire and anxiety.

"I am so ashamed!" Margaret said. "I just want to run away."

"Mum said to go and talk to her," Graham reminded.

"Do you think I should?" Margaret asked.

"Yes," croaked Graham. He was dry in the throat and his heart pumped furiously. The sight of her distress was upsetting him and he began to fear that she would get into terrible trouble from her own parents. *Oh, what have I done?* he thought unhappily.

After Margaret had dressed and stepped fearfully out of the room Graham climbed out of the bath and slowly towelled himself dry. By this time he had lost all desire and was feeling sick with anxiety and guilt. *Margaret is too nice—and too young! I should not have done that with her. I deserve all I get but I must try to save her,* he told himself.

Sick at heart but determined to do what he could to retrieve the situation, he dressed. For a minute he studied himself in the mirror, feeling very much like how he imagined a condemned man might feel. Then he took a deep breath and left the bathroom.

To his relief he found Margaret and his mother sitting quietly talking in the kitchen. He saw that Margaret was still red-eyed but she did not look too unhappy. His mother called him to join them, then said, "This applies to you too Graham. Now, I know you two are good friends but you are both reaching an age where you could get each other into real trouble. Do you understand?"

Graham nodded and blushed fiercely. His mother went on: "I want you both to promise me you won't do the wrong thing please."

"Yes mum. Sorry mum. I promise," Graham said.

"It was my fault Mrs Kirk," Margaret sobbed. Tears started coursing down her cheeks. "I won't do it again."

Mrs Kirk reached forward and hugged Margaret. "It's all right. What you did was entirely natural. You are just too young, that's all. I think you are a good girl. Besides, if Graham is going to play those sorts of games I would rather it was with someone like you that he loves and cares about than some cheap tart. I want you to be his friend. OK?"

Margaret nodded and wiped her eyes. Graham was gripped by even stronger guilt as visions of Cindy filled his mind.

Then his mother looked over Margaret's head while she stroked her hair. "And you, young man, remember what your father said to you about the age of consent. Don't you start playing around with girls who are under age or you will find yourself in trouble with the police. Now go and get changed ready to go to cadets. Margaret, would you help me ice some cup cakes please?"

So Margaret stayed for lunch. The two of them were both embarrassed, but to Graham's relief his mother said nothing more about the incident. By then he felt heartily ashamed of himself and he made a vow to behave in future. *But it was wonderful,* he thought, conscious that being with Margaret was much less stressful than being with other girls.

Alex joined them, then Kylie but by then Graham was distracted by clock watching. As the minutes ticked over bringing his attendance at the navy cadets closer he became more and more tense and excited. He barely heard what Kylie had to say about her shopping trip and found he was biting his nails with anxiety.

Mrs Kirk also looked at the clock. "Hurry up and finish eating your lunch Graham," she said. "I have your enrolment forms here." She pointed to the top of the fridge.

"Thanks mum." Graham sprang up to collect the enrolment documents. For a moment he stood looking from Margaret to his mother, his emotions all in turmoil. Then he said to Margaret, "It will be all right Margaret."

Margaret nodded, smiled and burst into tears. His mother smiled and said, "She will be fine, now you get going."

Graham felt his eyes prickle and fearing tears he fled. He was both scared and relieved. And confused. Who did he really love? When he had been with Margaret he had felt quite natural and happy. So what about Thelma? Cindy he discounted. *That wasn't love,* he thought. Even at his age he could tell pure lust. He shrugged. It was all very difficult.

He got out his bike and set off for the navy cadet depot.

***

When he arrived at the navy cadet's depot Graham felt very shy. He placed his bike against the fence and looked nervously around, hoping to see one of the cadets he knew so he could go in with him. There was no-one he knew. Several other navy cadets arrived, either dropped by parents from cars, or riding bikes. They wore uniforms and looked very smart and superior. Some glanced at Graham, making him even more self-conscious.

A bugle tune suddenly blared out from a loudspeaker and cadets came running out of a doorway onto the parade ground. A large cadet with very shiny boots and a peaked cap marched out and started calling orders. Two other cadets took up a position in front of him and about 20 paces apart and also began to bellow orders. The ordinary cadets quickly formed up in ranks in front of the two cadets.

I'm late! Graham thought. That made him even more nervous. He watched as a bearded man wearing white shirt and shorts and a peaked cap strode around growling corrections to minor faults of drill. Graham could tell by the rank badges on his sleeves that he was a Chief Petty Officer and his tough appearance gave Graham considerable misgivings about ever meeting him.

To his dismay the bearded CPO cast a glance at him, then turned and marched over. Graham swallowed and felt like running away.

"Can I help you lad?" the CPO asked.

"I... I've come to join sir," Graham replied.

"Ah! Good! Got an enrolment form have you?"

"Yes sir. I got it last week."

"Excellent. Follow me then. Petty Officer Pike, get your watch dressed by the right!" this last directed at a bellow to one of the two cadets standing in front of the uniformed groups. Graham walked in through the entrance and followed the CPO, very aware that all the cadets were watching his progress. It made him even more nervous and he broke into a cold sweat.

He was led into the office where several adult staff and a couple of cadets were working. One of the adults was Lt Ryan, the bearded XO (Executive Officer or 2ic). Another was a cheerful looking tubby lady wearing Sub Lieutenant's rank. Next to her was Sub Lt Sheldon. The sight of him made Graham relax a little.

The CPO saluted the XO. "Excuse me sir, lad here to enrol," he said.

Lt Ryan looked up and nodded. "Thank you CPO. Ah yes, young Kirk. Have a seat there and I'll look after you in a minute."

Feeling very nervous and not wanting to do the wrong thing Graham sat down. The tubby female Sub Lt gave him a friendly smile, then went on with her paperwork.

Sub Lt Sheldon finished writing and sent a cadet out with a message, then saw Graham. "We've met. You are the lad who rescued my model from under the wharf on Sunday. Sorry, I can't remember your name," he said.

"Graham Kirk sir."

"Ah. That's right. Your dad is captain of the *Malita*."

"Yes sir."

"And you are here to join?" Sub Lt Sheldon asked.

"Yes sir."

"Good lad. Excuse me. Cadet Midshipman Wainwright!" this last directed at the top of his voice.

"Sir!" A lad of about seventeen, dressed in whites with a single white bar on each black epaulet appeared from another office.

"This training program you gave me," Sub Lt Sheldon said, waving a paper at the youth. The two began a detailed discussion which Graham could not follow. He was left sitting there and felt conspicuous and embarrassed. It did, however, give him time to look around. He noted the two doors on the other side of the office, one marked 'Commanding Officer' and the other 'Wardroom'. To the left were other offices and some sort of corridor which must have led through to the rear of the building as several cadets came and went, as well as a very shapely lady Petty Officer in her twenties. Around the walls were various nautical pictures, ships' crests, lifebuoys and charts. There were two models, one of the World War 2 cruiser HMAS *Hobart*, and one of an aircraft carrier. Graham could not identify it and was too nervous to walk over and look.

Looks American though, he decided.

At that moment the cadets came off parade and went past outside to lessons in the lecture room at the rear. Graham was still left sitting amid the bustle till the first training period had begun. Then Lt Ryan came back and sat down opposite him.

"OK young feller, let's see your enrolment form."

Graham handed it over, beset by fears there would be something wrong with it. The officer scanned it quickly, nodding as he did.

"That looks fine. Now, the CO will meet you in a minute when he has finished briefing the Cadet Midshipmen. Meanwhile we will organize you into the Watch and Quarter Bill."

Graham nodded. He knew roughly what that meant. He badly wanted to be in the same group as Andrew Collins but was too shy to say anything. Lt Ryan studied the wall behind Graham, then nodded.

"Port Watch are due to get the next recruit. The unit is organized into two watches, like a ship, Port and Starboard. Each Watch is subdivided into two parts as well. I will put you in the Second Part of Port Watch. Remember that," Lt Ryan explained.

"Yes sir."

"You mean Aye aye sir," Lt Ryan corrected with a smile.

"Er... ye... aye aye sir," Graham replied. He blushed and felt slightly foolish using such quaint language.

Lt Ryan went on: "Cadet Midshipman Wainwright is your Divisional Officer and Petty Officer Armstrong is your P.O... Now, you will rank as a Recruit until you have passed the tests for Ordinary Seaman. That means when the others go to specialist training you go to the recruit squad."

"How long will I be a recruit sir?" Graham asked.

"Usually about three months. It depends how regularly you turn up and how quickly you pass the tests. Obviously the more reliable you are at attendance the faster you get promoted."

Graham nodded, unsure whether to say 'Aye aye' or 'yes sir' in answer. He blushed and hoped Lt Ryan had not noticed. Lt Ryan handed him a sheet of paper with the unit's program of parades on it. "That isn't complete," he explained. "Sometimes things come up which cause changes. For example we have been lucky enough to organize a day trip on a landing craft next Saturday."

Graham felt a thrill of excitement, tinged with worry. He asked: "Are... are recruits allowed to go sir?"

"Yes they are. Permission forms will be handed out at final parade," Lt Ryan replied. "Now, let's go and meet the CO, Lt Cdr Hazard."

Graham was led across to where a man of middle age stood in the doorway of the office titled, Commanding Officer. The CO wore lieutenant commander's rank badges on his epaulets and had three medal ribbons on his white shirt front. He looked to be a very fit and cheerful man and looked quite the part to Graham.

Lt Ryan introduced him: "Recruit Graham er... Graham Kirk sir. I have put him in Port Watch."

"Good. Thanks XO. Come in Recruit Kirk and take a seat," Lt Cdr Hazard replied. He put out his hand to Graham who reacted in surprise with a fumbling handshake. The CO's grip was firm and friendly. Graham sat on the edge of the chair in front of his desk.

For a few seconds Lt Cdr Hazard studied him. Then he said, "Now, tell me about yourself, family, school, interests, hobbies, and so on."

Graham did as he was asked, growing more fluent as his confidence returned. When he mentioned his father Lt Cdr Hazard, nodded and grinned. "Know him well. Often see him around. I run a ship's chandlery and we do business all the time."

That both pleased and worried Graham. He didn't want too close a connection in case he got into trouble and his dad heard of it. He went on to describe his hobby of model ship building, then ended by stating his ambition to be a naval officer.

Lt Cdr Hazard nodded with approval. "Good for you. That's what we want," he said, smiling. "Stick to it and you should do well. We will help of course. Now, all I want you to do is make me two promises, and I don't want you to make them today. I want you to think about them for a week. The first is that you will be a reliable attender. If I enrol you it causes us a lot of paperwork if you then just lose interest or don't turn up. Is that clear?"

"Yes sir, er... Aye aye sir," Graham replied, blushing in confusion over what the correct reply should have been.

Lt Cdr Hazard went on: "The other promise is to behave yourself. The adult staff are all volunteers and give up their spare time, mostly without pay, to run the unit. In return your part of the bargain is to not give us any grief by misbehaviour. OK?"

"Yes sir," Graham replied.

"Fine. I will ask you about it next Saturday. Now, if you go out there and ask for my Coxswain, Petty Officer Nevis, he will take you to join the others. Thank you."

Graham nodded and stood up. He wondered if he should be saluting or doing drill as he left but decided not to. He was supposed to be a recruit who knew nothing. *Besides, I'm not in uniform,* he reasoned. He went out and found the cadet PO who asked him what Watch and Part of Watch he had been allocated to. Then he led Graham through the side door and into another office where some older cadets were sitting.

Graham was introduced to Cadet Midshipman Mainwaring and was instantly impressed. The Cadet Midshipman was a tall, fair haired lad of about seventeen. To Graham he looked fit and handsome and fitted his image of what a junior officer should look like. He discovered that

Mainwaring attended the Trinity Anglican School and was a Year 12 there. Next Graham met his Divisional Petty Officer, PO Bob Armstrong. Bob was a solid, black haired lad with a cheerful grin. He was a Year 11 at Smithfield State High School.

PO Armstrong wrote Graham's name into his notebook and, after asking permission to do so, also his address, phone number and school. That done he led him to the rear of the building to where a squad was being instructed in drill: How to Off caps and On caps. Graham saw that the squad included a boy named Porter from his own school, a very attractive girl with nice big boobs, and a Torres Strait Islander who went to his school.

Graham was put on the end of the line without being introduced and the lesson went on. He had no cap so was told to pretend he had one by the Leading Seaman teaching the lesson. After 10 minutes the lesson ended and the Leading Seaman introduced himself. "I'm Ken George," he said. "I've seen you at school. Are you in Year 9?"

"No, Year 8," Graham replied. He was introduced to the others and stood self-consciously to one side while they talked during the break. More cadets joined them and Graham was relieved to see Andrew Collins and Arthur Blake.

Andrew waved and came over to him. "Good to see you Graham. What watch are you in?"

"Second Part of Port Watch," Graham replied.

"Oh good. So are we. This is Anthony Simmonds. He's a Year 8 at Trinity Bay State High," Andrew replied, introducing a tall, thin lad.

Graham felt immensely relieved. He knew some of the people and was in the same group as Andrew. Also they all seemed friendly and did not seem to look down on him.

A lesson on knot tying followed. This was taught by another Leading Seaman named Josh Neville who went to St Augustine's College. Graham found the lesson a bit embarrassing as he already knew all the knots from Scouts and from working on his father's ships, but he did not want to appear a know-all when he was a new recruit. He did the knots competently without showing off, and when questioned, explained why he knew them so well. To his relief, his explanation was accepted without any problems.

While they worked Graham looked around. A large shed nearby

contained three sail boats, a power boat and several canoes, all on trailers. A squad of cadets from the Starboard Watch was working on one of the sail boats, a corsair. The impression was quickly conveyed to him that the Starboard Watch were somewhat more than friendly rivals, but less than mortal enemies.

The afternoon finished with a parade. Graham was stood in the ranks and told what to do by PO Armstrong. He felt both proud and embarrassed; because he was only a new recruit, and because he was not in uniform. The Buffer, CPO Carpenter, a Year 12 from Woree, took over.

"Ship's company... Ho! Ship's company... Right dress!"

Graham shuffled as best he could, glancing at the others to watch what to do. He was in the rear rank. Seeing the front rank put their left arms up to get the spacing he put his up as well.

"Put your arm down," hissed Andrew beside him. Graham did so, blushing furiously at his mistake.

"Ship's company... Stand at... Ease!"

CPO Carpenter handed over to the Training Officer who distributed a bundle of permission forms. "These are to go out on the Landing Craft Heavy next Saturday. That is abbreviated LCH. The LCH's name is HMAS *Tarakan*. It is an all-day trip and you will need to bring your own lunch and the things listed on the form."

Graham folded the form and placed it in his pocket. The parade was then handed over to the CO and the flag lowered while they stood at attention, the officers saluting.

"Ship's company... Dis... miss!"

Chapter 25

BIRTHDAY PARTY

A t 6:30pm that evening, Graham stood nervously on the top step waiting for his guests to arrive. He was dressed in a new pair of long trousers, a gift from his father, and that alone made him feel different and uncomfortable as he usually wore shorts. He also wore a new shirt, a gift from his mother. Fresh from the bath and with his hair neatly combed he was as ready as he could make himself.

As the minutes ticked by tension built up as he worried over who might not come; or about what might happen at the party. It was enough to make him feel sick in the stomach. He continually checked the time and fidgeted, then bit his nails. There was also residual guilt and anxiety about whether Margaret's parents knew about the bath incident and over what repercussions might follow.

A car pulled up. Graham recognized it and felt a mixed sense of annoyance and apprehension. It was driven by Margaret's dad. Graham fervently hoped she had not said anything.

Margaret hopped out and gave him a cheery wave and a smile. Graham grinned mechanically in return. Relief swept through him. Obviously she had not and nor had his mother. He noted that Margaret wore a pink party frock made of some sort of thin cloth. A large pink ribbon was tied in the side of her hair. Clutching a present she made her way to the gate. Graham walked down to meet her.

"Happy birthday Graham," she replied, handing him the present. As he took it she leaned forward and gave him a tender little kiss on the cheek. The waft of a pleasant perfume filled his nostrils. His heart beat faster as he took the present and after saying an embarrassed thanks led her inside to the Ship Room.

The lights were now on and Margaret looked around then clapped her hands. "It looks lovely Graham," she said. She began to chatter happily while all he could do was remember the two of them in the bath earlier in the day. That made him start to get aroused. He struggled against this, wishing someone else would arrive as he did not want to be alone with her.

Then Max arrived. "Hello, What are you two doing down here alone?" he said in a bantering tone. Graham jumped with fright and went red with guilt. He had not heard Max arrive. Cindy was behind him, which increased his guilt.

"Hi Max. Hello Cindy. I didn't hear you arrive," he said.

"Happy birthday!" they chorused. Both then passed him presents and Cindy stepped forward, put her arms around Graham's neck and kissed him on the lips. More perfume smells assailed his senses. He flushed as the delightful sensation of being kissed, and the feel of Cindy rubbing against him made his heart pound. He also felt sorry for Margaret, who stood watching, trying to pretend she wasn't jealous and hurt. Worse still, scorching memories of being with Cindy flooded his mind and he became even more aroused. This increased his confusion. To gain time to recover he took the presents and placed them on a side table.

Max gestured to the presents "Well, open them," he insisted.

"Margaret's first," Graham said. He unwrapped the present, uncomfortably aware of his physical state.

It was a bundle of balsa sheets, small tins of Humbrol paints, paint thinner and several small brushes.

Graham smiled at her. "Thanks very much Margaret. I can certainly use these," he replied. Margaret blushed and smiled shyly.

As Graham unwrapped Cindy's present Kylie appeared and began to talk to Margaret. Cindy's present was a nice dress shirt. Graham said thanks and managed to meet her eyes. She grinned and winked and said in reply: "If there is any other little thing you might like let me know."

Graham thought immediately of what he really did want and blushed furiously. He wondered if that was what Cindy meant. *Or is she just saying that to tease me?*

Max's present was a plastic model kit; a 1:600 scale of the British cruiser HMS *Sheffield* of World War 2. While they were discussing it Peter and Stephen both arrived.

"Hello sailor!" Stephen cried. "Did you join the navy cadets?"

Graham nodded and blushed with embarrassment. "Yes. Thanks Steve," the last as he took Stephen's present. It was also a plastic ship kit; a 1:700 scale model of the British Battlecruiser HMS *Hood* of World War 2.

Peter's present was a book. As soon as he unwrapped it Graham wanted the party to end so he could sit and read it. It was a book entitled *Battleship Design and Development* by Norman Friedman and was crammed with facts, photos and fascinating diagrams. It took him an effort to put it down and be civil to his guests. At least it took his mind off girls and allowed his body to return to normal.

Roger arrived next, dressed up with a tie as well as long sleeves and looking very overdressed. Wayne and George followed him in. Wayne gave Graham a pocket knife with lots of useful attachments and George gave him a HO scale passenger wagon for the model railway.

"You are always playing trains," George said.

Max laughed and added: "He's taken to playing submarines recently."

Cindy burst into giggles and gave Graham a wicked grin. Graham noticed a puzzled, worried look cross Margaret's face. To add to his concern his mother came in with Alex and started circulating with plates of savoury biscuits. Kylie was roped in to help and Margaret went with her. Two more girls arrived: Rowena, looking absolutely beautiful with her black hair shining in the light; and Louise, mousy hair bobbed short and an infectious grin on her freckled face. They gave Graham a new video game on naval warfare and a DVD called *Battleships at War*. Graham studied the cover intently and wanted to rush up to the TV to watch it. Reluctantly he put it on the table with the other presents.

Rhonda and Dawn arrived soon after, with Michael and Chris on their heels. Rhonda wore a white blouse and a black dress and had a ribbon around her throat which Graham found very eye-catching and attractive. Dawn wore an emerald green dress which was cut to hug her body. She also wore make-up and a necklace which gave her the appearance of a little girl dressing up. Rhonda gave Graham a box of aftershave lotion. Dawn presented chocolates and new handkerchiefs, while the boys gave him a computer game and a novel with a picture of a battleship firing its guns on the front cover: *The Blooding of the Guns* by Alexander Fullerton. Graham managed to look pleased with all of them; although he puzzled over the aftershave and soap. *I haven't started shaving yet,* he thought, rubbing his jaw to feel if there was any bristle. Then he worried if they were trying to tactfully hint that he smelt and needed it.

By now it was 7pm and Graham was continually eyeing the door and worrying. Was Thelma going to come or not? His hopes kept see-sawing. Two more people arrived: Carmen and Andrew Collins. Carmen was the oldest girl there, by a year, and she looked it. She was very nicely dressed but had a grown up look about her. Carmen gave Graham a book: *A Pictorial History of the Royal Australian Navy*; while Andrew gave him another plastic model kit, this time of the German battleship *Bismarck*.

While Graham was looking at these his mother said to him: "It is time we started the party dear."

Graham looked at his watch. 7:10. He nodded. *Thelma mustn't be coming,* he thought sadly. It was a real disappointment. Swallowing his hurt he stepped into the middle of the room and raised his voice. "OK people, thank you for coming. Now the party can really start. First, as a way of saying thank you, we will have a lucky clothes colour prize."

There were groans and cheers. Graham took an envelope from his mother and opened it. "Green," he read. Everyone's eyes swept around, to settle on Dawn, with her tight emerald green dress. Graham picked up a prize and took it over to her. She unwrapped it and blushed furiously at all the attention. The prize included a variety of little things: chocolates, small toys, soap and so on. Next there was a lucky door prize.

Stephen laughed and called out: "This goes to the luckiest door in the room!"

Laughter greeted this quip. Graham grinned and opened another envelope. "Last person in," he read.

"That's me!" Andrew cried.

"No it's not! It's me!" called Janet from the doorway. Graham looked and his heart jumped. Thelma stood just inside the doorway with Janet behind her. Thelma looked very pretty, with a yellow party frock which set off her skin nicely. Janet, in contrast, wore jeans and a white turtle neck sweater which made her look much older and very cool.

"Sorry we are late," Janet said, "We had trouble with dad's car."

Graham couldn't have cared less what they had had trouble with; they were there—or at least Thelma was. He gave Janet the prize and accepted presents from them. Janet gave him a book, *Saving the Environment,* while Thelma gave him a nice dress shirt. "Blue, to match your eyes," she said, smiling at him as he looked at it. The shirt, till then just a boring item of apparel, became his instant favourite.

Max interrupted. "Come on, get on with the party!" he called. Graham started. He had been standing staring into Thelma's eyes. He blushed and went to read out the lucky spot prize. Roger won this and was suitably pleased.

Alex now took over. "Righto you lot, grab those chairs and sit in a circle."

They did as they were told. Graham tried to manoeuvre to sit beside Thelma but ended up between Rhonda and Dawn. He sat and looked around the circle of smiling faces. Every person he had asked was there. It gave him a warm feeling inside. Alex then announced the first party game: Pass the parcel. This resulted in a few jeers and comments from kids who believed they were too old for such stuff, but they all took part anyway.

Michael ended up the winner. Alex then had them stand to play a game of musical chairs. This announcement caused Max to sneer and Dawn looked down her nose. Janet said, "I thought Graham was turning thirteen, not three!"

Graham blushed but Alex didn't turn a hair. "You don't have to play," he said. The music began. They all did play, and Janet ended up winning. Graham actually enjoyed it as he got to bump against several of the girls during it.

"Righto!" Alex called. "Next is hide and seek. The birthday boy is 'in'. The rules are: you can hide anywhere in the house or in the yard but no going outside the fence. When a person is found they come back here. Last person found wins a prize. Count to a hundred Graham. Come on you lot! Get going!"

There was a mad scramble as kids realized the game had begun. Graham began counting aloud, listening to voices out in the garden and feet thudding up the stairs and into rooms overhead. As soon as he had counted and called the traditional "Coming, ready or not!" he raced outside and began searching. To his surprise he found the first person almost immediately. Cindy was standing just in the shadows under the front veranda.

"Here I am Graham," she whispered. He stopped and wondered what he should do. She decided that for him by stepping forward and kissing him, setting his senses on fire.

"I... I've got to keep looking," Graham said, trying to break free.

"They can wait another minute," Cindy replied. Her voice had a peculiar husky timbre to it which frightened Graham. She kissed him again, more passionately this time, rubbing herself against him so that he became quickly aroused.

"They will wonder where I am," he gasped when she stopped kissing. His heart was now thumping madly and he could feel his resistance crumbling. But Thelma was here somewhere. *Thelma! It is Thelma I love,* he told himself in desperation. He managed to free himself without too obviously fleeing and went on with the search.

The game was good fun. Most kids were easily found but a few, who knew the house, were harder to find. Alex hung like a gibbon ape from the pipes outside the bathroom. Kylie was in Alex's clothes cupboard. Max was under Alex's bed and Margaret was under Graham's bed. He wondered about that. Did she want to be in it? *Nah! She is just a little kid. She wouldn't understand,* he told himself.

When all had been rounded up and cold drinks consumed they played a game that involved blindfolding all the boys who then had to grope their way around the room until they touched someone. They then had to identify the person, and, if they were a girl, kiss them. Graham was very keen to play this game. By now he was in quite a state of emotional turmoil; torn between affection for Margaret, adoration for Thelma and lust for Cindy. As luck would have it the person he first grabbed was Stephen. Stephen uttered loud shrieks about not being one of them. Graham insisted on a second go. This time he was luckier and touched Rhonda. He gently felt her face but wasn't sure who she was. She whispered her name very softly, which surprised him.

Does she like me enough for me to want to kiss her? he wondered. He said "Rhonda" and removed his blindfold. Rhonda stood and waited. Graham licked his lips and hesitated. Suddenly he realized that he really wanted to kiss her, but Thelma was watching, and so was Margaret (not to mention little sister Kylie!). After hesitating for a few seconds he plucked up courage and gave her a gentle peck on the cheek.

Cindy jeered. "Oh Graham! You can do better than that!" she called. Graham blushed.

Louise grinned and turned to Cindy. "How do you know?" she queried. Hot memories made Graham blush even more. Feeling quite flustered he tried again. This time Rhonda put her arms around his neck and pressed against him. Her lips tasted sweet and she kissed very well. Graham's heart began to pound furiously. He was sorry when she stopped.

The game was a great success, with much shrieking and laughter. At the end of it they trooped upstairs to the dining room where the table was loaded with food. A huge cake, shaped like an ocean liner, was the centrepiece. Graham was very excited by this and enjoying himself immensely. Only with an effort did he recall his plans to win Thelma's attention.

They ate merrily and the candles were lit. Graham blew them out in one big puff and *Happy Birthday* was sung. During this he stood in the centre, flushed with pleasure and excitement. As he stood there Cindy stepped forward, put her arms around his neck and kissed him passionately on the lips. Graham squirmed with pleasure and mental agony. *What will Thelma think?* he fretted, yet he did not want Cindy to stop. There were cheers and cries of "Behave yourself!"

Max called: "If you eat any more of that you'll be sick!"

Amid the laughter Graham was released. He was blushing furiously and did not know what to do or say. His eyes met Margaret's and he felt a stab of sympathy. Hers were misted with misery. With her lips trembling she stepped forward and put her arms around him and kissed him.

"I love you," she murmured. Graham responded and put his arms around her too. The kiss was very nice and he had to admit he felt great affection for her. *But she is too young,* he told himself. When she stepped back he noted tears in her eyes. *Poor kid! She is jealous,* he thought.

Rhonda stepped forward and Stephen cried: "You've already had two goes Rhonda!" In reply she poked her tongue at him and put her arms around Graham's neck. A mischievous look glinted in her eye and she pressed herself against him before kissing him long and hard. By then Graham was also hard and was in total confusion. *This is a disaster,* he thought. *What will Thelma think?* But it was nice!

Dawn took Rhonda's place and pressed against him in a way that sent Graham into a mixture of panic and delight.

Then all the girls lined up to kiss him. Kylie gave him a sisterly peck. Carmen smiled and gave him a good smooch but did not rub against him.

Louise did and she even inserted her tongue into his mouth. Rowena was even more sultry. She kissed and went on kissing.

"Hey, don't be greedy!" Stephen called. "What about us?"

Rhonda grinned. "You can kiss Graham if you like," she replied. They all laughed. Rowena moved away and Graham's mind registered that Thelma was standing in front of him. *Here she is.* It was the moment he had dreamed about; and all he could do was stand there like a dummy while she gave him a friendly peck on the cheek. She stepped back and the kissing ended. Graham realized later that only Janet had not kissed him. He felt more hot and confused than he could ever remember.

Alex clapped his hands. "Time for another game," he called. "Sardines!"

"Yes!" they shouted. Sardines was a form of hide-and-seek in which as many people as possible tried to squeeze into the same hiding place. They raced off, leaving Alex 'in'.

"This way," Graham called to Thelma. But it was Cindy, Margaret and Rhonda who followed him. He led them through to the front veranda, then circled into his parent's bedroom and moved in behind the door to the lounge room. The lights were out in the bedroom and several coats and other items of clothing hung from the back of the door. They burrowed in amongst these. Graham found himself wedged in the corner with Margaret against one side, Rhonda against the other and Cindy pressing against him from the front.

Even in his aroused and excited state Graham could sense that there was a degree of rivalry and hostility between the girls. It did wonders for his ego but made him even more confused about who he liked. His emotional and physical states were even more upset by Cindy pressing against him.

It was almost a relief to get discovered, but not quite. He now had to move out into the light with the others, hoping no-one would see he was aroused. That Louise and Dawn noticed was embarrassingly obvious by the way Louise's eyes moved, and how she then whispered to Dawn, who also looked. Graham's cheeks scorched and he hurried from the room.

The next game was a form of tiggy. This resulted in kids running all around and through the house, with lots of laughing and yelling. Graham tried to stay near Thelma and he felt he was getting somewhere when she talked to him. They ran around the lawn in the moonlight and he badly wanted to kiss her. Lack of encouragement as well as lack of courage stopped him. He also became aware that Margaret and Kylie were following them. He wanted to tell them to stop it but did not want to make it obvious to Thelma that he wanted to be alone with her.

In the end he had no chance to say anything private to Thelma. They all ended up, hot and puffing, back in the Ship Room. Supper was served: ice cream, fruit salad, cakes and cold soft drinks. Graham stood eating and basking in the pleasure of the occasion. The party was plainly a success and that made him feel good.

As the group stood around eating and talking about the games George and Michael studied Graham's model ships.

"These are very good Graham. What are they?" Michael asked. Graham was both embarrassed and proud. He named his battleship and aircraft carrier and the tiny planes were duly picked up and admired. Janet and Thelma stood nearby. Thelma looked at the models and seemed impressed. She bent down to study the collection of sailing ships grouped on the table.

"Did you make these Graham?" she asked.

Graham nodded. "When I was younger," he replied, trying to give the impression he was now grown up and no longer did such childish things.

"I love these little people," she said. "What are they made of?"

Graham explained his plasticine people, a bit worried that she might think him still a little boy. However she just nodded with interest and picked several up to examine them.

Janet looked over the ships with the beginnings of a sneer curling her upper lip. "Do you only make models of warships?" she asked, hostility evident in her tone.

"No. There are some merchant ships too," Graham replied, but he felt uncomfortable about it as they were few and far between.

At that moment Stephen joined them. "What's this? Navy Day?"

"We were just looking at Graham's model ships," Thelma replied in a way that sent Graham's hopes soaring.

George joined them. "Yeah, they are good aren't they?" he said. He turned to Graham. "Did you join the Navy Cadets Graham?"

"Yes I did. This afternoon. I'm a recruit in the Port Watch."

Stephen laughed. "Port Watch! Which port do you watch; the Port of Cairns or a bottle of port?"

Graham made a face and blushed. He did not enjoy being teased. Janet then drove in another barb. "We will have to say 'Hello Sailor!' when we see you now."

Before Graham could reply, Stephen quipped: "I didn't know you were one of those sorts of girls Janet."

Janet turned on him furiously and almost spat her anger at him. "Watch your tongue or I'll scratch your eyes out!" she snarled. While the two argued Graham met Cindy's eye and he saw she was blushing. He blushed too. Peter came over and smoothed down the situation, getting Stephen to apologize.

Somehow the incident spoiled the atmosphere of the party. No-one felt like playing any more games so music was put on instead and they stood or sat and talked. Graham found himself next to Margaret and Peter and this put him in a bad mood too. He wanted to be with Thelma but did not know how to extricate himself from the social situation. To his jealous annoyance, he saw that she was deep in earnest conversation with Wayne about music.

The party was ended at 10pm by Graham's mum. Parents began arriving to take kids home and he stood and farewelled them. All he managed to achieve with Thelma was to thank her as she and Janet left. She gave him a nice smile but nothing more. Cindy gave Graham a kiss as she left, to the obvious jealousy of Margaret who was helping Kylie tidy up. Margaret was the last guest to leave. Her father seemed happy to talk to Graham's mum over a cup of tea. Graham helped carry plates and food upstairs. Margaret then stood at the door to say goodnight.

Graham could see she was very tense and her eyes sparkled. *She wants to impress me. And she wants a kiss,* he thought. He shifted uncomfortably from one foot to the other and blushed, thinking of Thelma; and of Cindy. *Oh! Why is life so complicated?* he thought.

In the end her father solved the problem by saying: "Come on moppet. Give your boyfriend a kiss and let's go. It's way past your bedtime."

Boyfriend! Graham thought. *Is that what the adults think? And is that what Margaret wants?* Graham knew it was. He leaned forward and gave her a gentle peck on the cheek. Her attitude told him she wanted more but he did not dare with the adults watching. *Besides, I don't want to encourage her.*

Chapter 26

DEVELOPMENTS

The following morning Graham sat in church feeling thoroughly confused. He did not know if he was happy or sad. The reason for this was girls. Which girl? He had never realized something so apparently simple could be so complex. *There are so many pretty girls to choose from!* he thought. To add to his dilemma was the issue of what it was that he really wanted: love or lust? To complicate his thinking processes two of the girls in question, Margaret and Cindy, sat near him in church. So did his sister and mother. And what about Thelma? *I adore her. I worship her!* he thought. But was it love? Or was he just a fool; a juvenile with a crush? He shook his head. *No. It is Thelma I am in love with!* he told himself.

It had taken an effort to attend church. To start with he had only woken up at 8 o'clock. Then there had been all those presents to distract him, particularly the book on battleship design, and the video on *Battleships at War*. As soon as the service was over Graham fled. He merely grunted a reply to Margaret's greeting and brushed past Roger. As quickly as he could he walked home.

Max and Alex were already there, working in Alex's room on model tanks and planes for their countries. They chased Graham out and then came to see what he was doing at his desk. Graham hid the plans of the second battleship and instead leafed through the book on battleship design. Peter arrived just after 11 o'clock and they all then settled in front of the TV to watch the video.

The video was all old black and white newsreel but with a narrative and Graham was fascinated. It dealt with the British King George V-class battleships of World War 2 and had some incredible footage. To begin with there were long and detailed scenes of the ships being built and leaving dock, then actual film of the *Bismarck* blowing up the HMS *Hood*. Later it showed the HMS *Prince of Wales* being sunk by the Japanese in 1941. The concluding section showing the fleet in the Arctic Ocean in 1942 was quite awe inspiring, the way the massive waves battered at the ships.

When the video was finished the boys were quite excited.

"Wasn't that something!" Max cried, "See that aircraft carrier run into that colossal wave and dip its flight deck in!"

Peter nodded. "And that bit about the *Hood* blowing up. Incredible!" he added.

Graham agreed. That scene had particularly moved him. He had always admired the *Hood*, ever since he had seen a picture of her in one of his granddad's books. It somehow rankled that the pride of the Royal Navy could have been sunk so easily. Now he wasn't so sure if he liked the ship or not. Likewise he had previously formed a fairly low opinion of the KGV-class ships because they had been smaller and had smaller guns than American battleships of the same era but now he decided they looked really good. *I will build one of them as well as the Nelson,* he decided.

It was lunch time by then and the boys all went to the kitchen at Mrs Kirk's call. Afterwards they went downstairs and helped clean up the Ship Room. The furniture was all taken back where it belonged and the concrete floor was swept and then hosed and scrubbed again. This left only faint chalk marks to show where the coastlines of Graham's Little World had been.

Peter looked around. "Are we still going to set up our game here?" he asked.

Alex answered at once: "You bet. We will lay it out now."

"Who gets what?" Max asked.

"We all have to have an equal share," Graham insisted.

"How will we do it?" Max asked.

Peter suggested: "Let's plan it on paper first. How big is it?"

Graham did not know. They obtained a tape measure and notepaper and set to work to make a plan. The area turned out to be about 10 metres by 12 with two rows of posts, three in each row.

"Why not exactly 12 metres?" Alex asked.

Peter answered. "Because it is an old house. It would have been built when we still used Imperial measurement; you know, feet and inches," he replied.

Armed with the data Peter drew up a grid on a sheet of paper, then set to work to plot the coastlines that were faintly visible.

"Why are you bothering with them?" Max asked.

Peter shrugged. "Because they are there and already have countries Graham has been using for years. We can just move forward in time from the Napoleonic Era to modern times."

"But who gets what?" Max persisted.

"We can negotiate that," Peter replied.

Once they had the map the boys took themselves upstairs to the comfort of the veranda and sat down to haggle over territory. The map showed a most peculiar hodge-podge which bore almost no relationship to the real geography of the world. As Peter pointed to each country, then labelled it with the name nominated by Graham he shook his head.

"Boy! You certainly didn't bother to open an Atlas when you planned this Graham," he said.

Graham could only shrug and blush. "It just sort of grew," he replied.

The rough layout had four main features. Along both the front and back walls were two irregular land masses representing Europe and America. In between were two large islands. The one to the north was an oval shaped Britain with huge harbours for ships and the other was a potato shaped Africa with only one big river.

"The Congo," Graham replied.

Peter gave a wry grin. "Why not the Nile or the Niger or the Zambezi?" he asked with humorous sarcasm. Graham could only shrug with embarrassment.

A narrow strait led between Europe and Africa. This had the huge Rock of Gibraltar dominating it. Turning east led into the Mediterranean and to the island of Malta (just a square harbour). Turning west led to the Atlantic via the bottom of Africa. There was no Red Sea or Indian Ocean. Between Britain and Africa was a scattering of six islands. Five belonged to Britain and one to France.

"Are we having France in the game?" Alex asked.

"No. The Trogs can take their place," Graham replied.

"Trogs-Frogs! Hah, hah, hah!" laughed Max.

Peter frowned. "Don't you like the French?" he asked.

Max shook his head. "Nah. Mob of arrogant trouble makers. I can't stand them," he replied.

Into Graham's mind flashed a searing image of Cindy and the French sailor and he nearly retorted that his sister really liked them. With an effort of will he managed to hold his tongue.

Once the map was drawn the hard bargaining began. Peter made the obvious statement that they all had to have at least one big country each.

"I am having the Trogs and Britain," Graham said.

"I will have the Germans and the Alexians," Alex said.

"Where are the Alexians?" Peter asked. Alex pointed to what had been North America, an almost rectangular country with two huge harbours and an east and south coast. No one objected to this. Graham pointed to five islands off the south coast of Alexia, and said, "These are the West Indies and they belong to Britain and France."

"What about Spain?" Peter asked.

"They used to own them but lost them in the wars," Graham said

"Is there a Spain?" Max asked.

"Yes, this country here between the Trogs and the Rock."

"So what's this one here?" Max asked, pointing to the next peninsular of Europe.

"Italy," Graham replied.

"What if I have them?" Max asked.

Again there was no objection. Peter now pointed to the area north east of Germany. This was in the small storeroom. "Is that Russia?"

"Yes," Graham answered.

"Must be mine then," Peter replied. They all laughed and no one disputed the claim. Peter's surname was Bronsky and his great grandparents had fled from Russia at the time of the Communist Revolution in 1917.

Peter again studied the map. "Now, everyone else has two countries so I would like that big bit there which I take it used to be South America?"

"Yes it was," Graham agreed.

Alex laughed. "You can set up a Banana Republic," he suggested.

"No I won't," Peter replied. "It is not South America. It is the fabled land of Atlantis."

That got some laughs. Graham said, "So we can sink your country as well as your ships!"

"You can try," Peter said.

"What about this skinny bit here; Central America?" Alex asked.

"We can divide it into a couple of small countries and fight over them," Peter suggested.

"Same with Africa," Max said.

"The top half is all desert," Graham added.

Alex stepped over onto it and swept his hand across it. "Cut it into four and we can draw straws to decide who gets which bit," he suggested.

They did this. The whole of the top half became the desert country of Erg-el-Domia. "The Domain or Kingdom of the Sand," Peter explained. That went to Max. Graham got West Africa which he called Nepa after a country in a *Phantom* comic. The south central country went to Alex as Simba, the Lion Kingdom; and the one opposite the Straits of Gibraltar went to Peter as Mauretania.

Lucrania, wedged in between Germany, Italy and a small country right near the door was allocated to Graham, who insisted that it really belonged to Kylie.

Alex pointed to the small country near the door. "That only leaves this one over in the corner between Germany and Italy," Alex said. "What is it?"

"Romania?" Graham suggested.

"Good idea," Peter agreed. "It will be flat and have a huge oil field, so we can fight over the oil."

"Who gets it?" Max asked.

"Me," Peter said. "You can't or you would have two countries side by side and that is silly."

Max had to accept this. They then drew two copies of the map. The first was coloured in four colours, one for each of them to show ownership. The names were added. The second had every colour in the spectrum to denote particular countries. This led to some argument about national colours.

"Black for Germany," Alex said.

"Why?"

"Because they have black crosses for markings, and the SS wore black uniforms," Graham replied.

"And yellow for Italy," Max added.

"Why yellow? Their flag is red, white and green," Peter asked.

Max shrugged. "Because it is my favourite colour, and because the Trogs are going to be blue, white and green and the British are red, white and blue," he explained.

"And Lucrania is green and white," Graham added. "So we need different colours. Yellow will do, and brown for the Russians because that is the colour their uniforms were."

"With a red flag and red stars on their planes and tanks," Peter added.

"Let's mark it out now," Alex said. They all agreed with this idea and rushed downstairs. Chalk was found and Graham set to work going over the coastlines. He was very pleased that the original coastlines of his earlier game were to stay, and was happy with his allocation of countries.

"What about the topography?" Peter asked, "You know, mountains and rivers?"

"The Rock goes back," Graham said. He went out to the garden and lugged the football sized rock back in and positioned it.

Max pointed down. "We must have the Pyrenees between France and Spain," he insisted. "Where are those rocks you had there Graham?"

These were found and a line of stones was placed along the 2 metres of border, with two very obvious passes left. "This is the Pass of Rosconvales, where Roland blew his horn," Graham explained, pointing to a gap in the stones.

Peter walked over to the border between the Trogs and Germany. "The Rhine River should run along here."

An almost straight Rhine about 3 metres long and 10cms wide was chalked in. Other rivers were added and a range of mountains piled up between Italy and the Trogs (the Alps). More mountains were placed between Italy, Lucrania, Germany and Romania.

"The Transylvanian Alps," Peter explained.

"I've heard of them," Alex said. "Why are they famous?"

Max laughed. "That is where the Vampires come from," he replied. For a few moments he imitated Count Dracula biting a victim.

Peter smiled. "Suits you," he observed.

Graham went to the work bench in the corner over Russia and lifted down his battleship. He placed her in the main harbour of Britain. "Portsmouth," he said.

Max laughed. "The ship is half as long as the country!"

"Doesn't matter," Graham replied. "It is only a game."

Alex walked to his own main harbour in Alexia. "The battleships will be able to fight each other without even leaving port," he said.

Peter nodded. "Yes, there is a scale problem," he agreed.

"How much?" Max asked. "How far could a battleship really shoot?"

Graham answered that: "A long way. At the Battle of Calabria in 1940 the *Warspite* opened fire at 26,000 yards; and she hit the Italian flagship with her first or second salvo. *Warspite* had 15" guns."

Peter tugged at his chin and made some mental calculations. "If the ship is about 250 metres long and it can fire say 25,000 metres and our model is about a metre long, and a scale of 1:240, then... hmmm... er... then if the model could shoot it could fire 100 metres."

"How far is that?" Alex asked.

"Well, a swimming pool is 50 metres and a football field is 100 metres long so 100 metres would be from here to the houses over the road," Peter answered.

There was silence for a moment while they digested this. Graham then shrugged and said, "So we just ignore it. We can always play with the ships outside on the lawn or on a map using tokens instead of models."

"Map would be best," Peter agreed.

Max pointed to his feet. He was standing in the Straits of Gibraltar. "Ships will have trouble getting through these narrow channels too," he said. "One big gun in a fort will stop them."

"Or a torpedo tube," Graham agreed.

"You can't put torpedo tubes on land!" Max cried.

"You can so!" Graham replied heatedly. "The Norwegians did it. That is how they sank the German heavy cruiser *Blucher* in 1940. And the Turks had them on the wharf at the Dardanelles in 1915. I've seen photos my dad took when he visited the place."

Max had to concede this. Peter then added. "A single mine will block up any of these straits."

"My oath!" Alex agreed. "And if a big ship was sunk in the channel then nothing could get through."

Max frowned. "How will we have mines? How can we show where they are without everyone else knowing?" he asked.

"Same way as submerged submarines," Peter answered. "Mark them on a map and get an adjudicator to decide."

"We should ban them," Alex suggested.

They considered this for a minute. Graham studied the narrow straits and harbour entrances and was appalled. His fleets would have great difficulty moving around if there were mines. *I will need minesweepers at every port,* he thought. He wasn't quite sure how minesweepers worked. He knew there were several types of underwater mines: the old fashioned contact type anchored to the seabed, which had horns protruding for ships to bump; magnetic mines which went off when a steel ship went over them; and acoustic mines which were set off by the sound of a ship's machinery and propellers. His mind wandered onto the problem of building model minesweepers.

It was agreed at length that it would be unrealistic to ban either mines or submarines. "Aircraft give us the same problem as big guns," Peter pointed out. "A fast plane could cover this whole game area in a few minutes. We can't ban planes."

"Unless we move the game back in time to before World War 1," Graham said. He was happy to do that, but then the problem of armies arose.

Peter shook his head. "Then we have no tanks. They weren't invented until 1916." So it was decided to keep the game in the 1940s. "Before guided missiles and all that electronics," Peter added.

Peter then raised the issue of the countries having economies and money. "That way a country could only have the armed forces it could afford," he explained.

"Did you work out those prices?" Graham asked.

"Yes I did. Here they are," Peter said. Opening a folder he took out a sheet of paper. He held this so the others could read it. "It isn't exact," he explained. "I had to guess at some of the prices of things like tanks and bombers. The ships are roughly correct though."

Graham ran his eye down the list and was surprised by the differences in price. One battleship for 700 points as against a destroyer for 35. *You could get twenty destroyers for the price of one battleship!* he marvelled. It was food for thought. Inshore minesweepers, he noted, were only 2 points. *Cheap enough to lose a few.*

Peter held up another price list. "These are costs of World War 1 ships. We can use them for map games where there are no aeroplanes."

Graham looked at them and was surprised to see that the price of ships had risen dramatically from World War 1 to World War 2. A Tribal-class destroyer of 1939 cost as much as a World War 1 light cruiser; and battleships had risen from about £2,500,000 to £7,000,000.

Max asked: "We are going to need a lot of money for each country if we do this. How much would a large country need?"

"Thousands," Peter replied. "I did up some rules and calculations." He took out a sheaf of papers covered with tables of figures and lists. These were passed around. To Graham it seemed a good idea but a bit complex.

Alex didn't like it. "This will get too bloody complicated," he objected. "I don't want to waste half my time doing bloody sums and paperwork. I get enough of that at school!"

Max seconded this: "I just want to play with models."

"So how do we control how much any country has?" Peter asked.

"By how hard the owner works," Graham suggested. "If they work hard and make lots of models then good luck to them."

"Yes, but then we will get people just whacking together cheap and nasty models of low quality," Peter objected.

We have a few already, Graham thought, with Max's battleship in mind. He said, "We can have some sort of minimum standard for quality, and if there is any argument then we can put it to the vote."

This was agreed to. Peter then said, "We can still use these prices for map games. We can try out a series of games where each player has the same amount of money but can select their own fleet secretly before the game."

"That will be interesting," Graham agreed. "I'd like to try that."

Max shook his head. "Let's get this game here set up first," he said.

They each set to work planning and moving things. Graham carried all his models down and placed them on the concrete. Alex did likewise and Max went home to get his. When all the ships, tanks and planes were placed on the floor they looked very sparse and scattered.

Graham had divided his few British ships up to have two fleets: Home Fleet and Mediterranean Fleet. *I need another battleship and another carrier,* he mused, *And some small ships for escorts and jobs like the West Indies Guardship.*

Next he deployed his Trog ships, with the same problem. Trogolitia, like France, had two coasts, and also some overseas territories. Alex added some wooden blocks for buildings and chalked in a few roads.

Then he added a couple of plastic caps off insect spray cans as oil tanks. The others did likewise but the supply of blocks soon ran out.

It was afternoon tea time by then so they trooped upstairs and sat discussing the game. After that Peter suggested a game of Battleships on maps as he had no models to play with yet. This was agreed to. Graham agreed to be the adjudicator and they ruled up sheets of white paper into 1cm squares and quickly cut out two sets of balsa tokens. Alex lost interest at this stage and went off so Peter and Max played. They used Mr Conkey's rules and Peter's World War 1 price list. Both players were allowed 1000 points.

While Max and Peter cut out more tokens Graham moved the flower vase off the dining room table and stuck down the maps with sticky tape. Then he used two marble book ends to hold up a sheet of plywood between the two maps. The respective fleets were then positioned by the two players so that they could not see what the opponent had, or where it was placed. As they finished this Graham did a quick count, interested to see what ships each had decided to have. He noted that both had an armoured cruiser and three light cruisers but that Peter had opted for only two battleships whereas Max had three. This allowed Peter ten destroyers and thirteen subs against Max's four destroyers and five subs.

It was an interesting battle. Peter won, and it was the extra subs and destroyers that gave him the victory, but only just. Graham filed away the results for when it was his turn to play. By the time the game was finished it was time for the others to go home. After they had gone Graham sat and read for a while, feeling quite contented. It had been a good day.

After tea Graham went to his desk and considered minesweepers. He found a photo of a British Algerine-class minesweeper and went to the scrap box to find a suitable hull. A nice piece of soft white pine caught his eye. It was 3cm wide, 2cm high and 15cm long. He decided it would do. Without drawing any plans he cut off and shaped the bow and stern, then rasped and sandpapered them. With a saw he cut away the back to give a lower quarterdeck. A small block provided the bridge.

Then he returned to his desk and added a cardboard funnel, bamboo mast, a balsa 4" gun in a small turret, two AA guns, searchlight, two lifeboats, five depth charges and a crane for the paravanes. By bedtime the minesweeper was completed and he really liked it. It looked just the job. He placed it on the table and went to bed very happy.

Chapter 27

A CHANGE OF HEART ?

Graham took his new book on battleship design to school. During the breaks he sat and read it. In class he jotted notes on the models he needed to make for each of his new countries. This kept him pleasantly occupied and out of mischief for the whole day. Several times he met Thelma's eye and smiled. She smiled back but it was only a perfunctory good manners smile.

How can I ask her out? What can I do to impress her? he wondered. He was sure she had enjoyed the party and that she did not find him repulsive so he still had hopes.

Goaded by urgent physical desire he also had vague hopes of enjoying a bit more with Cindy so at lunch time he went looking for her. He found her all right, but got a rude shock. She was sitting with two of her friends—and with three Year 11 boys. The boys were obviously trying to impress the girls, to win on. Equally obviously the girls were responding. One of the boys had his arm around Cindy's shoulders. The sight made Graham seethe with jealousy. With his ego somewhat deflated, Graham wandered back to join his mates in their usual place.

After school he went straight home and set to work on his second battleship, the HMS *Nelson*. For the hull he had found a plank of pine that was nearly a metre long, 12cm wide and 2.5cm thick. He marked out the hull shape with pencil and went down to the Ship Room to saw it to shape. While he was engaged in this task Alex came in and watched. Graham made no attempt to hide it.

He will see it on my desk anyway, he thought.

Alex said, "Can you go to town to pay the electricity bill? I have to go to footy practice."

"Why can't you do it while you are out?" Graham asked.

"Don't be silly! That is on the other side of town," Alex answered. "You go. Mum wants it done today. It should have been paid on Friday but she forgot."

With bad grace Graham took the money and bill and went upstairs to put on his shoes again. Then he wheeled out his bike and set off In town he parked his bike and walked along, alternately looking in shops and admiring the girls.

As he approached a cafe with tables on the footpath he noted several girls in the uniform of his school. When he was close he looked to see who they were, and his heart leapt. The one facing him was Thelma. With her were Janet and a girl he did not know. Then his heart fell with a thud. They were with Jerry Denham, Edmonson, and a youth who looked to be about twenty.

Thelma saw him first. For an instant Graham got the impression she was just going to look away and ignore him, but she nodded and gave a little smile.

Plucking up his courage Graham smiled back. "Hello Thelma, hello Janet," he said as he passed. He would have dearly liked to stop but did not dare.

Thelma nodded but did not answer. Edmonson turned to see who it was and a look of dislike crossed his face. Graham tensed ready for a fight. Then Janet looked up. "Hello sailor!" she called in a sarcastic tone.

Graham went red and Janet laughed mischievously. As he walked on Graham heard the youth ask: "Why did you say that to him?"

"'Cause he's in the navy cadets," Janet explained.

Graham did not hear any more but felt uncomfortable as long as he was in sight of the cafe. He was particularly worried that Edmonson might follow him to give him more grief. But he didn't so Graham went on to the shop and payed the bill. Outside again he hesitated on which way to go back to his bike. For a moment he considered walking right around the block as he did not want to be teased again. Then he gritted his teeth. *No. That is stupid. Worse, it's gutless. I'll go back the way I came.*

Steeling himself for a bad time he set off along the footpath. By the time he was approaching the café his heart was beating fast and his palms were sweaty but he was determined to not let Thelma think he was a coward. *Even if it means a few bruises and teeth knocked out,* he thought.

Feeling very self-conscious and afraid he rounded the corner. From half way along the block he saw that the girls were still seated there but Edmonson was gone. Anxiously Graham approached, ready for trouble. But he need not have bothered. This time they barely responded to his greeting. Janet did not even look at him but continued her conversation with the youth. That gave Graham the chance to learn his name; or at least his nickname, as Janet called him.

"Pinky! What a stupid nickname," Graham muttered angrily as he walked on. His anger was increased by the knowledge that he was jealous. Pinky was doing just what he longed to do: sit at the cafe with the girls!

In a grumpy mood he rode home and resumed work on the new model battleship. By tea time he had planed and sanded the hull and marked out in pencil where the main items were to be placed on the deck. Then he slid the hull under his bed and took his new minesweeper: the HMS *Seagull*, down to the Ship Room. He placed her at Gibraltar to keep the straits open.

For 10 minutes Graham stood there and considered what else he needed. The weakness of the Trog army and navy were glaringly obvious. "They have overseas territories and no-one to defend them," he told himself. With that in mind he went upstairs and set to work to make five small armoured cars for the Trog Foreign Legion. Having completed these he then had the idea to give them a Beau Geste type fort as their base.

Using white cardboard he cut out four walls each 10cms long and 2cms high. A doorway was cut out and then crenellations to show the battlements. The sides were glued together and he then made a tower 4cm square and 5cm high to place in one corner for the living accommodation. A flagpole and Trog flag were added as the finishing touches. He was very pleased with this and took it down to place it in West Africa (Nepa), right on the desert border of the Erg.

When he went to school on Tuesday Graham took a small tin box in which he had pieces of balsa of various thicknesses, plus pins, razor blades, wire, tweezers and other odd items. His plan was to use his spare time making more tanks and aircraft. His priority was the Trogs but somehow he sidetracked himself into only making one tank, a British Crusader, copied from a war comic.

But what really blew his building program was the fact that Thelma smiled at him and said hello. *She spoke to me!* he thought in astonishment. He was so surprised he could not think straight for the next 10 minutes. In class he glanced over towards her frequently, and was rewarded by her meeting his eye and grinning. For the rest of that lesson his mind was in turmoil. *She has noticed me! Oh my God! What do I do now?*

He did not know. But that did not matter. When they were dismissed for morning break Thelma came over and talked to him.

"Hi Graham. Where were you going yesterday afternoon?"

"Just going to pay the electricity bill for mum," he explained. He knew he should not ask but he was so curious he did: "Who was that with you yesterday?"

"Who, Jerry?"

"No. That other bloke?"

"Oh Pinky? He's a Uni student. He's a friend of Janet's sister," Thelma replied. She smiled and said, "Thanks for inviting me to your party. I really enjoyed it. It was the best party I've been to for a long time."

"Gee! Thanks Thelma," Graham replied. He blushed and glowed at the same time. She chattered on about the party for a few minutes while they walked downstairs. Graham expected her to wander off to her friends at that point but she didn't. To his delight she stayed and stood talking to him. She even laughed at one of his jokes. Standing talking to Thelma made Graham feel very self-conscious as he could see Stephen and Angus looking at them, but despite this he listened happily to what she had to say.

By the time they went in to class again Graham was on cloud nine. His hopes soared and he began to reconsider his plans to ask her for a date. But what to say? And where to go?

At lunch time Thelma again spoke to him. Graham was thrilled. *I didn't even have to go over to her! She came to me!* That gave him a problem of what to talk about. He had enough common sense, and enough self-control, to avoid talking about ships and the navy. Instead he clowned, told jokes, and described the family pets (Kylie's really: the pup Skip, the two budgerigars, the guinea pigs and the fish). This sufficed to keep them going without awkward pauses.

While Graham was packing his bag after the last lesson he found Thelma again beside him talking. That tore him in two directions as he had promised Peter he would go over to his house to play Battleships after school. *Bugger Battleships!* he thought. Now that Thelma was talking to him he did not want to miss one second of it.

What followed just seemed to develop naturally. Thelma packed her bag and picked it up and the pair went down the stairs together, still talking. At the bottom she paused to turn right. Normally Graham would have turned left but to get to Peter's he also had to turn right.

Thelma stopped. "See you tomorrow then Graham."

"Sure. Yes. I mean... I am going this way too. I am going over to Peter Bronsky's," he stammered.

"He's nice. He's very brainy isn't he?" Thelma said, starting to walk. Graham walked with her, experiencing a twinge of panic, lest she not want him to walk with her, and jealousy, about Peter. Thus he walked nearly all the way to her home with her. She only lived four blocks away, one from Peter's. They even stopped on the corner near her house to talk for 5 minutes before she said goodbye.

Blissfully happy, Graham strode on to Peter's. Peter and his little brother Paul were busy in their workshop under the house when he knocked. Peter turned to see who it was and cried out: "You can't come in here. We shoot spies. Go upstairs."

Graham did so, wondering what secret Peter was hatching below. After a few minutes Peter and Paul came up. Refreshments followed then the game was set up on a table in the front room. The game was played by the same rules as before and using the same price list. Peter handed Graham a photocopy of it to work from. Paul was the adjudicator, on the understanding he would get a game another day.

Graham took out a notebook and the checked over his ideas for the ideal fleet. Using his 1000 points he selected four battleships, five destroyers and ten subs. Using his razor he cut tokens for these out of the balsa in his box and placed these on his half of the map, wondering what Peter was laying out on the other side of the screen.

"OK, ready." he said, taking another gulp of cold lime cordial. Paul wrote on a notepad and said, "It is 0600 hours. This is what you can see."

He then measured the 20cm visibility distance and began to place tokens on the two maps of what the opposing fleets could see of each other. Graham was pleased to discover five enemy destroyers immediately. He thought Peter could only see three of his. All were out of range so Paul noted the new time.

"It is 0615. You can both move."

Graham moved all his tokens forward the allowed distances, keeping the battle squadron in a tight line astern. Peter seemed to take a long time to move, which was worrying to Graham. He speculated on what the composition of Peter's fleet might be. When both had moved Paul did the visibility and added more tokens to both maps. From watching Paul's eye movements and body Graham decided that all five of his destroyers and probably one of his battleships were then in sight of the enemy. A quick check led him to deduce that the destroyers were 8cm apart and the leading battleship 18cm from the nearest enemy destroyer. By then ten destroyers were marked from Peter's fleet, spread right across the map.

Aha! Pete has opted for less battleships and lots of destroyers, Graham thought.

All ships were still out of range so they moved again: 0630. At the end of this Graham's whole fleet was visible to Peter but he had only found thirteen of Peter's destroyers and no larger ships. By then the destroyers had closed so that some of them were within 4cm of each other and firing began. The dice rattled and notes were made of hits and losses. Three of Graham's battleships were able to fire as well as all his destroyers but at the end of the round he had lost three destroyers and only sunk four of Peter's.

They were told to move again. Seven more destroyers appeared on Peter's side. Graham was appalled at how rapidly a dozen of these were closing the range on his battleships and he turned the line to starboard. Even so the move ended with four of Peter's destroyers only 3cm away from his leading battleship. The dice rattled as torpedoes were launched and guns blazed. There were loud, excited cries as ships were hit. Graham was gripped by alarm as his first battleship was torpedoed and sunk and his second damaged so that it could only move at half speed. In return the battleships blasted all of the attacking destroyers, plus three more. Graham did a count and saw that Peter still had ten destroyers on the map.

They moved again and five more destroyers joined Peter's headlong attack. Six got within torpedo range of the battleships. One of Graham's destroyers had slipped through Peter's ships and could see the back of the maps. No large enemy ships were visible to it. *Hasn't Peter got any large ships?* Graham wondered. A sinking suspicion formed in his mind about the composition of the rest of Peter's fleet. *Submarines! And lots of them.*

This was confirmed immediately when Paul placed three submerged sub tokens near his two destroyers. Suddenly those two destroyers became vital assets—and one was right behind the enemy fleet!

Firing was done. Graham lost his slow battleship and the third battleship, all to torpedoes from the attacking destroyers. In return he managed to blast another six of them. One enemy sub was sunk by his closest destroyer.

With only one battleship left, plus two destroyers, Graham began a withdrawal. On the next move his last battleship was sunk, along with one destroyer. They took six enemy destroyers with them, leaving only two. But Graham's sole surviving ship was now in contact with four subs, all of which fired torpedoes at it.

During the next two moves Graham struggled desperately to extricate his destroyer. He sank another sub but detected three more! *And Peter's two surviving destroyers are now on their way back and closing the range fast!*

The end was inevitable. Graham sank one more enemy sub before three of them torpedoed his ship. They agreed that submerged subs could not harm each other, not using the technology of 1914, so the game was over.

Despite his defeat Graham was happy. "That was a bloody good game!" he cried. "What did you have in your fleet Pete?"

"Fifty subs and twenty-five destroyers," Peter replied.

It was on the tip of Graham's tongue to retort that that wasn't fair; but he knew it was. Ruefully he conceded that Peter was a smart bugger all right. *I should have guessed. I've known him long enough,* he thought.

The game had taken two hours and Graham had thoroughly enjoyed it. "That was fun," he said. "Can we play again tomorrow?"

"If you like. Paul will get his go then if that's all right?"

"Sure. I'd better go. It will be dark soon and mum will start to worry," Graham replied.

He collected his tokens and packed them, then set off home. On the way he looked longingly up Thelma's street, hoping for a glimpse of her. Sweet fantasies of true love filled his mind as he walked. It was a fair distance and he considered whether he should have brought his bike to school. *No. Then I wouldn't be able to walk with Thelma,* he decided.

At home that night he resumed work on his new battleship model.

The superstructure was built up using a piece of 1cm thick balsa cut to shape for the lowest level, and the one above. On top of that he placed a tower of cardboard with the bridge and various projections on it. The fire control range finders and fighting tops were added, made out of balsa and with pins down through them so they could rotate. A cardboard funnel was added which had the effect of transforming it into a ship.

He went to bed very pleased with his day.

***

Graham went to school full of hope and expectation the next day. He sang and whistled as he walked along, his mind full of dreams. As soon as he got to school he looked for Thelma. She was with Janet and another girl. As Graham hesitated he saw Janet nudge Thelma and nod in his direction. Thelma looked. then smiled and stood up. To Graham's surprise and relief Thelma walked over to him so he did not have to talk to her with the other girls listening.

When she started talking happily to him Graham's fears that yesterday had just been some sort of mistake evaporated. *She really must like me!* he decided.

His happiness grew as the day went on. Thelma talked to him at little lunch and again at big lunch and seemed to be happy. Graham glowed, aware that others were noticing. It made him feel good. He was even more thrilled when, after he told a silly joke to Thelma, she impulsively put out her hand and touched his forearm.

That made him tingle and his pulses race. His hopes grew. He began to dream of the golden moment when they might actually kiss.

But I mustn't rush it. That might put her off, he cautioned himself. He began to agonize again over asking her for a date.

The crown was placed on his happiness when even that trial suddenly evaporated. She suggested he might like to walk her home. So as soon as classes were over Graham hurried down and waited near the bike racks. While he stood waiting he had another slightly upsetting experience. Nearby the army cadets were getting ready for their weekly Home Training parade. Among the camouflage army uniforms Graham noted several people in school uniform.

That is Cindy, he noted. For the next few minutes he watched her.

At first he thought she must be considering joining the army cadets but that seemed unlikely. But when the cadets were all called to move on parade and she waved to one of the Year 11 boys he realized it wasn't that at all. *She is flirting,* he thought and felt quite sad and jealous. Despite that he found he was glad when she went the other way and did not see him waiting.

A few minutes later Thelma appeared and he walked her home again and when they reached the corner where they had to go their separate ways Thelma turned to him and asked: "Graham, what are you doing on Friday night?"

Friday night! he thought in a rush of panic. *What does she want?* He was about to say 'Scouts' but instead said, "Whatever you want."

She smiled at that and he felt very pleased that it had come out sounding so natural. She said, "Some of us are going to the movies. I wondered if you would like to come?"

A date! She is asking me! Graham was almost stunned into silence. There was a flash of disappointment that it would be some sort of group thing but he told himself that was only normal. At her age parents did not like serious dating. He replied: "I'd love to come. What is the movie?"

Thelma told him. He had never heard of it. "It is a love story," she said. She explained the outline but Graham could not have cared what it was about. He asked: "Who else will be going?"

"Oh, Janet and her sister and a couple of other kids," she replied.

Graham resolved to give Scouts a miss for one night. *I might never get another chance!* They settled the arrangements of when and where to meet and he went off to Peter's floating on air.

The battle against Paul went well. Paul tried Peter's tactics only with more destroyers. Graham opted for one less battleship and ten more destroyers himself. He lost all of his battleships but managed to sink all of Paul's destroyers and most of his subs before they ran out of time. It was a very happy boy that walked home that evening.

Work resumed in the shipyards on the *Nelson*. Six turrets, each mounting two 6" guns were positioned either side of the superstructure. Searchlight platforms and ladders were added to the sides of the funnel. Boats and small details were added, then the tripod mast and AA guns. By the time he went to bed the model was starting to look like a very powerful ship. *I will make the main armament tomorrow,* he thought.

After tea he faced a difficult moment when he asked his mother if he could go to the movies instead of to Scouts.

Mrs Kirk raised an eyebrow. "Who with?" she asked, once she had been told which movie.

Graham told her. She nodded and said, "Thelma was the girl in the nice yellow frock at your party wasn't she?"

Graham swallowed and nodded. "Yes mum," he replied. He was sweating now, worried she would say no. His heart beat faster with anxiety and he clenched his hands, bracing himself for bad news.

"Yes, I suppose so," she said. Graham's spirits leapt. Yes!

Milo and bed; and wonderful fantasies. And a dilemma. He became hot and horny but could not imagine a nice girl like Thelma doing crude things like that. He found himself in the grip of lust and was torn between keeping his love for Thelma pure or gaining satisfaction by fantasizing about some other girl, like Cindy.

Thursday was a good day too. As soon as he got to school Graham told Thelma he was allowed to go to the movies.

Her face broke into a smile. "That's great Graham. You will really like it," she replied. To his delight Thelma talked to him during the breaks and even sat next to him at lunch time, to the amusement of his mates. After school he walked her all the way home.

As they strolled along Thelma turned to him. "Are you playing Battleship games with Peter again?" she asked.

"No. I just wanted to be with you," Graham blurted out.

"Oh, that's sweet!" Thelma replied. Her eyes crinkled into a grin and her mouth dimpled. She touched his arm and gave it a gentle squeeze. As before the touch was like an electric shock.

After seeing Thelma home, Graham returned to his house and set to work on the model of the battleship HMS *Nelson*. To make the three main armament turrets he cut out blocks of balsa 8cm x 5cm x 6mm thick. The nine 16" gun barrels he made from 5mm balsa. He sliced a very long strip of it, shaved it and sandpapered it into a long cylinder, then cut it into nine equal lengths. To make them look bigger than the 12" guns on the *Iron Duke* he measured the length of those guns and made the new ones longer, 8cm instead of 6cm. Each barrel was then shaved and sanded to make it as close to perfectly round as he could manage, and tapered towards the muzzle. Using a black biro Graham pushed a small black hole in the end to represent the bore. Graham was almost finished when Max bounded up the stairs. There was no time to hide the ship. Max looked at it with admiring interest but to Graham's surprise he did not ask about it.

Instead he said, "Who was that girl you were with this afternoon?"

At that moment Kylie came through from the lounge room. Instantly she was all interest. "What girl?" she asked.

"Never you mind," Graham replied, going red.

Kylie lifted her nose. "Doesn't matter if you don't tell me. I'll find out, you two-timing toad!" she retorted.

That stung! "I am not!" Graham cried.

"You are too! There was that Joany girl a few weeks ago. And what about Cindy? You two were all over each other last week; you fickle cad! And what about poor Margaret?"

Graham blushed even more. Cindy! What did Kylie know? And Max? He broke into a guilty sweat. "Margaret doesn't own me. I can do as I like," he replied, hoping to take the subject off Cindy.

Kylie pursed her lips. "She loves you, though I sometimes wonder why," she replied angrily.

"She's only a kid," Graham replied hotly.

"Oh yeah? And you are all grown up?"

"But she's only in primary school," Graham replied defensively.

Kylie bristled. "Oh, a shame job to the big boy is it?" she retorted sarcastically. "She's a wonderful person, much nicer than you deserve!"

Luckily the arrival of their mother ended the argument, but it made Graham feel very uncomfortable. He and Max discussed their game and Max showed Graham some buildings he wanted to place in one of his countries. They went down to the Ship Room and Graham showed Max the Foreign Legion fort. It was obvious he was impressed, but also annoyed and jealous.

That evening Graham finished the main armament of the *Nelson* and positioned it on the model. *Only some minor details to add,* he thought. *Now, what will I build next?* It occurred to him that he had no merchant ships to group into convoys. That sent him to the plan book to draw one; a simple Three Island steamship typical of that era.

In bed that night he was again aroused and torn by emotions. Only one more day and he would be at the pictures with Thelma! But what

Kylie had said about Margaret and Cindy gnawed at him. *Damn! It is Thelma I love. I will decide,* he told himself.

But guilt over Cindy would not go away so easily. He could not rid himself of the idea that his attempts to get her to misbehave had contributed to her downfall. The idea made him feel awful and he wondered what he could do to repair the damage. *But how?* he agonized.

Very unhappy and mixed-up, he finally drifted into a restless sleep.

Chapter 28

FIRST DATE

For the whole of Friday Graham was a-tingle with anticipation. All he could think about was Thelma and the coming date. Pleasant and exciting fantasies floated through his imagination, fuelled by her smiling at him and talking to him during the breaks. The only fly in the ointment was his body which seemed to be out of his control. He became continually aroused and became deeply worried that Thelma would somehow become aware of this and be disgusted.

After school he rushed home. By then he was actually trembling with nervous tension and barely suppressed excitement. *Tonight! I will be with Thelma tonight!* he thought. Then time seemed to drag. He worked on the final details of the *Nelson*, adding breakwaters, bollards, capstans and other small details to the focsle.

The best touch was to use tiny chains, bought from a shop which sold jewellery for young girls, as the anchor chains. These were cut to the correct length and glued on so that they led from a hole in the foredeck, around a small balsa capstan and then forward to another hole which represented the hawse hole. The finished product looked very good and he felt particularly pleased.

When Alex had finished reading the *Phantom* comic their mother had bought (big brother's prerogative to read it first!) Graham lay and read that. Then he fidgeted and fretted.

During tea Kylie pretended to ignore him and let him know she did not approve. Graham did not care. He was about to achieve a long cherished dream. To ensure he did not smell he took special care over his shower and used some of the aftershave he had been given. He even used some of his mum's antiseptic mouth wash to ensure he did not have bad breath.

Then he dressed with particular care, wearing the new long trousers, new shirt and his black leather shoes which he polished specially.

At last it was time to go. Alex took no apparent interest but Kylie scowled when his mother checked that he was suitably dressed. By then Graham was a bundle of nerves. Should he have a little gift? Or flowers? He dimly knew that men sometimes gave ladies flowers when they took them out but wasn't sure of the etiquette of it all. He felt uncomfortable and worried about his appearance (that pimple on his cheek that he had only noticed after his shower!).

His mother drove him to the theatre, dropping him off with strict instructions to wait there for her to pick him up. "Cairns isn't the nice little safe town it was when I was your age," she said. "Now it is full of riff-raff from the south." It was one of her constant themes: how tourism had done little for the locals other than destroy their lifestyle and the environment.

Graham stood on the footpath outside the theatre feeling very self-conscious and nervous. He read the adverts for coming attractions and tried to pretend he was relaxed. Every few seconds he looked around, hoping to see the girls, prey to the deep fear that it was all some sort of a joke or misunderstanding and they weren't coming. For a while he agonized over being left standing there like a fool; 'stood up' was the term he had heard used to describe the situation. Glance after glance at his watch showed him that it was almost 7pm; time for the movie to start.

He chewed another fingernail and began to pace up and down. His stomach felt unsettled and he had a sudden urge to go to the toilet. He rushed in and emptied his bladder, then raced back outside to find the girls arriving in the foyer. Relief coursed through him.

There were five people: Thelma, Janet and Jerry, Danelle and Pinky. Thelma saw him and waved. "There he is. Hi Graham! Have you got your ticket?"

Graham shuddered with relief. He had not bought his ticket for fear they might not turn up. Smiling he shook his head and joined them in the queue at the ticket office. Pinky was introduced and shook hands perfunctorily. Obviously Graham was too unimportant for him to worry about. Graham smiled nervously at Thelma and she gave him a worried smile back.

She is nervous too! he realized. That thought made him feel better. He tried to think of things to talk about but was tongue-tied. Luckily Danelle did enough talking for all of them. Graham studied her covertly. She looked very grown up and sophisticated. *About seventeen or eighteen,* he decided. To Graham she looked very attractive, her hair shining in the lamplight. But something about her attitude and poise scared him.

They made their way inside just as the lights dimmed and had to bump and jostle to find their seats. Luckily the theatre was only half full so they had a choice of where they sat. All Graham wanted to do was sit beside Thelma but in the confusion she went into the row of seats first and Janet followed her. Only when the others began sitting was it realized that Graham was still standing in the aisle.

Danelle noticed this. "Move along one," she called.

"No," Pinky replied. "You don't want him sitting beside you. You never know what sailors pick up down the waterfront. Move past kid and sit with Thelma."

Graham blushed furiously, glad it was dark so it would not be noticed. He climbed past over their knees and feet feeling very embarrassed. There were several spare seats past Thelma and he slumped thankfully into the one next to her. In the light from the screen he saw her eyes watching him nervously.

He tried to make a joke to ease the tension but Jerry said, "Ssh! Shut up! I want to follow the story."

Graham lapsed into flustered silence. Through his shirt sleeve he could just feel Thelma's elbow on the arm rest. He moved away and leaned on the other side, fearful she might think him too pushy or forward. Later he could barely remember the movie but every detail of what followed was clear in his mind.

Thelma's proximity dominated everything. Graham could hear her breathing, could feel her move in her seat. Out of the corner of his eye he noted every tiny movement of her hands. She crossed her legs, then uncrossed them. She gripped her hands together, then placed them in her lap, then to her mouth as the movie moved into high drama. By this time Graham was in a lather over what to do. When Thelma spoke to him he turned his head and noted that Jerry had his arm around Janet's shoulders.

That was what he dearly longed to do, or at least to hold Thelma's hand, but he did not know how to go about it. He decided that the slow approach was the one to use, where he could pretend the contact was accidental and could withdraw with some semblance of pride if she hinted his advance wasn't what she wanted. Very slowly he moved in his seat until he was leaning on the same armrest as her. After about 10 minutes he eased across to actually touch her arm.

To his enormous relief she did not move away. Instead she seemed to lean against him so that their upper arms were in contact. It felt wonderful and Graham felt his pulses race with excitement and delight. This turned to consternation when he discovered he was getting aroused. *Not now!* he thought in horror. He tried to will his body to subside but the more he thought about it the worse it seemed to get.

Interval arrived, throwing Graham into a flap. *Will she expect me to buy her a drink or something?* he wondered. He had brought money for this but was scared to ask; and did not want to stand up lest she notice he was aroused. So he sat up and pretended to stretch, then smiled at her. Jerry stood up and asked Janet what she wanted.

Graham took that as his cue. "Would you like a drink or some chocolates Thelma?" he asked. His palms were so sweaty he wiped them on his trousers.

She smiled and nodded. "An orange drink would be nice. I need to go out anyway. Come on Janet."

Both Thelma and Janet both stood up. To his relief his body relaxed. He followed the girls along the row. As he passed Pinky and Danelle he got a shock. Pinky had his arm over Danelle's shoulder and his left hand was resting firmly on her front.

Graham tried to pretend he had not seen. *I wonder if Thelma noticed?* he thought. That set his mind racing. Girl's bosoms fascinated him and now played a major role in his thoughts and fantasies and he had a fervent desire to touch them. Hot memories of fondling Cindy surged in his mind, making him both guilty and excited. But Thelma's? He recoiled from that. *She is a nice girl. She wouldn't approve of me trying to do anything like that,* he thought.

Out in the foyer he joined the queue at the refreshment counter while the girls went to the toilet. By the time they reappeared, giggling and chattering, he had purchased two orange drinks and some chocolate Smarties. He offered a packet to Thelma. "I didn't know if you liked them or not," he explained apologetically.

Thelma smiled. "Thanks, I do," she replied. She smiled again and took them and the drink. They walked around looking at the 'Coming Attractions' posters and Graham found he could not think of anything to say. The girls chattered to each other and he followed them, feeling a bit like a spare wheel. It was a relief when they went back inside and sat down.

The problem of whether to make any physical advance to Thelma then re-asserted itself as his number one priority. The lights dimmed and the main movie began. Graham fidgeted and kept glancing sideways. He saw Jerry casually place his arm around Janet. She snuggled up against him. Graham sighed. If only! It looked so easy, but he was terrified of making a mistake. He sat almost rigid and watched the movie, trying to summon up the courage to make a move.

Thelma laughed at a scene in the movie and turned to him. "That was good," she whispered, her arm nudging his.

Graham nodded and found difficulty answering. His throat seemed to be constricted. He felt very tense. Cautiously he put his arm up on the arm rest. It bumped against hers, which was already there.

"Oh sorry!" he said, pulling it away.

"It's all right," she said. She turned and he met her eyes. For a moment hers searched his face. "Relax Graham. I don't bite."

He flushed with embarrassment and could only mumble a reply. For the next 10 minutes he sat in a state of growing turmoil. Time was slipping away and he was doing nothing! *She asked me. She must like me,* he told himself. But that wasn't much help. All sorts of old sayings he had heard over the years flitted through his brain: 'Nothing ventured, nothing gained'; 'Faint heart never won fair lady'; 'It is better to try your luck early to save wasting time and money.'

He took a deep breath and reached over to take her hand. For a moment he thought she was going to snatch it away. Then she let him hold it and leaned against his shoulder. He trembled with released tension and delight. Her hand felt very warm and slightly moist, not at all like he had expected. *Not like Margaret's,* he thought. Hers were warm but smooth and dry. And Cindy's were cool and smooth.

Movement further along the row caught his eye. When he looked his eyes opened wide in surprise. Janet and Jerry were in a passionate embrace and were stroking each other. *I wonder if Thelma can see them?* he worried. Then he decided she could. *She must be able to, she is closer.*

That was an exciting shock to him. The thought of it, added to the touch and smell of Thelma, soon had him aroused again. Then he realized he was being ridiculous. *I did far more with Cindy, and even with little Margaret, and all without this stress!* he told himself. But thinking of them just made him feel very guilty and increased his arousal. Then he was torn. Would Thelma ever do anything like that to him? He knew he did not dare ask or even suggest it. Nor did he want to. In his mind his love for Thelma was something noble and pure. *She is too perfect for anything sordid like that,* he thought.

But her touch was arousing and so was the situation. Jerry was obviously fondling Janet. This made Graham feel indignant. *She is only in Year 8!* he thought. But he knew he was a hypocrite and felt saddened by the knowledge.

The movie came to an end before Graham could nerve himself to make another advance. Thelma released his hand when they stood up but once outside she remained close beside him. While they stood talking and her hand brushed his. Greatly daring he took hers again, noting that Jerry was holding Janet's, and that Pinky had his arm around Danelle's waist. To his relief Thelma let him hold it. That made him feel very proud and happy.

Thelma had obviously enjoyed the movie. This saved Graham from having to make conversation as she talked about it to the others. Graham saw his mother drive past and waved, hoping she would wait while he said goodnight. That raised a whole host of new problems: How to say goodnight; how to ask if he could take her out again. *Should I try to kiss her?* he worried. *Not on a first date,* he decided. *I don't want to rush her and frighten her off.*

All his problems were solved in a few minutes. Thelma waved to a car and said, "There's mum. Come on you kids." She led them along the footpath into the darkness, still holding Graham's hand. When they reached the parked car, Thelma opened the door and said, "Mum, this is Graham."

Graham looked at her with interest, remembering his father's advice about looking at the mother because that was what the daughter was going to end up like. He saw that Mrs Severin was an older version of Thelma all right; same eyes, hair and colouring; just a crinkling of numerous small wrinkles around her eyes and mouth.

She smiled and nodded. "Hello. Now hop in you girls."

Janet moved to get into the car. As she did she gave Thelma a look and gestured towards Graham with her head. Thelma then turned to him and said, "Graham that was nice. Look, we are having a games night at Janet's tomorrow night. Would you like to come? That's all right isn't it Janet?"

Graham couldn't believe his ears. Two nights in a row! His immediate fear was whether his mum would allow it. "What kind of games?" he asked, knowing his mum would ask.

"Oh, Snakes and Ladders, Monopoly, Uno, that sort of thing," Thelma replied.

Janet giggled. "Uno, you know!" she quipped and laughed again.

"Who will be there?" Graham asked.

Thelma shrugged. "Same crowd as tonight and a couple of Danelle's friends," she replied.

Graham was thrilled. "I'd love to come."

"Tomorrow night then, 7:30, at Janet's. Just wear old clothes. It isn't a party. See you then," Thelma said. Before Graham realized what she was doing she reached up and kissed him on the cheek. The warmth and waft of her perfume made his senses reel. He couldn't believe it. It was too good to be true!

Thelma, Janet and Danelle climbed into the car. Pinky and Jerry waved as the car drove off but then just turned and walked away. Graham was left in an ecstatic daze. He walked slowly along to where his mother had parked and got in.

"Good movie dear?" she asked.

"Mmm. Yes. Great mum," he said. Then he paused, arranged his thoughts and said, "Mum, Thelma has asked if I can come over tomorrow night to Janet's to play games." He described the games. "May I?"

Mrs Kirk put the car in gear and pulled out before answering. That made Graham's heart palpitate with anxiety. "Will the parents be home?" she asked.

Graham hadn't thought to ask that. He felt his hopes crash. "I don't know. I suppose so," he replied.

"Don't forget you have your day out on the Landing Craft tomorrow. You might be very tired after that, or late. We will see how you feel when you get home from that," she said.

Graham had forgotten the trip on the LCH. For a moment his interest quickened. He resolved that no matter how tired he was he would not show it. *I want to be with Thelma!*

At home he had to tell his mother about the movie over a cup of Milo. He made no mention of holding Thelma's hand, or of what the others had been doing. All he wanted to do was get away on his own to dream of Thelma. It was with relief that he made his way to the toilet, and then to bed.

Once there he was too excited to sleep and lay fantasizing for what seemed like hours, until he slipped into a sleep filled with erotic dreams— about Cindy.

Chapter 29

HMAS TARAKAN

Graham stood self-consciously among the naval cadets standing on the wharf at HMAS *Cairns*, the naval base on Trinity Inlet. In front of him was the Landing Craft Heavy HMAS *Tarakan*. On either side were berthed other naval vessels: two Patrol Boats and a survey ship. It was 0830hrs and the sun was shining down from a clear blue sky. It was a prefect winter day in Cairns, just cool enough to cause a person to shiver in the sea breeze when not wearing a jumper.

In fact it was what he was wearing that largely contributed to Graham's self-consciousness. Because he had not been issued a uniform he wore civilian clothes: a pair of dark blue longs and a blue long-sleeved work shirt. But he felt very conspicuous as all the others wore the mottled grey and black navy camouflage work dress. On his feet he wore rubber soled gym boots and old socks. All the other cadets wore navy issue caps and Graham's was the only head with a non-regulation piece of headgear. His mother had insisted he wear a hat in the sun and the only hat available had been an old felt hat.

Before arriving at cadets Graham had taken the hat off but Lt Ryan had asked him if he had a hat and then insisted that he wear it. So now he stood among the others, wishing fervently that he looked the same as them. On the wharf in front of him stood a navy sub lieutenant in white shirt, white shorts and cap. He looked very trim and fit and had a friendly smile.

Lt Cdr Hazard introduced him. "This is Sub Lt Richards and he will be our host for the day. He will now explain the ship to you and what is going to happen, thank you Sub Lt Richards."

Sub Lt Richards nodded and cleared his throat then spoke loudly and clearly. "Well, hello cadets and welcome aboard HMAS *Tarakan*. In a moment I will have PO Wilkins give you more details and then he and his team will take you on a guided tour. Before he does that there are a number of things I must stress. First is safety. This ship is a working naval vessel and we are going to do a job of work. If you are told to go somewhere, or to stay somewhere, then obey. We don't want any accidents."

He listed things they must not do, and places they were not to go then said, "You will do a couple of safety drills before we leave the wharf including how to put on lifejackets and man overboard drill. But I will say again, just do what you are told and you will be safe. Now, the task; the ship is going out to investigate a report from some tourists of an unexploded bomb on a reef near Michaelmas Cay. That is about 20 nautical miles and will take us roughly 2 hours. There is a team of Clearance Divers on board and they will look around when we arrive. OK, this is PO Wilkins."

The Petty Officer, a chunky man with close cropped grey hair, took over. He had a seaman hand out pamphlets with the basic data on the vessel. Graham took one and looked at it. He had looked up the facts about the LCH in one of his dad's reference books the night before so already knew most of it. Even so he read the pamphlet to make sure he knew as much as he could.

'Landing Craft Heavy: Displacement 323 tonnes (loaded 511 tonnes); length 44.73 metres; beam 10.06 metres, draft 1.75 metres,' he read. *That's not much,* he thought. *She will float in water that is only just over my head!* He knew from his dad's barge that such vessels usually drew slightly more aft than forward, so that they could slip more easily back off the beach after unloading.

He noted that she was armed with two 0.5" machine guns but these were not visible. That did not surprise him as he knew that those types of small weapons were stored out of the weather until needed. The speed was given as 9.5 knots and he saw that she had a ship's company of two officers and 11 ratings. *If Sub Lt Richards is the XO then the CO must be a Lieutenant,* he reasoned.

The pamphlet mentioned that 8 LCHs were built in the 1970s and that two of them: *Salamaua* and *Buna* were transferred to the PNG Defence Force in 1974. The pamphlet listed three that were decommissioned in December 2012 and made the point that the remaining three were due to be paid off in the next few years. The three still in commission were *Tarakan, Brunei* and *Labuan*. The three decommissioned LCHs were *Balipapan, Betano* and *Wewak*.

Wewak, Graham noted. *That is the name of my dad's landing barge.*

These names obviously caught the attention of another cadet who asked: "Please sir, why do they all have these funny foreign names?"

PO Wilkins smiled and explained: "They are all named after places where Australian forces carried out amphibious landings during World War 2. Most are in Borneo and a couple in Papua New Guinea."

The cadets were then divided into four groups, by watches and part of watch, and handed over to young sailors to care for them. Officers of Cadets went with each group. The rating in charge of Graham's group was a pimply faced young man who looked like he had just left school. He said his name was Ken and they were stick to him like glue. While he talked Graham studied the details of the LCH with an eye to making a model of her.

She had a very distinctive profile. About two thirds of her length was the well deck for cargo. This was open on top. The sides of the well deck were raised towards the bow and the pennant number was painted on this; white paint with black edging on one side to make it stand out. L129. She had a flat ramp as her bow. The stern section had a deck over it and on this was a double story superstructure.

Ken led them up the gangplank onto the deck, then along a walkway on top of the sides above the well deck. Graham looked down and was disappointed to see that all she was carrying were two aluminium dinghies and two rigid inflatable boats with outboard motors. Several men were working on a litter of diving gear laid out on the deck. Most of these men wore shorts, shirt and sandals but some wore only shorts. Graham studied them with interest. They were the clearance divers. Mostly they looked very ordinary men but were certainly fit, with muscles rippling under their tanned skin.

Graham turned to Ken. "How many army tanks can she carry?"

"Three main battle tanks. Or she can carry about six APCs or eight trucks," Ken replied.

Andrew had been listening to Ken, and asked. "Do you carry them very often?"

Ken shook his head. "No. Only once last year, to an exercise at

Shoalwater Bay. Normally we carry trucks and stores. We also do a lot of support for the hydrographic people."

"Who are they?" asked a cadet.

"Survey. They are the people who study the ocean and make the charts," Ken explained. "And we also do a fair bit of this sort of thing, supporting diving teams."

"What do they do?" asked a girl.

"Rescue, salvage, you know, diving down to recover crashed planes, sunken ships and so on, and a lot of mine clearance. They will give you a talk once we are under way. Follow me aft and we will check out the lifejackets."

Graham would have liked to stay and watch the clearance divers preparing but had to follow the others. They went under the bridge and were each handed a lifejacket and shown how to put it on. Graham had no trouble with this, having done it many times on his father's ships. However one of the girls, Tina Babcock, who was another Year 8 at Graham's school, seemed to be having difficulty. Ken sprang to her assistance in a way that made Graham smile.

As soon as they had been briefed on safety the barge got under way. The mooring lines were cast off and she eased out into the current. Graham stood at the taffrail and thrilled to the feel and smell. The deck trembled as the engines were engaged. He gripped the rail and sniffed deeply at the sea smell: the familiar odours of oil, salt, decaying marine life, paint and diesel. Below his feet water swirled as the propellers churned up the muddy tidal water. The bow swung out into the current and the voyage had begun.

As soon as they were well down the channel their tour was resumed. They were taken into the superstructure and shown the interior layout: cabins, galley, wardroom, senior ratings mess, heads and so on. As they made their way through these spaces Graham experienced several searing flashbacks to the French destroyer and then of Cindy and the *matelot*. *Oh! I wish I had been able to stop her,* he thought.

Ken led them down a steep ladder into the engine room. Here they were handed ear protection and had things pointed out but were not taken close to the machinery. As always Graham marvelled that men liked machines and were content to work in such a place instead of up in the clean fresh air. He watched with fascination the rippling movements of the tappets and rocker arms on top of the huge diesels. *Incredible,* he thought, *how engines can run for hundreds of hours non stop.*

They were led up to the upper deck again, then up to the top of the wheelhouse to see the masts, aerials and radar scanners. By this time the LCH was nearing the end of the long shipping channel and were starting to butt into larger waves. Graham screwed his eyes up against the glare and looked out to sea. *We are in for a bit of rough water when we get out of the lee of False Cape,* he thought, observing the tumbled state of the waves further out.

Next came a visit to the bridge and an introduction to the captain; Lt Howe. He reminded Graham very much of his dad. He had the same stance, feet apart to balance himself against the roll, hands gripping his binoculars which were slung around his neck; the same weather-beaten complexion and the same distant horizon look in the eyes.

The bridge held no mysteries for Graham. Even so he listened carefully and looked at each instrument as it was explained.

Lt Howe looked out and said, "OK, we are out of the channel now. Who would like to have a go at steering her? Who is the youngest; your newest recruit?"

PO Armstrong pointed to Graham. "Recruit Kirk sir. He only joined last week."

Lt Howe smiled and nodded. "Fine. Relieve the wheel please Recruit."

Graham swallowed. He was embarrassed but mostly because he did not want to show off. The quartermaster at the wheel grinned and stepped aside. "OK son, take over," he said.

Graham stepped forward and gripped the wheel and looked down into the compass repeater. "Aye, aye, sir," he managed to croak.

"Steer zero two five," the quartermaster said, watching carefully from beside him.

"Zero two five, aye, aye, sir," Graham replied. He gripped the small wheel and carefully studied the numbers on the compass. With a minor adjustment he lined the pointer up then looked out, feeling very self-conscious.

After a minute Lt Howe said, "You are doing very well young fellow." He turned to the quartermaster and said, "You want to watch out Swain. This young bloke can steer as straight as you."

A bearded Chief Petty Officer guffawed: "That wouldn't be hard!"

The quartermaster looked aggrieved and said accusingly to Graham: "You've done this before."

"Yes I have," admitted Graham. "A lot."

He then had to describe how he had spent many weeks at sea on voyages with his father and often did a full watch at the wheel.

"Who is your dad?" Lt Howe asked.

"Captain Kirk sir. He owns a coaster named the *Malita* and a landing craft the *Wewak*. She is a landing craft like this one," Graham replied. He deliberately, and somewhat defensively gave his father the title of Captain, although his real ranking was as Master Mariner.

Lt Howe laughed. "We picked the wrong nipper here Swain! I know your dad young Kirk. We often pass his ships. In fact, the *Wewak* is due in today. I heard her chattering on the radio a while ago." He turned and said to a rating at the back of the bridge: "Brian, call up the *Wewak*, the one that carries freight to the gulf ports, and ask her where she is now."

"Aye, aye, sir."

Graham meanwhile continued to steer the barge with the effortless ease of long practice. The 'Swain said, "OK young fella, step aside and let someone else have a go. Who else wants to try?"

Andrew stepped forward. "Me please sir."

Thankfully Graham stepped aside. As he did he deliberately showed off. "Steer zero two five. Wheel relieved sir."

Lt Howe nodded with approval. "Good."

Graham edged to the rear of the bridge, blushing but also glowing at the praise. For the next 20 minutes he stood quietly at the back while the others in the group had a turn at steering. By this time they were running into larger waves, the flat bow thumping into them with a crash which made the ship shudder and pitch. Several of the cadets began to look a bit green around the gills. Their evident discomfiture gave Graham a real sense of superiority to offset his recruit status. At least he did not get seasick, no matter how rough it got.

It was the turn of another group by then so they were ushered out and down to the main deck where they sheltered on the lee side of the superstructure out of the wind and spray. Graham sat quietly beside Andrew and Blake and just enjoyed it all: the sparkling blue waves, the fresh cool air, the tang and taste of salt spray. It was good to be alive; great to be a navy cadet.

***

At 11:00 the LCH nosed into a narrow channel in a coral reef. By then they were in calm water, sheltered from the wind behind the line of reefs which made up the Great Barrier Reef. Graham had often been out to The Reef and was not particularly interested. He stood at the rail and looked down into the crystal clear water with an eye to navigation rather than marine beauty. The brown and black shadows off to port he knew were coral, the yellowish to pale green below indicated sand. A few fish flitted past but nothing of any interest.

As soon as LCH was inside the shelter of the lagoon she was turned hard to port and made her way slowly to where a red pontoon with a flag on it was moored. The LCH was made fast to this and the engines stopped. All cadets were then called to move to the well deck.

Here they found the clearance divers with all their gear laid out. The divers were all now dressed in wetsuits, with knives strapped to their ankles and lead weighted belts around their waists. A huge bear of a diver with a massive black beard stepped forward when they were all seated.

"I am Warrant Officer Crabb," he said in a deep voice. "This is Naval Clearance Diving Team Four, the best in the navy."

His men grinned and held their thumbs up. WO Crabb then proceeded to explain exactly what clearance divers do. "Our main job is to destroy mines which cannot be swept by conventional minesweepers," he explained. "You know, the old fashioned sort of mines which you see in the movies. They are a big round thing with horns on it. They are anchored to the seabed by a wire or chain and can be cut loose by a minesweeper using an Oropesa sweep or paravane. But most modern mines aren't like that. Modern mines often lie on the seabed and some are like a torpedo. They have propellers and controls and when their sensors pick up what their on-board computer determines is a target their engine starts and they head off to meet it."

This was all new to Graham and he found it fascinating. With frank admiration he carefully studied the men and their equipment. Frogmen was the popular name for such divers, and the movie image of them was swimming into enemy harbours to place explosives on the bottoms of enemy ships to sink them. Blake thought this and asked if they ever did that.

WO Crabb grinned and said, "We could, but most of our training is to search the bottoms of our own ships, and their anchor chains, to find and remove such things. Some of the army Commando types and the Special Air Service are trained as assault swimmers. We also do reconnaissance of enemy coasts for planning amphibious landings."

Graham remembered stories his father had told him about when he had been a young officer on supply ships to the Vietnam War. The ship had anchored in the muddy waters of the Mekong Delta at a place called Vung Tau. Navy clearance divers had then swum around underneath her day and night to stop enemy frogmen placing limpet mines on the hull. On one occasion they had even met some enemy frogmen doing this and had fought them underwater. It sounded like the bravest possible thing to do as a job. In Graham's mind the divers were heroes and he had it in his mind that he might like to be one.

Anthony Simmonds asked: "How do you actually find the mines?"

"Some mines are laid on the sea bed and are exploded by the sound of a ship going over it, or by the change in water pressure from its passage. Those sorts of mines can't be swept by minesweepers. They have to be located by a mine hunter's sonar, or by a remote controlled robot sub. Once the mine has been located a diver goes down to look at it. He either disarms it, if he thinks it is safe to do that; or he places explosives on it and blows it up," WO Crabb explained.

"What if it blows up when he touches it?" a girl asked.

All the divers laughed and WO Crabb said, "Then he is dead."

When the black humour had subsided WO Crabb went on: "Don't get the wrong idea. Today will be a lovely day for us, diving on the Great Barrier Reef. Ideal conditions, calm sea, bright sunlight, clear water, shallow. I mean, tourists actually pay to come and do this for fun. Most of our work is very boring, dirty and hard. Most jobs are in some muddy harbour, often at night where you can't see your hand in front of your face and you have to work by feel."

Blake looked horrified. "You swim underwater at night?" he cried.

"Yes."

"Aren't you scared of sharks?"

"Yes. But they don't bother working divers much. Gropers and crocs are more of a worry. And none of them compare with worrying that some engineer might turn over a ship's engines when you are near the propellers." He made a sucking, scrunching noise and a twisting motion with his hands. Graham shuddered. What a horrible way to die!

WO Crabb explained that much of their work was checking the bottoms of ships that had run aground or hit some object, to see what the damage was; or untangling mooring lines and tow ropes from around propellers, picking up tools that idiots had dropped in the harbour, or removing obstructions from the cooling inlets to ship's engines.

"Had to do that in Hong Kong once," he said, "Main inlet to a frigate was blocked. Turned out to be a dead baby."

There was a collective shudder of horror and several gasps. He explained: "Girl baby of course. The Chinese apparently value boy babies more and sometimes throw the girl babies in the river, which is how it came to be sucked into a ship's engines. We see a lot of bodies. If you don't like dead bodies don't become a professional diver. We are always being called in to extract them from wrecked planes, cars that run of bridges, boats that sink, even from drain pipes and sewers."

That got more gasps and shudders of revulsion. Apparently the last job the team had done had been to raise a sunken helicopter and one of them named Jacko had tugged at an arm and it had pulled off the body. This description caused more gasps of horror and Graham saw a few cadets looking quite anxious and pale. *Could I cope with recovering mangled dead bodies?* he wondered. He decided he could.

At the end of the lecture Graham was sold. What an exciting job: Salvage, searching, finding things—real adventure! He began to consider whether that might be the branch of the navy he wanted to go into.

The cadets were now all moved back up to the main deck and the divers got to work. The bow ramp of the LCH was lowered until it was just past horizontal. That put the end of the ramp just in the water. The divers were then able to carry their rubber boats along and launch them with no trouble. Their gear was placed aboard, the outboard started and they headed off.

"Where are they going?" Tina asked.

"To that yellow buoy," Ken said, pointing to where a tiny yellow flag fluttered above the sea about a kilometre away.

Hoyle, a cadet in the Starboard Watch said to Tina: "Why do girls wear T-shirts over their bathers when they go swimming?"

Tina looked puzzled and blushed. "Why?" she asked.

"Because the air gets trapped under it and acts like a boy. Ya get it? Acts like a buoy!" Hoyle said with a snigger.

Graham couldn't help glancing at Tina's front. She was a very busty young lady for her age and his mouth went dry at the thought of acting like a boy with her bosom. Tina blushed and scowled.

Hoyle then said, "You all heard the one about the homosexual sailor?" They shook their heads. Hoyle went on: "He fell overboard and was found clinging to a buoy. Ya get it? Found clinging to a boy. Hah! Hah!"

There was laughter but Graham could see that Tina was very embarrassed. The situation made him feel uncomfortable but being only a new recruit he did not know what to do in the circumstances.

Carmen Collins did though. "You boys stop that disgusting talk! That is sexual harassment and I won't have it. You don't have to put up with that Tina; and you shouldn't pretend you aren't offended if you are."

That shut the boys up, even the ones of higher rank than Carmen. Graham saw PO Armstrong look embarrassed. *He should have stopped those jokes,* Graham thought.

Lunch followed. The navy did not feed them. The cadets had all brought their own cut lunch. They sat around the decks and talked happily while they ate. The divers came back and went off to their own lunch below, then returned to the reef in their inflatable boats.

Graham sat and watched hungrily, wishing he was out there with them.

Chapter 30

SHOCKS AND SURPRISES

The divers reported back at 1300hrs. The cadets were able to overhear the conversation from vantage points along the walkways. The divers had indeed found an unexploded bomb. "An old 250 pound aerial bomb," said WO Crabb, relaying the news to the CO. "Dropped way back in the Second World War I'd say. She's all covered with coral and only parts of the fins are visible."

Lt Howe chuckled. "They weren't very environmentally friendly in those days."

Blake interrupted. "Excuse me sir, why would they drop bombs here?" he asked.

"Probably using the reef as a practice target for attacks on ships. They may even have had a target set up on the reef," Lt Howe replied.

"But World War 2 was over seventy years ago. Surely the bomb wouldn't be dangerous now," Blake said.

WO Crabb and his divers laughed. "Don't you believe it son. That stuff can last for donkey's years. And usually it becomes more unstable with age."

Lt Howe asked: "So what do you propose to do with her Crabby?"

"We are cutting the coral away now sir. Once we can get at the casing we will drill a hole to let the water in. Should have no problem securing a line to it. We will then haul it free. If it doesn't go bang we will suspend it from a boat and take it out into the deep water beyond the reef and blow it. Should be safe then," WO Crabb replied. He said it very matter-of-factly but Graham appreciated there was a degree of tension about the divers.

They went back to where the other boat was anchored and the work went on. All that the cadets could see were two tiny black dots and the yellow marker buoy. After about an hour the cadets were told, the news having been passed by radio, that the bomb had been pulled free and was now hanging under one of the boats. This was seen to head off out through the gap in the reef. Watching it put an awful feeling of dread into Graham's stomach. In anticipation of the blast all of the ship's company and the cadets lined the rails to watch. Graham remained tense until he saw the small boat move well away from the place where it had released the bomb in deep water. There was a nail-biting delay of another 5 minutes or so before the distant sea suddenly erupted in a column of white water. It wasn't as big as Graham had hoped for, his mind full of old newsreel images of depth charges exploding, but it was still very satisfying to see. The water quickly subsided and the muffled sound was barely noticed. The two dive boats then returned to the LCH.

As soon as they were aboard, the bow ramp was winched up, the anchor raised and the LCH got under way. As she nosed her way out through the reef Graham stood and watched with the wide eyes of hero-worship as the divers took off their dive equipment, then checked and packed it. By then it was after 2pm and the wind had got up with the afternoon sun so that the waves were even bigger as the LCH left the shelter of the reef. The distant coastal mountains looked a long way away as the first big wave burst over the bow in a splatter of spray.

The cadets fled to the stern and to the lee of the superstructure. Several soon became seasick, including Hoyle. The LCH began to batter into every wave as she moved further from the lee of the reef. The waves slammed against the flat ramp with a force that made the whole vessel shudder. This was no novelty to Graham who had endured days of slogging into 'Sou-Easters' on week-long voyages back from T.I. Some of the other cadets however looked positively worried. He could only smile and enjoy the whole experience.

As they got closer to Cairns the sea moderated as they got behind Cape Grafton, and then False Cape. By then they were sharing the water with a variety of other craft. A big Bulk Carrier passed on its way northwards. Several large sail yachts went racing by with fine feathers of spray at their bows. A Big Cat ferry went past towards Green Island.

"Cadet Recruit Kirk to the bridge!" boomed the loudspeaker.

Graham was so surprised that for a moment he could not respond.

Andrew nudged him. "That's you."

"I know," Graham replied. He examined his conscience, wondering what he had done wrong. Quickly he made his way up the ladder to the bridge. Lt Howe greeted him. He pointed over the starboard quarter and said, "*Wewak*," then proffered a pair of binoculars.

Graham took the binoculars and focused them. Into the lenses came a long, low black hull with a white painted box of a superstructure at the stern and bursts of white spray at her bows. The barge was about three miles off, just passing to seaward of Double Island and heading in the same direction.

Graham studied her for a few minutes, then stood leaning on the wing of the bridge staring across the tumbling water towards her. *Is that my future?* he wondered. He had some unpleasant memories of uncomfortable voyages on his father's ships: long hours and hard work with tough, unsympathetic men who cared little for children.

Below him on the main deck stood a young rating who turned and called to a friend: "Hey Nobby! Come and get an eyeful of this."

Graham looked where the rating was pointing. He saw that the LCH was overhauling a large sailing yacht. The yacht was less than 50 metres away, both vessels on converging courses as they headed for the channel markers. For a moment Graham wondered what had excited the sailor's interest; then his eye detected girls. He raised the binoculars and focused them.

Not just girls but half naked girls! On the foredeck of the yacht reclined two big-breasted girls who wore no tops. They began waving at the LCH as it drew abeam. Graham felt his mouth go dry and his heart started to pound faster as he watched the girl's breasts quiver as they waved. He moved his gaze aft to see if there were any more girls on the yacht. There were. Then he froze with shock. Sitting on the roof of the cabin were Janet and Thelma! Janet wore only a pair of brief black bikini pants and no top. And Thelma wore only a pair of shorts!

Graham was stunned. He licked his lips and refocused the binoculars, his hands trembling from the shock and a rush of desire. Then he felt a surge of jealousy that left him feeling sick. Seated beside the girls were Jerry Denham, Edmonson, Pinky and another lad: a good looking fellow of about twenty. They all wore only bathers. Seated in the cockpit was a blowsy, middle-aged woman who looked badly sunburnt. Standing in the cockpit steering the yacht was a thin, tanned, middle-aged man with short grey hair. He wore only a pair of brief bathers.

Graham moved his vision back to Thelma. She turned to look then waved, making no attempt to cover herself. Graham was stunned. *That can't be her!* he thought. *She's not like that!*

A hand clapped him on the shoulders. It was the Swain. "Give us those binos young fella. You are too young to be looking at things like that. It'll make you go blind before your time," he said with a chuckle.

Graham handed over the binoculars and blushed, then went even redder when the CO and lookout both laughed. They all focused binoculars on the yacht. Graham turned back to look at the yacht, gripping the rail as his mind whirled with ugly speculation.

The yacht's name caught his eye: *Frolicker*, he read. That sounded ominous. He had an idea that word meant something to do with sex; like orgies. He screwed up his eyes to squint as the glare of the afternoon sun sparkled off the water. Tears formed and he moved hastily away lest anyone see.

It was Thelma. And the girl next to her definitely was Janet. Graham felt sick; and also aroused. The two girls on the foredeck were Danelle and her friend. They looked very attractive, even at that distance. Graham slipped off down the port ladder lest they recognize him. Thelma! Topless on a yacht with Jerry Denham, Edmonson and some dirty old man!

The LCH drew ahead as they passed between the first channel markers. Graham stood and stared at the jungle covered mountains to the east of the inlet, his emotions and thoughts in sickening upheaval. The remainder of the voyage into harbour passed in a blur. He gave monosyllabic answers to people who spoke to him and was only glad when they were at last tied up at the naval base and he could get ashore. By then the yacht was far behind and nosing into the marina.

Once the LCH was tied up Lt Cdr Hazard said 'thank you' to the navy. The cadets were then lined up on the edge of the parade ground. Lt Cdr Hazard then said, "You must be the luckiest cadets afloat. Next weekend there are two US warships coming to Cairns. One is the nuclear powered cruiser USS *Ticonderoga*. The other is the frigate USS *Samuel P McGillicuddy*. We have made arrangements to visit them next Saturday. We won't get a trip on them but we should have a good look around. They arrive next Friday afternoon and we would like you to be at the wharf to give them a warm welcome. Now here are the details." He went on to give the cadets timings and details of where to be and what to wear. The ships were staying for five days to give their crews some deserved R & R. Graham heard all this in a sort of a daze. It really was of no importance at all.

The cadets were then called to attention and dismissed. As they made their way to the gate Andrew spoke to him: "Did you enjoy the trip Graham?"

"Yes, yes I did," Graham replied distractedly.

Blake joined them: "Did you see those topless sheilas! I reckon a couple of them go to our school; that Janet and her friend Thelma. Aren't they in your class Graham?"

Carmen arrived and overheard this: "It was them, the little tarts!"

Graham felt sick. Thelma a tart! He could only mumble and pretend he wasn't interested. Carmen's presence ended the discussion anyway and he was able to get away on his own. He was now gripped by fierce jealousy and felt an almost frantic urge to rush to the marina to see if they were there. That made him extremely edgy. He immediately sprang on his bike and pedalled off as fast as he could go.

On arrival at the marina he just dumped his bike and raced out onto the boardwalk. Almost at once he saw the yacht. It was berthed out at one of the long pontoons. No-one appeared to be aboard. As the security gate to the pontoon pier was open Graham walked out along the pontoon past several other yachts until he came to it. At any moment he expected to see Thelma or Janet appear on deck. He was now so distressed he thought he might throw up. In case they appeared he prepared a story to explain why he was there. He need not have bothered. The yacht was locked up and deserted.

For several minutes he stood on the pontoon looking down at the yacht, his thoughts tormented by images of half-naked girls; of Thelma.

Then a man spoke to him: "What do you want kid?"

Graham turned. The man looked like some sort of marina official. "I was just looking."

The man sneered then laughed. "Just looking eh? What for? Thinking of buying; or planning to pinch something?"

Anger and embarrassment seethed in Graham. "Neither," he snapped. "Would you please tell me who owns this yacht?"

"It's none of your business, now get off the pontoon unless you have some legitimate reason to be here," the man replied.

Angry and embarrassed Graham turned and walked off, watched by the man. As Graham strode along the floating walkway towards the shore a man glanced up at him from the next yacht. He looked a friendly old cove so Graham stopped and asked: "Excuse me sir, can you tell me who owns the *Frolicker*?"

"Sure son. She belongs to that greenie environmentalist, Doctor Metcalf, the bloke who is standing for parliament. You've just missed them. They all left just a few minutes ago."

"Thank you sir," Graham said. Puzzled and sad he continued on his way. A doctor who was an environmental radical? Yes, he had heard of Dr Metcalf. He was often in the news acting as spokesperson for some issue or other. Presumably Thelma was on the yacht because Janet and her sister were. *They might even be family friends,* Graham pondered unhappily. That made him realize that he knew almost nothing about Thelma or her family.

When he reached the boardwalk Graham stopped and sat down, so upset he was ready to burst into tears. What to do now? *Should I go to this games evening tonight?* he pondered. *Did they see me on the LCH?* He decided they had not. *I doubt if they realized all us navy cadets were on board. If they had they would surely have covered up. Gosh, they are in for a time at school when word gets out.* That was an unhappy prospect which raised another dilemma: Should he warn them?

As Graham sat there the old *Wewak* came churning past on her way up to Portsmith. Distracted by his emotional turmoil he barely noted her as she went by. *Dad is back,* he thought, but otherwise wasn't interested. For a few minutes he stood, staring unseeingly across the Inlet at the line of mountains that had been the backdrop to his whole life.

Sadly, he hopped on his bike and pedalled slowly home.

***

Arriving home raised new problems. He had to pretend he was happy and that he had enjoyed the day. Somehow he was able to chatter away about the LCH and the clearance divers without letting on he was deeply distressed.

Then he had to greet his father and talk normally. This time it was easier as he was able to use details from the trip on the LCH. As he had his shower he contemplated his options, then realized that he just had to go to Janet's that evening. *No matter how much it hurts I have to know,* he thought. The decision made, he cheered up somewhat and settled down to read his book on battleships.

To get to Janet's Graham was allowed to ride his bike as it was not into the city. He set out after tea feeling so tense he was almost ill. He was dressed in shorts and a good shirt and hoped it would be suitable for the occasion.

It was. Most of the other people there were just in jeans and T-shirt, or shorts and T-shirt. Graham had never been to Janet's. Her home was on the lower slopes of Mt Whitfield at Edge Hill, a pretty suburb with lush gardens and many trees. He had been past the house but never really noticed it. It was a renovated 'Old Queenslander' with a terraced garden lush with ferns, tropical palms and flower beds.

Feeling very scared Graham placed his bike inside the gate and walked up the steps. The sound of laughter and loud music drifted out of the front door. Graham gave a hesitant knock which drew no response so he had to nerve himself and knock louder. Danelle Ozgood appeared, wearing some sort of wrap-around caftan thing.

"Hi! Are you the boy Thelma invited; the navy cadet?" she asked.

"Yes," croaked Graham. He was regretting he had come and regretted it even more when he followed her through to a back room. There a dozen people sat around the table or against the walls. Most were years older than him and looked about twenty. Graham saw Jerry Denham, Pinky and the young man who had been on the yacht that afternoon. Edmonson sat in a corner talking to several people and he met his eye and started to scowl before looking away. There were also several girls, including the other big girl who had been topless. She was almost in that state now, wearing a thin cotton blouse that barely restrained her large bosom. She was smoking and held a stubby of beer in her hand. Graham now learned that her name was Sonja, and that she was Dr Metcalf's daughter. She was in Year 12 at a private school.

To Graham's relief he saw Thelma sitting over to one side with Janet. She waved and beckoned him over. Feeling very self-conscious and out of place he made his way over to her, noting as he did that Janet was also smoking. There was no sign of any board games, only lots of beer bottles and wine casks. That made Graham feel even more worried and sicker than ever. For a moment he contemplated leaving. What bothered him most was the puzzle over how Thelma and Janet could be at a party like this, as no older adults were to be seen.

Thelma smiled. "Hi Graham. Have a good day?" she asked.

"Yes thanks, most of the time," he replied, his mind racing. *Should I mention the LCH?* he wondered. *What will I say if they asked me what I did?* To his own shame he decided to say nothing. Janet smiled and pointed to the fridge.

"There is beer in the fridge." she said.

Graham's mind raced. Beer? *If I drink beer mum will be able to smell it,* he thought. His father drank plenty of it but Graham did not like the taste very much. He shook his head.

Janet shrugged and said, "Suit yourself. There are softdrinks in there as well. Do you want a smoke?"

"No thanks," Graham replied hastily.

Thelma gave a wry smile. "Wise boy. Get a drink and join us."

Graham selected a can of lemonade. Thelma moved along on the sofa and indicated he should sit beside her. He did so, finding it a squeeze so that he ended up pressed against her. She did not seem to mind and began to chatter happily away.

"We went sailing today," she said. "What did you do?"

"Went to navy cadets," Graham replied.

"Oh yeah," she replied. She was not really interested. "What did you do there?"

Graham gulped some softdrink before answering. "We went out on a landing craft for the day. We saw you."

Thelma's cheeks tinged red. "Saw us?"

Graham nodded, feeling utterly miserable. "Yes. When you were on that yacht coming back into harbour."

"Oh!"

Janet leaned across and smirked. "Were you one of those sailors leering at us from that navy barge?"

Graham nodded. He was too upset to answer. Thelma's facial expression appeared a bit strained but Janet just shrugged. "Lucky them! I'll bet they had a good look."

At that moment, more people came in. Graham looked up and started with surprise. It was the black-bearded demonstrator and his girlfriend. Graham now learned that his name was Sean O'Malley, and that hers was Paula. Paula wore a very loose, flowing wrap-around which was so thin he could see through it. From some angles she may as well have been naked. Their arrival made Graham even more uncomfortable. He felt as though he had inadvertently stumbled into the enemy camp.

Introductions were made and Sean and Paula were handed beers and what Graham guessed were marijuana joints. Pinky turned to the four youngsters and said, "You kids piss off outside for a while. We want to talk business. Go for a walk in the garden or something."

"Or something!" giggled Janet. She took Denham's hand and he hauled her to her feet. Edmonson also stood up and helped another girl to her feet, giving Graham a vaguely hostile look as he did. They then left the room arm in arm. Graham blushed fiercely but was glad of the opportunity to stand up. It was an enormous relief to get out of that room, now rapidly filling with marijuana smoke. Thelma stood and followed Janet and Denham. Feeling very flustered and mixed up, Graham followed. He had half a mind to make an excuse and say goodnight but once they were outside Thelma took his hand. Instantly his emotions went into overdrive and he was lost.

Edmonson and his girl went off towards the back of the house and Janet and Jerry wandered off along a path in the garden. Thelma stopped in the front garden and whispered to Graham: "Let's sit here. They won't want us with them."

That set Graham's imagination racing, wondering what Janet and Denham might be heading off to do. Thelma indicated a seat in a nice dark nook amongst the shrubs. Before Graham knew what was happening she had embraced him and started kissing. His already stunned senses reeled. She tasted, smelt and felt wonderful. All he could do was respond, uncomfortably aware that he was fast becoming aroused. That she must be able to feel it was obvious, but she pressed firmly against him and did not seem to mind.

Perhaps if she goes topless at times she is not as innocent as I thought? he pondered. It came to him that his goddess had developed more than just feet of clay and he was immensely saddened. But he was also a hot-blooded lad and she seemed willing. He responded.

After a few minutes Thelma eased them apart and sat on the seat. Graham sat beside her and she leaned on him. Feeling very daring he put his arm around her shoulders. She murmured and snuggled closer, her hand coming to rest on his thigh.

That hand seemed to burn through his skin, to heat his blood. His heart pounded and he became aroused even more. She turned up her face and they kissed again. To Graham it seemed that his dearest wishes had come true. He was actually kissing Thelma! Graham's blood pounced in his skull. He had an urgent desire to go further but did not dare, even though he could feel her right breast firmly pressed against him. It was obvious she was not wearing a bra and that got his imagination flaring as well. His mind was filled with the remembered images of her breasts from that afternoon and that, combined with her touch, helped fire his blood.

After another bout of kissing Graham summoned up the courage to try for more. He edged his right hand up her side until it was close to her breast. She immediately reached up and firmly moved it away. Graham flushed at the rebuff, but as she didn't stop kissing he decided that perhaps he was trying too soon. After a few minutes they stopped kissing and sat together in silence. To Graham that was wonderful.

Then, to his annoyance, he heard men's voices nearby. He wondered if he should stop but Thelma reached up and held his head firmly and kept on kissing. The men had come out of the house and strolled along the garden path, stopping just the other side of the large shrub.

One of them was Sean, the demo leader. He said to his companions, who turned out to be Pinky and a man named Frank, "I brought you two out here because I don't want all those guys inside to hear this. I don't trust them all and we don't want the coppers to get to hear of our plans."

At that Graham's mind went into racing speed. *The demonstrators are going to discuss their secret plans and I can hear them!* he thought. That aroused his interest enormously, but also his fears. *I don't want to get into trouble for eavesdropping. Maybe I should let them know we are here?*

Easing back a few centimetres he whispered to Thelma: "We'd better move away."

Thelma shook her head. "No. Don't move. They don't care about us," she replied. With that she resumed kissing, her tongue now probing his lips.

Graham could only acquiesce. The men stopped nearby and leaned on the fence. One burped and grunted. Sean said, "Are you drunk Frank? I'm not going to waste time briefing you if you are."

"I'm not drunk," Frank answered grumpily. "Just get on with it so we can get back inside."

Frank? Graham wondered. *Who is he?* He was also appalled that Thelma was hearing their crude language. He didn't want her to be subjected to that. But what could he do? Once again he considered letting the men know they were there. To his surprise and enormous delight, Thelma took his right hand and placed it gently on her left breast. Graham felt the blood pounding in his skull and he responded to his instincts, gently caressing and fondling. Thelma sighed and moved to allow him more room, then kissed him fiercely and urgently and he was set on fire and responded.

Sean continued. "Now listen to me, it's like this. On Friday afternoon those two Yankee warships are coming in and we are going to give them a reception that will grab us world headlines. This will be the best demo we have ever done."

By now Graham's mouth had gone dry from desire and fear. He was intensely interested, as well as intensely aroused. Thelma added to this by nibbling his ear lobe while she kissed him. His mind bubbled with the sheer pleasure of it. That made it enormously difficult for him to concentrate on what the men were saying, particularly as he had to pretend he wasn't interested.

Sean said, "That mob inside think that only one thing is going to happen, the demo on the wharf. But they haven't been told the whole plan. The real plan is this: at 4pm the two warships enter the channel and head for the wharves. The police and security people will establish a no go zone around them for half a kilometre—no boats of any sort allowed into that. At that time I form up the main demo crowd at the City Library buildings and we start marching towards the wharf. That will attract the attention of most of the coppers and we will have the media people with us and give them a good show. Then, at about 4:30, Frank, your two Zodiacs will start their decoy job, just when the first ship is passing the Yacht Club. You will come out from behind the small craft moored along the other side of the inlet at full speed and head for the ship. You know where I mean?"

"Yeah. I had a look today," Frank replied.

"Good. Have flags up, and placards. Lead the police launches a real run around and try to get right over to throw paint bombs on the sides of the ship."

"That will be very risky," Frank said. "The Yanks might open fire on us. They are very touchy about small boats going near their ships ever since that terrorist attack on the USS *Cole* at Aden. I don't want to get shot."

Sean grunted and went on: "You will be all right. Just angle slowly in and don't do an obvious charge at them. Give them time to see the placards. Now, remember you are the decoys. Your job is to attract the attention of the police boats. Once they are worrying about you we send in our third group. This is another bit I have kept secret from the mob inside. Pinky, this is your part of the operation."

Pinky grunted something Graham could not hear. Sean went on: "You are to have your six canoes and your people at the Yacht Club. Move there early in the morning and pretend to be working on them. Then, at my call on the radio, launch your boats and slip out. The first warship should just be easing into the wharf at that point, and the second one getting close. You are to get between them and the wharf so they can't berth. Throw paint and use your spray cans to paint our logo on their side. You can withdraw in under the wharf if you have to. Go and do a recon in your canoe in the next couple of days but don't attract any attention."

Pinky assured him that he would not. The conspirators went on to discuss details of numbers of people, and things like radio channels and codes. All the while Graham was gently stroking Thelma's back and she had begun to caress his face and neck.

Sean then said, "Any questions? No? Good! OK, let's go back in. I need another beer. And remember, keep all this secret. It is most important the cops don't get to hear of it."

With that the three made their way back to the house; leaving Graham in the throes of utter turmoil. He was so aroused he wanted to do things to Thelma; and he was torn up over what he had just overheard. *I know their secret plans. What should I do? Should I tell?* In his heart he knew he should, but who?

There was also the dilemma of what to do with Thelma. *What does she want?* he wondered. And how far would she let him go?

Suddenly, Thelma released him and sat up. She murmured, "We'd better be getting back to the others before they come looking for us."

To Graham's relief and regret she disentangled herself. They had only just done this when there were voices and footsteps and Janet and Denham appeared out of the darkness at the back of the garden.

"Where are you two?" Janet giggled. "Is it all right if we join you?"

"Yes," Thelma replied. Graham was engulfed by waves of hot shame and repressed urges. Thelma stood up and he had to stand up as well. Releasing his hand, Thelma said, "We'd better go back inside."

Graham did not want to do that. "I'd rather stay out here with you," he managed to say, his heart beating frantically.

Thelma hugged him and murmured, "All right."

Janet overheard this. She smirked and said, "You two behave; and don't do anything I wouldn't do." With that she shrilled with laughter and led Denham on towards the house.

After they had gone, Thelma said, "I don't want to sit down. Let's walk for a bit."

That wasn't really what Graham wanted, but he was relieved all the same. So he walked with her to the front gate and out along the footpath. They held hands and she chatted about her pets while Graham cooled down. They didn't go far, just down to Collins Avenue and along to the nearest shops and back, allowing Graham to return to something like normal. When they returned to the house they did not go inside but stayed sitting on the front steps talking. Thelma seemed to have gone cold and kept her distance, but Graham didn't mind. He needed a break too.

She is probably regretting she let me go so far, he surmised.

Janet and Denham came out and joined them. Several of the older people left. There was much laughter and singing inside. Then Thelma's father arrived in his car to pick her up. Thelma smiled and gave Graham a warm goodnight kiss and said, "See you on Monday." He had been hoping to see her the next day but had to accept this.

After she had gone, Graham hastily made his goodbyes to Janet, who was as stand-offish as ever. Then he jumped on his bike and pedalled away, his emotions and thoughts in great confusion. Once his body had calmed down, his mind concentrated on one thing: what to do about the secret plans he had overheard?

Chapter 31

TORN

All the way home Graham was in a fever of emotion. He had achieved Stage 2 of his heart's desire: he had kissed Thelma! But he had also overheard the demonstrator's plans and was torn over what to do about them. Out of loyalty to Thelma he thought he should keep it to himself. *After all, nobody will know,* he rationalized. But that did not sit easily on his conscience. His sense of duty, and his liking for navies, even foreign ones, caused him to consider telling the authorities.

But who? And how? *And will they believe me anyway?* he worried. It all seemed very difficult and threatened to spoil his memories of those moments of ecstasy in the garden. *I will make up my mind what to do tomorrow,* he decided. *Anyway, they aren't Australian ships, only Yanks; and they get demonstrated against all the time. They must be used to it.*

When he got home Graham was thankful in not having to face an inquisition from Kylie as she was at the ballet with Margaret and his mother was only pleasantly interested and did not ask any awkward questions. She just smiled at his apparent happiness.

Later, in bed, Graham relived every moment, brushing aside the intrusive problem of what he had overheard. Harder to push out were thoughts that told him, against his will, that Thelma had been kissed before. That unleashed a storm of jealousy and gnawing doubt that left him feeling quite sick. The images of her topless on the yacht floated up to haunt him. How often had she done that before? And who with? And who was that good-looking bloke? Graham had not found out his name. It was all very upsetting.

The next morning he felt wrung out and tired. Dreams had tormented his restless sleep; taunting, erotic dreams. He was in no mood to go to church and face Margaret's hurt little smile. The thought that he was causing her pain bothered him and he tried to brush that uncomfortable thought aside.

It is Thelma I love, he told himself. *And she must like me, or she wouldn't have kissed me.* He lay in bed and had daydreams about Thelma, but which now had a sharper, more sexual edge to them. She was no longer a distant cold Goddess, but a warm memory.

After a shower and leisurely breakfast Graham finally stirred himself. The day had been given over to playing Battleships. He finished a few details on his new model of the battleship *Nelson*, adding small paper flags drawn with coloured pens to indicate she was British, and that she had an Admiral on board. He then carried her downstairs and placed her in the Naval Base.

A few minutes later Max arrived. He had a large cardboard box which contained smaller butter containers. He opened one to reveal models for his country of Italy. These included six fighter planes and a really good little model of a tri-motor SM79 torpedo bomber; ten tanks painted a sand colour with yellow marks on top, three armoured cars and three trucks. As well he had an MAS Boat, a type of small Motor Torpedo Boat. Another box contained vehicles and aircraft painted light brown and with red and yellow markings: Spaniards. They included three fighters, three bombers, eight heavy and four light tanks and four trucks.

A third box contained about twenty small trees made of green cardboard stuck to matchsticks. They were planted upright in dobs of plasticine to represent the jungle of the Central American country of Andesia. "That jungle is so thick that tanks can't get through it," Max declared.

What a good idea! Graham thought, envious that he had not done the same.

Alex now joined them, carrying his latest increases, all German. These included a model of a Heinkel III bomber which had clear plastic glued over its nose to represent the crew compartment and cockpit. It looked very realistic and was by far the best model Alex had yet made. A twin-engine ME 110 fighter and four of the dreaded Stuka JU87 Dive Bombers, plus four more ME109 fighters joined the other German planes on the airfields.

Almost at once the war began. Without further ado Alex launched a massive air raid on the Trogs. Max joined in. In the middle of this Peter arrived lugging his new models. These caused a lull in the action while they were inspected. Graham was at once amazed, appalled and envious. Peter had been very busy. He had constructed a huge battleship, two cruisers, six destroyers and a Seaplane Tender, as well as numerous tanks and planes.

The battleship was named the *Avron* and was based on the American Iowa-class. "Nine 16" guns," Peter told them. There was no disputing that fact at all. The *Avron* was the largest ship so far. The cruisers were just as much of a blow to Graham. One was an absolute monster with 9 x 8" guns, based, so Peter said, on the US Baltimore-class. The other was a light cruiser nearly as large, of the US Brooklyn-class, armed with 15 x 6" guns.

They make my two old cruisers look pretty sick, Graham thought ruefully. *Thank God I have made the* Nelson. *At least she can match the* Avron *in guns and armour.*

Peter's model destroyers were also a sight to see. They were identical, all mass-produced, of the US Gearing-class with 6 x 5" guns and ten torpedo tubes. When they were berthed side by side in Peter's main harbour they looked very impressive and powerful. Graham resolved to make more destroyers as a top priority.

Peter had also made dozens of planes and tanks. Graham tried to count them but gave up when he reached one hundredd for the Russians. Peter had made these all the same and had painted them a dark brown and put red markings on them. As Peter placed them along the Russian border Max and Alex both looked worried. Almost at once they broke off the air battle with the Trogs.

The Russian planes joined in. Then their tanks rolled over the border. Furious battles broke out. Max and Alex set about re-grouping their armies to face in both directions. Graham started building a pontoon bridge of balsa and matches over the Rhine, while loading British tanks on the Trog landing craft for shipment across the Channel.

The battle raged for two hours before Alex and Max were defeated. The huge guns of the battleships played a major part in this, as did a strike by Graham's carrier planes on Italy. The boys all enjoyed it enormously and emerged grimy on hands and knees from crawling around on the concrete. It was agreed to put everything back the way it was before another game after lunch.

At lunch time Graham had to finally face Kylie. She looked at him hard but he said nothing about the previous night. Luckily she did not press the matter with questions but she was obviously not in favour of Thelma. It was a relief to get back to the Ship Room to continue the battles.

These raged for the next three hours, and followed quite a different pattern. Graham sent an invasion force to seize the Erg, which annoyed Max enormously. Alex invaded Romania. Max tried to capture the Rock but was beaten off by the battleships guns after his own was sunk. Then his Spanish army tried to force the passes in the Pyrenees and fierce fighting ensued until both passes were blocked by piles of dead tanks. In the end Graham and Peter won again, but only when the Atlantis army was shipped over to invade Spain. Towards the end tempers began to fray a little and there were some cross words, but the use of the dice kept most disputes to a minimum.

All in all it was a very enjoyable day. Graham was pleasantly tired when he farewelled the others after arranging to play games after school during the week. Before going to have his bath he stood alone in the Ship Room and savoured the atmosphere, and admired his models.

Peter's might be bigger and better made but I still like my own, he told himself. He now felt quite affectionate towards them.

After tea he settled, very unwillingly, at his desk to do some homework. Then he started work on three Lancaster heavy bombers. He made these out of balsa wood and wire. They measured 12cm across the wings and looked very impressive when they were painted brown and green camouflage and had tiny wire guns stuck in their turrets. He went to bed a tired but happy boy, his happiness increased by the thought that he would see Thelma again within a few hours.

She was almost the first person he saw when he got to school on Monday. As he walked towards her he noticed her face under go quite a dramatic change. Initially she appeared to frown; then she gave him a big smile. "Hi Graham! How was Sunday?" she asked.

"Fine. We had lots of fun," Graham replied. "What about you?" He was careful not to talk war games to her, suspecting she would not approve. They chatted away until the bell went. All the time Graham's mind worked on the problem of when and how to ask her for another date.

It was apparent that they were now an item of gossip in the class.

That made Graham feel very good. He wanted Thelma to be his girlfriend and was happy that people were starting to assume they were. Thelma did not seem to mind as she sat with him at morning break and again at lunch time. This sent his hopes soaring that there might be more of those heavenly kisses not too far in the future. Memories of their embrace in the garden flooded his mind; along with the fact that he had overheard the demonstrators plotting. The thought that he should decide what to do about that niggled irritably till he consciously pushed it aside.

After school he walked with Thelma. She seemed to accept this and appeared happy. As they walked along Graham really wanted to hold her hand, but he had to wheel his bike; and was not game anyway. All the time he was in a fever of anxiety about asking her for another date. Finally, when they reached her street, he asked her. She shook her head.

"Sorry Graham. Not this weekend. I am already booked up with things," she said.

"What about during the week?"

"No. My mum wouldn't let me go out on week nights. I have to do my homework. What about the week after?" she suggested.

It seemed a long way off to Graham in his disappointment, but he snatched gratefully at the crumbs he was offered. After all he had made great progress over the last few weeks. "OK, what about going to the movies again?" he asked.

To his relief Thelma nodded. "Yes, all right. I'll let you know."

With that Graham had to be content. His disappointment must have shown on his face for her expression softened and she put her hand on his arm. "Would you like to have afternoon tea at my place?" she asked.

For a moment Graham was torn. He would have loved to say yes but he had to shake his head. "I'd love to, but I've arranged to go over to Peter's straight after school."

Thelma gave a little curl of the lip and said, "Suit yourself."

Even to Graham's inexperienced eye she was plainly miffed at his reply. He was also a bit annoyed. "Be fair Thelma. I promised Pete I'd come over. I can come to your place tomorrow if you like." In his own mind he instantly relegated games of Battleships to a low priority. If it meant being with Thelma he would never play again!

Thelma gave a wry smile. "All right. I will see you tomorrow then," she replied.

Graham had been hoping there might be a little kiss for him as they said farewell but she just turned and walked off. He shrugged and went on his way to Peter's, unsure whether he was happy or sad.

***

Mrs Bronsky provided afternoon tea for the boys while they set up for another map battle. This time Graham was to adjudicate while Peter played against his little brother Paul. Adjudicating was a whole new experience. So was the type of battle. Peter had drawn maps which had land on both sides, and added a centre map to make the playing area bigger. The land had harbours and harbour defences were included on the price list. Paul had the job of getting a convoy of troop transports, supply ships and oil tankers across from one harbour to the other. Peter had the job of stopping them. To defend the convoy Paul had a fleet which included one heavy and two light cruisers, four destroyers, two anti-sub frigates and four corvettes. Peter's force comprised only one heavy cruiser and eight submarines.

It was an interesting battle for Graham as it gave him a new insight into Peter's mental processes and personality. Peter was mathematical and ruthlessly rational, working to a definite plan. He soon located the convoy, then waited till so-called dark (each move being 15 minutes of time). The Panzer Kreuzer then charged in and wreaked havoc before it was sunk. Its primary targets were the small anti-sub vessels. Paul was left with only his cruisers and one destroyer and one corvette to beat off the U-boat pack. Peter won resoundingly.

By then it was nearly dark. Graham thanked them and went down to his bike. Peter came out with him to say goodbye.

"Are we playing again tomorrow afternoon?" he asked.

That gave Graham a jolt. He hesitated then shook his head. "Sorry. I... I'm going over to Thelma's after school."

It was Peter's turn to shake his head. "You'll be sorry," he commented. Graham indignantly refuted this and said good night, then pedalled happily home, detouring to pass Thelma's on the way. He hoped to get a glimpse of her but was out of luck.

That evening he sat at his work table and resumed work on his model merchant ship. One of the weaknesses revealed in the Sunday battle had been the old one of not enough sea transport. Also watching the convoy battle had inspired him. He drew simple plans, then went downstairs and cut out the bows and stern of a cargo ship from a piece of redwood 30cm long x 6cm wide x 4cm high. Holes for masts were drilled and he then rasped and sanded it to shape. 1 cm thick balsa was glued on in three places to give the raised focsle, midships section and poop deck of an old fashioned Three Island steamship. By the time that was completed it was time for bed.

At school on Tuesday Thelma again sat with him during the breaks and was very friendly. Janet scowled a bit but Graham didn't mind. The good-natured jibes of his mates he just shrugged off. The day seemed to fly by. After school Graham walked with Thelma to the bike racks and then wheeled his bike beside her while they walked to her house.

He had never been there; nor met her parents other than the one fleeting introduction after the movies, so he was quite nervous as he followed her in through the front gate. Her house looked to be an ordinary old Cairns type high block house and was very clean and pleasant inside. Thelma's mum said hello and offered them afternoon tea so they sat in the lounge room; Graham feeling very self-conscious and nervous. He sat on the edge of his chair and sweated and Thelma did most of the talking. She put on some music and Graham tried to discuss it intelligently.

After half an hour they both seemed to run out of things to say. Graham fidgeted and felt uncomfortable. He groped in his mind for witty and funny things to say but dried up after a few more minutes. A glance at the clock showed him it was only 4:30 pm but he now decided he should not outdo his welcome.

"I'd better be getting home," he said.

Thelma's face brightened perceptibly. "Yes, I should get on with my homework."

Graham agreed. Now that he had made the move he couldn't leave fast enough. He thanked Thelma's mum and she smiled. Thelma did too but she looked very tired.

"See you tomorrow," Graham said.

"Yes, see you. Goodbye," Thelma replied. She walked to the front door with him but did not walk down the steps.

No kiss again, Graham thought. *Oh well, it is daytime and we don't know each other that well.*

Feeling quite unsure of himself he mounted his bike and rode off, glancing back frequently to wave. Thelma stood in the doorway and watched him until he was out of sight. Freed from the bonds of social constraint, Graham's spirits soared. "I think her mum likes me," he told himself as he pedalled along. That had been a bit of advice from his dad: 'Get the mother on side first son and you'll be in like Flynn!'

At home he settled to work on his new cargo ship model. A block of wood was glued on for the superstructure, and another on the poop. Cardboard was cut to form the wheel house and a thin balsa bridge with cardboard screen was glued across. A cardboard funnel, painted red and black, was glued on behind the wheelhouse, with a lifeboat either side. Wire davits for the boats were stuck on. Then balsa hatch covers and some small details like capstans, bollards and winches were added. Two masts of tapered bamboo were stuck in the holes and then derricks of thin bamboo (The type used for meat skewers in cooking) were fastened on with wire and black cotton.

The cargo ship was finished by bedtime and he named her the SS *Africa Star*. She looked good and he liked her immediately. Before he climbed into bed he studied photos of destroyers, finally deciding that he would build a British Tribal-class ship of World War 2. The most famous appeared to be the HMS *Cossack*, so he started to sketch out some plans but his mother came out and chased him to bed.

"You get some sleep my boy. These blasted battleships and models won't get you a good job when you leave school," she said.

"But I'm going to join the navy mum," Graham replied.

"Hmmm. Maybe, but you need good maths for that," she replied. "And let's hope those eyes of yours are good enough."

That left Graham lying in the dark with the niggling worry that perhaps his eyes might let him down. He knew his left eye wasn't perfect, and that sometimes it went a bit blurry, but he didn't think it would matter.

Wednesday was almost a repeat of Tuesday, except that when Graham hinted to Thelma that he might come over to her place again she shook her head and said she was going over to Janet's. That gave him a bit of a jolt. Not only did it leave him feeling disappointed, but it reminded him that he had done nothing about telling anyone in authority about the demonstrator's plans.

It doesn't matter if I don't, he told himself. *They aren't doing any harm. They have every right to demonstrate. It is a free country after all.* But he knew it wasn't quite that simple. There was another side to the coin. *The Americans are guests in Australia. We shouldn't abuse them or give them a hard time. Besides, it was the US Navy that saved Australia from the Japanese in World War 2. We should be grateful,* he rationalized.

But he knew that wasn't the whole story either. The real reason he felt he should do something, he had to admit to himself, was that he just liked navies and warships and therefore anyone opposed to them he saw as an enemy.

That led to another uncomfortable train of thought: Thelma was opposed to navies and armies. He didn't know what to do about that, sensing that he was unlikely to change her mind. That raised the issue of loyalty. *I was with her when I overheard her friend's plans. Do I want to hurt her and her friends?* he thought. Then another worrying idea came to him. *Gosh! I wonder if she and Janet are planning to take part in this demo on Friday when the American ships come in?* he wondered.

It was a question he knew he had to find the answer to but did not know how to broach the subject. Instead he went off to find Peter. To the query whether he was interested in playing another Battleships game that afternoon Peter replied 'yes'.

So after school Graham watched sadly from a distance when Thelma hopped into a car with Janet. Then he made his way to Peter's. Peter had organized another game, with Graham pitted against Paul, while he adjudicated. This time the map was even bigger and had several islands drawn on it, as well as the nice safe harbours. Both sides were allowed to choose any fleet they liked from the price list. Graham chose a balanced mixture: two battleships, three cruisers, six destroyers, two corvettes, six subs and a boom defence vessel to keep his harbour safe.

The tokens were deployed and the game began. Graham soon made a stunning discovery: Paul had purchased a minelayer and had laid a minefield in a narrow strait between two islands. Graham's leading destroyer was blown up and his advance turned into a milling shambles, just as Paul's battle fleet came into range.

Graham had to withdraw out of range as fast as he could, but ran into a submarine ambush. He lost a cruiser and had a battleship damaged before his fleet won clear. Two subs were sunk in return. Then further disaster struck: another minefield. This time Graham lost a cruiser. Paul's two battleships and three cruisers closed to gun range and opened with immediate fire.

For a few moves Graham thought he was doomed but he managed to sink one of Paul's battleships and the others withdrew out of range. But an attempt to use his subs to catch them also ended in disaster. Once again it was a minefield. A sub was blown up and Paul's fleet retired safely out of range behind an island.

The next move of Paul's was for his fast minelayer to appear from behind an island well to the rear of Graham's fleet. It proceeded to lay a minefield right across the entrance to his harbour, sinking the boom defence vessel in the process. Simultaneously, five of Paul's subs were detected moving towards Graham's big ships.

"Bloody mines!" Graham growled. "What have we got that can sweep mines?" He was uncomfortably aware that he had not purchased any minesweepers, even though they were on the price list.

"Any ship could, by streaming Oropesa sweeps or paravanes," Peter explained. "Although they risk hitting a mine while they do it."

"Only if they are moored contact mines," Graham said, remembering the lecture on the LCH. "If they are Influence Mines they have to be located by a minehunter, then blown up by divers or robot subs."

"These are the old types anchored on a wire," Peter replied. "Our game is before all those new types."

"But how did the minesweepers get rid of the mines without being blown up themselves?" Paul asked.

Graham could answer that. "They couldn't. They just had to run the risk; but they were small and cheap so the navy could afford to lose them. But they could sweep a wide channel and mark it with buoys."

"Sounds pretty dangerous then," Paul commented.

"I think it was," Graham agreed. He had been grappling with how to get his fleet of big ships safely back to harbour, at least till he could deal with the subs. In the end he had to use his two corvettes as minesweepers while the destroyers held off the subs and counter-attacked them. Graham managed to get his fleet in, but lost one of the corvettes on a mine. The other had to stay to replace the missing boom defence vessel. The big ships were saved but the game came to an inconclusive end from lack of time, the mines and subs having driven both battle squadrons to the safety of their harbours.

"That was a bloody good game," Graham replied, "but I hated those mines. We should ban the bloody things."

"No! They were good!" Paul cried.

"I will get a few minesweepers next time," Graham said.

As Graham went downstairs with Peter he glanced into the workshop under the house. "What model is that Pete?" he asked, catching sight of another ship under construction.

"You weren't supposed to see that till Sunday," Peter laughed. "Come and look. She is my new carrier."

The model was of an aircraft carrier. It was fully 80cm long and already had a flight deck crammed with thirty planes and lined with AA guns. It was a model of a US Essex-class carrier and really excited Graham's envy. He noted that Peter had glued the cardboard flight deck to a thin sheet of balsa, which made it much smoother and stronger. He had also lined the hull with cardboard to hide the rough wood and that made it look even better. By comparison, Graham's model of the *Glorious* looked quite shabby.

That inspired him to another burst of model building. As he rode home he vowed to match Peter's carrier. As soon as he got there he opened books with pictures of carriers and decided that he would make the British equivalent: HMS *Indomitable*. Plans were hastily drawn and a baulk of pine found for the hull. It was only 75cm long but was the best he could find. He set to work to saw and rasp it into shape.

Once again his mother ordered him to bed. He retired resentfully and lay dreaming of the models he would make and how he would beat Alex and Max next weekend.

Next weekend! That is when these Yank ships arrive. What on earth should I do? he worried. But he dropped off to sleep undecided.

Chapter 32

DECISION

As he rode to school on Thursday Graham knew he had to make a decision about the conversation he had overheard. All the arguments for and against churned around in his brain. He tried to tell himself it was none of his business; but he knew that was not true. *The fact that it bothers me so much means I can't just ignore it and hope it will go away,* he thought.

On arrival at school he met Thelma and she helped increase the pressure he felt. She smiled and was friendly and even brushed against him several times so that his heart began to thump eagerly and his hopes shot up. Somehow he kept talking about anything but ships, but all the while he turned over in his mind how to find out if Thelma was going to be involved in the demonstration. The question was becoming urgent.

Those two ships arrive tomorrow, he thought. *I have to know. Oh! What should I do?*

At that moment Graham made his decision: he would tell someone in authority. But who? As he puzzled over this he saw Andrew Collins in the distance. *Andrew might know,* he thought. So he caught up with Andrew, who grinned and said, "Hi Graham! Not sitting with the love of your life today?"

Is it that obvious? Graham wondered. He shrugged and grunted, then said, "Andrew, I've got a bit of a problem. Could you spare me a minute?"

"Sure. What is it?"

Graham led Andrew out of the stream of students and outlined what he had overheard. As he finished he asked: "Who do you think I should tell?"

Andrew rubbed his chin and frowned. "You could tell the CO. He would know who to pass it on to. Let's ask big sister. She will know."

So they sought out Carmen and Graham had to retell the story. He found it harder this time as it involved recounting how he had been kissing Thelma and that hurt as it was private and very personal. He glossed over what he and Thelma were doing in the garden and concentrated on what he had overheard.

Carmen agreed with Andrew. "I think you should tell Commander Hazard. He will know what to do. But you had better hurry. The ships come in tomorrow afternoon."

"How do I get in touch with him?" Graham asked.

"At his work I suppose. He has a ship's chandlery down near Portsmith," Carmen replied.

Graham did rapid calculations. To get to Portsmith he needed his bike. *I was hoping to walk home with Thelma after school,* he thought, but his estimation of timings made it rapidly apparent he would not have time to do both. He bit his lip as the cruel choice became clear. "Perhaps I could phone him?" he suggested.

Carmen nodded. "Yes, do that first," she agreed. "Come on, there's the bell. We will be late for class."

Graham made his way unhappily to class. *What will I say to Thelma? Will I even tell her?* he agonized. He felt very much the traitor yet perversely felt relieved at having made the decision and told someone. On arrival at the classroom he saw that Thelma was already seated with Janet. Thelma met his eye and smiled quizzically.

Graham smiled back but he felt sick inside as he did. *Will I tell her? What will I say?* he wondered. All through the morning lessons he sat mulling over his options, steadily becoming more and more miserable. *How will I face her?* he wondered.

At morning break he got part of the answer. He went to the tuckshop but Thelma wasn't there. So he walked over to where she normally sat. As he came around the corner he saw Janet talking to Jerry Denham. He heard Janet say: "She says he is SO boring; and that he is such a..."

Denham saw Graham and flicked his eyes significantly. Janet stopped in mid-sentence and turned. Her lip curled and she said sarcastically, "Oh hello sailor. How is your battleship this morning?"

"Fine thanks," Graham replied, trying to sound off-hand. He was hurt but did not want to show it. *Was she talking about me?* he wondered. Was Janet repeating something Thelma had told her? What was he? He felt annoyed and embarrassed. But still hopeful he kept on walking, his mind seething with worry and resentment.

Then, in the distance Graham saw Thelma, but it took him an effort of will to walk over to her. He wanted to find out if what he had overheard was about him but could not think of a way to even hint at it.

Thelma smiled and seemed quite happy to see him which calmed his fears somewhat. They sat and chatted until the bell went. But during the middle session classes Graham sat with maggots of doubt crawling in his brain.

At lunch time he got part of his answer. He saw Denham talking to Edmonson and he made a point of walking past close enough to overhear them. As Graham approached, neither Denham nor Edmonson noticed him. Denham said, "You bring the placards and..." At that moment he saw Graham and he stopped talking and gave Graham a sidelong glance that had no friendliness in it.

Edmonson was worse. "What do you want anal cadet? Piss off and mind your own business."

Graham went red. He made no reply but kept on walking. The insult had cut deep and he resented it very much. *Mongrels,* he thought. *I'll show you! I will tell the authorities. That will spoil your plans.*

After that Graham had to sit through the boring afternoon lessons while all he wanted to do was rush off to tell Lt Cdr Hazard. As he sat there mulling over his options he became steadily more and more miserable.

When the final bell went Graham packed up slowly, still hoping he could somehow find the time to walk Thelma home, and then go to see Lt Cdr Hazard. To add to the pressure she put him on a spot immediately by asking: "Are you walking with me Graham?"

Faced with her bright eyes and smile he gave in. "Yes, if you like," he replied.

She smiled again and while chatting about nothing continued to pack her school bag. They walked down the stairs together and Graham collected his bike and met her at the side gate. For the next 20 minutes they strolled slowly along. As they did he agonized over the possible future of their relationship.

Thelma suddenly said, "What's wrong? You seem a bit unhappy."

Graham nodded. His throat choked up and he blurted out, "I am. I'm worried about tomorrow. Are you going to be in this demonstration against the American ships?"

Thelma raised her eyebrows then said, "Yes, I am. Do you object?"

That put him right on the spot. His mind raced. *If I answer this wrong I could lose her,* he thought desperately. But equally he did not want to lie. "I would prefer you didn't," he replied.

"Well I'm going to. I might like you, but I don't like warships, particularly nuclear armed ones," she replied.

Graham was about to bite back and ask her how she knew they were nuclear armed but he held his tongue. He did not want a fight with her. After all he now had his answer. "I am just worrying. I don't want you to get hurt, or to get into trouble," he said.

"How could I get into trouble?" she asked.

"The police might arrest you," Graham replied lamely.

Thelma snorted. "Piffle! They only arrest one or two and they never charge them with anything."

Graham struggled for words but did not want to remind her of what she may have overheard in the garden too. Instead, he said, "I will be going to watch them tie up."

Thelma grinned. "Ooh good! You can join us then."

Graham shook his head. "I will be with the navy cadets."

She turned her nose up. "Oh them!"

They walked in uncomfortable silence for a while. Graham managed to change the subject. It was too painful and he did not want to let on what he was planning to do. He felt a real Judas. At the corner of her street they stopped. She asked, "Are you coming over for afternoon tea?"

Graham shook his head. "No. I... I'm going to Peter's again," he lied. The words nearly choked in his throat.

Thelma nodded and said, "OK. Have a good time. See you tomorrow."

Graham nodded. He felt so miserable he did not trust himself to speak. Thelma turned abruptly and walked off and he stood and watched her for a minute. Once she looked back, frowned then waved. He waved and turned away. For the next block he struggled with his conscience.

I can still change my mind. I don't have to tell anyone, he argued.

But sadly he realized he already had. Carmen and Andrew knew. The heart of the matter, he admitted to himself, was that he did not want to betray or hurt Thelma. With a great sigh he stopped at Peter's. He was at home and busy mass-producing another hundred Russian tanks. He came to the door at Graham's knock.

"G'day Graham. I didn't think you were coming over this arvo. Paul's not here so we can't play."

"That's all right Pete. I just wanted to use your telephone if I could," Graham replied.

Peter grinned. "Sure, as long as you aren't ringing London long distance," he replied. He led Graham in to the phone. "Afternoon tea?" he asked then tactfully withdrew, leaving Graham alone. For several minutes Graham stood and looked at the phone as though it was something liable to bite him. Tears were close and he felt terribly torn. With a shudder he reached down and picked up the phone book. A minute of searching provided him with the number he needed. Then he sat and again looked at the phone.

Peter put his head in the door. "Go on, ring her. She can only say no," he said. He went away again. The comment struck deep. Graham sighed and picked up the handset. His secret hope that Lt Cdr Hazard might not be there was squashed instantly. The CO answered the call.

"Hello, who's that speaking?" he asked.

"Recruit Kirk sir," Graham replied. He faltered, even now wishing he had not made the call and wanting to back out.

"Yes? What do you want? Graham isn't it?"

"Yes sir. Sir, it's... it's something I've heard. I... I don't want to say over the phone. But I think you should know about it."

"I see. Is it about cadets?" Lt Cdr Hazard asked, plainly puzzled and concerned.

"Well... sort of sir. It concerns those two American ships that are arriving tomorrow. I have overheard the demonstrator's plans. They are going to cause trouble and have a big demo planned. I... I wondered who I should tell," Graham said.

There was a moments silence while the CO absorbed this. Then he said, "Can you tell me more?"

"Yes sir," Graham replied. Now that he had started he felt the need to explain. Taking care with his wording he gave an outline of what he had heard. This took quite a while and during it Peter twice glanced in to see if he was finished and to tell him afternoon tea was ready.

When Graham finished, Lt Cdr Hazard said, "This sounds serious Graham. Where are you now?"

"At my friend's place sir. I can come over if you wish," he answered.

"No. That is a long way for you to ride. I'll tell you what; I will do some enquiring. Could you be home at your house after 5 o'clock? I can't just leave work. Would that be all right?" Lt Cdr Hazard asked.

"Yes sir. I will do that."

"Fine. What is your address?"

Graham gave the CO his home address and phone number. Lt Cdr Hazard then thanked him and rang off. Feeling both relieved and upset Graham hung up.

Peter appeared in the doorway. "Did she turn you down?" he asked sympathetically, seeing Graham's long face.

"It wasn't a girl," Graham replied. "It was the CO of the navy cadets. Sorry. I can't tell you about it. How is your aircraft carrier coming along?"

"Finished," Peter replied. "Come and eat."

He led the way to the kitchen. Graham glanced at the wall clock and saw that it was only 4pm—an hour yet. Feeling nervous and tense he sat down and began to discuss model ships over cordial and biscuits.

Peter asked: "Are we still going to play Battleships on Sunday?"

"Yes," Graham replied. He hesitated then asked in turn: "I am going down to the wharf tomorrow afternoon to watch these two American warships come in. Would you like to come?"

"Yeah. Should be quite an event," Peter replied. "I've heard that there is going to be a real demo against them. Apparently there are several busloads of demonstrators coming from Townsville and other places to take part."

"Who told you that?" Graham asked sharply.

Peter raised his eyes at Graham's tone but replied: "I heard two of the Year 12 girls talking about it; that Ozgood sheila and another one," Peter replied.

Graham nodded and felt even more unhappy. Peter looked hard at him then said, "That's what is bugging you isn't it? Your beloved is friends with Janet Ozgood and they are both anti-navy."

Struggling to hold back tears Graham nodded again. "I'd better go home. I am expecting visitors at 5 o'clock," he said.

They said goodbye and Graham got on his bike and pedalled home.

This time he detoured away from Thelma's street. Without thinking about it he went along the street Margaret lived in and, as luck would have it, she was out in her front yard. She saw him and her face lit up. She waved. He waved back, feeling a sharp stab of guilt as he did.

"I can't stop," he called. "I have to be home by 5 o'clock." *Poor kid!* he thought. He felt a heel.

At home Graham found Alex making more German tanks. He chased Graham out of his room. Feeling very upset Graham retreated to his veranda and sat to work on his new model aircraft carrier. By then he was strongly regretting having contacted Lt Cdr Hazard and wished he could somehow back out. As he worked he continually kept glancing out at the street. Kylie came home with another friend, Emma. She put her bike away and came up the steps.

"Home already?" she asked.

"Yes," Graham replied defensively.

"Did you walk little Miss Rabble Rouser home again?"

Graham was shocked. How did Kylie know he had walked Thelma home? He reacted. "She isn't a rabble-rouser!"

Kylie curled her lip. "Yes she is. I saw her with a group of them yesterday afternoon; that bearded fellow who led the demo the day we visited the HMAS *Hobart*. Besides, I've heard even worse about her," she said.

Graham went red, remembering the scene of Thelma and the other girls topless on the yacht. There had been quite a few comments about it at school. He was appalled that the gossip might have gone from his High School to Kylie's Primary School.

At that moment their mother arrived home. As soon as she came upstairs Graham met her. "Hello mum. I hope you don't mind but Lt Cdr Hazard is coming over to see me soon."

His mother at once frowned and looked worried. "You aren't in some sort of trouble?"

"No mum. It... it's something I heard. He wants to hear the full story. It's not about cadets."

Kylie heard the tail end of this and Graham did not want her or Alex to know any more so he clammed up. To avoid further questioning he went out to the front and waited. The minutes then dragged past, Graham becoming more anxious with every one.

At last two cars pulled up out front. That in itself was an unpleasant surprise. *Two?* Graham thought. He saw that the first was driven by Lt Cdr Hazard, wearing his business clothes, but was worried to note the two men in suits who climbed out of the second car. Both had a distinctly police-type look about them. Then he stared at the solid, middle-aged one in the suit.

He looks like the spook who was there when I was interviewed on the HMAS *Hobart,* he thought.

He wasn't wrong. Exactly what government department the men worked for he never did learn but they introduced themselves to his mother by showing badges in leather wallets, the sight of which instantly put creases in her forehead.

The solid one said, "I am Mr Cartwright. We met a few weeks ago after the flag incident on the HMAS *Hobart.*"

Mrs Kirk nodded and said, "Yes, I remember."

The other man was then introduced as Mr Baxter. He was a thin, hard-faced man in a suit of lighter grey and of better cut.

Mr Cartwright indicated Graham. "We need to question your son over something he says he has heard," he explained. Then he glanced at Alex and Kylie who both come out to see who was visiting. "Without anyone else listening in please."

"Yes, but I will stay," Mrs Kirk said firmly.

"Oh yes, certainly. I meant the other children."

Alex and Kylie were told to go away and not to interrupt. Mrs Kirk led the three men into the lounge room. They all seated themselves and the policemen, or security men, or whatever they were, took out notebooks and a recorder. Lt Cdr Hazard seated himself to one side.

Cartwright did most of the questioning, but Graham sensed that Baxter was the real boss. Graham did not like either man. There was something about them that made him feel scared. By then his regrets were even stronger and he felt trapped.

Cartwright met his eyes. "OK son, tell us the story. Start at the beginning, and leave nothing out," he said. Graham licked his lips, ordered his thoughts and began. He described how he had gone to Janet's and who he had seen there. At that point Cartwright interrupted.

"Hang on. How did you know who these people were? Go back a bit and explain how you got to know they were demonstrators."

That stopped Graham for a minute. Then he resumed, explaining how he been on the HMAS *Hobart* with the girls, including Thelma and Janet. Several more questions settled minor points. Graham then returned to the night at Janet's. He glossed over the fact that Janet's parents had not been there. Feeling very uncomfortable with his mother present he said, "I went outside with Thelma and we sat down in the garden... and..."

The men all smiled and Cartwright said, "We can imagine why you were in the garden with a girl. Go on."

Graham blushed furiously and tried to avoid meeting his mother's eyes. He went on to describe how the three men had come out and how he had overheard their plans.

Cartwright made some notes and then looked at him. "Did these men know you were there?" he asked.

Graham remembered the scene vividly and blushed. Then he shook his head. "No. I'm sure they did not. We were sitting behind a big bush."

"And they wanted to keep their plans secret even from their own people?"

"That's what they said sir," Graham replied. He was perspiring now and feeling very anxious, not least over what his mother might have to say afterwards.

Cartwright looked thoughtful. "I see. So what was this secret plan again?"

"They have told their people there will only be one thing happening but there will be three. There is to be a march from the Council Chambers to the wharf led by the bearded man, Sean."

"Sean O'Malley?" Baxter queried.

Graham nodded and went on: "And they are going to have a couple of those fast inflatable runabouts, Zodiacs they called them. You know, the inflatable boats with outboard motors on them. They are to hide behind the boats on the other side of the Inlet but they are only a decoy to draw the police boats away. That is when the group of canoeists led by this Frank fellow are going to head out from the Yacht Club."

Graham also mentioned the story Peter had told him of overhearing Danelle Ozgood talking about the busloads of demonstrators coming from Townsville. The two men looked at each other and Cartwright nodded. "Yes. We know about that thank you. Can you tell us more about Danelle Ozgood? Who does she associate with?"

Graham told them about Jerry Denham, Edmonson and Peabrain Pondorsky, then remembered Sonja Metcalf and her group. By then he felt awful as he had to mention when he had seen them. He carefully made no mention of the actual scene on the yacht.

The two men asked several more questions. Cartwright then said, "It is most important that nobody knows you have told this to us. The USA is in the process of reviewing all of its alliances and trade deals at the moment and it is most important we do not annoy them at this moment. Since the 'War on Terror' they are very nervous about the security of their ships. With this information we should be able to nip any trouble in the bud. So, not a word to anyone, particularly to this little girlfriend of yours. We can't afford any leaks."

Graham nodded and swallowed. "Yes sir," he replied in a tiny voice.

The two men then thanked Graham's mother and took their leave. Lt Cdr Hazard also stood up. "Thank you for your time Mrs Kirk. Thank you Graham for that. It could be very important. Will I see you down at the wharf tomorrow afternoon when the ships come in?"

Graham glanced at his mother who nodded. "Yes sir," he said.

"Good. See you then."

After Lt Cdr Hazard had gone Graham felt very mixed emotions: relief; and regret. To his great relief his mother said nothing about Thelma. Sadly he went to have his bath while tea was cooked. Later he saw mention of the two American ships on the TV news. That prompted him to dig out his father's *Jane's Fighting Ships* to look them up. The USS *Samuel P. McGillicuddy* was just an old FFG 7 similar to the ones in the Australian Navy. But the USS *Ticonderoga* was a major warship by any standards. She was a guided missile cruiser of about 10,000 tons; one of a class designated as AEGIS, which were specially designed for the air defence of naval Task Forces.

As he read the details Graham became very keen to see the cruiser. She was 171 metres long, which was 40 metres longer than a frigate and three times the weight. He noted that she was armed with surface-to-surface missiles: sixteen harpoons as well as SAMs and ASMs. She had 2 x 5" automatic guns and two of the multi-barrelled 20mm Gatling guns called Phalanx, plus AS torpedo tubes. She also carried two heavily armed helicopters.

The next paragraph made Graham stop and think. He then re-read it. This concerned the ship's propulsion plant. It was provided by four General Electric LM 2500 gas turbines.

"She's not nuclear powered at all!" he muttered, trying to remember who had said she was. He read it a third time to check. Definitely conventional propulsion: 80,000 horse power; 30 knots; complement 316 (27 officers and 289 enlisted men).

He noted the information about the ship's sophisticated electronics and fire control systems. *She certainly sounds like a very capable and powerful ship,* he decided.

For a minute or so he studied the photos of the ship. *She isn't a battleship but she is nearly as big. She will be really something to visit,* he thought.

He took himself to bed feeling quite excited. Friday promised to be a very interesting day.

Chapter 33

THE BIG DEMO

Friday. At school. Janet in full flight. "We must all make a statement for peace! We must show the warmongers that they cannot just walk on people. They should take their horrible weapons of destruction away and scrap them. We don't need them here; and we don't want them."

The class listened with interest. Old Wily raised his eyebrows and waited. Janet was really angry and seemed to be very worked up. She glared at Graham. "You should not support such evil by offering your bodies as a sacrifice. There will only be peace when the ordinary people all refuse to serve. If there were no armies there would be no wars."

Graham went red but held his tongue. He glanced at Thelma but she seemed withdrawn. Stephen was grinning. He nudged Graham and whispered: "She might make a sacrifice of her body—for me!"

Janet did not hear what he said but saw his smirk and turned on him. "You can laugh Stephen Bell! But if you really care you will come to the wharf this afternoon and help demonstrate against this invasion of filthy evil!"

"I'll be there," Stephen replied cheerfully. "I wouldn't miss it for quids."

Janet waved her arms. "It will be the biggest peace demonstration this city has ever seen," she continued. "I call on all of you to come and support the anti-war cause. We must let the government know they cannot just trample on our rights. They cannot just sail their disgusting nuclear battleships into our harbour."

Graham shook his head and finally spoke. "It is not a battleship. The *Ticonderoga* is an air defence cruiser; and she isn't nuclear. She runs on gas turbines."

Janet turned and spat savagely: "Lies! That is just what they want you to believe. It is a nuclear ship."

Graham shrugged and blushed. He could not prove it. Michael put more heat on him by adding, "The ship may not be nuclear powered but it probably carries nuclear weapons."

"Possibly," Graham conceded. He wished the subject had never come up. Janet started again but now Old Wily cut in.

"Thank you Janet. You have had your say. Now let us get on with the lesson. You can get on your soap box again at lunch time."

Janet started to argue but Old Wily firmly told her to be quiet and resumed the interrupted lesson. Graham sat back and breathed more easily. Out of the corner of his eye he watched Thelma, wondering exactly where he now stood with her. She did not look happy; and he certainly did not feel that way.

At lunch time when Graham plucked up the courage to approach Thelma she immediately asked, "Have you changed your mind about joining us Graham?"

Graham shook his head. "Sorry. No. I will be with the navy cadets and I will welcome the Americans." He said it with a feeling of sinking desperation but could not bring himself to pretend. In his heart he felt it was bad enough having to keep a guard on his tongue over the fact that he had betrayed the secrets of Thelma's friends.

Janet joined Thelma and that put an end to any personal conversation. Graham gave up trying and took the first opportunity to drift away. After that he sat on his own down at the oval till Peter saw him and came to sit with him.

"Woman trouble mate?" Peter asked.

"Yeah," Graham replied. He did not want to talk about it. Sensing this Peter tried to change the subject but immediately struck right onto Graham's sore spot. "You going down the wharf this arvo? They reckon it is going to be the biggest anti-American demo ever. It should be really something."

"Who told you that?" Graham asked.

"Oh I dunno. That's what everyone is saying. I reckon the whole town will be down there. Are you coming?"

Graham nodded. "Yes. Stephen and I are going straight after school. The navy cadets are part of the welcoming committee."

Peter also nodded. "Aah! And the girl of your dreams is on the opposing team. I see the problem," he said.

Graham grunted and didn't want to talk about it. He was just glad when the bell sent them back into classes. *Only an hour and a half to go,* he thought, anxiety about the event now gripping him.

That time was one of slowly building tension for Graham. He glanced frequently at Thelma but she appeared to concentrate on her work. Try as he might he could not think of any plan to coax her into a possible change of mind. When the bell went she met his eyes just once, blushed and turned away. To Graham she appeared to be quite unhappy. He had no chance to talk to her as Janet almost dragged her off.

Feeling baffled and upset Graham went downstairs with Stephen. They met up with Peter and Roger and went over to Roger's to dump their school bags and bikes before heading downtown. At Graham's suggestion they detoured to walk along the Esplanade. As soon as the sea came into view Graham's eyes scanned the horizon.

Two distant grey shapes, unmistakably warships, were at the far end of the channel. Graham felt his pulse quicken. He cried out "There they are!" and increased his pace. Their route led them a block clear of the City Library but as they crossed the intersection with Aplin Street Graham looked earnestly in that direction. He was hoping to see Thelma but all he saw was a throng of what appeared to be hundreds of people. There were police and placards very much in evidence. The big demo had begun.

The boys hurried on at Graham's urging. "We want to be on the wharf well before the ships got in close, just in case the police close it off or something," he explained. There were certainly plenty of police, some on point duty in the intersections, which was most unusual. There also seemed to be more traffic than usual and a steadily thickening stream of pedestrians all flowing towards the wharves.

As they reached the Yacht Club Graham excused himself for a minute and detoured into the driveway of the Green Island Terminal. As he walked quickly along he glanced left and was gratified to see two trucks in the Yacht Club driveway with several canoes on them. A number of people were busy unloading these. Two kayaks already floated in the Yacht Club Basin. Re-assured that what he had overheard was actually happening Graham hurried back to join the others.

The boys walked on, along with what Graham guessed were hundreds of other people. Graham saw Andrew, Carmen and Blake up ahead and wanted to catch them up but by the time they did they were in the gate at the wharves.

Getting in was more difficult. There were security guards and police and no-one was allowed to take any sort of bag. Everyone was scanned by metal detectors and only then allowed through the gates. Inside there were more police, in pairs and threes with radios. A TV camera team was setting up on a van in the car park. Interested tourists gawked at the growing crowd.

Graham led the way out onto the wharf. At least a dozen police stood there and they had set up barricades to keep people well clear of the area where the two ships were to berth. Graham squeezed through the throng over to the seaward edge of the wharf. From there he could see right down the shipping channel. From where he stood the long lines of pilings and lights marking the shipping channel were even more obvious. The two ships were now half way in, details becoming visible to the naked eye. The second ship appeared to be much larger than the leading one so he surmised she was the cruiser.

From the edge of the wharf Graham was able to scan the Inlet. He noted the police launches keeping all small boats well away and knew from the TV news that people had been warned to stay out of the 500m exclusion zone or risk prosecution. There had even been a warning that the Americans might fire at any boat that came too close to their ships. Even though that would be self-defence there was the possibility of innocent people being killed and that had made many people angry.

"What right have these Yanks got to come into our harbour with loaded guns?" muttered one middle-aged man.

A band started playing in the open area beyond the barricades and Graham saw a gathering of officials, police, media and naval personnel. He looked anxiously around and saw several other navy cadets in the crowd but no sign of their officers. To make matters worse the crowd was growing by the minute. Then Graham saw Lt Cdr Hazard and Lt Ryan, both in uniform, walk out to join the officials.

A police launch surged past only 20 metres from the wharf. Graham scanned the waters of the Inlet for the inflatable boats of the demonstrators. There were none to be seen. He began to worry that what he had been told was not going to happen. A helicopter clattered overhead: TV news. A second circled higher up: Police.

Another fast boat surged past: navy this time in a Rigid Raider-type inflatable runabout. In it were four divers in wetsuits plus a crew of two. Again Graham anxiously scanned the inlet. No sign of anything, just a few small boats well away from the channel and several launches leading the two warships in. As these got closer he saw they were the pilot launch and another police launch, a large, sea-going Shark Cat type. The crowd grew larger.

Someone had a pocket radio and Graham started to hear snippets of a live broadcast about the demonstration, which was now moving through the city. The tension mounted. It seemed everyone expected something to happen.

Ah! Two fast boats had appeared from behind the rows of moored yachts across the Inlet. Graham felt his chest tighten then relax. The demonstrators had started their decoy act. The boats were inflatable types with powerful outboard motors. They carried four people in each and bright coloured anti-nuclear flags waved from them. The two craft came zipping across the channel towards the wharf. In response the two police launches increased speed and turned to intercept them.

For a moment it looked as though one of the demonstrator's boats might collide with the police Rigid Raider but at the last instant it sheered away. Both inflatables then tore off up the Inlet with the police in pursuit, keeping between them and the wharf. Cries of surprise attracted Graham's attention. Two more inflatables had appeared from behind the moored yachts across the channel and were scudding towards the first of the warships, now only half a kilometre away.

Two more? That makes four, Graham thought. A niggling worm of doubt crept into his brain.

The big police Shark Cat spun round and headed to cut them off. The two police launches further up the inlet gave up their chase and turned back. The first two inflatables followed suit and came powering back. Fierce excitement gripped Graham as he watched. The police managed to head off the demonstrator's inflatables, but only by some dramatic and risky manoeuvres. The four inflatables suddenly swung round and headed back across the Inlet.

The three police boats swung round to follow. "Don't follow them!"

Graham muttered. He began to sweat. Had the police forgotten the canoes at the Yacht Club? At that moment there was a burst of noise and hundreds of demonstrators began surging onto the wharf into an area blocked off by police barricades. Graham turned to scan the crowd anxiously, hoping to see Thelma.

He picked her out almost at once. She was right up the front with Sean O'Malley, Sonja, Danelle and Janet. Sean O'Malley had a loudspeaker and was shouting directions. The demonstrators were chanting and waved hundreds of placards. More police appeared from a doorway as the demonstrators started to push past the wooden barricades at Sean's urging. In an instant the whole wharf was swamped by hundreds of cheering, shouting people. Graham was both thrilled and appalled. He had never seen a really big crowd and it frightened him.

How on earth will the police control them? he wondered, anxious for Thelma who was now in the midst of the surging mob.

The frigate was now in mid-stream off the wharf and had slowed down to berth. A tug moved out to assist. Graham looked anxiously downstream and noted that the three police boats were now right across the far side of the Inlet, apparently playing catch with the four inflatables, which were zig-zagging through the lines of moored small craft.

A loudspeaker boomed: "Please all move back behind the barricades. The ships will not attempt to berth while there are people in the out-of-bounds area."

For a few minutes the demonstrators ignored this and the request was repeated. The frigate and tug swung and then slowed to stem the outgoing tide. The cruiser came to a standstill in the end of the channel and a tug moved to assist her.

Sean O'Malley raised his loudspeaker and called and the demonstrators suddenly turned and began moving back away from the edge of the wharf. To Graham the discipline and organization of the demonstrators was a revelation. That both alarmed and impressed him.

Within a minute all the demonstrators were back where the barricades had been erected and they even helped the police to stand them up again. The chanting stopped and a sort of calm descended on the crowd.

Graham now turned his attention to his left, staring back along the edge of the wharf towards the Yacht Club and marina.

"Here come the canoes!" he muttered. "Oh come back you fools!"

Eight kayaks, each with two protestors in it, had come sliding out of the Yacht Club basin. These now paddled furiously in the direction of the frigate which was edging in towards the wharf. An American officer stood right up in her bows, pointing at the kayaks and talking on a hand-held radio. Beside him stood two sailors with rifles. At the officer's command they cocked the rifles and aimed them at the kayaks. Graham felt his chest tighten. Dread and ghoulish fascination mingled in his emotions: fearing to see someone shot, yet morbidly curious about it!

From the marina downstream two more fast craft appeared—Police Rigid Raiders. Graham heaved a sigh of relief and leaned over to watch, his excitement growing to a fever pitch. The two new police Rigid Raiders rapidly overtook the kayaks and cut in between them and the frigate. Two kayaks slipped in under the wharf but so did one of the Rigid Raiders. Graham noted the other three police boats still holding off the four inflatables across the inlet. The frigate stopped then resumed slowly moving in towards the wharves, the swirl of her propeller showing clearly in the murky water. The ship was facing upstream so that her stern would end up just past where Graham stood and her bow further along the wharf.

The cruiser must be going to berth further along, he decided, noting the empty wharf space in the distance. *Tide is on the ebb,* he observed, noting how fast the outgoing current was. By now the two crowds had merged and formed one huge milling throng which the police were struggling to keep back from the stretch of wharf which the frigate was nosing in towards.

Police loudspeakers began to order the crowd to move back. The frigate came to a standstill 50 metres out, stemming the tide with the aid of the tug. Graham saw more armed sailors at her stern and also noted several parties of sailors with fire hoses. Even more thrilling was the sight of a group of three sailors in helmets grouped around an automatic gun up on the superstructure.

The Americans are anxious all right, he thought.

The frigate remained out in the stream until all of the demonstrators had been pushed back again behind the barricades. This caused a lot of jostling, shoving and bad-tempered pushing. Graham caught a glimpse of Thelma and pushed his way along towards her. He saw that her face was alive with the excitement of the event. Her focus was the ships and while she occasionally looked around at the crowd she did not see him. Janet, Denham and Sean O'Malley appeared behind her.

When Graham reached Thelma he tapped her on the arm.

Thelma glanced at him. "You came then?" she cried. "Isn't it great? There are more than a thousand demonstrators here. It is the biggest demo ever. We will really make the government take notice now."

Graham made a non-committal grunt, still anxious not to offend her. Thelma turned to Janet who was now beside her. "Gosh that ship is big!"

Graham turned to look. The cruiser was now stopped in mid channel a few hundred metres away and it did look big. Then Janet scowled. "I don't care how big it is. It's still a battleship and it isn't welcome here."

Graham could not help himself. "It's not a battleship. It's only a cruiser," he explained. "A battleship would have trouble fitting into Cairns Harbour. The channel is too shallow and narrow and the Inlet isn't really wide enough for one to safely swing."

"Swing!" Janet sneered. "It's a warship so I'll call it a battleship if I like." She pushed in front of him and began to wave a placard. "Yankee go home!" she shouted in Graham's ear. "Ban nuclear weapons! No atomic bombs in our town! Go away, you aren't welcome here!"

"Yes you are!" Graham shouted to the sailors lining the deck of the frigate, now only 5 metres out. The ship had slid slowly past so that now he was level with the helicopter deck on her stern. The bow was nudged in against the wharf. From the stern opposite where Graham stood a heaving line was tossed to waiting seamen from the RAN but several demonstrators dodged past the police and grabbed it and a tug-of-war began. This ended with the rope being tossed into the water. An officer with a radio spoke and the swirl under the frigate's stern stopped before the rope was wrapped around her propeller.

At that moment two kayaks appeared from under the wharf. From the deck of the frigate fire hoses spurted a powerful jet down on them, driving them back under cover. A police Rigid Raider popped out briefly then also vanished under the wharf.

The mooring line was hauled back and thrown again. This time it came close to where Graham was. The RAN sailor nearest reached for it but was jostled out of the way by Denham and Edmonson. The line fell on the wharf near Graham's feet. Quickly he reached down to grab it. People around him began to push and shove, but he clung on tightly.

Suddenly he felt a savage shove in the middle of his back. There was a scream and Graham felt himself stumble. Before he realized what was happening he was over the edge of the wharf. Below him was the turgid water of the Inlet.

As he fell his mind registered the grey painted steel of the frigate's side, the black of her boot-topping, the swirl of water along her sides, churned up by the propeller. He clung onto the rope but realized an instant too late that this was a mistake as it swung him violently against the steel side. The impact came as a savage blow.

Stunned, he lost his grip and fell into the water.

***

Even as he struck the surface, Graham's mind screamed in panic: *Propellers!* His eyes were open but he was so surprised and stunned that he could only note, in a detached sort of way, the black of the ship's bottom, the darkness below and the murk under the wharf. Sheer terror gripped him as he was tumbled over and over by the suction of the propeller.

Stop it! Oh please God, stop it! his mind cried.

Frantic to live he struggled to swim but found he was quite powerless in the grip of the suction. Then he whacked his head on the steel hull and felt blackness threatening to engulf him.

Some part of his struggling brain told him that the turbulence had ceased—the propeller had stopped. There was a swirl of bubbles near him as he tried to orient himself to find which way was up. Now other fears gripped him, his old enemies: sharks, crocodiles and gropers. Something grabbed him and he screamed underwater.

The scream was cut off as he swallowed salt water. A burning, choking sensation seared down his throat and into his lungs. His vision blurred. Then he realized it was a diver who had him in his grip. The man was a powerful swimmer and hauled Graham quickly upwards. Graham still had his wits about him sufficiently to recognize the lightness which indicated the surface, and for him to continue to hold his breath.

They broke surface and Graham had an impression of the side of the frigate, a strip of sky, and the edge of the wharf lined with faces peering down. The diver held him in a firm grip. From under the wharf a navy Rigid Raider slid out to come to a stop next to him. The rubber nudged Graham's cheek. Hands grabbed him and he was hauled aboard. The diver followed.

For a while all Graham could do was lie and be sick. He vomited up what seemed like an enormous amount of seawater while strong hands held him. The boat meanwhile slid out from under the wharf and out past the stern of the frigate. An anxious face looked into Graham's. He recognized it: Warrant Officer Crabb's.

"You OK son? How do you feel?"

"I'm OK sir. I..." Graham began. Then he retched again, this time over the side, still held by the strong hands.

Warrant Officer Crabb shook his head. "That was a bloody silly thing to do; you nearly went through the props then," he said.

"I was pushed sir," Graham replied indignantly, wishing fiercely that he did not feel like vomiting again, and that his eyes weren't misting with tears. Ashamed of showing weakness he tried to stop himself trembling.

WO Crabb looked at him. "I've met you before. Who are you?"

"Graham Kirk sir. I'm a navy cadet. I was on the LCH HMAS *Tarakan* last weekend."

"Ah yes. You are the kid who asked all the questions and whose dad owned the old LCT," WO Crabb replied. "Now, are you sure you are alright? Have you hurt yourself anywhere?"

"Bumped my head sir, that's all," Graham replied stiffly, burning with shame as two tears trickled down his cheeks, their tracks made more obvious to him by the chill of the cool breeze.

At that moment one of the other men in the boat called out and pointed. Graham struggled to sit up and look around. The man holding him, another navy diver, helped him up. WO Crabb swore, then picked up a radio and started talking. First he informed whoever he was talking to that Graham was all right, and gave his name then he said, "There are a whole swarm of kayaks coming down the inlet past the navy base."

Graham focused against the wind and stared. There they were; a dozen or more, all being paddled furiously. The sunlight flashed on the rapidly moving paddles. An awful doubt slid into Graham's mind.

These kayaks weren't in the plan I overheard, he thought. Had the protesters changed their plan?

Radios chattered. The Rigid Raider still under the wharf reported it could not leave as it was only just managing to keep the eight kayaks there away from the frigate, which was now against the wharf. The three police boats holding off the four inflatables were called on. The large Shark Cat was left to keep the inflatables away while the other two headed back up the inlet, throwing up showers of spray as they drove into the chop.

"Cunning buggers!" WO Crabb said. "They have timed it well. They have the tide on their side. Look how fast they are moving."

Graham could see what he meant. The canoes were slipping along with quite astonishing speed. With a roar their own motor surged into life and they set off to intercept them. For Graham the next 10 minutes was one of wild excitement. He was handed a life jacket and told to put it on and then hang on. Quickly he put the jacket on and was glad of it for several times they came close to tipping over as they executed violent manoeuvres to cut off kayaks. Spray soaked him but he barely noticed it.

Most of the kayaks were kept at bay but three slipped in close enough to mark the side of the frigate with paint. They were unable to paint slogans as the crew of the frigate hosed them with high pressure hoses, driving them off in a waterlogged condition.

WO Crabb swore and said, "I dunno where these buggers have come from. They weren't mentioned in the briefing."

That gave Graham an uneasy feeling. This turned to apprehension a moment later when the radio crackled again and the wet-suited man holding it called, "Hey, Crabby, they need us back there. The cruiser is in trouble."

"What sort of trouble?" WO Crabb asked as they spun round to face down channel.

"They've got a rope or something wrapped round their props and they are being sprayed with paint," the diver replied.

"How the bloody hell...?"

"That launch apparently," the radio man replied pointing. Graham saw an old motor boat on the eastern side of the channel. One of the inflatables had stopped alongside it. Two men scrambled out of the motor launch and into the inflatable. Two other inflatables could be seen skimming across the cruiser's bows in the other direction, with the Shark Cat heading them off. The fourth inflatable was nowhere to be seen. The inflatable at the old motor launch suddenly shot away and headed towards the mangroves on the eastern shore.

"That one, follow him!" WO Crabb shouted.

The bow turned slightly but it was apparent even to Graham that they had little chance of catching the craft. It was moving just as fast and had a good lead of about a kilometre.

Graham heard a series of short, sharp noises. WO Crabb listened to the radio, then said, "The Yanks are firing warning shots at those inflatables. They are not happy! This could get very ugly."

"No uglier than you, Crabby!" called the other diver.

The men all laughed and Graham envied them their sense of purpose and comradeship. He turned and looked at the cruiser and saw to his astonishment that coloured paint was spraying out from hoses or pumps which were mounted on the channel markers on either side of it. One hose was showering the forward half of the cruiser with bright pink paint and the other was covering parts of the deck and superstructure with luminous yellow.

At that moment the other two inflatables shot into view from around the stern of the cruiser, still with the Shark Cat in pursuit. These two separated and both headed for the lines of moored boats across the inlet.

The radio ordered their Rigid Raider to try to catch one. They turned and headed for the closest. The motor bellowed and spray flew past as the boat skimmed and bumped across the waves. Graham found it the most exhilarating ride he had ever had. He gripped the side in excitement, willing them to go faster.

But it was no good. The inflatable they were pursuing raced through the lines of moored boats and vanished from sight up a mangrove creek. The Rigid Raider sped up the creek after them, the mangroves flashing past only metres away on either side. The police helicopter buzzed low overhead.

A few minutes later they caught up with the inflatable. It had been beached at a gap in the mangroves and the men were gone. The Rigid Raider surged ashore, its engine dying. The divers sprang out.

"You stay here young Kirk," WO Crabb ordered. Graham jumped out too but did as he was told. He went to the top of the bank to watch and was in time to see a white 4WD vanishing around the bend of a rough track along the top of an earthen embankment. The police helicopter circled low over the vehicle.

WO Crabb and the other three divers, two of whom were apparently policemen, gave up the chase and returned in disgust to the boat. "The chopper boys will track them," one of the policemen said. "We should catch them at a road block."

Graham followed the annoyed group back to the boat. One of the policemen secured the abandoned inflatable with a painter and they set off back down the mangrove creek with it in tow. It was very apparent to Graham that the men were feeling they had been outsmarted. That made him feel guilty as he presumed it had been his information that their defensive strategy had been based on.

They motored out into the Inlet and across to where the huge cruiser lay stationary in the channel. The pink and yellow paint made it look ridiculous and Graham felt deeply anxious. The ship was now surrounded by two tugs, a pilot boat, two boats with TV crews and the police Shark Cat. As the diver's rigid raider approached another large, powerful launch came racing out from the marina to stop alongside.

Now Graham clearly understood what had happened. The dredged shipping channel leading into the port of Cairns is 10 kilometres long, its course marked by two rows of pilings and lights. The pilings are in pairs on either side of the channel and are spaced along it at intervals of about a kilometre. The demonstrators had secured a rope to a post on the western side of the channel and then laid it on the seabed across the channel to a piling on the eastern side. To each piling they had fastened a pressure pack of coloured paint. They had then attached a long rope and a pulley and moved their launch further to the east to be out of the exclusion zone. When the cruiser had begun passing between the pair of pilings the launch had moved away, pulling the rope tight so that it rose up to scrape along the bottom of the cruiser until it was caught by the propellers. Then the paint packs had been activated.

Very cunning, Graham had to concede, but as it wasn't part of the plan he had overheard he felt very anxious.

Close up the cruiser was huge. Graham stared up at her in awe, his eyes drinking in all the details and shaking his head at the coloured paint that now covered large areas of the ship and even some of the crew. By now he was feeling too uneasy to enjoy the spectacle. He had an awful feeling that something had gone very wrong.

This was soon confirmed. He was passed up to the large launch which had just arrived, to find himself confronted by the two security men: Mr Cartwright and Mr Baxter. They glared at him then told him to sit while they went up the gangway to the deck of the cruiser. A plain clothes policemen stood over Graham and told him not to move. That gave him an awful shock and he wondered what he had done wrong.

All he could do was sit and shiver as the wind dried his wet clothes. He was able to see over the stern of the launch and watched WO Crabb and another diver don their scuba gear and slip into the water at the cruiser's stern. A group of a dozen American officers and ratings, plus the two security men, were visible leaning over the stern rail watching and discussing the problem. They were not in a good mood.

After a while WO Crabb and his mate surfaced and climbed up into their boat. They and the officers and security men discussed their findings. The security men shook their heads. After some more discussion with the American officers the two security men, plus an American lieutenant commander came back to the launch.

As they approached him Graham swallowed, feeling sick with apprehension at the hostile look on their faces. Mr Cartwright stood over him with his hands on his hips and chewed his lip. Then he said, "Well, that wasn't in the plan you told us young Kirk. It seems they had a rope fastened to the post marking that side of the channel, with its other end attached to that old motor boat. They let it hang slack so that the frigate could pass over. The cunning bastards even had an American flag and waved a welcome."

He pointed angrily to the old motor boat which was now tied to the channel marker nearby. "Then, when all our boats were decoyed away they waited for the cruiser to come past and pulled the rope up under her so that it caught in her propellers. Then they set off those paint sprayers."

He shook his head angrily and Mr Baxter swore. The American naval officer went red in the face and became hostile. Cartwright went on, "Then the two men in the old motor boat were picked up by one of their inflatables and have got clean away. All four of the boats have reached shore in a different place and they had cars waiting. We haven't caught a single one—yet. It's plainly obvious to me that we have been fed a line because our whole plan was wrong. There weren't three lots of demonstrators; there were five. That second lot of canoes wasn't in the story you told us; and nor was this bit of sabotage. Now, the question is this: did you deliberately feed us a line? Or are you a dupe, who has been used to pass us false information?"

Chapter 34

MISERY

"I'm not lying! That is exactly what I heard!" Graham cried miserably. The questioning had now gone for over two hours and he was feeling very upset.

Mr Cartwright leaned back and gave him a hard stare. "Then that means you were set-up; that you were used to trick us with false information."

As that ugly thought sank in Graham's mind recoiled from its deeper implications. *Used!* If so then Thelma had been a party to the plot. The idea made him feel physically ill.

Graham's mother, who had been present during the questioning at Police HQ, now spoke up. "I think that is enough of an interrogation thank you. I'm sure Graham has not lied to you, that whatever he told you he did in good faith. You people should be efficient enough to cross-check your sources of information. We will go now thank you."

The security men looked uncomfortable at the suggestion they were not efficient. "Bloody shambles the whole thing," muttered a uniformed Inspector. "We should never have allowed anyone onto the wharf." This last was delivered in a tone Graham detected as definitely of the 'I told you so' type.

Mrs Kirk led the very unhappy boy out without any objection from the police or security men. It was dark outside by then, after 7pm. They drove home in silence. Graham was tormented by the idea that Thelma had been a party to the deception. *Surely she wouldn't?* he asked himself, sensing the deeper levels of deceit implicit in that. *That would mean she did not like me at all and was only pretending!* At that the tears began.

On arrival at home both Alex and Kylie wanted to know the story. "We saw it all on TV," Alex cried. "When you went off the wharf we were sure you were a goner. They must have stopped the propellers just in time."

"Propeller," Graham replied gruffly. "FFGs only have a single screw." He did not want to talk to Alex at that moment. The tears threatened to start again.

Kylie looked sympathetic. "Was that you in the little runabout?"

"Yes."

"Well, tell us about it!" Alex cried.

Mrs Kirk intervened. "That is enough. We have just spent two hours telling the police. Leave Graham alone. He can tell you when he feels like it. You get ready for Scouts Alex or you will be late."

Graham sniffled and looked up. "What happened to the cruiser?"

"The USS *Ticonderoga*?" Alex asked. "She got towed in by a tug." Then he laughed. "Boy! Doesn't it look funny all painted party colours!"

That confirmed what Graham had suspected. *My information helped to decoy the security people away from the real threat,* he thought. The humiliation and shame made him burn. He turned and walked out to his bed, threw himself on it and began to sob.

About half an hour later his mother came out and gently stroked his hair and told him it would be all right. "It is only politics, nobody got hurt," she said. "Now come and have some tea."

Graham shuddered with sobs again. "I was nearly killed!" he cried. "Someone pushed me off the wharf."

"You can't be sure of that. There was a big crowd all jostling," his mother replied.

"I was pushed, I am sure of it," Graham replied. The memory of that hard shove came back to him clearly. The thought that someone might want him dead sent shivers of dread through him but he could not think who it was. *Who was standing behind me?* he wondered.

"You told the police that. Let them investigate," his mother said soothingly. "Now calm down and forget about it."

It was then that what was really troubling him caused him to blurt out: "But... but you... I... she... It means that I was deceived by Thelma. That... that she doesn't... (sniff) doesn't like me at all!"

Graham's mother had no answer to that. She gently stroked his hair as he lay face down in the darkness. After a time, Graham calmed down and followed her out to the kitchen. It was too late for him to go to Scouts and he did not want to go anyway. The wound to his pride was too raw and painful.

Then the phone rang. Graham's heart leapt. Perhaps it was Thelma? But it was not. It was Peter, wanting to know how he was; and what had happened. Graham gave only a short outline, aware that Peter did not know of his part in informing the authorities. Graham asked Peter if he had seen who pushed him but Peter answered in the negative. "I was too busy looking at the ships," he replied.

No sooner had Graham hung up than the phone went again; Roger this time, also wanting to know the story. Another uncomfortable conversation followed. Later he sat and watched the mid-evening news on TV and saw himself on a video clip from a helicopter as he went down between the wharf and the frigate. As soon as he saw it he wished he had recorded it to the HDD so he could watch again.

I might see who pushed me, he thought. Then he decided to make sure the police viewed the footage. *That could have been murder,* he told himself. Then he shuddered and broke into sobs again as misery engulfed him. The fact that the demonstration was the major item on the national news and was headlines around the world did nothing to ease his conscience.

As he watched the helicopter view of the chase and then of the disabled and multi-coloured cruiser being towed in by tugs Graham burned with shame and a sick feeling at being used. The demonstrators had certainly made headlines!

Graham went early to bed and lay wracked by misery as he grappled with the ugly thoughts about whether Thelma had known and gone along with the plan willingly. He replayed every incident for the previous week and that made him feel very uncomfortable. Thelma had seemed very friendly but had still been stand-offish even then. The incident in the garden was the one that bothered him most. She had let him kiss her— and more.

"But when those men came out and I suggested we move somewhere else she said no and then she let me..." he muttered. As the memories of her taking his hand and placing it on her breast came to him he felt physically sick.

Was that part of the plan, so that she could make sure I was there to 'accidentally' overhear the false plan? he wondered.

He mulled over everything he could remember, annoyed that some of it he could not recall clearly. *That drunk, Frank, he could have just been pretending. I thought he had not noticed us but he might have really been checking that we were in the right place before they began their play act.*

Then an ugly thought made him wonder about the type of relationship Thelma might have with those men. *After all she was topless with some of them. Perhaps they...?*

The ideas were too painful. It made his insides writhe with jealousy and disgust. Surely it was all just a horrible mistake? *The demonstrators might have just changed their plans,* he told himself.

He considered the likelihood of him actually passing on the information to the authorities. That seemed to him a weakness in the plot. *What if I didn't? How would they know?* That thought led him to the idea that perhaps there was a double-agent in the police or security service who could tell the demonstrators. *No. Too far fetched. All they had to do was keep the other part of their plan secret. It would probably have worked nearly as well even if I had not told the police.*

At length Graham fell into a troubled sleep. When he woke on Saturday morning he felt drained and sick. As the recollections of the previous day's events flooded back his misery returned. This was compounded by the realization that he had another ordeal ahead. After lunch he was due to go to navy cadets; and they were to visit the USS *Ticonderoga*!

"I won't go. I couldn't face them," he told himself. The very thought of going onto the ship he had helped to sabotage made him feel miserable and sick. He voiced this opinion to his mother over breakfast.

She was not impressed. "It wasn't your fault. You acted in good faith. Besides, you don't solve life's problems by running away. If you don't have the courage to face them you lose your self-respect. Then you start to lose life's battle," she said.

Graham's mind squirmed on that for a while and he knew she was right: he would have to go whatever the humiliation. To fill in the morning he threw himself into chores: mowing the lawn, cleaning the guinea pig cage, tidying his room, sweeping, scrubbing the bath. He was involved in the latter task, clad only in a pair of wet shorts when Margaret arrived.

She knocked and looked in the door at his call. When Graham saw who it was he flushed with embarrassment, remembering the last time the two of them had been together in the bathroom. She was full of concern but, apart from saying hello, said nothing about the previous day's events. It was evident she knew something had happened but was unsure what. She had heard part of the story at Guides from Kylie the night before but not the full details. Graham did not enlighten her and she went off with Kylie to her room. He went on with the scrubbing, feeling more confused and upset than ever.

As he worked Graham turned over various strategies to try to find out what Thelma really thought about him. He still could not accept that she had simply befriended him to use him to pass false information to the police. *It is just too much work,* he tried to tell himself, *and too unreliable. They couldn't be sure I would actually do anything about things I heard.*

But the idea would not go away. It nagged at him all morning, tormenting him until it induced a sort of sick rage. This was exacerbated by his inability to formulate a plan for finding out where Thelma fitted into all this. A niggling thought in the back of his mind told him that if she was really his girlfriend, or if she even liked him, she would have at least phoned to see how he was, if not actually come over (as Margaret had done). He tried to push this idea out, but however he thought about it it still hurt.

***

Lunch time came. Kylie and Alex both wanted to know more details and Margaret sat opposite with concern all over her face. Graham managed to put on a brave face and talk about the chase in the Rigid Raider with some semblance of enthusiasm. He carefully avoided any reference to his part in passing information to the authorities.

Then it was time to go to navy cadets. Graham dressed in blue shorts and an old khaki shirt and gym boots. His mother drove him to the depot. As they pulled up Graham saw Andrew and Carmen near the entrance and he quailed at the coming ordeal. For a moment he sat in the car, too scared to get out. Then he met his mother's anxious eyes and she gave him a smile and nodded. He licked his lips and got out. With an effort he walked briskly forward with his head up.

Andrew called to him as he approached, "Hi Graham! That was a good dive yesterday. What happened?"

Graham stopped and began to relate his version of what had occurred. As he did he saw Lt Ryan approaching. The sight of the officer made Graham's heart palpitate with anxiety.

The officer stopped and said to him, "Recruit Kirk, the CO would like to see you. Follow me please."

Graham swallowed and felt sick. With a sinking heart he followed the officer into the office. As he went in the people inside all seemed to stare at him, although later he could not name who they had been. Everything except the door to the CO's office seemed to be misty. The next thing he knew he was inside with Lt Cdr Hazard seated behind his desk and Lt Ryan seating himself to one side.

Lt Cdr Hazard looked up, a grim set to his mouth. He did not invite Graham to sit. "Well Recruit Kirk, I have had a very uncomfortable morning on account of you. I have spent over an hour with the security men listening to how your little story led them to adopting a plan which resulted in the fiasco yesterday afternoon. They are of the strong impression that you deliberately fed them a line to help the demonstrators."

"No sir! That's not..."

"Wait till I finish. That is their opinion as you have been frequently seen in the company of several of the key leaders of the demonstrators. I gather your girlfriend is one of them?"

Graham's mind raced. Was she his girlfriend? He did not know. "I don't think she is sir. She..." He could not finish he was so upset.

Lt Cdr Hazard made a face and went on, "Anyhow, that is your business. I have also spent an hour down at the USS *Ticonderoga* convincing the Americans that we are their friends and that the visit to the ships should not be cancelled on account of yesterday. After all we were there to welcome them. But, because of the doubts about your role in yesterday's rather humiliating shambles, it has been made very clear to me that you will not be welcome on their ships. I'm sorry, but you are not allowed to go with us on the visit."

It took Graham a moment to absorb this. He flamed with shame and knew he was trembling with emotion. Then other awful thoughts crowded into his mind. "Does that mean I am going to be chucked out of the cadets sir?" he asked in a croaking whisper.

Lt Cdr Hazard shook his head. "No it doesn't. But it does mean you are under a bit of a cloud. Now, you had better phone your mother and get her to come and get you. We are closing the depot while we all go to the wharf and you can't stay here."

Graham heard this as though from a distance. Hot shame pounded in his cheeks. Outside he could hear the cadets being formed up on parade. He did not want to go out and be an object of curiosity or hostility to them. He managed to point and ask: "Do... do the other cadets know what I am being sent home for sir?"

Lt Cdr Hazard again shook his head. "No. You can tell them you are sick if you like. The only people who know anything about your role in this are myself, Lt Ryan and AB Collins and her brother; and I have already spoken to them. They promise not to say anything."

"Yes sir," Graham mumbled. His throat now choked up and he was further humiliated when his eyes filled with tears. He tried to hold back the sobs but couldn't. Lt Cdr Hazard stood up and went out.

Lt Ryan stayed with him till he had mastered his tears. "Go to the heads and wash your face, then ring your parents using this phone," he said, his voice hard.

Graham stumbled blindly out and made his way to the heads, hoping desperately that no-one had seen him. From that sanctuary he heard the cadets being called outside. While he waited, his mind and emotions whirling, he decided he did not want to phone his mother. He just wanted to be alone in his misery.

So he walked out of the depot, hoping that Lt Ryan did not see him. By then the other cadets were filing onto a bus outside. Rather than face them Graham detoured and went past the back of the bus and along the road away from the depot, the bulk sugar terminal on his left. From 200 paces along the road he watched the bus drive off, the happy faces of the cadets visible through the windows.

After they had gone, Graham turned around and walked back along the side of the road, oblivious to the traffic and feeling more wretched than he could ever remember. Anxious about his little deception, he hurried past the now locked depot and on past the navy base.

In spite of everything his steps led him in the direction of the main wharf. Several times he became so upset he could not see properly from the tears and he took himself into corners away from the traffic till his eyes dried and he felt able to continue. It was several kilometres walk and the sun was hot, blazing down from a clear blue sky.

On arrival at the wharves, he discovered that the whole area was now sealed off by police and security guards. No-one was being allowed inside the fence. Vehicles were checked carefully as to who their occupants were. To add to his emotions he saw that a large group of protesters with banners and placards stood opposite the main gate. From time to time they burst into songs or chanted slogans, particularly when small groups of uniformed American sailors came out to go on leave.

From a distance Graham loitered and watched them. He was looking for Thelma, and at the same time mentally scratching at his emotional wounds. There was no sign of her, but he did see the big-breasted blonde in the caftan who had been with O'Malley during the previous demos. The sight of her encouraged him to stay and he sat down across the street to watch.

His patience was rewarded half an hour later when he saw Thelma. But as he watched, Graham's whole body froze—she was holding hands with Edmonson! With them were Janet, Danelle, Denham and Pinky. They had come into view from the direction of the Esplanade. Graham stood up and walked towards them. He was so upset he did not care if he was making a spectacle of himself. As he got closer, Janet saw him and said something to the others. Graham got a very clear impression of hostility on the faces of most of them; and was that a flash of guilt on Thelma's?

Graham reached them and stopped, his eyes focused on Thelma. She avoided his eyes and went to keep on walking, which made Graham's stomach lurch sickeningly. "Thelma," he croaked. "Can I talk to you?"

Thelma met his eyes briefly and Graham saw that she appeared to have tears in them. She certainly looked unhappy and quickly looked away again. Janet stepped between them. "She doesn't want to talk to you."

"But... I need to know. Thelma, don't you like me anymore?" Graham blurted out.

Janet again answered for her. "She never did, you idiot, now clear out and leave us alone!"

The words seemed to slam into Graham's skull. All he was conscious of was Thelma turning away with Janet, and of Edmonson and Denham standing in front of him. Edmonson thrust out his arm and pushed Graham hard in the chest, making him stagger backwards.

"Bugger off Kirk or you'll regret it!" he said.

Stubbornly, Graham stood his ground. His eyes met Edmonson's and in a flash of revelation, he cried, "You! You pushed me off the wharf."

Edmonson's reaction confirmed it. He made no reply but the way his eyes moved and the blank look on his face told Graham he was right. "You could have killed me!" he added.

Edmonson curled his lip and raised his fists. "Clear out! And don't make wild accusations you can't prove," he retorted.

For a moment Graham was tempted to lash out but then he saw Thelma looking back with horror on her face. Emboldened he cried, "I'll do what I like!"

Edmonson moved to punch him but Denham stepped between them. He stood chest to chest with Graham and glared. "Leave Thelma alone, or else!" he snarled.

Graham wanted to fight now. Hurt and angry, a sort of red mist seemed to envelop him. To add to his misery, he saw Thelma again turn away and go hurrying off, Janet on her heels. Furious at his betrayal and near death, Graham tried to confront Edmonson.

But Denham and Pinky blocked him and also held Edmonson back. "Cool it mate," Denham snapped at Edmonson. "Walk away before the cops come over to investigate. They are looking at us. We don't want trouble yet."

Denham and Edmonson both glared and sneered at Graham, then turned and walked off. Graham stood in stunned misery as the youths followed the girls across the road towards the crowd of jeering and chanting demonstrators. He glanced around and saw that the bus with the navy cadets was just making its way across the car park inside the wharf enclosure.

That was the final straw to his emotions. Rather than have the cadets see him standing there in misery and defeat, Graham turned and ran along the footpath. He ran for a whole block, tears streaming down his face, the stares of tourists and curious onlookers adding to his humiliation. To avoid them he turned and fled into the park near the Green Island terminal and slumped down on a seat where he had some privacy. The thought that Cindy had been nearby with the French sailor only added to his distress. Overcome by utter misery, he broke down and sobbed uncontrollably.

Thelma does not love me! She has used me! he thought.

Chapter 35

WHAT TO DO ?

Graham lost track of how long he sat in the park. Several people walked past and looked at him but he turned his tear-streaked face away and hugged his misery to himself. It was true—he had been used. *Thelma doesn't love me!* he thought. He felt utterly devastated and defiled. More tears flowed and he briefly contemplated walking through to the wharf and throwing himself into the sea. He could never remember feeling so completely depressed.

Then fate twisted another emotional knife in his gut. Through the park walked an American sailor—with Cindy! She wore a very short skirt and he had his arm around her. She was laughing and he was telling her what a wonderful time she would have. Graham hid his face and felt physically ill; but she did not even glance at him. After they had gone he sat and brooded, thinking the darkest thoughts of his life.

Then it came to him that he should try to stop her. "I must save her," he muttered. "Her behaviour is partly my fault." With that in mind he stood up and ran in the direction Cindy and the American sailor had gone. But they were nowhere to be seen. Driven by an urgent desire to right the earlier wrong and to prevent more harm he ran on, rounding several blocks and drawing many curious glances.

Maybe they didn't leave the waterfront area? he thought. With that idea he hurried back to where he had last seen them. But then he could not decide which way to go and he came to a panting standstill.

The pain in his chest was so intense he trembled. He stood there, clutching his arms about himself, and looked anxiously in all directions. Once again misery overwhelmed him and tears came. To gain some privacy he walked unsteadily through to the Green Island Terminal. But a ferry was just nosing in with a load of tourists. In his current mood he did not wish anyone to witness his shame and defeat. He wanted to be alone, to brood, to summon up the courage to end it all. Barely able to see where he was going through his tears he fled through the yard of the Yacht Club.

That put him on the boardwalk along the side of the marina. There he paused as there was a boat ramp and roadway ahead. Rather than walk past the people there he stopped and leaned on the railing, bowing his head to hide his misery. For over half an hour he stood staring down at the swiftly flowing water of the outgoing tide. It looked dark green and murky with the scourings of the mangroves upstream. By turning his head he could see the stern of the American frigate at the main wharf. Beyond the frigate the superstructure and masts of the cruiser were visible. Sailors were visible re-painting the side of the cruiser.

For several minutes Graham looked at these symbols of his defeat and betrayal and felt the pain surge anew. Again he contemplated the dark water. He shivered. *I could end it all!* he thought.

Behind him a man laughed. The man said to his companion: "We really got them that time Brad. Boy, did I enjoy tying those bloody Yanks in knots!"

Graham's ears pricked up and he glanced around as the two men walked past behind him. The speaker was a middle-aged man wearing non-descript old blue shorts and singlet. He had grey hair and a hairy chest and back; the hairs also mostly grey. With a shock Graham recognized him. *He is the man I saw under the wharf with Sean O'Malley the day I retrieved the model ship,* he remembered.

The man named Brad was a thin, tanned man in his thirties. He had a beard and looked very fit. Brad laughed and agreed. "You should have seen their faces when we came paddling down past them. It was worth a million bucks. Your plan really worked. We had the stupid bastards fooled all right."

The middle-aged man nodded and replied, "What we have to do now is hit the buggers again. Our next blow will really make the world take notice. This time we..." But Graham could not hear anymore. The two men continued on as far as the roadway near the Pier. They had taken no notice of Graham and he was able to study them as they stopped to talk. Their words had burned into his shame.

I am one of the stupid bastards! he told himself fiercely. A wave of anger surged up. These were the men responsible for his humiliation and pain!

The middle-aged man climbed down into a grimy little runabout, started the outboard motor, and went sputtering off across the Inlet towards the boats moored on the other side. Graham watched intently. *He said he enjoyed tying the Yanks in knots. Was he the man on the old motor launch who wrapped the rope around the cruiser's propellers?*

Graham was seized with an intense desire to act. He looked around for a boat that he might be able to use to follow the man. *I need to know where he lives. Does he live on one of those boats over there?* he wondered. He eyed the rows of boats on the other side of the Inlet. There were dozens of them, of all types and sizes: yachts, fishing boats, motor launches.

Then another idea came to him: follow Brad and see if he could find out more about this organization that was plotting the protests. By this time Brad had vanished up a flight of stairs onto a low terrace at the large building which Graham recognized as a hotel. As a local he rarely went to such a touristy place so he did not know its layout. He hurried along the walkway to the stairs—and came almost face to face with Brad.

Brad was seating himself at a table on the terrace outside some sort of bar or restaurant. Already seated at the table was fat little man with a cheerful, ruddy face. The chubby man was dressed like a tourist: Hawaiian shirt, shorts, sunglasses; a camera slung round his neck. That the two knew each other was obvious. Graham stopped on the steps, which he realized instantly was a mistake as the chubby man glanced at him. Furious at his error Graham turned and went on along the walkway.

As soon as he was sure he could not be seen by the men Graham stopped. *How can I eavesdrop without them becoming suspicious?* he thought. A quick look along the walkway indicated the props he needed for his subterfuge: an old reel of fishing line, the end of which looked to be in a hopeless tangle. He walked along and scooped it up, then walked back along the walkway until he was just below the place where the two men sat. A low railing and ornamental plants gave him the cover he needed. His heart beating rapidly with excitement he seated himself near the steps with his back to the concrete retaining wall and pretended to be untangling the fishing line.

By moving his head a bit Graham could just see the man called Brad but could only just see the feet and legs of the chubby man. To Graham's annoyance he could only hear snatches of their conversation; and what he could was largely recollections of the previous day's events, interspersed with gossip and crude jokes.

Graham became engrossed in untangling the line and started to lose focus on why he was there. Several tourists walked past but they barely glanced at him. He looked out over the moored yachts and the water of the Inlet. The afternoon sun was now bright on the jungle clad slopes of the mountains and the air was fresh and cool. He shivered and realized it was getting late.

I'd better go home, he thought. *Mum will start to worry otherwise.*

Graham stood up to go and took a last peek through the pot plants at the two men, who were now leaning over the table in earnest conversation. At that moment a waiter, conventionally dressed in black trousers, white shirt and black bow tie, came out with a tray of drinks. The waiter stopped at the table and the two men looked up.

The chubby man said, "Thanks Rico. OK, we've decided on Monday's plan. Will your group still be available?"

"Monday eh? Sure," replied Rico, a swarthy skinned man with shiny black hair. "What time you want us? I gotta be at work by midday."

"About 10 o'clock will be fine," the chubby man replied. He paused and looked around to check no-one was near. "This is the plan; O'Malley's group will start a really rowdy demo at the main entrance to the wharf. They will try to break in. When all the cops are busy and the media have arrived Brad here will come up the Inlet with a dozen canoes and will try a paint job on both ships, mostly from under the wharf."

"Good!" Rico nodded approvingly. "Where will you put your canoes in this time Brad?"

"Just the other side of this building, over near that helipad at the seaward end of the marina," Brad replied. "We will bring them in on a truck again and our people will be waiting to unload them."

"The cops will be watching out for you," Rico replied.

Brad nodded. "I know. Our people will move there on foot in ones and twos beforehand," he replied.

The chubby man went on: "OK Rico, this is where you and your group come in. As soon as Brad's canoes have distracted the cops your team are to use those ladders and ropes to scale the fence at the far end of the wharf, then climb onto the roof of the warehouses. You can walk along on the roof all the way to the two warships then. Once you are there have a team paint slogans on the roof of the warehouse, big letters so the news helicopters can read them easily; and have another team throw paint bombs and insults at the ships."

"Got that," Rico replied with a grin. Graham listened to his accent and decided he was European, Spanish or Italian or something like that. Rico then asked: "How do we get away? I don't want to end up in jail. The cops might find out who I am then."

"Metcalf is organizing that. I have to see him tonight to see if he has things set up," Chubby replied. "I am meeting him at 8:00 on his yacht. As soon as I have the details I will come over to the bar here and will let you know, OK?"

"Sure," Rico grinned. He pretended to wipe the table clean and pick up empty glasses, then walked away. Graham watched him go in through the glass doors to the bar. By now his heart was pounding furiously. *I am overhearing the demonstrator's plans. And this time it can't be a set up. They surely can't know I am here,* he thought.

At that moment Brad stood up and it was obvious that he was saying farewell. Graham felt a surge of panic then forced himself to move. He scuttled 10 metres along the walkway, keeping bent double, then stopped and sat on the edge with his feet hanging over the water. The end of the fishing line was dropped into the water and he sat holding the reel, leaning on the railings. A post was used to half hide his face.

He was not a moment too soon as Brad came down the steps. Graham did not dare turn his head to look as Brad walked towards him. The man passed behind him and kept on going. Graham breathed out and watched out of the corner of his eye till Brad was out of sight in the direction of the helipad.

"Now what do I do?" Graham muttered. The obvious thing was to take the information to the security men, but the thought of meeting Mr Cartwright and Mr Baxter again chilled him. "They won't believe me anyway," he said bitterly.

He waited for a few more minutes, then moved back to peek through to the patio. Chubby was nowhere to be seen. Graham decided he had better go home. Deep in thought he walked quickly along to the entrance road to the marina, tossed his fishing line in the bin, and set off home at a brisk walk. Only then did he remember that his mother would have driven to cadets to pick him up at 4:30. Feeling sick at heart he broke into a jog.

It was dusk by the time he arrived home. To his surprise Margaret was sitting in the kitchen with Kylie and his mother.

"Where have you been? I've been worried sick about you," his mother said.

"I walked home."

"I can see that. Why didn't you phone me from cadets?"

Graham shrugged and had to fight back tears. "I... I went for a walk. Sorry mum. I was a bit upset," he replied. He glanced at Kylie and Margaret wondering what they knew. The thought of his exclusion from the ship visit brought back the pain in a rush. Did his mother know?

She did. She nodded. "I can imagine how you felt. I had a talk to Commander Hazard. He was a bit annoyed you had not called me."

That gave Graham another jolt. *I am not giving a very good impression at cadets,* he thought. Again he looked at Kylie and Margaret. His mother said, "Oh it's all right. They both know a bit of what happened."

Again tears prickled. Graham battled with them. He bit his lip. His mother noted these signs and said, "You go and have a bath and change and we will talk about it after tea. It is not the end of the world. I would like an apology though, for causing me the worry and inconvenience."

"Yes mum. Sorry mum," Graham replied. His eyes watered and he fled to the bathroom.

In the sanctuary of the bathroom Graham wept and agonized over the situation. Thelma: gone beyond any hope; Cindy: a tart, and moving way out of his league. And Margaret? He thrust the thought aside. She was just a nice little kid. And what to do about what he had just overheard?

That started another train of thought as he went over all he had heard. *I don't have all the information. Rico's group have to escape from the roof of the warehouse. How can they do that I wonder?* That reminded him that Chubby was meeting Dr Metcalf on his yacht at the marina at 8:30. *I wonder if I could get to hear what they say?* he thought.

The moment that idea crossed his mind it seized on him. *I must try. Then I might be able to go to the coppers with all the facts and they will have to believe me then,* he decided.

Energized by his plan he hurried through his bath and dressed. All the while his mind raced with plans: how to get out, what to wear, how to get within listening distance? To his annoyance Alex came out of his room and began chatting about the game they were to play against Peter and Max the next day. The last thing Graham was interested in at that moment was playing silly games. But he hid his irritation and talked as sensibly as he could.

At tea he got another surprise. Margaret was sleeping over, sharing Kylie's room. *I wonder if that was her idea; or was it mum's?* he speculated. Margaret gave him a shy little smile and he forced a smile back. As they ate he kept glancing at the clock. It was already past 7pm. Impatiently he wolfed down his food, until rebuked for his poor table manners by his mother.

As soon as he could Graham went and changed back into his old blue shorts, shirt and gym boots. His mother looked up in surprise when he came through to the kitchen. "Why are you wearing those dirty clothes again?" she asked.

"I'm just going for a walk mum. I want to be on my own for a bit," Graham replied, feeling guilty at lying.

"Hmm. You'd be better off here with us. Don't you be gone long," she said.

"No mum," Graham replied. Then he fled down the back stairs. 7:40! Knowing speed was vital he took his bike, checked the light and wheeled it out. Alex called after him to come back and do the washing up but he ignored this and set off, pedalling as fast as he could.

It was a cool night but by the time he arrived at the Esplanade he was a lather of sweat. His first problem was what to do with his bike so it wouldn't be stolen by the undesirables who lurked along the Esplanade at night. He solved this by wheeling it into the ornamental garden and hiding it in a garden bed. That done he walked quickly across to the road leading to the marina.

Another obstacle reared up. A civilian security man stopped him at the entrance. "Where do you think you are going kid?"

"Fishing," Graham replied.

"Oh yeah! What with? Clear off!"

Graham retreated to the car park and considered his next move. For a few minutes he stood in the shadows of a garden bed and noted that the security guard was patrolling, not stationary. As soon as the guard was out of sight Graham walked forward and out onto the walkway along the edge of the water. He sought out the rubbish bin he had dumped his fishing gear into and retrieved it, then moved along towards the Yacht Club into a patch of shadows. From there he could watch the entrance road and the pier leading out to the pontoons.

Settling himself as though fishing, he began careful observation of the area. The place was reasonably well lit but virtually deserted. In 10 minutes the only people he saw were a man and a woman who sauntered past arm in arm, stopping to kiss every 20 metres or so.

Lucky bugger! Graham thought morosely.

A man walked through the pool of light under the streetlight at the end of the pier and walked out towards the moored yachts. Graham strained his eyes. He did not recognize the man, who did not go anywhere near the *Frolicker*. More time passed. A cold wind blew down the Inlet and began to chill Graham. It was enough to make his eyes water and he regretted not wearing a pullover.

Another man appeared on the walkway. Yes! It was the chubby tourist. He spoke briefly to the security guard who directed him on. Graham's eyes followed Chubby as he made his way out along the pier and down along one of the floating mooring pontoons. Yes! He was going to Metcalf's yacht.

Soon after that Brad appeared. He strode straight out to the yacht which showed that he had been there before. Graham's excitement mounted. The meeting was going to take place! A noise behind him made him glance back. Two people were strolling along the walkway from the Yacht Club, a man and a woman. At first he thought it was the same couple as before but then he espied them in passionate embrace in a patch of shadow. With a shock Graham realized the two newcomers were Sean O'Malley and his girlfriend Paula.

Fearful they would recognize him Graham looked away, bending over to look down at the dark water gurgling just below his feet. As the couple drew closer Graham's heart began to hammer anxiously. They strolled past close behind him and he heard Sean say, "I will be as quick as I can. Sorry you can't come but the boss doesn't want too many people there."

Graham could not hear what else was said but Sean took Paula along to the steps leading up to the bar. The pair vanished up them and a minute later Sean returned alone, striding fast. He also made his way out to Metcalf's yacht.

"Time I moved," Graham muttered. He looked carefully around for the security guard but could not see him. *Nothing for it but to walk quickly along, hoping it is dark enough to give me some cover,* he thought. He strode to the start of the pier and out along it. Now his heart really began to hammer, sensing that he would get a very unpleasant reception if he was caught eavesdropping.

The security guard! The man was at the far end of the pontoon shining a torch over a yacht moored there. What to do? Where to hide? Beside Graham was another yacht which was in darkness. In an instant he had stepped over its rail and lay flat behind its deckhouse. Now he was afraid and he lay there ready to run as the security guard walked slowly back. The beam of the torch passed over the cockpit of the yacht and then on.

As the security guard strolled back to the pier Graham released his breath with a slow gasp. Picking his moment he stood and scuttled back onto the pontoon and continued on along it. Now his attention was concentrated on the *Frolicker* which was the second last yacht in the line. Lights shone out of the cabin door and the portholes but no-one was visible on deck.

Graham stopped on the pontoon beside the yacht and bent down to peer in the portholes. His mouth was now dry and his heart hammered rapidly. Yes! He could see Metcalf, Chubby and Sean. Brad was not visible but must have been in there because people kept turning their heads to look at someone Graham couldn't see. To Graham's annoyance he was unable to hear anything. The sound of voices could just be made out but was lost on the background sounds of rigging slatting in the breeze, the tide gurgling around hulls and moorings and distant music from a nightclub.

How on earth can I get to overhear them? he wondered. For a moment he contemplated creeping onto the deck of the yacht so as to listen at the companionway but he hesitated. He knew from experience how easily movement could be felt in a small vessel. Besides, it would be a serious risk. What possible excuse could he give for being there if caught?

At that moment voices attracted his attention back to the shore end of the pontoon. Under the lamp there stood the security guard and he was talking to a man in a white shirt: Rico! Graham did an instant appraisal of his position. *I have to hide, and quickly!* he thought. Glancing around for a hiding place he considered moving to the far end of the pontoon but instantly rejected it. There was a lamp there too and he would be silhouetted by it if he tried. It would also betray him if he tried to cross the pontoon to the yacht opposite. That was ruled out anyway as there were lights on in the cabin.

Here they come! he thought in alarm as he saw Rico and the security guard start walking along the pontoon. There was only one place to go and Graham took it before he had time to think too much about it—over the side into the water. Grasping the mooring rope at a bollard Graham lowered himself into the water near the stern of the yacht. The water was cold and made him gasp with shock. But it was fear that really chilled him; fear of the sharks and crocodiles as much as of the men.

There was a concrete piling at that point and he slid close to it. Careful testing showed it to be relatively free of barnacles. He presumed that was because the pontoons slid up and down the pilings with the rise and fall of the tide.

It is some sort of protection, he told himself.

Moving his grip so that his hand was hidden close to the piling, he hung up to his waist in the water. The tug of the current was an unpleasant surprise but he clung on.

Rico walked to the yacht and jumped aboard. Graham heard him being greeted. The security guard stopped just nearby and shone his torch around. Graham held his breath and prepared to slip under if spotted. A large fish went plop, attracting the man's torch, and making Graham's blood run cold with fear.

Big fish jump to escape even bigger fish, he thought.

Then another sound came to Graham; the splutter of an outboard. Into view around the last yacht came the black shape of a dinghy with a man in it, silhouetted against the lights of the hotel. For a moment Graham thought it was just some yachtsman or fisherman; then realization struck hard. It was the middle-aged man in the blue singlet and shorts; and he was heading straight for where Graham was hiding!

There was only one thing to do. Graham let go. He slid soundlessly under into total blackness. Panic stirred but he managed to keep control. As he rose to the surface he drifted on the current. The next yacht was only 3 metres away and he was carried into the gap between the pontoon and its stern. His arm went up and gripped the low rail before he was wedged in against the fenders.

By the time Graham had himself under control the dinghy had reached the piling he had just left. Graham saw the security guard take to painter thrown to him and make it fast. The middle-aged man climbed up onto the pontoon and spoke briefly to the guard who nodded. They obviously knew each other. The middle-aged man went down into the cabin of the yacht. To Graham's consternation and annoyance the security guard took up post on the pontoon facing towards the shore.

He looks like he is on guard. Is he part of the organization too? Graham wondered.

It looked as though his plan had failed completely. He gave up hope of getting to overhear anything and started planning how to get out of his predicament. The simplest thing was to climb onto another boat and to wait. So he waited till the security guard was definitely looking the other way, then he tried to haul himself out of the water onto the deck of the yacht he was clinging to. It was a hard lift but fear lent him strength. Even so he stopped half way because of the noise he was making.

This won't do. That bloke will hear me, Graham told himself. Carefully he lowered himself back into the water and thought again. *I will wait till he moves away.*

Having decided that, Graham hauled his legs up beside the pontoon and tried not to dangle down as a tempting morsel for every passing predator. It took a real effort to push the fear down to manageable levels. So as not to attract attention from denizens of the deep he stayed as still as possible.

After a time boredom, cold and cramp began to replace fear as his main concerns. It seemed as though he would have to cling there all night. His teeth began to chatter and his fingers started to cramp so he alternately flexed them. To Graham's annoyance the guard stayed in position.

After what seemed like hours men appeared on the deck of the yacht. Graham saw them briefly in the cabin light, then dimly as they stepped across onto the pontoon. The meeting was over and he had not heard anything! He swore under his breath. Then he lowered himself as far as he could while still holding onto a fender as the middle-aged man and Rico appeared on the pontoon above the dinghy.

The two men stopped only a few metres from Graham. He saw Rico look around to check they were alone. Rico then said, "So, is Steinwehr going ahead with his mad plan?"

"The Stonefish? Yes he is," the middle-aged man replied.

"Then you make sure I get off that wharf Mellish. I want to be well out of the country before he uses that," Rico replied.

"Don't worry Rico. We will really screw the coppers up. O'Malley has another group who are going to crash the fence down. They will all be in skeleton costumes and will saturate the place in coloured smoke. It is going to cause pandemonium. Those suckers of demonstrators are going to get a real surprise." Mellish replied.

Rico laughed and said, "Now I must be sure. At the signal from O'Malley I start all my people sliding down ropes onto the wharf, but I then run back and slip down the other side at the south end to where your costume party is covering me?"

"That's right. By then there will be a couple of hundred people inside the yard and the cops will be too busy to notice one person. There will be a car waiting near the Criterion Hotel. It will take you directly to the airport."

"Good. That is what I want. OK I had better get back to work. See you on Monday," Rico replied.

"Not me. I'll watch it on TV," Mellish laughed. "I'll leave the protesting to the suckers. Besides I will have the Stonefish on board by then."

"When do you collect it?" Rico asked.

"Tomorrow morning," Mellish replied.

"Steinwehr must be insane," Rico said.

"He certainly has a grudge against the US Navy, but then so do I," Mellish replied.

Rico laughed. "It will certainly put the cork in the bottle. I wish I could be here to see it."

"It will teach the bastards a lesson," Mellish said savagely.

At that he stepped down into his dinghy. The motor spluttered into life and Rico cast off the painter. Graham ducked down so that only a hand was out of the water. He heard the motor surge and that told him that the dinghy had reversed out. The sound died, then charged and from underwater Graham was able to clearly follow the sound as the dinghy headed off out of the marina. When he could hold his breath no longer he slowly surfaced and breathed out in a long, slow breath, as quietly as he possibly could.

After blinking water out of his eyes he scanned the yacht. There was no sign of anyone. *Time to get out of here,* he told himself.

But that was easier said than done. First he had to locate the security guard and the other men. Only when he saw a man walk under a lamp near the shore did he make a move. With an effort he hauled himself dripping onto the deck of the yacht he had been clinging to. Then he lay in cover till he was sure the pontoon and pier were clear.

With a rapidly beating heart and mouth dry with fear Graham stepped onto the pontoon and walked as quickly as he could, very conscious he was leaving a trail of drips and wet footprints. He almost ran to the shore and off along the walkway to the Yacht Club. He was chilled through but exultant. He had heard the demonstrator's plans: and better than he had hoped.

They are obviously not telling everyone in their groups the whole plan, he mused. *Now, what do I do?*

Chapter 36

YOU KEEP OUT OF THINGS!

When Graham arrived home his clothes were still damp. Worse it was nearly 10pm and he was met by a very worried and angry mother. "Where have you been? I've been worried sick about you! I was just about to ring the police to start a search."

Graham bit his lip and met her eye. "Maybe you'd better phone the police anyway. I have overheard more of what these demonstrators are planning," he said.

"Where have you been? What have you been doing?" his mother exploded. "Why are you all wet?"

"I've been down the wharf; and I hid to listen to some of those men. I know what they are going to do. I will have to tell the police."

His mother went pale. Alex, Kylie and Margaret craned forward to listen. Graham could never remember a time when his mother had been so angry. "You've been listening to those men! And you've been swimming in the harbour! In the dark! Are you crazy! You are lucky you didn't get caught. Or eaten by something! You stupid boy!"

Graham recoiled from his mother's anger but stood his ground. When she paused he said, "It is important mum. I did hear them; and this time they didn't know I was there, so they are the real plans."

His mother shook her head in dismay and sat down. Graham sat as well. He shivered and Margaret came to stand beside him.

"You are all cold," she said. "Would you like a hot drink?"

"Yes please. Milo," Graham replied.

At that his mother calmed down. "Go and have a hot shower and change, then tell me the story."

Graham did this. A warm shower and dry pyjamas restored his

physical well-being. He sat at the kitchen table and sipped the warm Milo. Margaret sat beside him and looked at him with sympathetic and loving eyes. Alex and Kylie sat at the end of the table, agog at the fuss.

When they were all settled Mrs Kirk said, "All right, tell us the whole story, from start to finish."

Graham did so. It took him over half an hour. The others kept breaking in with questions as they did not know all the background but Mrs Kirk silenced them. As Graham described how he had slid into the sea to hide from the security guard her face paled and her dismay was clear to see. She shook her head in disbelief as he recounted the conversation between Mellish and Rico.

"I think they are going to do something really serious and dramatic mum, this stonefish thing they have talked about a couple of times. We have to tell someone. I don't think they are just ordinary demonstrators. I think they are going to really cause trouble."

"Yes, I think you are right," his mother agreed. "But the demonstration isn't till Monday so you can go to bed now and sleep on it. We can decide in the morning what to do."

"Yes mum," Graham replied, both glad and sad for that. He did not relish being questioned by Mr Cartwright at this time of night. In fact he felt quite wrung out. Without protest he took himself off to bed. As he slid into his sheets Margaret came out to stand beside his bed. She was also in her pyjamas. She stood there uncertainly and the thought crossed his mind that she possibly wanted a goodnight kiss. *She probably wants to be reassured,* he thought. On an impulse he reached out and took her hand. Margaret let out a little sob and moved to sit on his bed.

"Poor kid," Graham murmured. Then he put his arms around her and gently pulled her down. She came willingly and they kissed. Graham could feel her heart beating and suddenly felt very comforted. She kissed him again and half lay on him. It felt very nice—just right. But there were tears too.

After a few minutes Graham gently wiped her cheek and said, "You had better go to bed."

"I want to be with you," she whispered, choked with emotion.

"You can't sleep with me," he said, both shocked and pleased at the idea.

"Why not? We don't have to do... to do anything naughty," she said.

Graham nodded but then shook his head. "It wouldn't be right. People wouldn't understand. Besides, I'm not sure if I could control myself."

At that she hugged him tightly and put her head beside his. "That would be all right. I won't mind."

"Margaret! You are too young," Graham cried, half shocked at this confirmation of what he had suspected. "Besides, I like you too much to hurt you," he added.

"You can, anytime you like," she said matter-of-factly as she sat up.

"When we are older," Graham replied. At that moment he did not feel like any more harrowing struggles with his conscience. "Anyway, mum won't allow it."

"I know, but it is nice to think about," she said, standing up after kissing his forehead.

"Go to bed!" he said, but kindly.

"Good night Graham. I think you were very brave," Margaret said. She hesitated, then at last turned and went back to Kylie's room. Graham lay back to think over all he had heard; and was asleep in minutes.

***

He slept soundly the whole night and was only roused for breakfast at 8am. First he made his way to the bathroom and changed, not wishing to appear in front of Kylie and Margaret in his pyjamas.

His mother called from the kitchen, "Hurry up and eat your breakfast. We have to leave for church in half an hour."

"I don't want to go," Graham replied.

"Too bad! You are going and that's final. You are not staying here on your own," his mother replied flatly.

So Graham went, squashed into the back seat of the car between Margaret and Kylie. At church he sat between his mother and Margaret. He was more embarrassed and upset to see Max and Cindy with their parents. *How can Cindy just sit there and look so innocent?* he wondered. All through the service Graham was tormented by memories of Cindy and sex; by thoughts of Thelma's betrayal; and by doubts over what to do next.

Afterwards, his mother bundled them into the car and drove them home. On arrival Graham was dismayed to find that Lt Cdr Hazard and the two security men were waiting. "I phoned them as soon as I got up," his mother explained.

Alex, Kylie and Margaret were sent downstairs and the adults and Graham seated themselves in the lounge room. Graham now felt scared as the two security men were looking at him with very hard faces. As he told his story their faces became even stonier.

When Graham was finished Mr Cartwright said angrily: "You have been causing us a lot of trouble. We know you have been down at the marina. Now, answer these questions. Who is Steinwehr? How does he come into the picture?"

"I don't know sir, except that he has the stonefish and he has a grudge against the American Navy. So does the middle-aged man Mellish," Graham replied.

"What is this stonefish thing? Is it a code name?"

Graham had wracked his brains over that but to no avail. "Some sort of radio perhaps? Do they listen in on your police radios?" Graham suggested. It could have been anything, a brand name, or a codeword. He shook his head.

Mr Baxter leaned forward. "Tell us about Rico again."

"He is a waiter in the hotel there," Graham replied. Once again he went over everything he could remember. At length the security men finished their questioning. Cartwright then said, "Now, not a word of this to anyone. That includes your brother and sister."

"They already know. I told them the story last night."

"Damn!" swore Baxter. "I'll speak to them." He got up and went downstairs. Cartwright went on: "Now, you keep out of this from now on. It is police business. We don't want kids mucking things up. So stay away from those people; you hear me?"

"Yes sir," Graham replied. He swallowed and felt very small. The security man said goodbye and went downstairs. He and Baxter got in their car and drove off.

Lt Cdr Hazard had lingered and he said, "Now Recruit Kirk, next time I tell you to do something, like phone your mother, you do it. If you give us any more trouble I will discharge you from the unit. And do as the security men said; stay away from those demonstrators. I have to tell you I don't think they believed you. It is my belief they think you are trying to plant another story."

"I'm not sir!" Graham cried. "Honest I'm not."

"Maybe, but it doesn't look good. You are the friend of these demonstrators. You were seen talking to them again yesterday afternoon down at the main wharf; and seen again at the marina. It is the police view that you were acting as a sentry for the plotters while they were talking."

Graham was appalled. "No sir. That isn't true." He was stunned by the accusations, and also by the realization that he had been under police surveillance yesterday afternoon. "They have to believe me sir. I really did overhear it all."

"I am sure the police will take your information into account, and compare it with what they get from other sources. Now do as they say and stay right out of things. Keep your nose clean and I will see you at cadets next Saturday. Thank you Mrs Kirk. Good morning."

After Lt Cdr Hazard had gone, Graham again tried to tell his mother he wasn't in league with the demonstrators. She agreed with him but was worried. "Just stay out of it all."

***

Alex and the girls came up to see if the security people were gone. None made mention of what Mr Baxter might have said to them as they had a late morning tea. Peter then arrived in his mother's car with more model ships and models in a cardboard box.

Damn! Graham thought. He did not feel like playing games. All he wanted to do was lie down and brood. But Peter was full of cheerfulness and Alex and he began talking games so Graham was dragged in. Soon after that Max arrived. His presence made Graham very uneasy. *I wonder if he knows Cindy was with an American sailor yesterday afternoon?*

The boys retired to the Ship Room to play. Margaret and Kylie came down as well. Margaret plainly wanted to be with Graham but he ignored her and threw himself into the game. The two girls then helped the others to move their balsa models around the concrete floor as the battles raged.

Peter had several new ships: four MTBs and a larger destroyer-type ship, which he said was a minelayer. He made this announcement after declaring that Graham's battleship *Nelson* had struck a mine in the Straits of Gibraltar.

"So how did the mines get there?" Graham asked.

That was when Peter took his minelayer out of the box. Graham bent to study it and was jealously impressed. It was a good model. The mines were tiny balls of plasticine the size of small peas. These had tiny pieces of fuze wire stuck in them to represent the contact horns. The mines were glued on flat balsa bases which represented the anchors. Tiny wire rails were laid along the deck on both sides of the ship. Twenty mines sat on each rail. There could be no real argument. Peter really did have a minelayer.

But Graham tried. "How did she lay them without being seen from Gibraltar?" he queried, indicating the huge rock beside the strait.

"At night, during fog," Peter answered.

Graham muttered about searchlights but was pointedly asked where they were. Unable to show any he tried another tack. "But I have a minesweeper which is there to keep the strait clear," he said, pointing to the HMS *Seagull*.

Peter shook his head. "But she is tied up at the wharf and I laid the mines last night," he replied.

"She did an early morning sweep," Graham insisted.

Alex now intervened. "No. Our game begins at daylight unless we agree beforehand. Play the game Graham."

Reluctantly Graham agreed. Dice were thrown and Graham cursed as a '1' indicated his ship was indeed mined; and a subsequent '6' said it was sunk.

Max crowed aloud. "Beauty! That means she is now completely blocking the channel. No other ships can get in or out."

"The water is deep," Graham insisted. "She has sunk so far down that other ships can pass over the wreck."

"Can't!"

"Can so!"

"Can't!"

Peter put up a hand. "Stop it you two," he said. "I reckon the channel is blocked. What do you think Alex?"

Alex agreed and the game went on, but Graham was now in a foul mood and had a headache. He played, but not with any enthusiasm, and disputed every action or throw of the dice which went against him.

Peter shook his head. "God, you're a grizzle-puss today Graham," he said. "What's the matter? Did you get out of bed the wrong side?"

Graham shrugged and met Alex's eye. Then he made a face and said nothing. The game went on till lunch time, resulting in a resounding defeat for Graham. The Trogs were all overrun and even England was invaded. It was not a happy morning.

Lunch was provided for all of them. As they ate sandwiches Alex asked Peter where he had got the plans for the minelayer. Peter pointed to the box he had brought. "I found a magazine article in a Navy journal. It is all about mines and minelaying and had some good photos. I'll show you."

Peter went and picked up the magazine and leafed through it to the photo he had mentioned. Graham glanced at it out of curiosity. It was of a Russian destroyer and clearly showed the arrangement of rails and mines on her deck. Alex also noted the nationality of the ship in the photo.

"That is a Russian ship Pete. I thought your ships were all based on American designs?"

Peter laughed. "I am also Russia don't forget. Besides my Atlantis Navy are smart enough to use any good idea."

Graham made a face at that. How true! *Pete is a smart bugger all right!* he thought. Idly he watched as Alex flicked over to the next page of the magazine. This showed an aircraft, a Hercules, dropping a long, cylindrical mine by parachute.

Alex studied the picture and then looked up. "I didn't know you could lay mines from an aircraft," he said.

"Oh yes," Peter replied. "That was how the Germans laid most of their magnetic mines back in World War 2. It is one of the most common methods of laying mines these days."

Alex flicked to the next page. It showed a line of trolleys laden with bright orange mines behind the open rear doors of another Hercules. Out of habit Graham read the caption, and felt his blood go cold from shock. The caption read: STONEFISH being loaded into a C-130. This mine is available in five sizes.

Stonefish! Surely that was not what those men meant? He reached over. "Can I read that please Alex."

Alex held the magazine out of reach. "In a minute. Wait your turn wart," he replied. With an effort Graham mastered his tongue and waited. When Alex finished flicking through the magazine Graham snatched it and began to read. The article described in detail the development of mines, with long descriptions of how the various types of initiating systems worked. Under the heading of Influence Mines, which were laid as ground mines, were a number Graham had never heard of. He read with astonishment of the American CAPTOR mine; which was an encapsulated Mk 46 Torpedo, which lay on the bottom till its sensors detected the correct target (using a computer memory to determine by propeller and machinery noises whether it was an enemy sub or vessel or not); upon which it fired the torpedo. With a range of several kilometres it gave the word 'mine' a whole new meaning.

Then Graham came to the paragraph describing the STONEFISH. It was a British mine developed by Marconi and had a near relative named SEA URCHIN and a later version named SEA DRAGON.

'It has a shelf life of 20 years and an underwater life of about 2 years,' he read. 'It is designed to operate in water from 10 to 200 metres deep and has two basic charges in its warhead: 100kg and 300kg, but with a capacity for assembly into packages up to 600kg.'

His mind now in turmoil, Graham studied the photos of the modern mines. They were like torpedoes without fins or obvious propellers. One photo of a British Aerospace Versatile Exercise Mine was bright blue. It looked so shiny and pretty that it was hard to imagine it might be something deadly. His suspicion that they must be extremely expensive objects was confirmed by a paragraph describing a contract for the German navy for two hundred mines at the cost of about $12,000 each.

Graham re-read the article and bit his lip, oblivious of the curious stares and questions of the others. *These people are peace demonstrators. They are protesting about weapons. They wouldn't use them,* he thought. Or would they? It hit him that some of these people were using lies and deception as propaganda weapons. *They are lying to their own followers and deceiving them,* he thought.

Was it possible they were planning some new act—an act of terror? Graham was so appalled he shook his head. No. It was unthinkable. To use a thing like a sea mine was not protesting. It was terrorism.

They could not possibly hope to use it and not kill people, Graham thought. He had a mental image of the men in the engine room of the American cruiser as the mine exploded, blasting them with steel splinters and then the great inrush of water to drown them.

Again he shook his head. No. They couldn't be planning that. That would be sheer murder. No-one would do such a terrible thing. But his mind told him mockingly that there were people who could and would. He thought of all the bomb outrages on the TV news. Almost every week some band of fanatics let off a bomb somewhere, usually in a bus or crowded street. But they were all in places like the Middle East and South America.

That couldn't happen here. Not in sleepy little North Queensland, he tried to tell himself.

His thoughts were interrupted by the others calling on him to go down to the Ship Room for another battle. Graham did not want to but saw no way to easily get out of it. Reluctantly he followed them down stairs and they plunged into another game. This time there was an exciting carrier battle between planes from Peter's new carrier *Hornet* and Graham's *Glorious*. Peter won but it was a good battle and Graham found he felt curiously happy at having given his friend the enjoyment.

Alex and Max started another battle. This one went on for nearly two hours before the fighting ground to a stalemate in the desert of North Africa. Graham stood up and stretched. His hands and knees were grimy from crawling around on the concrete all that time. All the while he had played his mind had been busy on the problem of the Stonefish. Now his mind was made up.

I have to contact the security men and tell them what I suspect, he thought gloomily. He bit his lip. He did not want to meet Mr Cartwright or Mr Baxter again. *I wish I could be certain.* Phrases kept echoing in his mind: Steinwehr's grudge, and his 'mad plan'; and Rico's insistence he wanted to be out of the country before the Stonefish was used.

If it is a mine it will certainly make world headlines for the demonstrators. But it won't do their cause much good, he thought.

It was that which made him most doubtful. What could the peace protesters hope to gain by an act of sabotage which killed people? He pictured the cruiser being torn open and sinking in the harbour. That was a new train of thought: where would the terrorists use the thing? How could they get it close enough? With a sick feeling he realized he had stopped thinking of the demonstrators as peace protesters and had mentally labelled them as terrorists. That gave him an answer.

If they are terrorists, they don't care about the peace protests. They may have some other aim altogether and are just using the demonstrators!

And it was clear to Graham where they would use it. The long, narrow shipping channel was the obvious place. *If they sink the first ship the other one will be trapped in Cairns for days, or weeks, until they can clear the channel, or dredge a new one.*

Peter was speaking to him. He sounded annoyed. Graham turned to him. "Sorry Pete. I was miles away. Can I borrow that magazine? I want to read that article on mines again," he asked.

Peter was packing up to go home. "Sure. Time I was gone anyway. This sounds like mum now," he said.

But it wasn't. It was Max's parents in their car. Max was astonished. "It's my oldies. I wonder what they want?"

Mr and Mrs Pullford came in with a worried Mrs Kirk a few minutes later. Mr Pullford asked the children: "Have any of you seen Cindy? She went out this morning and hasn't come home and we don't know where she is."

Graham felt his stomach turn over. He swallowed and felt so sick he almost threw up. Beads of perspiration broke out on his brow. *Oh my God! If they find out she has been going with sailors it is going to destroy them,* he thought.

His mind raced and he licked his lips, and said, "I think I know where she might be."

Chapter 37

SEARCHING

Graham felt so sick he wanted to throw up. Remembered images of Cindy swirled in his consciousness: laughing up at the American sailor; sitting with the French matelot; with him downstairs. His mind screamed as it raced. *How can I tell them? It will hurt so many people!* But what else could he do? If the parents went to the police she would soon be found. And there were her parents staring anxiously at him.

Once again he said, "I think I might know where she is." As he said it he broke into a cold sweat and began to tremble.

"Where?" cried Mrs Pullford.

Graham could see she was very upset and worried. "I... I saw her. Yesterday afternoon. Down at the wharf," he replied.

"Down at the wharf?" said Mr Pullford in a puzzled voice. "At the wharf! What on earth?" Then he gasped and added, "She isn't with those demonstrators is she?"

Graham grasped at this straw. He did not want to lie; but nor did he want to get Cindy into trouble, or at least more trouble than she was making for herself anyway. "Could be. It was near there that I saw her."

Mrs Pullford turned to Mrs Kirk: "She vanished as soon as we got home from church; never said a word, just went out. I didn't realize she was gone till lunchtime. I've phoned all her friends. I am so worried."

Mr Pullford broke in. "If she is with that rabble of trouble makers who are protesting I will tan her hide by Jove!"

"I could go and look," Graham suggested. The thought crossed his mind that if he could find her first it might save a lot of grief.

"We could all go," Alex added, which made Graham curse silently.

Mr Pullford nodded. "We shall go there at once," he said. He turned and led Mrs Pullford out. Graham became so agitated he could not stand still. *I have to find Cindy first,* he thought; *and I have to warn those horrible security men about Stonefish.* Without asking permission he turned to go to get his bike.

His mother called to him. "Where are you going Graham?"

"To help find Cindy. Don't worry mum. I won't get into any trouble."

"We will come with you," Kylie offered. Margaret agreed. So did Alex. Peter had no bike and had to wait for his mother. Max hesitated and then ran out to go with his parents in their car. Graham grabbed his bike. He did not want any of the others with him but could not think of any sensible reason to say so.

"I will go quickly. I think I might be able to find her before she gets into trouble," he said. He did not wait but wheeled his bike out, ignoring the calls from the others. His mother told him to get a hat and he became aware that he wore only a shirt and shorts and had nothing on his feet. Instead he shrugged and began pedalling as fast as he could, aware that the others must think his behaviour odd at the very least.

All the way his mind conjured up sickening images of Cindy in the clutches of some sailor. "They will probably be in some hotel room," he decided. Even with his limited experience he had heard that was how it was done. But which hotel? And how would he find out? That slowed him down. Suddenly the search looked hopeless.

In spite of that he resumed pedalling as fast as he could. His plan was to search the area around the wharf to begin with, then the streets closest to it. On arrival at the main entrance to the wharf the first thing he saw was the crowd of demonstrators and the Pullfords' car.

Graham stopped to one side and scanned the crowd. There appeared to be about thirty people only, most sitting in groups. A few banners and some placards were propped against the fence. The only person he could recognize was Pondorski. To Graham's relief there was no sign of Thelma or Janet.

Graham had not really expected Cindy to be there. From across the street he watched Mr and Mrs Pullford questioning the demonstrators. *They will soon find out she is not one of them,* he decided. *I'd better move.* So he rode off along to the ornamental garden where he had seen Cindy with the French matelot. No sign of her. Scorching memories made him feel insanely jealous and annoyingly aroused when he viewed the seat where he had seen them. These emotions were then replaced by scarifying guilt and the urge to save her.

Spurred by this, Graham rode quickly around the Yacht Club and along the waterfront walkway past the marina and hotels. *They are probably in there,* he thought. But it was obvious he wouldn't even get in the door, dressed as he was, so he rode on. With every passing minute he became more and more upset and sick. His eyes roved everywhere, hoping desperately he would spot her. He did a lap of the main block. Several white sailor suits attracted his eyes instantly but they had no girl with them. Another flash of white showed down at the end of the block: a sailor with a girl; but it was a huge African American sailor with an Aboriginal girl.

Feeling increasingly frustrated and desperate Graham rode on around the next two blocks. By then he was starting to sob and tears trickled unnoticed down his cheeks.

He turned from Spence Street into Sheridan Street. Being a Sunday afternoon there was very little traffic and only a few pedestrians. There was no sign of Cindy anywhere. Then Graham got another shock. Just ahead on the right was the Police HQ. That made him pause.

I'd better tell those security men what I think, he decided.

It took some courage for him to pull up and walk in. He felt very small and was acutely conscious he looked like the original grubby urchin. A very large sergeant looked down at him over the front desk.

"What do you want?" the sergeant asked.

"Can I please see Mr Cartwright or Mr Baxter?" Graham asked. He licked his lips nervously.

"Who are they and who are you?" the sergeant asked.

"They are the two security men looking after the American warships," Graham replied. "And my name is Graham Kirk."

The sergeant shot him a penetrating look, then turned and spoke into a telephone. "Wait there," he ordered. Graham stood, feeling very dirty and insignificant. The urge to run was very strong.

After a few minutes a plain clothes policeman Graham had never seen came out of a side door. "Who wants to see Mr Baxter?"

Graham put his hand up. "Me sir."

The plain clothes man frowned and looked him up and down, a sneer barely concealed. "What for?"

"It... it's about the Stonefish," Graham replied.

"Stonefish? What on earth is that?" the plain clothes man replied.

"If you don't know I probably shouldn't tell you," Graham replied. "I should only tell Mr Cartwright or Mr Baxter."

"They are not here at the moment. You had better tell me and I will contact them if I think it is important enough. What did you say your name was?"

Graham told him again. He was led through into a room and seated at a table. There he outlined his story to the policeman. As he described his theory about the Stonefish a look of obvious disbelief crossed the man's face. When Graham finished he was told to wait and the man went out. A wall clock told Graham it was now almost 4pm.

I shouldn't have wasted my time, he thought. *I should have kept on looking for Cindy. This bloke doesn't believe me.*

A few minutes later the plain clothes man came back and told him Mr Cartwright was on his way. Graham sat and fidgeted under the scrutiny of the policeman for 20 minutes. As he waited he began to get upset and restless again. Once he asked if he could go and the man said he should wait. Graham suspected that it was within his rights to just walk out if he wished but did not have the courage to put it to the test; or even to ask.

At last a very grumpy Mr Cartwright arrived. "This had better be good kid. You have dragged me out of my afternoon snooze," he growled.

Graham swallowed and proceeded to tell him his idea about the Stonefish. As he spoke Graham was interested to see that Cartwright's reaction was very different. He tried to pretend he was bored but Graham got the impression that the security man was in fact intensely interested.

When Graham finished Mr Cartwright asked: "And do you have any fresh evidence on which to base this wild theory?"

Graham had to admit he did not. "It just came to me while I was reading the article in the magazine sir," he replied. He again had to describe the magazine and how he had read it.

Cartwright made a face indicating disbelief, but his eyes were alive. "If that is all then you can go. Now, remember what I told you this morning; don't talk about this to anyone. We don't want this sort of rumour circulating causing alarm. Just go home and keep out of things."

"Don't you believe me?" Graham asked, annoyed at the man's off-handed manner.

Cartwright made another face and looked at the other policeman. "Well, it does sound pretty far-fetched; and you have fed us a line before. Just go home. We will look into it."

Graham was shown out. He seethed with anger at not being believed.

Well bugger you! he thought. *I had better get on with looking for Cindy.*

The thought crossed his mind that she was probably home by this time but as he mounted his bike he saw the Pullfords' car pull up at the kerb and a glance showed no Cindy inside. They hadn't seen him so he pedalled quickly off in the direction of the wharf. *They haven't found her. They must be going in to report her missing to the police,* he decided.

That lent new urgency to his search so he rode quickly along to Wharf Street and left along it past the main gate and the small crowd of demonstrators.

Once again he pedalled through the park and past the Yacht Club. Next he rode along the walkway beside the marina, his attention half on Metcalf's yacht. It appeared to be deserted. Ahead of him two people came down the steps from the hotel: an American sailor in white and a girl in a very short skirt: Cindy.

Graham skidded to stop in front of them. Cindy glared at him and went very red. She opened her mouth to speak and the sailor looked mystified. Graham spoke first. "Cindy, your mum and dad are looking for you. They are at the police station now. Quick, go home!"

Cindy shut her mouth with a snap. She paled and swallowed. The sailor looked at her quizzically. After a moment Cindy asked: "Do... do they know where I've been?"

Graham shook his head. "They think you're with the demonstrators."

The sailor became angry. "Those trouble-making shits!" he snarled. "Why don't you piss off kid?"

Graham shook his head. He was scared of the man but stood his ground. "Because I am here to look after Cindy. She is only fifteen Mister. You are in deep trouble if you aren't careful."

"Fifteen! Holy shit! Why you lying little bitch! You told me you were seventeen!" the sailor cried. He stepped away from her, aghast.

"What about my money?" Cindy shrieked. She looked frightened but very determined.

The sailor shook his head. "Be stuffed! I ain't paying you money in front of witnesses," he replied; confirming Graham's worst fears about what Cindy had been doing.

"Pay her or I'll tell," Graham said. "I've just come from the police station and her parents are there now."

The sailor blanched. He was a nice looking young man of about twenty. Graham studied the red and black badges on the sleeves of the sailor's white jacket, wondering what they meant, while the sailor dug out his wallet and hastily peeled off notes to give to Cindy. As he did so, Graham was distracted by seeing people emerge onto the deck of Metcalf's yacht: Metcalf and Mellish.

Graham said, "Quick Cindy. Go over and join the demonstrators in front of the main gate to the wharf. Tell your parents you went for a hamburger or a milk shake or something. Say that you have been with them all the time," Graham said.

"You won't tell?" Cindy asked anxiously.

"No, but only if you promise to stop doing what you are doing," Graham answered.

Cindy blushed and tears sprang to her eyes. Sniffling she nodded. "I promise," she replied.

The sailor shook his head and strode quickly away. Cindy stayed with Graham for a moment, her head hung in shame. Graham was moved to hug her for comfort but was repelled by the thought of what she had been doing. Standing that close he could smell that she had just had a bath. Out of the corner of his eye, he watched as Mellish came striding along the pier from the yacht.

He said he was collecting the Stonefish this morning. I wonder if he did? Graham thought. As the man got closer Graham said, "Cindy, stay with me for a minute please. Pretend we are lovers. I don't want that man to see me."

Cindy looked around while Graham turned his back. Then Cindy moved beside him and put her arm around his shoulders, shielding his face. "Why?" she asked.

"Tell you later," Graham muttered. Out of the corner of his eye he watched as Mellish went out onto the roadway. As soon as he was out of sight Graham released Cindy. "Get going and join the demonstrators at the wharf, quick! I will see you later," he said.

An idea had come to Graham and he acted on it. *I will follow him. He might lead me to the Stonefish. Then I will have some real evidence for Cartwright. Then he will have to believe me,* he thought.

Without waiting to see if Cindy acted on his instructions Graham sprang onto his bike and pedalled along to the roadway, just in time to see Mellish getting into a battered old brown station wagon in the car park. That made his spirits drop.

I won't be able to follow a car, he thought glumly.

But he tried. As Mellish drove off he followed. Mellish turned left onto Wharf Street and drove along past the main wharves. As Graham pedalled rapidly past the group of demonstrators, he looked to see if Thelma or Janet were there but saw no sign of them. Mellish's car drew rapidly away and soon vanished from sight around the bend at the railway crossing. Graham kept on pedalling and was rewarded by seeing the car turn left at Draper Street.

He's heading for Portsmith. I wonder if his boat is there? Graham mused. The idea fired him to keep on pedalling, ignoring his pounding heart and gasping breath. Within a minute he was at the Draper Street intersection and went round to the left. He raced on as fast as he could ride, past the Naval Base and the Navy Cadet depot, then right into Cook Street and past the Bulk Sugar Terminal.

There was almost no traffic on the road but no sign of the brown car. On arriving at the next intersection Graham had to think fast. *He might have gone to the Trawler Base. I'll just check,* he decided.

Turning left he pedalled the short distance to Smiths Creek. At the car park there he stopped and looked.

Yes! There was the brown car. And there was Mellish, walking out along the first concrete pier between the moored trawlers. Graham dumped his bike against a garden bed and ran over to the seawall to watch.

Mellish went to where a small, grubby trawler was moored alongside the end of the pier, *Pelican Pride,* proclaimed in faded painting on the soiled stern. Mellish jumped down and was met by another man who emerged from the wheelhouse forward of the clump of nets and booms which comprised the fishing gear. The two men spoke for a while then Mellish walked with him to the stern. To Graham's intense interest Mellish hauled up a tangle of nets and then a canvas cover and bent to peer underneath.

I wonder if the Stonefish is under that? Graham speculated.

Mellish dropped the covers back into place and the two men stood talking. Graham sat down on the rocks of the retaining wall where he could see but was hidden by another trawler's gear. After a few minutes both men climbed up onto the wharf and walked back along it. That put Graham into a quandary. Should he run, or hide? He chose to just sit and pretend he was fishing.

Out of the corner of his eye he watched the two men. To his relief they did not walk towards the car park but turned the other way and vanished into the small cafe beyond.

They've gone to the shop. This is my chance! Graham told himself. Heart pounding with excitement he sprang up and walked briskly towards the end of the pier. *I don't think Mellish knows me at all so I should be safe,* he thought.

As he hurried along the pier Graham looked around. Upstream the *Wewak* was moored alongside the next wharf. *I will just say I am off the Wewak and waiting for someone,* he thought.

Within a minute he was standing on the end of the pier looking down at the untidy deck of the trawler. Close up the trawler looked even dirtier, the decks filthy with muck and grease and the sides streaked with rust. She was a typical small trawler: bow raked high, small deckhouse with wheelhouse at the front, masts and rigging, then the stern half taken up by the working deck for fishing. The hold was covered by a tangle of nets and a tarpaulin. It was this which interested Graham the most. He stared down at the shapeless heap.

Will I risk a look? he thought. His heart was now pounding furiously and his throat went dry. *What will I do if they come back?* he worried. Then he shrugged. *I will just run away or escape by diving overboard.*

One quick glance around confirmed the men were still in the shop. Before he had really considered what he was doing Graham had scrambled down onto the trawler's deck.

In five swift steps he reached the pile of nets and canvas. He reached down and lifted. It was very heavy and he could see nothing except some timber baulks. *Must be on the other side,* he thought. Quickly he strode around to the outboard side and grabbed the edge of the tarpaulin. He lifted it and let out a gasp.

"Yes! The Stonefish!"

The thing lay there in a wooden frame, a shiny cylinder about 4 metres long and 1 metre in diameter. To Graham's surprise it was bright yellow, with a black nose cap. The one in the picture in the magazine had been orange. He shrugged and bent to examine it more closely.

As he did a noise alerted him. He froze in fright as a door banged open at the side of the deckhouse and a man came out to hurl some scraps over the side. Graham stared in horror as the man swilled water around in the pail he was carrying.

I must hide. He will see me! But where? There was only one place. The man was only 5 paces away and would see him at any moment if he turned. In a flash Graham had dropped flat and rolled in under the tarpaulin against the frame of the Stonefish. He heard the man walk towards him and his heart pounded so hard it sounded like drums in his ears. He tensed for discovery. The mine felt very cold and smooth against his skin.

The man padded by on bare feet and did something at the stern of the boat. Graham could hear him scraping something but did not dare lift the canvas to risk a peek. *Go away!* he thought desperately. But the man didn't. He scraped and banged at something metal, all the while muttering obscenities. Minutes dragged past and Graham became really worried. *What if Mellish returns?*

Then his fears were realized as he heard voices and the thump of people jumping down onto the deck. Mellish had returned with the other man! Graham broke into a sweat and tensed ready to run. To his annoyance and consternation the men stood talking nearby. The topic was spare parts for a pump, which didn't interest Graham in the slightest.

Then Mellish said, "Ah! Good! Here's Steinwehr."

The men moved away and Graham heard more muffled voices. Steinwehr! The mad American! *I'd better get out of here. He is sure to want to see the Stonefish,* Graham thought. He moved to slide out from under the tarpaulin, thinking to slip over the side and then swim in under the wharf and along to the next trawler. But before he could move he heard footsteps and the tarpaulin was suddenly lifted.

Graham found himself staring into the astonished faces of four men, one a thin man wearing sunglasses and a Hawaiian shirt.

Mellish gasped and cried: "What the bloody hell?".

Chapter 38

MELLISH

For a stunned instant Graham stared up at the four men. Then he tried to rise. Before he was even half way up Mellish slammed him back to the deck by thumping his boot onto his chest.

"What the bloody hell! Who are you?" Mellish demanded, his boot still firmly on Graham's chest. Graham lay, winded and bruised, so afraid and surprised that for a moment he was quite unable to speak, even if he had wanted to.

Mellish lifted the boot and slammed it down again. "Hey! I'm talkin' to you kid. Who are you and what are you doin' here?" he demanded, his voice a harsh grate. Graham met the man's eyes and shook his head. Anger began to replace the surprise and fear that had initially shown on Mellish's face. Once again he lifted his boot and rammed it down hard, the heel grinding against Graham's ribs painfully. "Answer me kid!"

Graham again shook his head. At that Mellish looked quickly in all directions. "Get him below out of sight," he snapped to the two men in dirty old clothes. They bent at once to seize Graham by the arms. At that Graham opened his mouth to scream.

"Help! Help... ugh!"

Mellish kicked him hard in the face, loosening several teeth and slamming his jaw shut with a painful snap. One of the men clamped a hand over his face.

"Gag the little bugger," Mellish ordered.

"Who is he?" One of the men asked. "Do ya reckon he's workin' fer the coppers?"

"Shut up, Roper! Get him into the cabin out of sight," Mellish said.

Strong hands quickly bound Graham hand and foot with short lengths of rope. An old rag was shoved hard into his mouth, further loosening several teeth and causing blood to seep down Graham's gullet. The men then lifted him and roughly bundled him along the deck past the fishing nets and into the outboard door. Inside a cabin he was dumped on a bunk covered by rough and smelly blankets.

The four men crowded into the cabin. Graham was very scared now. It came to him that these were very dangerous men. *If they are planning to sink a ship and kill people with a mine then they might kill me,* he thought. At that he began to sweat and shiver. Desperately he looked around for a way of escape. His gag was hauled out, half ripping a tooth from his gums. Blood welled into his mouth adding to his growing feeling of nausea.

Mellish stepped forward and slapped him hard on the face. "OK kid. Who are you? What are you doin' on my boat?"

Graham still refused to answer. Mellish snapped at the man named Roper: "Search the little shit."

Roper turned out Graham's pockets but found nothing. Mellish and Steinwehr moved into the wheelhouse next door and muttered in low tones. After a few minutes Mellish came back into the cabin and said, "Find out who he is and what he was doing here. I'll be back in a few minutes."

Mellish again left the cabin. Roper stepped forward. "Righto kid, you'd better tell us or you are gunna get hurt. Got it? You can make this easy on yourself or hard. Either way we will find out. So, what's your name?"

Graham went cold with fear. Even so, he refused to answer. He swallowed blood and saliva to stop himself gagging and tried to push the loose tooth back into place with his tongue. Roper grinned and slapped him on both cheeks; fast, stinging blows which made Graham's head reel. Still Graham would not answer, so he was slapped again and again till his cheeks and forehead throbbed and began to go numb.

Mellish returned to the cabin alone. He gestured the men aside and grabbed Graham's shirt front with strong hands stinking of fish and tobacco. "Now kid, start to co-operate. Answer the questions or I'll make it so painful you will wish you had never been born."

To reinforce the threat, Mellish produced a wicked looking fish knife and laid the blade on Graham's cheek. At the touch of the cold steel Graham flinched and real terror gripped him. He felt his testicles contract and his bowels went loose. Only with an effort did he avoid emptying them.

Mellish gestured to the two men. "Get his shirt off."

Graham felt almost paralysed with fear and shook his head in disbelief. "No. Don't!" he cried. The men ignored him and tore his shirt off, leaving the rags around his arms. Graham began to tremble from fear and shame.

Mellish leaned down and Graham felt the point of the knife dig in under the fingernail on his left thumb. The pain was so sudden and so sharp he cried out and found it hard to believe something so small could hurt so much.

"No, don't, please. I haven't stolen anything. Let me go please!" Graham pleaded. In his mind raced mortal dread, along with a shocked realization that he might never get to live another day.

Mellish inserted the knife point under his left forefinger fingernail and pushed. His eyes were flat and hard and so was the expression on his face. "Are you a thief then?" he queried, jabbing with the knife so that Graham felt a hot pain in his left hand which made him gasp in shock.

"Yes. Yes. I... I was just looking for things to pinch," Graham lied.

"So what were you hiding under the tarp for?"

"Because that man there came out on deck and it was the closest hiding place," Graham replied. The knife point was pressing in harder causing a searing pain to shoot through him. Nausea welled up causing his stomach to heave. He managed to swallow the bile and vomit but could feel his resistance rapidly crumbling. His mind raced, trying to decide whether it mattered if he told the men who he was. In the end he decided he should say nothing as the men seemed doubtful.

Mellish eased the pressure then suddenly reapplied it, sending searing waves of sheer agony through Graham. "So what's your name?" Mellish persisted. The knife point jabbed and twisted again. Graham felt completely humiliated as well as helpless. Stubbornly, he refused to answer. When Mellish realized this he jabbed harder. Waves of pain engulfed Graham and he vomited and almost blacked out.

Suddenly Roper cried out, "There's a name on his shirt boss."

The rags were jerked loose savagely and Graham watched through a swimming mist of nausea as Mellish snatched the torn cloth and read the name tag inside the collar. "Graham Kirk eh? Now where have I heard that name? Come on kid, cough up or I will really hurt you."

The knife jabbed in again and Graham tried to squirm away. The pain seared through him again and he groaned and began to cry. Somehow he managed to shake his head.

These mongrels won't let me go, he thought bitterly. *They will kill me. I'll be damned if I will give them the satisfaction of finding out.*

But then sheer terror swamped his mind and he was left trembling and on the verge of begging for his life.

To his relief, Mellish withdrew the knife and said, "Make sure the little toad doesn't escape. I need to make a phone call." He left the cabin and Graham could tell by the sounds and movement of the trawler that he had climbed up onto the wharf. The two men sat down.

Roper said to the other, "Make us a brew Sam, I'm bloody parched."

Sam went through another door into a tiny cubby-hole of a galley and began making tea. Roper remained watching Graham, warning him to talk while he still could. By this time Graham was feeling almost numb with the battering and shock. The chill dread of possible death grew in him. Time crept by, each second seeming an hour.

At last Mellish returned. He grunted and accepted a cup of tea, then sat to glare at Graham. He explained nothing to the other two. Graham tried to relax. He started to feel chilled and numb in the hands and feet. His mind was now concentrated alternately on prayer and on thoughts of how he might escape. Bitterly, he decided no-one was likely to come to his rescue.

I didn't tell anyone where I was going. They will never find me in time!

Footsteps sounded and two people knocked and were let in. The light was switched on and Graham realized with a shock that it was Sean O'Malley and his girl friend Paula. They stared at him curiously and for a moment Graham experienced a shaft of hope.

Then Paula said something and Mellish laughed harshly, lacerating Graham's hopes. O'Malley leaned over and peered at Graham. "That's him all right. What are you doing snooping around here Kirk? Did the cops put you up to this?"

Graham shook his head and suffered the knife again. They tried several more questions before O'Malley said, "That will do Mellish. It doesn't matter. We will be gone before he is missed. Let's get the show on the road."

Mellish grunted and swore, but withdrew the knife and slid it back into a sheath on his belt. "So what do we do with the little rat? We can't let him go. I reckon he's a spy for the cops; and he knows too much."

O'Malley tugged at his beard and his black eyes glinted hate at Graham. After a moment he said, "Take him with you and toss him overboard somewhere. Make sure the body isn't found."

Graham was stunned at the callous death sentence. He started to cry. "Please let me go," he pleaded. "I don't know anything."

"Like hell!" Mellish snarled. "I just remembered where I seen ya. You was down at the marina the other day. You been watchin' us."

Graham looked at the girl but she sneered and turned her back. O'Malley followed her out with a curt "Get on with it!" to Mellish.

Roper turned to Mellish. "I don't like this boss. What do we do after we have laid this bloody mine?"

"We sail out to meet up with Steinwehr's yacht of Upolo Cay. Then we scuttle this tub in deep water and skedaddle in the yacht. Now let's get moving."

Mellish went out as well. Graham saw that it was now dark outside. *Mum will be starting to worry now,* he thought miserably. Then another thought occurred to him: *I wonder if Cindy got home all right?* He hoped she had.

After a few minutes, Mellish returned and called to the two men. "Let's get this tub moving. Make sure those knots are tight and go and stand by the lines Sam. Get the engine going Roper."

Graham was left alone, trussed hand and foot. Waves of utter terror swept over him, almost paralyzing him. *I don't want to die! It can't be true. It must be just a bad dream. I will wake up in a minute! Please God, don't let me die! I'm sorry I did rude things with Cindy. I promise I will behave in future!*

Frantically, he looked around for a way of escape. He tried to wriggle free but the ropes were too tight and expertly tied. All he could do was wait in a state of mounting panic and fear as the trawler's engines rumbled to life below him. As the motion of the vessel indicated that it had been cast off and was heading out into Smiths Creek Graham's imagination sent him into the depths of absolute desperation and fear.

Into his mind came fearful images of death, a jumble of ideas from every sermon he had ever heard, and of books and stories. He tried to come to terms with the fact that he would die very soon but still found it difficult to accept the reality of his situation.

Images of what death might be like tormented him. The thought of his flesh rotting and being gnawed and torn by fish so repelled him that he closed his mind to the possibility. It was all he could do to keep from whimpering cravenly. Instead he turned to prayer, begging God for forgiveness.

The trawler heeled to starboard and began to pitch slightly. This told Graham that they had turned to port out in the Inlet and that they were now heading down channel. With every passing second he became more and more desperate, his mind searching frantically for some escape. None presented itself and the dreadful journey continued. Graham began to compose himself for the inevitable end. One of the images that formed in his mind was of him and Margaret in the bath. He pictured her snuggling up to him in bed and somehow that felt just right and gave him great comfort, but also intense regret.

I will never know what it might have been like; and she will be very hurt when I am gone, he thought.

After about 20 minutes, the trawler's engines suddenly slowed and the vessel turned to starboard before coming to a rocking standstill. *Oh no! It is time!* Graham's mind screamed. He bit his lip and prayed aloud till the door banged open and Roper came in with Mellish.

"Time to take your dive kid. Sorry about this, but you know too much," Mellish said. Graham made no comment. There was something about the men's manner which indicated that any plea would be futile.

They grabbed his arms and dragged him off the bunk and roughly hauled him out through the door.

***

It was dark outside and a bright red light glowed in the sky. For a moment Graham was disoriented. Then he realized the light was on top of one of the channel marker pylons. The lights of Cairns took up half the horizon still and he estimated they were only about a kilometre or so offshore. It was a cool night and a gentle breeze was pushing up a small lop.

"Boat coming in," Sam said as the two men dumped Graham on the deck near the stern.

Mellish looked. "Only a Green Island ferry. Hurry up, tie the kid to the mine."

Shock and revulsion coursed through Graham. *Tie me to the mine!* It was so horrible he could only gasp and retch as spasms of terror gripped him.

Roper bent and passed a roped around Graham's waist and tied it firmly. He said, "This is a good idea boss. When it goes bang there will be no evidence left." Then he gave a chuckle which sent paralyzing tremors up Graham's spine.

The trawler rocked in the wash of the passing ferry. Mellish watched it, then peered in all directions. "OK. I can't see any stray fishermen or anything. Get the Stonefish over the side."

The aft deck of the trawler was in darkness, but in the glow of the riding light on her mast and the light from the wheelhouse Graham could see the men's faces as they worked. They looked hard and pitiless. The nets were dragged aside then the tarpaulin lifted and dragged clear. The rope around Graham's waist was tied securely to the mine's frame. Mellish produced a torch and knelt beside the mine. In the beam of the torch the mine shone a shiny, sinister yellow. Mellish began making adjustments to something near the nose of the weapon.

"Right, the mine is armed," he said to the others. "Winch her up Sam and let's get her over." He paused and looked down at Graham, then shone his torch full in his face. "You got anything to say yet kid? No? Oh well, too bad. Sorry about this, but I gotta admit you've got guts. Pity really. Righto, Sam, wind her up."

Graham found his chest so tight he could not breathe properly. He was sweating and trembling and his mouth moved automatically in prayer. *Oh please God! Make it quick!* The winch grated and screeched as it started to wind up the steel wire rope now shackled to the top of the mine by a snap catch of some sort. The mine began to rise from its cradle on the deck.

"No, please," Graham gasped.

"Sorry kid. This is the way it's gotta be," Mellish replied.

As the mine lifted it swung with the vessel's movement, bumping painfully against Graham's chilled and clammy flesh. The winch rattled and scraped and the mine rose higher. Mellish switched off his torch and looked around.

Roper called out, "Another boat coming boss, fast, from over near the mangroves."

"Where? I can't see any lights," Mellish called anxiously.

Roper pointed. "Over there. He hasn't got any lights. You can just see the bow wave."

Mellish looked and then swore. "The bastard's moving fast, and heading this way. I don't like this. Get that bloody mine over the side, quick!" he snapped. He sprang forward and pushed to swing the boom of the derrick outboard. The mine swung out over the side and the rope around Graham's waist suddenly jerked tight, making him cry out in fear and pain. He was lifted from the deck, feet first, so that his head banged painfully on a cleat.

Sam suddenly looked up. "What's that bloody noise?" he shouted. Graham shook his head to clear the ringing from his ears and heard a deep, throbbing roar sounding above the noise of the winch.

Rope looked around and suddenly pointed back along the channel. "Another boat, big bugger too, and moving fast!" he cried.

"No! It's a bloody chopper!" Mellish cried.

Hope surged in Graham. Suddenly the trawler was bathed in a brilliant white light from a powerful searchlight and a loudspeaker boomed across the water: "This is the police. Stop! Do not move!"

The police! Graham thought, hope surging.

Mellish uttered an obscenity as another spotlight came on from the helicopter, which was now roaring overhead in the darkness. "Bloody cops! It's a trap! The bastards are onto us. You little rat! You were a bloody police spy!"

He kicked savagely at Graham's butt as he dangled from the rope. Loudspeakers boomed again and a brilliant flare burst high overhead, lighting everything up like day. Mellish swore and kicked Graham again, viciously. At that moment a boat thudded alongside and black clad figures came scrambling over the rail.

"Hands up! Don't move. This is the police!" shouted a man who crouched and pointed a pistol at Sam.

At that Mellish snatched up a large wrench and swung it savagely at the catch holding the mine, which now dangled out over the water. There was a loud metallic *tung!* and the mine suddenly dropped. Graham saw it fall with disbelief.

"No!" he screamed.

Before he could do more than scream, he was savagely jerked against the side, then up and over the bulwark. He had a fleeting glimpse of a large launch rushing alongside only metres away; of silver ripples as the light of the flare reflected on the waves.

Then he plunged into cold, black water.

Chapter 39

THE BATTLESHIP

Terror flooded through Graham. *It isn't true!* his mind screamed. It couldn't be possible! But he was under water and being dragged rapidly to the bottom of the sea! The rope around his waist cut sharply into him, firmly tied to the Stonefish mine. So rapidly did Graham and his lethal anchor sink that his ear drums ached painfully from the rapidly increasing pressure. He swallowed instinctively and somehow managed to keep from breathing in water.

I must get free or I will drown! he thought desperately; although he already felt it was hopeless. Death was only a minute or so away. Already it seemed it was enfolding him in its cold embrace. He squirmed and wriggled frantically but with both hands and feet tied he knew it was no use.

The worst thing was that his eyes were open and he could see. All around him was nothing but absolute blackness but above him he could see the blurred black silhouettes of the trawler and the launch beside it, outlined by the dazzling flare which flickered and shimmered overhead. He could even see bubbles and dark shapes swirling above him.

Now the pain in his ears was so intense he felt like crying aloud. The descent suddenly slowed and he slid to a stop in a layer of clammy ooze. *I'm on the bottom,* his mind registered. *On the bottom of the main shipping channel—and dead!* Already his lungs were bursting from the effort of holding his breath and he knew he could only last a few more seconds. The agony in his lungs built up as he struggled to hold out, even as his mind said to him *What's the use?*

Bright lights appeared in his vision and he started to release bubbles. His straining chest heaved and trembled as he struggled to squirm free.

Stars danced in his vision and he began to pray. *Please God, forgive me for being naughty with Cindy. Please take me to heaven.*

Something had him. His heart palpitated wildly as terror redoubled. Shark! No a groper, or an octopus. That was even worse. *Can't it even wait till I'm dead!* his tormented mind called. A bright light shone into his eyes and then something was rammed into his mouth, hard. Bubbles and pain. The taste of blood from his loose teeth which had just received another battering. And he could not hold his breath any longer. With a shudder he gave up and breathed out.

Something was clamped over his mouth and face. His reeling mind prepared for the terrible intake of water which would flood into his lungs to drown him. *They say drowning is peaceful—but I don't believe them. It hurts!* he thought. But instead he gasped air and felt something gripping him firmly around the neck and pinching his nose tight. The bright light moved, revealing a face mask with two bright eyes behind it.

A diver!

Graham's mind tried to grope with this. *Am I already dead? Is this hell, or what?* his shocked mind thought. No, it was a man. He was gripping Grahm and holding a mouthpiece in his mouth while reaching down past him. Another bright light appeared: another diver, and he was blowing bubbles. Graham realized that the thing in his mouth was the regulator from a SCUBA set. He gasped more compressed air and began to black out. Bile rose in his throat.

Don't vomit! Don't vomit! Don't black out! he told himself.

The diver hauled at him and Graham knew he was free, being hauled upwards. This was as painful as the descent as they went up fast. He tried to focus his eyes but the salt water was making his vision blurred. Two figures, both in black wetsuits, but the man gripping his face and arm had no regulator in his mouth. Even as Graham's mind registered this he saw the second diver take his regulator out and open his mouth to breathe out. Graham knew enough from his reading to understand that the man was releasing pressure to avoid the bends.

Graham felt his heart fluttering. *I might live! Please God, I want to live!* He took another breath, half fearing it would be a cruel trick and that water, not air, would swamp his lungs. As it was he began to cough. Bubbles swirled around him and his senses reeled. But the divers had him firmly in their grip and were swimming strongly upwards.

Suddenly his head broke surface. The two divers held him up but a wave slapped into his eyes and washed over him. Then his head was above water again, made evident by the chill wind blowing on him. He bumped against the side of a boat and hands grabbed him. The regulator was pulled out of his mouth and before he knew what was happening strong hands had lifted him up and dumped him on the deck of a launch.

He just had time to register people and lights and that the deck was made of non-skid green plastic before he spewed. Warm vomit and seawater flushed down onto his cold skin. Hands held him on his front as he heaved again. Then he began to shiver and retch alternately. A blanket was wrapped around him and hands touched him. He dimly knew that the ropes around his wrists and feet had been removed, but whether cut or undone he could not tell.

Another person was vomiting beside him. Graham glanced out of his aching eyes and saw it was one of the divers, a big, bearded man. Graham's head throbbed and his ears felt as though hot needles had been pushed into them. From the vibration he dimly understood that the launch was under way. A policeman bent down to help wipe slime from his face. In the light of a torch, Graham saw Cartwright's face.

Then he blacked out.

***

For the next period of time, he slid in and out of consciousness. Bright lights, the launch berthing, being carried quickly down a gangway on a stretcher, the back of an ambulance-siren wailing.

Graham came to in a hospital bed. His head throbbed and his ears ached terribly, but he knew at once he was alive. As his eyes shifted focus from the overhead light they looked at his mother's anxious face. She cried out and reached forward to embrace him. Nurses and doctors came running and he was checked all over.

"I'm alive mum!" he said in wonder.

"Yes," she sobbed, tears of joy running down her cheeks.

"Is Cindy all right?"

His mother frowned then nodded. "Yes, the little minx! She was down the wharf with those demonstrators. Never mind her. Margaret is here too," she replied.

Graham could only smile. He could hardly hear her. Once the doctors were through with their checks Margaret and Kylie came in. Margaret's smile quickly crumpled and she sobbed and rushed over to hug him. Graham could only murmur in reply, unsure what she had said. Kylie hugged him too and Margaret then sat beside him, holding his hand. Graham found it very comforting. Somehow it just felt right. Alex came in next and sat to one side.

Later Mr Cartwright and Mr Baxter came in and Graham learned that the police had been watching Mellish's trawler from the moment Graham had informed them of his involvement.

"We saw you go on board and get grabbed," Cartwright admitted. "And we followed every move, even at night with Night Vision equipment."

Graham's mother was appalled and became very angry. "You could have moved sooner to rescue him. He was nearly drowned!" she said.

Cartwright had the grace to blush. "Er... yes. We were about to move in when the trawler suddenly got under way. Then we could only follow."

"The divers..." Graham began.

"From the Naval Clearance Diving Team. They have recovered the Stonefish," Baxter replied. "Their leader, Warrant Officer Crabb, the man who rescued you, is in the next bed."

At that Graham insisted that the curtain be pulled back so he could thank his rescuer. WO Crabb was embarrassed and off-hand.

"I didn't think we would be in time," he said. "When I saw you go over the side tied to that mine I thought you were a goner."

"So did I!" Graham replied.

They laughed and WO Crabb went on to describe how he had grabbed his air tank and a toolkit and torch and jumped in. The toolkit was just a weight to take him down quickly. "It was damned lucky I was close enough to see your bubbles and follow you down, otherwise I would never have found you in time," he said.

Graham now learned that WO Crabb had given him his spare regulator and cut him free with his diver's knife. The arrival of his mate with another torch had saved him as they had been able get him free quickly. Because WO Crabb and his mate had dived so fast, and surfaced too quickly, they had both suffered some damage to their ears and a mild attack of the bends.

"Will you be all right?" Graham asked.

"Yes. The doctor says I will be diving again in a month," WO Crabb replied. Then he grinned and said, "You had better stop falling in the harbour. I can't guarantee that I'll be there next time!"

They laughed again and Graham blushed. He thought WO Crabb was the bravest man he had ever met. *I will try to be just like him when I grow up,* he vowed.

Cartwright then spoke: "So you see, we did take notice of you young Kirk."

"Did you get all the crooks?" Graham asked. He was damned if he would call the man 'sir'. *He could have rescued me and saved me all that trauma,* he thought. He felt distinctly used and aggrieved.

Cartwright shook his head. "No. We have arrested O'Malley and his girlfriend, and also Rico. We got him as he tried to board a plane. He is an international terrorist wanted in four countries, so we are particularly pleased to have him in the bag. We also have Dr Metcalf in custody, but we missed Steinwehr," Cartwright replied.

"He is waiting in his launch at Upolo Cay," Graham replied. "Mellish and his crew were to lay the mine, then sail out to meet him. The trawler was then to be sunk in deep water."

"How do you know that?" Cartwright asked.

"I overheard them talking while I was tied up—being tortured," Graham replied angrily.

Cartwright made a muttered ejaculation and stood up. As he walked to the door he pulled out a mobile phone and quickly called. Graham could not follow the conversation as his ears kept going deaf or fuzzy but he gathered the navy were being told.

A few minutes later, Cartwright returned. "A helicopter and patrol boat are on their way," he explained. "Our good friend Mr Steinwehr shouldn't get far."

"Who is this Mr Steinwehr?" Graham asked.

"This is classified, so don't mention it," Cartwright said. "He was a commander in the US Navy, an expert on mine warfare. He lost his commission after being caught in, well, let's say 'compromising' activities with a several sailors. This was before the US Navy changed its policy on homosexuals, and they wouldn't take him back. He's got a bit of a grudge over it and has been causing the navy a lot of grief ever since."

There was a stir in the corridor; and then white uniforms. More visitors came in. Graham noted the gold rank epaulets and officer's caps wreathed in gold braid and goggled. It was an American Admiral and the captains of both warships, plus their aides. Graham was introduced and had his hand shaken. He was a bit overwhelmed by it all: a real admiral! With row after row of medal ribbons and all that gold braid on his cap and shoulders.

The admiral shook his hand. "You did a great job son. You saved a lot of lives, not to mention one of our ships. We really appreciate what you did and I'd like to apologize for you being badly treated before."

"Sir?" Graham asked weakly, unsure what he was talking about.

Lt Cdr Hazard stepped forward. "For when you weren't allowed on the ship visit on Saturday, Graham," he explained.

Graham blushed. "Oh! Oh that's all right sir. It must have looked pretty fishy at the time," he replied.

The admiral nodded. "It did. But you have done a mighty job. When you brought in the information with Steinwehr's name, our security boys suddenly went ape; and when you told Mr Cartwright here about the Stonefish, we knew we had big trouble on our hands," he explained.

An American captain nodded and added, "A Stonefish went missing in transit from the factory in England last year and we've been in a sweat ever since worrying about when and where it would turn up. You found it for us. Well done!"

The admiral patted Graham's shoulder. "Yes son, we owe you," he said. "Is there anything you would like? We would like to repay you. Uncle Sam knows how to reward his friends."

An idea flitted into Graham's mind. He started, then stopped. "Well sir, I'd... I'd really like to see..." Again Graham dried up, thinking he was being silly and unreasonable.

"Like to see what?" the Admiral urged gently, a twinkle in his eye. "Would you like to visit America?"

Graham nodded. "Yes sir. I'd like to see a real battleship."

The admiral grinned. "A battleship! What a great idea. Why I was a gunnery officer on the Mighty Mo for two years. Consider it done son, if that's all right Mrs Kirk?"

It was. Graham could not believe his luck. In its own way it was as unbelievable as being thrown into the harbour to drown. The American captains both then invited Graham to visit their ships the next day. "As our honoured guest."

Thus it was that five weeks later Graham stood on the deck of the mighty Iowa-class battleship USS *Wisconsin* at the Hampton Roads Naval Museum in Virginia. He stared up at the massive 16" guns in their colossal turrets, then up over the steel mountain of upper works. It was a little disappointing to him that the battleship was no longer in service, but she was still massive and a most impressive ship. He turned to grin at Kylie and Alex. It was a dream come true!

And she was the second battleship he had visited. The Americans had flown the whole family across for two weeks during the September holidays and they had already visited the USS *Massachusetts*, also now a museum ship, at Fall River in her home state; and next they were to go to Wilmington, North Carolina, to see the USS *North Carolina*, then on to see the USS *Texas* at Houston. Their return journey would include a visit to Pear Harbour Naval Base in Hawaii to see the USS *Missouri* and the wreck of the USS *Arizona*; all of it as guests of the US Navy. Graham's greatest wish had come true.

For a few moments Graham relived the events that had led to this. There was a moment's wistful regret over Thelma. Then he breathed in deeply and looked up once more at the towering grey steel superstructure and tried to imagine what it must have been like to be aboard when she was at sea and heading in harm's way.

As for Cindy? Well, he did see Cindy again. When he got the chance he begged her for forgiveness. "I'm sorry Cindy," he sobbed.

"For what?" she asked quizzically.

"For persuading you to... to do things," he said.

Cindy snorted and curled her lip. "Huh! I'm not that weak! It is me who should be saying sorry to you. I was just using you to learn on. And it was nice, but I am sorry I used you that way."

"But why?" Graham cried.

Cindy shrugged. "Just stupid peer pressure I guess. A couple of my friends did it and said it was good and I wanted to be part of the 'in' crowd," she explained.

Graham was flabbergasted and did not know whether to be hurt or angry. "I thought you liked me," he muttered.

"I did. I do! If I hadn't I wouldn't have let you do anything. You are a really nice boy, and a brave one. That's another reason why I was going to let you. You had the guts to ask. Every other boy was thinking what they'd like to do with me but you were brave enough to say so. So don't feel bad about it."

"Please don't do it anymore, Cindy," Graham begged.

Cindy smiled. "I intend to do it a lot more. It can be fantastic fun, but I have learned my lesson. I will wait until I am old enough and until I meet the right man. So thank you Graham."

With that she leaned forward and kissed him, then walked away.

Enjoy more C.R. Cummings stories

The Cadet Under~Officer
by C.R. Cummings
The Army Cadet series

DoctorZed Publishing
www.doctorzed.com

ISBN: 978-0-9875975-5-7
2nd edition 2013

Fifteen-year-old Elizabeth has been handed a briefcase full of incriminating documents by her dying uncle, documents wanted by a gang of crooks. In desperation she flees into the bush, where she encounters seventeen-year-old Cadet Under-Officer Graham Kirk and his platoon of army cadets. Graham decides to hide Elizabeth until he can contact the authorities.

But how? And who can he trust? As the days go by the crooks become ever more desperate.

Now available in print and ebook.

www.ingramcontent.com/pod-product-compliance
Lightning Source LLC
Chambersburg PA
CBHW020833030726
47496CB00001B/221